THE THREE-
LEGGED STOOL

THE THREE-LEGGED STOOL

F. CHARLES WALTERS

Charleston, SC
www.PalmettoPublishing.com

The Three-Legged Stool

Copyright © 2021 by F. Charles Walters

All rights reserved

First Edition

Hardcover ISBN: 978-1-63837-291-2
Paperback ISBN: 978-1-63837-292-9
eBook ISBN: 978-1-63837-293-6

Table of Contents

Acknowledgments

To my wife Barbara, my family, and all my friends, who have encouraged me to write this book.

Chapter One

April 8, 1925: The Girl on the Train

A fifteen-year-old boy's heart raced as he descended shadowy stairs deep in the bowels of a Berlin apartment. And he burst out the door wide-eyed, flashing a toothy smile, imagining the farm he had left as a baby.

"Freddy, hurry," shouted a long-faced woman leaning from a sputtering taxi. "Did you lock the door?"

"I did, Mother," said the boy, quickstepping toward a whiskered man handing him a suitcase.

"Freddy, don't stand there. Hurry into the taxi; the train won't wait."

"Yes, Mother." And Freddy dashed through white puffs to reach the other side of the taxi. He yanked open the door, finding his mother twisting a silver ring and his father tapping his knees.

His face glowed, and wiggling into the seat, he said, "I'm going to see Grandpa Bauer, Grandma Hoffman, and uncles and cousins."

The driver stepped inside the cab, released the brake, ground the gears, and the taxi lurched forward. The driver slowed the taxi on a quiet street and pushed on the gas pedal, turning onto a thoroughfare.

With a weightless feeling, he felt cool air come through the cracked window, ruffling his blond hair. "I'm going home." And his face brightened, noticing the taxi speed over a stone bridge with ornate bronze railings and marbled figurines. At a congested boulevard with impatient drivers honking their horns, his mother bared her teeth, checking the time, and his expressionless father drummed his fingers.

"Barbara, stop worrying; we'll make the train."

"How can I, Wilhelm? We got off to a late start."

Freddy's eyes sparkled, and he bounced, admiring the train station through the driver's window. "Mother, I can see the train station."

The taxi's brakes screeched, stopping at the station, and the driver jumped out and opened the door. Freddy's father stepped out, placing two bags on the curb. "Freddy, please rush, leave nothing behind."

He trailed behind his mother into the station and stood motionless to admire a massive space lined with pillars and enormous windows, noticing the gray sky through glass panels overhead.

"Freddy, get a move on," said his father, tapping one foot. "The train won't wait."

His father purchased three tickets, paying close attention to the agent. "Sir, hurry to track two right away. Your train leaves in five minutes."

In ten breaths Freddy reached track two, overwhelmed at a gigantic black locomotive hissing white smoke.

With gleaming eyes, he stopped, swaying back and forth. "Look, Father, the train's gigantic. The white clouds resemble a dragon blasting smoke through its nose just before spitting fire."

His pleased father said lifting his chin, "Freddy, I'll never figure out what goes on in your head."

When he spotted a man wearing a dark blue uniform with a shiny hat, his father dashed his way.

The conductor pointed to a green car. "Sir, please go to passenger car number two."

A slow smile built on Freddy's lips as he edged close behind his mother between lacquered walls and rows of dark green seats till she found a place to sit.

The corners of Freddy's lips turned up when he heard the conductor's loud voice. "All aboard; next stop Koenig Station."

And he tilted his head toward his father. "How long will it take to reach the farm, Father?"

"Freddy, let your father relax."

He dropped his head, lowering his voice. "Sorry, Mother."

"Barbara, it's fine; Freddy's eager to see the farm where he was born."

"Wilhelm, Freddy shouldn't be bothering you while you are reading the newspaper."

"Barbara, it's okay, the news never changes—politicians argue with each other and you can't count on the weather forecast being right."

"Wilhelm, if we hadn't been to America, you could've fought in the war. I hate to think what could have happened to you if Otto talked you into joining the army with him. I could be a widow with a son to raise, and your poor mother lost two sons. It makes me sick to think of it. Yes, Wilhelm, I'm thankful we didn't live with the hardships Germany faced after the war."

His mother bit on her lip, twisting a length of golden hair.

"Wilhelm, don't overlook that when the war ended, people paid for bread with bags full of money," pointed out Freddy's mother, widening her eyes. "Can you imagine that? People starved, having no money for bread. Our families were lucky; they were farmers. Thank God it's better now that we're back in Germany."

His father stroked his chin. "You're right, Barbara."

"You found a wonderfully high-paying job."

Freddy's father eyed his mother. "What I learned at Ford landed me the job in Berlin. Without it, I'd be in a low-paying job."

"That's right, Wilhelm Bauer; they taught you to be a good machinist and be damn proud of it," said his mother, using a gruff tone of voice, nodding.

Uninterested in the conversation, Freddy sighed and glanced at the passengers. He discovered an amazing girl seated with an older man and woman. When the girl's head pivoted, he caught a sparkling butterfly clip holding a bunch of overlong blond hair together. When her head edged back, he sighed, believing he had never seen another girl who measured up to her angelic face. He gasped, tapped on the leg with a newspaper, and caught a grin and understanding nod from his father. And noticed his mother raise an eyebrow.

"Wilhelm, why'd you do that?"

"Freddy looked sleepy."

Freddy looked straight ahead, running fingers through his thick hair, afraid of getting caught gawking at the girl again. Outside the window at Koenig Station, Freddy laid eyes on a tearful young couple kissing goodbye. He pictured the flawless girl again.

His mother fidgeted with a button, clearing her throat. "Ahem, Freddy Bauer, I'm no fool; read your book."

He bared his teeth, catching a sly smile from his father.

And he dropped the book, overhearing the girl speak a foreign language.

His voice took a polite tone, and he furrowed his brows. "Mother, I know I'm being a nuisance, and promise it's the last time I'll bother you, but what language are the people across the aisle speaking?"

"Freddy Bauer, didn't I tell you to mind your business and read?"

A faint flush crossed his cheeks; he bowed his head. "You did, Mother, but I was curious."

"Freddy Bauer, idle curiosity is a waste of time."

With a hint of a frown, and a quick headshake, she leaned back wide-eyed, pursing her lips, eavesdropping on the strangers.

"Freddy picked up a word or two in Polish; they might be Poles heading for Poland."

"Mother, why Gorlitz?"

"Freddy, because that's where 'they'll connect with trains going to Poland."

"Oh, I didn't know that."

His mother's eyes narrowed, and she spoke in an irritated tone. "Freddy, this is the last time I'm telling you to read your book."

Freddy detected the train's wheels spin and screech, struggling for traction, and he caught puffs of white clouds shoot past the window. The thunderous train lurched forward, passing onlookers waving goodbyes to passengers, and moments later chugged by a line of coal cars. The train sped up, pushing Freddy against the seat.

"Tickets—please have tickets ready," called out the conductor.

The thin conductor swayed, moving along, punching tickets. He smiled, taking the tickets from his father, and lifted his voice above the train's noise. "Going to Gorlitz, are you?"

"No, headed for Bischofswerda," said his father with a faint smile.

"Oh, heading west from Gorlitz on a Saxon-Silesian train. I think it makes three stops before Bischofswerda check with the ticket agent at Gorlitz to make sure," said the conductor, grinning at him, nodding.

Freddy perked up. "Conductor, will it take long to reach Gorlitz?"

The conductor's eyes brightened. "No, be there at noon and not one minute later." And he raised his chest, saying to him, "Young man, you're traveling the German Imperial Railway, the finest train system in the entire world."

Not long after the conductor left, a slow smile crossed Freddy's mouth, and he peeked at her once more.

"Stop it, Freddy Bauer; keep reading," said his mother, taking on a sinister undertone in her voice.

His shoulders tightened, and with pursed lips he nodded and picked up a book, expecting her to remind him of the three-legged stool.

"Now that's the Freddy Bauer I know and love."

At a few minutes past eleven, Freddy's mother smeared brown sausage on a piece of bread and handed it to him.

"Wilhelm, want a piece of sausage?"

"No thanks; I'll wait till we arrive in Gorlitz."

A sheen came to Freddy's face as he caught his mother's head's last bounce and her eyes shut. A hard smile crossed his lips, and he ditched Greek mythology. Freed from prying eyes, Freddy beamed at the girl picking through pages of a magazine. The girl closed the magazine, discovering Freddy staring at her. He gasped. A tinge of red crept along his cheeks, and he swept his head to the window. Bored from glancing at endless hills, occasional woods, and never-ending wired poles, he raised his eyebrows at his father.

"Uh, Father, sorry to bother you, but how much longer to Gorlitz?"

His father ignored him, staring into space. Freddy made a face and repeated the question more loudly. His father's head shook, and his mouth sprung open, as he gave Freddy a dazed stare. "What?"

"When will we get to Gorlitz?"

"Freddy, at noon; check your watch," said his father, raising his voice and slanting his eyes at him.

The girl and her companions shot glances at Freddy and his father. Freddy forced a smile and gazed back out the window. A short time later, he yawned, hatching another question.

"Father, do you miss home?"

His father's face reddened, and he compressed his lips. Freddy gave him a bitter smile and crossed his arms, raising his voice. "Um, father, can you please answer my question, I want to know?"

"Ahem." The girl coughed, dropping her brows. Freddy's stomach hardened, and he moved his head toward the window.

"Freddy, I'm sorry, I avoided your question. It depressed me." His father's lips shivered; he stared at Freddy dull-eyed. "Freddy, I regret we arrived in Germany too late to see my mother before she died. It will be strange returning home without seeing Grandma and Uncle Otto's faces."

His father sniffled and wiped a corner of one eye dry. "Freddy, wars are terrible. Your Uncle Otto died in France, and your mother's brothers we're injured there."

He sorted out his father's words, recalling something brought up in American history. And he leaned closer to his father. "Can I ask you something else?"

His father swallowed, and he nodded, forming a straight line across his lips, pressing them together.

"In America Brother Pollak told the class in the Civil War brothers fought brothers; could you fight Uncle Tomas?"

His father gave him an icy stare without answering the question. He folded his arms across his chest. "Father, did you hear me?"

The corners of his father's mouth dropped as he glued his eyes to Freddy. "No, son, I couldn't fight Uncle Tomas.

7

I remember a priest saying the only reason for men to fight is to defeat evil."

With an uncontrollable shudder sweeping through his body, Freddy covered his face, reminded of a soldier's grave in a Detroit church cemetery.

"Was the priest Father Volker? Mother often mentions his name."

His father's cheeks rose, and he closed his eyes, giving his head a slow nod.

"Why isn't Grandfather Werner's name ever mentioned?"

A painful stare materialized on his father's face.

"Was mother's father a good man?"

"It's not the right time to discuss him; let's wait till you're older."

Freddy tapped his foot. "What of your mother?"

With a blank face, his father sat motionless. Freddy released a heavy sigh, collapsing his shoulders.

His father sat up. "I love your grandmother and miss her. When it feels right, I'll tell you what a wonderful woman she was."

Freddy sighed and gave him a slow nod, deciding to keep quiet.

His mother woke up yawning and circled her head, opening her eyes. Freddy grabbed a book quickly and started reading.

"Did the nap help?" his father asked.

His mother stretched out her arms, flexing her jaw, and wiggled her shoulders. "I needed it; it tired me packing the suitcases and cleaning the apartment this morning. Do you think we will we make Bischofswerda on time? I dread the long carriage ride home."

"I do. Did you forget the conductor told Freddy the German Imperial Railway is prompt; I hope the Saxon-Silesian railroad is just as good."

His mother frowned, tensing her voice. "Wilhelm, men are alike—ask them simple questions, and they complicate it. I'd be happy with a simple yes or no."

"Sorry, while you were sleeping, the conductor said we were on time."

His mother's eyes held him hostage, and he dipped his head with a slight shiver, expecting criticism from her.

A brief time passed, and Freddy's father checked the time. "Better tidy up; we're nearing Gorlitz."

The locomotive slowed, and the conductor cried out, "Gorlitzzzz, Gorlitz next stop. Please take your belongings with you when you leave the train. We will arrive at the Gorlitz Station at twelve o'clock."

Scattered houses and two warehouses lined up alongside the tracks. The locomotive's heart beat less frequently and lost speed approaching the station, and once more the conductor spoke with an excited catch in his loud voice. "Gorlitzzzz. Next stop, Gorlitzzzz."

The locomotive crept into the station and stopped with a slight jerk. Expressionless, Freddy checked on the girl, feeling his ribs tighten. Dressed in a yellow coat, the youthful girl glanced at Freddy and picked up her suitcase. His mouth opened wide, and he stared at her, guessing he'd never lay eyes on her again. The blond-haired girl caught him watching her and lifted the corners of her mouth. His face warmed, and he slid back, grinning.

"Freddy, hurry, we've another train to catch," said his mother, looking worried.

The girl hurried to the exit, followed by her companions. His mother eased up the aisle, falling behind the girl. On restless legs, Freddy huffed, wishing she'd hurry. The moment Freddy's feet touched ground his eyes hunted for the girl. And they twinkled, catching sight of the long-haired blonde in the yellow coat entering the station. He dashed for the doors, seeking one more peek at the girl. Inside the station, his eyes darted, auditing the crowded room. Freddy's father broke toward the ticket window, and Freddy spent the time hunting for the girl in the waiting room. She'd disappeared.

"Mother, I'm going to the restroom," said Freddy, unable to stand still.

He scooted through a majestic passageway, catching a stony stare from a police officer, and gazed at enormous doors at the other end of the station, talking to himself. "She's not here."

"Dresden train now boarding track two."

He eyed the overhead speaker, shaking his head. "Good grief, that's the train stopping in Bischofswerda."

Freddy made a quick pivot and double-timed it to the waiting room.

"That's splendid news; we should arrive at Bischofswerda at two," said his mother, grinning and nodding.

"Warsaw—last call for the train going to Warsaw."

"Oh no!" said Freddy, shifting his pupils. "I want to see the electric train leave the station."

He stopped outside the station doors, checking the platform for the girl. And he observed a man and woman step up into an electrified train, hearing the conductor's loud voice calling out strange city names. Freddy's lips pressed together, and he moved closer to the train. The electricity-juiced engine moved forward with less noise than a smoke-puffing locomotive. And his mouth fell open as he discovered the girl waving at him with a cheeky grin from one of the even-tempered beast's windows. He let out a gasp and ran alongside the train till it left the station. At the end of the platform, panting, he paid attention to the disappearing train, thinking he'd never get a glimpse of her again. The police officer he had encountered inside the station gave him an unpleasant smile and trailed behind him, heading toward the station.

"Freddy, didn't you hear the train to Bischofswerda announced? Your mother's mad, she's been looking for you."

His shoulders slumped. "I'm coming."

With a pained expression, he approached his father.

His father's voice firmed, and giving him a pained stare, he said, "Freddy, you better make up an excuse. Your mother's mad at you."

Freddy cringed, pulling together his thoughts.

Chapter Two

Enlightened

The Saxon-Silesian Railway's black locomotive puffing clouds of white smoke stopped at Bischofswerda Station. Excited, Freddy jumped up, staring at the people outside. His voice rang with excitement, focusing on a man leaning against a clock post. "That could be Uncle Tomas?"

His mother's forehead wrinkled, and she shifted in her seat, saying, "Uh, Freddy, are you sure? You haven't seen Uncle Tomas in a while."

His father's eyes bulged with a flash of red tinting his cheeks, and he jumped up to glance outward. "You're right; it's Uncle Tomas." And he stuck his head out the window. "Over here, Tomas, we're over here!"

The moment his mother stepped off the train, laugh lines formed in the corners of Uncle Tomas's eyes. "Barbara Bauer, you haven't changed one bit—still glamorous."

"Tomas, keep the sweet talk for Andrea and your daughters, and how are they? Andrea never writes," said his mother, cringing.

"Not surprised. She works hard on the farm, and the girls keep her busy."

She gave him a mocking snicker, shrugging. "Tomas, that's no excuse."

"Got wonderful news to tell you—Hanna's remarried," said Uncle Tomas, nodding.

"Wow, that's a surprise," replied his mother, pulling back her head with an open mouth.

The disheveled man wearing muddied boots assessed his father. "Wilhelm, I've missed you; we've lots to talk over."

"How's father coping?"

Uncle Tomas shook his head. "He's never been the same since mother died; you'll see for yourself. How was the trip from Berlin?"

His mother interrupted, crossing her arms and raising her voice. "The train ride took forever, and Freddy didn't mind his business the whole trip," she said, eyeing Freddy's father with pursed lips. "Hope he studied while I napped; university entrance exams are in two years."

Uncle Tomas nodded, a smile growing on his face. "Barbara, you'll never change."

"What does that mean?" she responded.

Freddy bounced from foot to foot, smiling at his uncle. "Do you remember me?"

Uncle Tomas's eyes shined. "Freddy, how could I forget you."

Uncle Tomas sighed, pulling out a tarnished watch. "Dammit, we better get going; it'll be dark in three hours."

Uncle Tomas led everyone inside a foul-smelling livery stable, heading for a muscular brown horse hooked up to an open black carriage.

Freddy squeezed his eyes shut, picturing a stable hand in Detroit, giving his best friend Rolf an apple to feed a horse.

A black-and-white sheepdog, tied up to a carriage, barked and did a somersault, trying to pull free. Uncle Tomas laughed and dropped onto one knee, letting the antsy animal lick his face. "I missed you too, Kaiser."

His mother frowned, tapping a foot. "Tomas, let's hurry. It stinks in here; don't they ever clean it? If this were summer, horseflies would bite us. Tomas, I will throw up if we don't leave."

"Why should it bother you?" said his uncle, displaying a wide grin, "you grew up on a farm."

His mother's brows drew together; she expelled a hard breath. "Tomas, I've been away from the farm too long; I'm a city girl now."

Uncle Tomas met her gaze. "Yeah, when I lived in Detroit, I stepped in horseshit."

"That was your fault. In fresh air you don't pinch your nose," said his mother, placing her hands on her hips.

His father snorted and grabbed hold of the fidgety horse's bridle and stroked the beast's head. "What's his name?"

"Browny."

The relaxed horse allowed his father to check inside its mouth. "Browny, you're an old geezer, aren't you? I bet your teeth chewed a mountain or two of grass in your lifetime."

His mother scrunched her nose and fanned her face hard. "Wilhelm, it stinks here; leave the horse alone and get into the carriage."

Once everyone had sat, Uncle Tomas picked up Kaiser and carried the dog up with him in the driver's seat and flicked Browny's reins. On a quiet road heading home, a green roadster pulled alongside Browny, and its laughing driver honked the horn, spooking Browny as it sped away, kicking up mud at the horse. Uncle Tomas yanked on the reins and cursed at him.

Freddy pointed his index finger at the falling sun. "How much longer? I'm hungry and my bottom hurts."

His father took on a concerned expression. "Not that much longer."

Freddy crossed his arms, firming his voice. "Father, how long is not much longer?"

Tongue-tied, his father glared at him.

Two fingers pinched his leg. "Freddy Bauer, leave your father alone; not much longer means what he said not much longer."

Freddy's mood plummeted, and his chin dropped. "Sorry, mother. I'll leave him alone."

Unexpectedly Browny passed wind, causing his mother to choke and fan her face. "For God's sake, Tomas, what do you feed that beast?"

Freddy's chest bounced as he held a giggle inside.

At sunset Uncle Tomas drew back on Browny's reins, yelling, "Whoa!" and the horse stopped, letting out a neigh and a loud snort, shaking its head. Uncle Tomas rose, smiling, pointing a finger at something. "See it? It's over there."

His father squinted, focusing on the spot. "What, where?"

"Wilhelm, over there, the church steeple sticking out above that hill," said his uncle, nodding.

His mother stood up to better observe. "Yes, I see it; right there, Wilhelm."

"Oh, yes, now I can see it."

Freddy crossed his arms and turned the other way. "Who cares?"

"Freddy, look the other way, and you'll find it." said Uncle Tomas, bright eyed.

He faced back, rolling his eyes. "It's a church, with a steeple and cross on top of it—that's nothing new."

Uncle Tomas glanced at him, grinning, seesawing his head. "Freddy, that's not just a church; that's where Father Vogel married your parents and baptized you."

Freddy's mouth fell open and his voice strengthened. "Wow, at that church?"

"Yes, Freddy, that's the church where it happened," said Uncle Tomas with a wide smile on his upturned face.

Freddy gasped, finding his parents kissing.

"Oh, Wilhelm, I'm happy to be home; it's been too long."

In darkness, with the moon and the stars the only source of light, they crossed over an old wooden bridge, the sounds of running water below them. Uncle Tomas rested Browny a scant distance from the bridge, in front of a candlelit white stone church. Freddy's mother jumped up, clasping her hands together. "Wilhelm, I'll cry when we visit Father Vogel tomorrow."

"We could never repay him for the kindness," said his father with a warm smile.

With sparkling eyes, she broadened her mouth into a smile.

Freddy's lips pressed into a slight grimace; his father's words confused him.

"Git up, Browny," yelled his uncle, and the horse's heavy hoofs jolted the carriage, moving forward till it veered right at a fork in the road.

"Freddy, guess what?" his mother said, grinning. "If we traveled the other road, we'd be heading for Grandma's farm."

With his stomach fluttering and fidgety hands, Freddy sized up the moonlit fields flanking him.

"We're close to home," said Uncle Tomas, keeping his eyes straight ahead.

His father leaped up with excitement in his voice, curving his head right. "I know where I am. There's the farm; we're home." In tears, he hugged his wife. "Barbara, we're back home, at last."

Freddy's eyes bulged, dazed by his father's unusual behavior, and his mouth opened wide.

With tears in her eyes, his mother pressed her quivering lips against his father's mouth.

Browny tramped closer to the house. And Freddy spotted a man and woman clutching flickering lanterns with two young girls standing in front of a bowed-roofed house made conspicuous by the moonlight. Freddy soared to his feet and sang out, feeling his insides vibrate. "It's them; I see them. It's grandfather, Aunt Andrea, Charlotte, and Maria."

His stomach churned, and he glanced at the moon. *Will Grandpa smile when he sees me?*

Uncle Tomas stopped Browny. Kaiser jumped off the carriage and dashed over to his cousins, barking at them. Freddy's mother sniffled, embracing Aunt Andrea, and kissed Charlotte and Maria. She stepped back, beaming, saying, "Andrea, the girls are adorable. I've missed them, they've grown, but how should I have known since you never write?"

Not long after, his mother backed away and raced over to his grandfather. She gripped the lamp in his grandfather's hand and grounded it, placing her head against the old man's chest, mumbling something inaudible. His grandfather cried, caressing her back with his better hand. Freddy's breaths grew louder, and he came closer and picked up the lantern, handing it to the old man. "Grandpa, it's me; its Freddy." The old man held the fickle flame in front of Freddy's face. "I think you take after your mother."

He looked over the nooks and crannies in his grandfather's weathered face; he had envisioned him differently.

With a shine in his eyes, his father approached, rubbing fingers together. "Hello, Father, it's good to see you again. I've missed you."

Speechless, the old man shed tears, studying his son. Freddy moved on, certain the men needed time alone.

"Is that you, Freddy Bauer? You're so handsome you could be in the cinemas; I'll bet you've got lots of girlfriends, don't you?" said Aunt Andrea, putting her fingers against her cheeks; her eyes twinkled as he discovered Freddy.

He did a double take at Aunt Andrea, believing she had added pounds around her waist and a few gray hairs. He blushed, wanting to flee as his aunt's kiss touched him on the cheek. His cousins wore the same brown dresses as his aunt, and he figured they had come from the same cloth. He inspected the girls, finding no similarities between them. And pictured Charlotte, little, tearing open a Christmas present in Detroit. Uncle Tomas and his father arrived, smiling. His father kissed Aunt Andrea and Charlotte. And he lifted Maria high, laughing, swinging her in a circle.

"Andrea, the girls are bigger than I imagined," said Freddy's father with an approving nod.

"Wilhelm, time doesn't stand still; it's been a while since you last looked at them."

Freddy's shoulders lowered, and he recalled one of his mother's overused thoughts.

A grin shot across Aunt Andrea's face. "We'd better go inside; the food is getting cold."

Within the four walls, a fireplace and four lanterns lit the room. Freddy dropped into a seat alongside Charlotte and Maria, observing the girls eating from bowls stuffed with meat and potatoes. His grandfather stabbed at a sausage with his good hand till he got lucky. His chin dipped as he caught Freddy scrutinizing him. Freddy's smile wavered, and he scratched his head. *Why didn't anyone help him? Maybe he'd holler at them if they did.* Hungry, Freddy wiped his wet lips and bit into a sausage.

Snuggled in a corner of the room, he read *Little Red-Cap* to Charlotte and Maria. Charlotte's mouth hung open on every word he read. "Cousin Freddy, the wolf scared me. I'm glad he drowned," said Maria, quivering. He gazed at Maria, covering his smile with his hand. And then he leaned back, beholding his mother and aunt, shelving clean dishes in a cupboard.

"Time for bed, girls. Thank Cousin Freddy for reading a story to you."

His cousins' voices harmonized. "Thank you, Cousin Freddy."

His mother yawned, pulling back her arms, jutting out her chest. "Freddy, I'm going to bed with Aunt Andrea and the girls; please read a book and leave the men alone—they've lots to discuss with each other."

"Yes, Mother; I won't bother them. Good night, everyone."

He dropped his book and slouched with a slow smile building on his lips, and he slid his chair toward the talking men. Unable to understand them, he inched his chair closer. With half-open eyelids and a swaying head, his grandfather picked himself up and limped off to bed. Uncle Tomas overlooked him, speaking with his brother. "Wilhelm, are you ready for tomorrow?"

His father's lips quivered, and he angled his head away, running his fingers through his hair. "How can I be, Tomas? I don't know if I can hold myself together at mother's grave. It won't be easy for Barbara either; it bothers her what happened to her brothers."

Uncle Tomas rested his chin between his hands. "It's hard seeing mother's grave; I cry each time."

His father let out a heavy sigh, eyeing his uncle. "Tomas, when I left, it was the last time I eyed Mother or Otto."

Uncle Tomas's head fell. "She understood when you left; Freddy and Barbara came first."

"Tomorrow Barbara wants to visit Werner's grave."

"Wilhelm, go with her."

"I can't; I hate him."

Freddy turned his head, closing his eyes, assessing a thought. *Maybe tomorrow I'll have answers to my questions.*

Sleepless, Freddy stretched on a lumpy mattress in a space no larger than a coffin, fenced in by three walls and double doors. Without distractions, his mind focused on the girl on the train. His eyes widened as he picked up the sound of squeaky floor planks, and he rose and opened the doors a tad, discovering Uncle Tomas holding a jug and dimming an oil lamp. He grinned, relaxing alongside his father, close by the warm stove. Kaiser wagged his tail, content, resting alongside his uncle's foot. Uncle Tomas's smile broadened as he uncorked the jug, speaking to his father loud enough he could make out his words. "Wilhelm, I've saved half the brandy, just for this day, but Andrea got mad at me for not giving it up for Lent."

"Tomas, pass me the jug; I need a taste right now." His father drank from it, and delight tinged his voice. "Ahh, Tomas, it tastes better than I remembered."

Uncle Tomas took a gulp and placed the jug beside Kaiser. Minutes passed without a word said. And Freddy's father broke the silence. "Hand me back the jug—I need another swallow."

"Go to bed, you look tired."

"You go; I've too much on my mind. Leave me the jug."

"Wilhelm, I'm not leaving you alone with excellent brandy. I didn't save it so you could finish it without me; we'll drink it together."

Freddy turned his head, making out loud snoring, figuring his grandfather was making the noise, and moved his eyes back to the doors, recognizing a cough. "Tomas, being home stirred up terrible memories. On the train Freddy wanted to know why we never mention Werner."

"He did? What did you tell him?"

"Nothing. I didn't want to tell him his mother's father was an evil man."

Freddy's lips parted, and his legs numbed with his father's words echoing in his brain.

"Wilhelm, he's dead; forget the bastard."

"I can't; his ghost lives in my soul."

Freddy caught a gulp and an "ah" from one man.

21

"Hey, save me a drink," said Wilhelm.

"Shush. Do you want to wake everyone?"

"Did you ever consider what could've happened to us if Nils never wrote to you from America?"

"Yes, I did. It was our only chance to better ourselves. Do you remember the trade union manager laughing at us when we applied for trainee positions in Dresden? And him telling us our education didn't meet union standards and to look elsewhere for a job."

"I will never not remember it; it depressed me."

"Yeah, it was depressing, wasn't it?"

Freddy covered his mouth with his palms. *Nils Keller, Rolf's father's letter, is the reason I went to America?*

"Tomas, could you ever imagine we'd both be assembling Model T automobiles in Highland Park, Michigan, or live in Detroit? I remember Mother shrugging when she heard the names?"

Freddy's mouth opened, and he was concentrating on a thought. *The letter changed my life too.*

"Why are you shaking your head?" Tomas asked.

"Father's hand was shaking."

"It started before mother died. He's lost without her. Wilhelm, his sly smiles and sense of humor died with her."

Freddy's eyes teared up, and he crossed his arms across his chest, pondering his uncle's words.

"Barbara is my life; without her I'm lost. I hope Freddy finds someone to love as good as her. Huh! That reminds me—on the train I caught him peeking at a gorgeous girl."

"Are you surprised? He's a man."

"When he finds the right girl, I hope he never puts up with someone as wicked as Werner."

"No one should. I guess it wasn't easy for Freddy to start a new life in Germany."

"At first, but he adjusted fast. His professor marvels at his brilliance, said Freddy stood above his peers."

"Wow! I'm sure that made Barbara happy."

"For a minute or two; she will never rest till he walks on water. The professor told us Freddy was his best student and will do well on the university entrance exams."

"Does she still pester him with the three-legged stool?"

"What do you think?"

"Go to sleep; we'll talk more tomorrow."

"Can't. I've lots on my mind."

"What is it? I'm sure I'll regret asking you at sunup."

"This house brings back so many bittersweet memories. I can picture mother reading to us fairy tales by the fire or chasing after us with the wooden spoon when we were naughty."

"Yes, Wilhelm." Uncle Tomas sniffled. "They were good times."

"And awful times too—the lot of us, plus Barbara, Hanna, and the baby struggling to get by under one roof. I ran to the outhouse when I needed to be alone to think."

"They were hard times, weren't they?"

"It was hard on Barbara, but she never complained. I worried and once thought of taking her and Freddy to stay with Werner."

"Barbara could never leave you; take another drink."

"Werner looked at me with hatred in his eyes."

A breath stuck in Freddy's throat as he mulled over his father's words.

"Wilhelm, Werner's gone. Saturday's the bonfire; Freddy's never been to one—it will be fun."

"Ah! The Easter bonfire, where Barbara and I fell in love, and the entire mess began."

"It was there?"

"Yes, it was there Barbara schemed a plot to deceive her father, believing Werner would never approve of me. It was there, using Gretchen as an excuse to take a walk she proposed meeting at the pond behind the schoolhouse."

"That's the Barbara Bauer I recall back then." Uncle Tomas snorted, sounding amused.

"Not funny, Tomas!"

"Shush! You'll wake up someone."

Freddy's skin tingled, and he gazed through the door's crack, beaming.

"Before Christmas Barbara decided she couldn't go on deceiving Werner. We went to see Werner and told him we were in love. With his cheeks reddening, he asked Barbara if she was pregnant." His father paused, blowing air in and out of his nose. "Barbara told Werner she loved me; he laughed at her, said she doesn't know what love is."

An uncontrollable shudder swept through his body, and he pressed his hands against his ears. *Am I a bastard?*

"Werner assumed Mother and Father were hiding us and rode off to face them. Barbara's brothers blocked the door, keeping me from leaving."

Freddy's head sunk into the mattress, and he tightened his fingers.

"What happened?"

"Barbara's mother ordered the boys to move away from the door saying, 'Wilhelm, leave before Werner comes back.' I left thinking, *I'll never see Barbara again.* I walked home sick to my stomach. Coming back from the farm, Werner caught me on the road, and he raced his horse. If I didn't jump out of the way, he might have killed me."

"Werner barged inside the house, cursing at Mother and Father. Otto was furious with him; I used every bit of strength in me to hold him back."

Freddy collapsed onto the mattress, agonizing over what had happened.

"Guess what Werner did the next day? Went to Father Vogel with the elders, insisting he keep us apart."

"Why haven't you mentioned this before?" said Uncle Tomas in an excited voice.

"Shh! Might wake someone. Drink more brandy."

Caged, a victim of circumstances, Freddy hashed over what they had said.

"Did you know one elder was Barbara's best friend Gretchen's father? He told Gretchen that Father Vogel had yelled at Werner for bringing the elders with him."

Freddy's stomach muscles contracted as he assessed his grandfather's dreadful behavior.

"Werner makes my skin crawl. What happened next?"

"Father Vogel summoned us to the church and asked Barbara if she was free from sin."

"No!"

"Yes, Barbara cried, saying she was virtuous."

Freddy felt a sense of release. *I'm not a bastard?*

"Barbara swore to Father Vogel Mother and Father didn't know what we were doing."

His eyes widened when the room quieted.

"Are you okay?" Uncle Tomas asked.

"Father Vogel asked her if she was certain that she loved me," said his father in a quiet, tense voice. "Barbara wept, nodding, saying she was happy when we were together and sad when we weren't. And she told him we had kissed and done nothing more. I recall Father Vogel's lips curving into a smile."

Freddy cringed, on the verge of tears, with a fluttering in the pit of his stomach. *This isn't right; I invaded my parent's privacy.*

"Father Vogel pleaded with Werner to let me court Barbara. Werner laughed at him, wanted to know what a poor boy living on a small farm could give his daughter. Father Vogel answered, 'Happiness.' Father Vogel reminded Werner that if his grandfather hadn't received a land grant from the church, he'd be no better than Mother and Father. And warned him if he didn't agree, Barbara might run off with me. That changed his mind."

He smiled, appreciating Father Vogel's significance in his parent's lives.

"The pigheaded fool made life miserable, never left you alone with Barbara; I can't blame you for hating him."

"It could've been different. He never tried to know me, and Barbara married me without him walking her to the altar. That I'll never forgive him for doing."

"Let's get some sleep; tomorrow's a busy day."

Overwhelmed by the day's circumstances, in dark silence, with heavy eyelids, Freddy drifted off to sleep.

Chapter Three

Freddy's Metamorphosis

A brown boxer's tail wagged as it barked, standing on Freddy's legs.

"Sit, Prince," an unseen man shouted at the dog. Prince whined and fell under a window, panting. Freddy stepped inside the house with a lopsided grin, catching a whiff of a pleasant odor. "Hmm, maybe a roast?" He scanned an immense room filled with beaming faces. Expressionless, his father drifted over to the window and stooped to pet Prince. Freddy's mouth dropped, imagining his heartache. Fussed over by her family, his mother cried happy tears and faced his father. "Wilhelm, come join us."

Once she completed a teary-eyed moment with her mother, she introduced Freddy, attempting a smile. Grandma Petra snatched him in her arms, planting a wet kiss on his mouth, turning his ears red. The gray-haired woman stepped back, grinning, admiring him. "Oh! Barbara, Friedrich takes after you!"

"Not so sure, Mother—I see Wilhelm in him."

A man with dirty blond hair scratched the back of his neck. "Nonsense, Barbara, he's you, m-m-mother's right."

Tongue-tied, examining his grandmother with a visibly flushed face, Freddy thought about the fact his mother possessed the same blue eyes and high cheekbones. "I think my mother resembles you." Grandma Petra blushed and kissed him once more. And he stepped back with a dropped jaw. *Ugh.*

Introduced to his uncles Dieter and Manfred, he gripped their hands hard, the way his father had taught him. And straightened up, figuring they stood near the spot where they had blocked his father from leaving that terrible night.

A legless man wheeled between his uncles. Freddy's chest lifted; he narrowed his eyes on the man standing in silence.

"Hello, Friedrich; I'm Uncle Heinz, and I'm glad to make your acquaintance." The vibrant man with a wide smile said extending his hand.

And Freddy strengthened his grip, cracking his voice. "It's nice to meet you, Uncle Heinz."

The black-haired man toyed with spokes on his wheelchair, reminding Freddy of someone strumming a guitar. Uncle Heinz shifted in the chair, noticing Freddy eyeing his stumps, and covered them. Freddy cringed, and his stomach hardened. Uncle Heinz gazed at him, smiling, putting him at ease. "Friedrich, I've many medals; bet you didn't know they awarded me an Iron Cross?" Uncle Heinz said, bobbing his head with creased cheeks. Freddy presumed the proud man had accepted his fate.

Uncle Manfred tapped his shoulder. "I-h-have m-medals too." Freddy checked out Manfred's head for signs of a war injury but couldn't find a mark on it. He examined his uncle's faces, figuring one might resemble Grandpa Werner. And he edged around, looking for his father, discovering the downcast man staring out the window.

Freddy let out a heavy sigh as he gazed at three curious children.

"Friedrich, these are cousins, Werner, Petra, and Barbara," said Uncle Dieter, curving his lips upward.

A loud-voiced woman wearing a stained apron with long, curly brown hair barged in and hugged his mother. "Barbara

Bauer, let's look at you?" Her eyes sparkled; she bounced on her toes. "You're still glamorous, and time has not changed your adorable face."

His mother's face blushed pink, and she bowed her head. "Stop, Gretchen, you're embarrassing me."

With a whimsical look, gazing between Gretchen and his mother, he pictured them sneaking out the door to meet his father behind the schoolhouse.

And he lowered himself on a long bench flanked by his mother and junior cousin Werner. His mouth watered as he swept his eyes over a variety of aromatic foods, and bottles of white wine lined up in the middle of the table. Served a plate of sliced lamb, Freddy grinned, putting a name on what had smelled good earlier. Antsy young Werner eyeballed him. "My mother said you were smart; I'm eleven, and I'm smart too. She told me we're cousins and you live far away in a building in Berlin."

Freddy smiled through narrowed eyes and stuffed a forkful of lamb in his mouth. Uncle Dieter rose, holding up a glass of wine. Freddy swallowed the lamb.

"Welcome home, Barbara, Wilhelm, and Friedrich; let's hope now that you 're back in Germany, you're no longer strangers in our home."

His smile wavered, and he gazed at his father's deadpanned face. He rubbed his teeth against his lip, grasping that his father's pain had just started. He smiled at Uncles Heinz and Manfred. Uncle Heinz wheeled alongside him, beaming at him. "The lamb's good, but don't forget to bite into one of those delicious sausages, my favorite."

Uncle Heinz giggled, snatching Barbara's one-eyed doll out of her hands. Everyone laughed out loud, watching him dance with the doll on the table while mouthing a girl's voice. His face glowed as he noticed Uncle Manfred's belly laugh. His muscles tensed, and his lips curled around his teeth, hating what the war had done to the gentle soul.

Freddy sighed, seeing that his father ate little. Then his eyes widened as he caught his mother squeezing his father's hand and whispering in his ear. His father attempted to smile and angled his head away from her. He nodded with a credible idea of what she had said to him.

The room quieted, and his eyes focused on his father, figuring more pain awaited him at the cemetery.

After lunch Freddy settled alongside his father, in a fancy black carriage with shiny leather seats, waiting for his mother and Grandma Petra. He watched Uncle Manfred finish harnessing a horse with a reddish-brown coat and black mane and tail. Two German shepherds barked at Uncle Dieter, hooking up the horse to the carriage. Freddy rubbed his hands together, when the woman arrived, worrying about what would happen at the church.

"Wilhelm, do you want to come up top?" said Uncle Dieter.

His father frowned. "No thanks, Dieter; I'll stay with Friedrich and the woman."

Speechless, Freddy grasped the dark-eyed man's predicament.

"Friedrich, come up top with me," said Uncle Dieter, giving him his hand and lugging him alongside him. His uncle smiled at Freddy and tugged on the reins, and the horse clip-clopped forward on the dirt road.

"Uncle Dieter, who takes after your father?"

Uncle Dieter peered at Freddy, saying, "My mother tells me I do."

Freddy's stomach quivered, and he slipped his hands inside his pockets.

The brief ride ended at a point overlooking the church he had visited last night. Uncle Dieter jumped off the carriage, helping the woman out with a sad demeanor. He took Grandma Petra by the hand and headed toward the grave-yard with her. Freddy's father smiled for the first time and gripped his wife's hand. Inside the church a gray-haired priest knelt in front of the altar, praying. The old priest's ears detected footsteps behind him, and he pivoted his head toward the noise. He rose, bright eyed, flashing a smile at his visitors. "Is that you, Barbara and Wilhelm Bauer? Tomas told me you were coming." The holy man rejoiced, raising his voice and clasping his hands together.

Freddy peered at the plump stranger whose name he had caught often at home. As he sat beside his parents in the church's front row, wiggling on the hardwood, he remembered it was here love triumphed over evil.

Father Vogel's eyes sparkled, and he pivoted toward the altar. "Did you know, Friedrich Bauer, at this altar I married your mother and father and baptized you? I recall the moments as if it were yesterday."

With an upturned face, Father Vogel chanted a prayer, leading everyone along a stoned pathway that ended at a rusty cemetery gate. The priest grew silent, pursing his lips. "I'll leave you now."

He walked slow behind his parents, speeding up his breathing. His stomach constricted as he caught sight of Grandma Petra and Uncle Dieter praying near a gravestone between tall, budding trees. His shoulders curled, and he cringed, locking eyes on Grandpa Werner's darkened head-stone. And continued toward his grandmother's grave, with eyes widened, viewing a few crooked headstones and sol-dier's graves.

At his grandmother's grave, his father's head bobbed, and he wiped tears from his cheeks. His mother squeezed his father's hand. "Barbara, I love her."

"I know you do, Wilhelm."

"Did we stay too long in America?"

She slumped, saying to him in a brittle voice, "No, we didn't; we lived a wonderful life in Detroit till it fell apart."

His father's eyes drifted to a patch of grass beside his mother's grave. "Barbara, she's alone; Otto should rest beside her. I wonder where he is, or how he died; did he suffer?" said his father in a disbelieving voice.

"Darling, please stop torturing yourself; let it be."

At the end of the visit, Freddy limped toward his grandfather's grave in grim silence, but at a fair distance from it, his father stopped and let go of his mother's hand.

Wet-eyed, his mother looked up at him and begged, sobbing, "Wilhelm, please come with me."

"I can't do it; I hate him,"

"W-Wilhelm, please, do it for me."

He followed his parents on the way to Grandpa Werner's grave. Halfway there, his father froze and freed his hand, shaking his head. His mother lowered her head and walked on.

His father pursed his lips, and his voice took on a bitter tone. "Freddy, go with your mother."

Freddy yawned, concentrating on his grandfather's headstone. He lowered his head, recalling what his father said about of the man under his feet. He swallowed, watching his grandmother face his father and navigate uneven ground heading for him. His father locked eyes on the dainty woman and crossed his arms. Often shaking his head, his father listened to her. When she finished, his father wept and latched onto her. Perplexed, Freddy stared at his dumbfounded mother. His father joined his mother alongside his grandfather's grave. His mother's cheeks moved up and down as she blinked a few tears from her eyes.

He moved along the pathway at a snail's pace within earshot of his parents.

"Wilhelm, what happened with mother?"

"She asked me to forgive your father."

"No, she didn't?" said his mother, furrowing her brows and covering her mouth.

"She told me you forgave him?"

"He was awful, but he loved me; I saw it in his eyes when he looked at me."

"Petra cried, said Werner asked for God's forgiveness before dying."

Surprise lifted his mother's brows.

"He didn't?" said his mother, covering her mouth with a hand.

A slight grimace came to his father's lips, and he dropped his head.

"I realized I had let hatred find a place in my heart. I didn't want it." His father squeezed his eyes shut. His voice softened. "Barbara, I pray for his soul."

Cold weather chilled bones as they waited for the wagon to move. Charlotte and Maria snuggled up next to Freddy, sharing their blanket with him. His lashes flickered; he recalled what the bonfire had meant to his father. Uncle Tomas finished tying last year's Christmas tree onto the back of the wagon. His father joined Uncle Tomas, and Browny got going. Charlotte jumped up and laughed loudly. "Bye, Grandpa; we'll miss you. Take care of Kaiser."

Freddy's heart warmed as they sang songs on the trip. His eyes shined as he beheld the merry faces. Browny came to a stop alongside Uncle Dieter's fancy carriage. Uncle Tomas untied the barren tree and dragged it over to a pile of trees and flung it on top. The orange and red sky dulled, and Uncle Dieter tossed a torch on the pile, setting off flames flickering light onto faces. The high-spirited people touched hands and whirled around the fire, laughing and singing aloud. Seated away from the roaring flames, his mother and aunt supervised his cousins. He sighed, spotting Aunt Gretchen giving Werner a tongue-lashing. Caught up in the festivities, he laughed with his father and Uncle Tomas. Uncle Dieter gulped from a jug and grinned, holding it out. "Wilhelm and Tomas, drink." His father drank from the jug, and said to Uncle Tomas. "Ahh, better than the stuff I drank last night."

Uncle Tomas laughed, shaking his head. "Liar."

Freddy glowed inside, happy the men put aside past differences. Freddy caught Uncle Manfred straining to push Uncle Heinz up an incline and helped him. He glanced back, discovering his father widening his grin.

"Freddy Bauer, come dance with us?" said his mother, motioning him toward her, standing alongside Grandma Petra.

Freddy giggled and joined hands with them, and in a line of people hopping and skipping, he laughed, singing around the fickle flame. Winded Grandma Petra stopped, panting. Freddy twisted toward his mother, but she disappeared. Open-mouthed, he shuffled back a step and searched for her. His eyes lit up as he watched her rushing up to his father, embracing and kissing him before yanking him to a secluded spot. Their lips touched, and she spun around in his arms, with the bonfire brightening her eyes. Freddy pressed his lips hard against each other, understanding why it was important for them to be here. And Freddy cringed, dipping his head, acknowledging he had invaded their privacy, having eavesdropped on his father and uncle's conversation. *Why didn't I cover my ears?*

Heavy-legged, he inched toward the men. Uncles Dieter and Tomas laughed, sharing the jug between them. Uncle Manfred rested beside Uncle Heinz, paying attention to the jumping flames. Close to tears, Freddy huddled with his uncles and whimpered, rubbing his fingers. "I'll miss you both."

Uncle Heinz shifted his weight towards Freddy with flickers of light shining on his face. "Freddy, we'll miss you too."

"Please write. I want to know how you're both doing and promise to write back." And with his vision clouding over, scrutinizing Uncle Manfred, he said. "Hope you get better, Uncle Manfred. I'll pray for you and Uncle Heinz every day."

* * *

A hard rain hit against the overhead canopy of the Gorlitz train station platform. Freddy backed off when drops found his shoes. His head edged around, spotting the noisy Berlin train entering the station. And with sagging eyes, he watched the black monster approach and thought of the captivating blond girl on the train. Inside one of the black monster's green tabernacles, he gazed outside his window at a youthful couple kissing under an umbrella.

"Freddy, you won't pass university exams looking out the window," said his mother in a harsh voice that matched the disgust on her face.

He lifted his chin and gave her a decisive nod, saying to her in a quiet voice, "Yes, I should study hard, while I can." He picked up a book with a serious expression.

"I'm glad you agree with me."

With a gleam in his eyes, his father's voice tensed, betraying his genuine feelings. "Freddy's maturing; the way he stared at the young girl on the train made me aware of it."

"Uh, why? Because he gawked at a girl on a train?"

With eyelids lifted, concentrating on Freddy, his father said, "No, that was just the beginning. Freddy acted like a responsible adult, and it pleased me to observe him with his younger cousins. And happy noticing him dote over my father, your mother, Heinz, and Manfred." And winking at

Freddy, his father said in a pleased voice, "Son, I'm proud of you."

His mother's gaze shifted to him; she looked pleased.

Freddy's blue eyes twinkled as he grinned at them. And he sighed with a sense of mental clarity, with the impression his spirit had been reborn.

Chapter Four

May 9, 1915: Detroit

F reddy rocked back and forth in the pew, flattening his lips, eyeing a slow-moving old priest approaching the altar. "You're in church, Freddy; sit still," said his mother in a quiet but tense voice. He glanced up, catching a frown. "Stay still."

His father squeezed his knee. And he flinched, making a sourpuss face. His father pinched him harder. "Ouch!" Within minutes, a smile flashed on his face as he noticed the priest vanish behind the altar. *Time for lunch with Rolf at the German Club.*

His father took him by the hand and steered him outside Saint Paul's church. Blinded by the sun's intense rays, and squinting, he moved his head the other way and stood with his parents and Aunt Andrea, waiting for Uncle Tomas to come with a baby buggy. Freddy roared, yanking on his father's coat. "Papa, want to see Rolf now?"

Uncle Tomas said with an upturned face, "I'm ready, Freddy; let's go to the German Club."

Freddy grinned, picturing eating a pretzel with Rolf.

Aware of a few of their big words and sad faces, he pieced together what the adults talked about as they headed for the German Club. Uncle pushed baby Charlotte across the road up onto the sidewalk. His father gripped his hand tightly as they crossed the bumpy street, followed by his gabbing mother and aunt. Freddy was mindful of angry faces tuned in to his mother and aunt's loud chitchat. Freddy's father smiled in a pleasing manner, strengthening his grip. A beefy old lady wearing a mammoth hat wore a sour expression on her face, pointing her finger at his mother. "That lady spoke German—I heard her. And all of them left the German-speaking church."

Freddy's blue eyes clouded, and his lips jiggled as he glanced at the strangers.

A tall, whiskered man's loud voice made him recoil. "Dirty Huns, go back to Germany; we don't want Huns here." And Freddy shed tears, hearing more angry screams without understanding what they meant. "Blockheads…Huns…sank the Lusitania."

"Papa, Papa!"

A skinny woman's voice rose to a scream, saying, "A baby from Detroit died on that boat; too bad you weren't on board."

Freddy wrapped his arms around his father's leg, squeezing tight with trembling lips. "Papa, I want to go home."

"Tomas, better hurry," said his father, gathering Freddy in his arms.

Pursued by mad people with distorted expressions screaming unfamiliar words, he bawled, locking his eyes on angry faces gaining ground on him.

His father's voice had risen almost to a scream. "Andrea and Tomas, keep up; Germantown is not far."

"Papa, I'm scared," Freddy said, in tears into his father's ear.

Uncle Tomas, his mother, and his aunt gasped, trying to keep up with his father.

Freddy's head recoiled at the sound of a bottle smashing on the ground. He squeezed his eyes shut, hearing loud, obscure screams. The screaming mob hounded them for two more blocks. His father crossed over into Germantown and put Freddy's feet on the ground, staring quietly at the mob parked the other side of the boulevard. Crowds of German-speaking people congregated, exchanging angry words with the mob. An adolescent man shouted, raising a fist, "Better never see you in Germantown."

His aunt and mother made loud squawking noises, catching their breath.

The furious mob turned round and started walking away. One man in the crowd raised a fist. "We don't want block-heads living here." Confused, Freddy frowned, agonizing over the bitter words and angry glances from people.

His father sighed, twitching his nostrils at them. "They won't dare cross into Germantown."

Aunt Andrea and Uncle Tomas glared at each other with wide gapes.

Big-eyed, giving his father a harsh look, his mother whined, pressing her open hand against her breastbone. "Wilhelm, why are they mad at us? We didn't sink the boat."

Wilhelm mulled over his wife's words. Freddy gazed at his mother. *What boat?*

"Because they think we're loyal to the kaiser, not America."

His mother opened and closed her mouth before words came from it. "But Wilhelm, we're not, and it upset us to read the German submarine sunk the Lusitania."

Freddy examined his mother with a blank face.

"You're reading it in German newspapers," said his uncle, "they fill English papers with anti-German hatred."

He gawked at his mother, tilting his head. "Huh?"

"No, Tomas, we read English papers too," said his mother, giving Uncle Tomas a displeased stare.

Freddy scrutinized Uncle Tomas, knowing what the word "hatred" meant.

"Tomas, we're now Americans citizens, no different from them, we renounced our allegiance to Germany," spoke his mother, shifting her eyes to his father.

Aunt Andrea crossed her arms. "Barbara, you're a dreamer—you speak English with an accent."

Freddy's lips pressed together, staring at Aunt Andrea, not understanding what she meant.

"B-b-but we love living in America. My English is good; I read American newspapers and practice my accent."

Freddy's smile widened as he recalled reading English papers with her.

Aunt Andrea pressed her lips together, tapping her foot. "Listen to me. I was born here, but I'm still considered a blockhead."

His mother's voice firmed, and she gave Aunt Andrea a hard nod. "Andrea, don't say that word in front of Freddy."

He caught sight of Aunt Andrea building, a slow smile on his lips. "Aunt Andrea, what's a blockhead?"

His mother's lips twisted, and her voice took a harsh tone. "Don't tell him. Freddy's only five; he won't understand you."

Freddy's lips pursed; he shot a glance at his mother with empty eyes.

* * *

And he continued walking toward the German Club but had lost the bounce in his step. He traveled past endless rows of wood-framed homes till he turned onto Lafayette Avenue. His father zigzagged through crowds; most people dressed for church. His ears picked up clanging cable car bells and the *eeeeee* sound of a police car in the distance. He sighed with satisfaction, fingering marbles in his pocket, stopping at a corner on Lafayette Avenue. His eyes sparkled identifying the Gratiot Avenue sign; he knew they were approaching the German Club. He giggled and yanked on his father's hand. "Papa, go faster."

His father leaned forward, nodding at him. "I'll hurry."

Inside the concrete building, Freddy stepped over a long passageway with his father, viewing large paintings of scenery and bright chandeliers.

Rolf Keller spotted him and bounced in his seat. Freddy freed his hand and hunkered beside Rolf, snatching a handful of marbles from his pocket. "Rolf, want one?"

Rolf's face glowed. "Freddy, this one."

Except for Rolf's parents, everyone gave each other a dirty look.

"It was scary!" said his mother, rolling her eyes.

"Nice to see you too, Barbara," said Rolf's father, frowning. "I've received warmer hellos from a dead horse."

Freddy's smile turned into a grimace. *Dead horse?*

"Nils, it was awful—you and Hilda should be glad you weren't with us. Freddy cried, listening to hysterical shouts."

He grimaced, not understanding what the word "hysterical" meant.

Rolf's mother's eyes bulged, and she said, slumping, "I'll never feel safe anymore."

His father tapped hard on the table. "Where's Ursula when you need her?"

"Wilhelm, she went into the kitchen," uttered Rolf's chunky mother.

Ass-first Ursula exited through the kitchen door, balancing trays of food.

Rolf's father rose, saying to the plump woman wearing her gray-streaked hair in a bun, "Ursula, six Pfeiffer and two root beers when you get around to it."

"Okay, Nils; give me a few secs."

Ursula hurried back with drinks, planting a kiss on Rolf's and Freddy's cheeks. "Rolf and Friedrich, you're the best-looking boys in the entire world."

He sipped his root beer, noticing Ursula had stepped back, rubbing her chin. "Thirsty bunch you are—what's the hurry?"

His mother wiped foam off her top lip. "Ursula, you'll never believe what happened to us after church."

"Let me tell Ursula what happened." Aunt Andrea interrupted, expelling a lengthy breath.

Ursula circled her eyes and moved closer. Rolf and Freddy finished drinking their root beers while she explained to Ursula what had happened.

Rolf raised his cheekbones. "Freddy, can I have one more marble?" Freddy snickered, reaching inside his pocket for another marble.

"Thanks for the marbles," said Rolf, teetering in his seat, smiling.

Rolf's mother frowned and spit in her hand, applying her slobber on her son's cowlick.

"Sit still, Rolf Keller; do you hear me?"

Rolf fidgeted with his hands, looking his mother in the eye. "Y-yes, mother."

Freddy crossed his arms, glaring at Rolf's mother. He mulled over Rolf's chance meeting with Sister Margaret at Saint Paul's playground. He pictured the angry nun's red face as she grabbed hold of Rolf's collar and twisted it till he cried. "Rolf Keller, stop sticking your tongue at the girls and calling them names; the next time I catch you, I'll wash your mouth with Ivory soap."

Aunt Andrea's high-pitched voice broke into his thoughts.

"Ursula, can you picture running away from angry people, afraid Charlotte's buggy might tip over?" complained Aunt Andrea, unable to sit still. "God only knows why my hat stayed put. I ask you, where's the police when you need them? I don't think I'll be safe walking anymore outside Germantown."

He frowned, unable to figure out the answer to Aunt Andrea's question.

"I hope people will calm themselves before it gets out of hand," said Rolf's father as he crossed and uncrossed his arms. And laugh lines broke at the corners of his mouth. "Drink up—I'm buying the next round of beers."

His father gave him a warm smile.

"Barbara, any news from Father Vogel?" asked Rolf's mother, fingering her short brown hair.

"Yes, got a letter from him Wednesday; he said little. The church needs painting, and the roof leaks. He couldn't wait for the weather to warm. He misses Sunday picnics."

"Oh, how are Heinz and Manfred doing? Is your mother well?"

His mother leaned back and said in a soft voice, "Thanks for asking, Hilda. Mother's fine. Heinz does most things for himself, lets Manfred help him if he needs it. Manfred's still having nightmares. I'm glad my father died before seeing what the war did to his sons."

Freddy frowned, glaring at his mother. "Mama, what's a nightmare? Why are you glad Grandpa died? Did you love him?"

"Freddy, I'm not glad Grandpa's dead; why don't you play with Rolf?"

Ursula reappeared, and the grown-ups chose the Sunday special—pork, potatoes, and sauerkraut.

Deep folds linked the corners of Rolf's father's lips with his nose, and he smiled. "Ursula, six more Pfeiffer please."

He bared his gums, watching Rolf dunk his pretzel in mustard, then lick it clean with a few fast swipes of his tongue. Rolf's mother sighed, spotting mustard on the tablecloth.

"Rolf Keller, watch what you're doing; want people to think you're a slob?" barked Rolf's mother, tensing her lips.

"Let him be, Hilda; he's having fun," said Rolf's father, grimacing at his wife.

Rolf's father's baritone voice brought a smile to Freddy's face. He loved visiting the Harmonie Club when Rolf's father sang in a choir. He always bought fizzy root beers for Freddy and Rolf when it ended.

* * *

Freddy and Rolf held hands, laughing and frolicking on familiar streets heading toward Germantown.

Inside Germantown his mother stopped walking and said in a sad voice, "I'll never be safe outside Germantown again."

"Stop talking that way, Barbara; it will get better," said his father, narrowing his brows and creasing his forehead.

Freddy tightened his grip on Rolf's hand, throwing frightened glances at the adults.

Chapter Five

1917: America Enters the War in Europe

"Freddy, where does time go, Easter Sunday will be here in less than two weeks."

He gave his mother a toothy smile and continued reading *Bunny Brown and His Sister Sue*. Loud footsteps surprised Freddy on the porch, and his brows jumped, and his head twitched. The front door flung open, and his father rushed inside, expelling rasping breaths with Uncle Tomas and Rolf's father behind him.

"Barbara, did you hear the news?" said his father, unable to stand still, adding shock to his voice.

"W-what news, Wilhelm?"

"Barbara, President Wilson declared war on Germany."

"What? That's not possible, Wilhelm?" said his mother in a doubting voice.

Uncle Tomas uncrossed his arms, and firmed his voice saying to his mother, "It's true, Barbara, he did."

"Do Andrea and Hilda know?"

"No. We stopped here first," said his father, rocking from one foot to the other.

His mother's chin trembled, and her voice took an anxious tone; she played with a strand of her hair. "My head's spinning; what could happen to us? I'm confused."

His father's head froze, and he said with a confused look on his face, sticking his hands inside his pant pockets, "Let me think."

Freddy shut his eyes, thinking back to his parent's discussions of dead and wounded soldiers in trenches in France.

"I'm scared. What might happen to us? We're German."

Freddy's lips curled as he took notice of the tremors in her voice.

His father's eyes narrowed; he considered Barbara's question. "What could go wrong? I work for Ford, and we're citizens."

"Are you sure of it?"

Freddy opened his eyes, spotting a frown on Rolf's father's face.

His mother sniveled, resting her fingertips on her chest. "It's been two years since the mob chased us inside Germantown, but I still see the hatred in their eyes."

Freddy shivered, recalling the awful day, and sighed, watching Uncle Tomas's head dip.

His father's lips formed a thin line as he looked at Uncle Tomas and Rolf's father. His head swayed, and he added delight to his voice. "I'll get us beers."

Rolf's father's shoulders slumped. "Wilhelm, I need something stronger—got whiskey?"

His father returned with two beers and a half-full glass of whiskey. Rolf's father emptied the glass in a few big swallows.

"Bring me the bottle." Rolf's father's face lit up as he eyed the label. "Ah, it's Old—"

But his mother interrupted him saying with a harsh edge to her voice, "Nils Keller, drop the bottle; Wilhelm and Tomas don't need to bring you home drunk. What will Hilda and Rolf think seeing you that way?"

* * *

Rolf slipped onto his head a dark blue Detroit Tigers baseball cap, nodding and smiling, saying to Freddy, "Throw me the ball, Freddy; I can catch it."

He angled his body toward Rolf, pulling back his right arm with his weight on his back foot, beaming. "Get ready; here it comes," said Freddy, throwing himself forward on his left foot, releasing the ball.

Rolf caught the ball and jumped, ecstatic. "You caught it, Rolf," said Freddy, grinning.

"Splendid catch, Rolf; I'm proud of you. Do it again," whooped Rolf's father, lifting his chest, nodding and smiling as he spoke.

"Freddy, throw the ball higher."

Freddy sucked in air as Rolf's father put a cigarette in his mouth, and he tossed the ball higher in the air. "Catch it, Rolf." Freddy's feet bounced, and his face glowed, seeing Rolf's glove squeeze the ball. "Wow, Rolf, you did it! You caught the ball!"

Rolf danced in place, eyeing his father, widening his smile.

His father jumped, dropping the cigarette he had been jiggling between his lips. "Rolf, you caught the ball." Rolf's father held his smile, picking up the cigarette, and relaxed in a wicker chair, puffing on it.

A black police car pulled up; two hostile-looking police officers dressed in dark blue uniforms stepped out of it and headed for the porch steps. Freddy's mouth fell open, with his blue eyes scrutinizing the police officers. Rolf's father rose, pulling the cigarette out of his mouth, squinting at the police officers. Rolf and Freddy followed the blue suits edging up the creaky steps.

One officer, tall and slender with a pointy nose, stopped, glancing at Rolf and Freddy before approaching Rolf's father. "Sir, are you Nils Keller?"

With a bit of a frown, Rolf's father threw his cigarette on the floor and crushed it with a shoe, speaking broken English. "I am Nils Keller; is something wrong?"

"I think so, Mr. Keller. I hold here a paper calling for your arrest," said the officer, puffing air in Rolf's father's face.

Rolf's father's eyes bulged. "A-arrest me? I-I-I do nothing wrong; y-you got the wrong person?"

"It says here you did," said the shorter officer, waving a piece of paper in front of Nils. "Is this you? Can you read your name?"

"Yeah, my name's Nils Keller. I can read my name on the paper, but I do nothing wrong."

"Mr. Keller, a judge called for your arrest on suspicion you're a German spy."

Rolf's father scratched his head. "Not me. I no spy; I work assembly line at Ford Motor Company. Everyone there tells you that."

"It says right here, Mr. Keller, you've got a brother fighting for the kaiser overseas. And that you might be a German sympathizer," argued the officer, placing his index finger on a line.

"Um, what 'sympathizer' means?"

"I'm sorry, can't spend the day answering questions, Mr. Keller. I must take you in; please don't give me any trouble."

Rolf shrugged, gawking. "What do police officers want with Papa; he looks sick?"

Rolf's mother hummed a tune, backing out the screen door with two Coca-Colas. When she turned, her eyes bulged and her mouth flew open as she discovered handcuffs around her husband's wrists. The Coca-Colas fell from her hands, fizzing with a foamy brown liquid when they hit the floor. Rolf's father's face whitened as he spoke to her in German. "Hilda, they think I'm a spy because Aldo's in the

German Army. The police are taking me downtown to jail. Hurry, go see Wilhelm and tell him what happened."

Rolf flinched and bawled, grasping his father's words, and grabbed hold of his teary-eyed mother's waist. The police car sped away, leaving a trail of smoke and dust behind it. Rolf's frantic mother whined, panting, blinking hard. "I don't understand; Nils is no spy." She grabbed Rolf and Freddy's hands, crying. "Come with me; we're going to see Freddy's father."

* * *

Bang, bang, bang. Rolf's mother's knuckles pounded on the door, puffing hard.

"Be patient; I'm coming," said Freddy's father from the other side of the door.

He peeked out the curtains, widening his gaze before opening the door. Rolf's mother burst inside, weeping.

"Hilda, what's wrong? Where...where's Nils?"

Her mouth opened and closed, and she struggled to find her voice. "W-W-Wilhelm."

Freddy's mother rushed inside the room with a quizzical expression on her face. His father fetched a glass of water for the panting woman. And she spilled drops on her dress, drinking it with a shaky hand.

"I want my papa," screamed Rolf, flailing his arms and stomping his feet. His mother placed her trembling fingers against her lips.

"Hilda, tell us what happened," said his mother, wrinkling her brows.

"It's Nils. Two police officers took him away in handcuffs."

Freddy's father perked up with a dazed expression covering his face. "What? Impossible What'd he do?"

"W-W-Wilhelm, Nils said, it's because Aldo's in the German Army and they think he's a spy."

"Hilda, that's absurd," said Freddy's mother, "Nil's no spy."

His father ran his hands through his hair. "The entire country's gone mad since the war started." And he pinched his lips, gazing at Rolf's mother. "I'll get Tomas and go downtown to city jail to see what's happening. Hilda, stay calm till we get back; I'm sure it's a big misunderstanding."

Sunlight penetrated the kitchen window, targeting a picture on the wall, at the time Freddy's father and uncle left the house. Hours passed before the kitchen door opened and shut.

"It's Papa!" said Rolf with a sparkle in his eyes.

Standing in front of the darkened kitchen window, his father bowed his head. Rolf's mother fell into a seat, burying her head in her shaking hands. "No, Wilhelm—where's Nils?"

Rolf wept, pulling on his mother's sleeve. "I want Papa."

His mother wrapped Rolf in her arms. "Papa will come home soon."

Freddy's father shook his head. "I'm sorry, Hilda, there's nothing we could do. They didn't let us see Nils. The police officer behind the desk said the Justice Department accused Nils of spying for Germany."

Rolf's mother sniveled, adjusting her grip on her son. "T-that's not true. I'm his wife; I should know if he's a spy."

With a bleak expression on his face, his father toyed with his watch. "Hilda, you know it, but they don't."

The woman twisted her mouth, expanding her chest. "Wilhelm, Nils is no spy."

* * *

Freddy rose, dimpling his cheek. He fluffed his pillow and laid his head back in its softness, reckoning the judge might free Rolf's father today.

His head moved sideways as he picked up on a knock on the door. "Freddy, breakfast is ready; are you up?"

He rose, eyeballing the shiny glass doorknob. "Yes, Mother; I'll get dressed."

"Did you forget Rolf's coming over today?"

With a warm smile, he stretched his arms. "No, Mother, I didn't forget."

Freddy's face shined as he listened to a knock on the kitchen door and placed his milk on the table. His father sighed, putting down his coffee, and answered the door. Puffy-faced, Hilda Keller rushed in, gripping Rolf's hand.

"Please sit," said his mother, giving her a pensive smile.

Rolf stood by his mother, dull-eyed, clutching her arm.

Aunt Andrea arrived minutes later, followed by Uncle Tomas with Charlotte in his arms. His mother smiled, taking the sleeping child from his uncle, and carried her to the bedroom. Freddy left his seat, making room for Aunt Andrea to sit.

"Tomas, I'm going, and that's it," argued Aunt Andrea, glaring at his uncle.

His uncle's nose and brows wrinkled. "Andrea, you're pregnant; it'll be too hot inside the courthouse. Nils will understand why you're not there."

Freddy's mouth popped open, and he turned an eye to Aunt Andrea's stomach.

With a hint of a frown, Aunt Andrea rolled her eyes. "Tomas, Barbara can watch Charlotte, and Freddy can play with Rolf."

"Okay, have it your way, be pigheaded," whined Uncle Tomas, blushing a rosy color.

Rolf's mother stood, pulling Rolf's hands away, and straightened the black belt wrapped around her ankle-length blue dress.

"Mama, don't go." Rolf sobbed, flapping his arms.

Freddy's mother seized Rolf's hand. "Hilda, he'll be fine; we'll take excellent care of him."

"Barbara, he might nap he cried a lot during the night."

Rolf fell to the floor, slapping it with his hands. "Mama, Mama, don't go," he screamed, trembling.

His mother patted Hilda Keller on her back. "You better get going; he'll quiet when you're gone."

Close to tears, with pain written on her face, Rolf's mother answered her with a slow nod.

After everyone left, Rolf calmed and fell asleep. Freddy tilted his head at his mother, dwelling on words he had overheard. "Mother, what's a trial?"

His mother kept her eyes on him for seconds. "You're too young to understand."

He curled his bottom lip. "Mother, please tell me."

"Okay, but pay close attention. Freddy, a man, sits behind a high bench and decides based on evidence if someone did something wrong; he's a problem solver. Did you understand me?"

"Think so—Rolf's father went to jail because he did something wrong."

"No Freddy, this time the judge made a mistake sending Rolf's father to jail. Rolf's father did nothing wrong."

Freddy shrugged, furrowing his brows.

With occasional tears, Rolf held onto his misery the whole morning. At lunch he just took two bites of his peanut butter and jelly sandwich and stared at his plate the rest of the time. "Rolf, do you want to look at my baseball cards?"

His lips rounded, and he buried his neck in his shoulders. "No, I don't won't to play with your baseball cards."

Rolf left the kitchen and curled up on the sofa. Freddy eased himself into the cushy rocker and read a book, often checking on Rolf while he slept.

The sky darkened, and Freddy caught the kitchen door open and close. He jumped off the rocker and dashed inside the kitchen, auditing four sad faces, figuring it had not gone well for Rolf's father in court. Rolf's mother scented the room with her sweat. Freddy's mother walked in silent, shooting her eyes in every direction.

"Andrea, Charlotte's napping, she's been good all day."

Aunt Andrea's face softened, and she gazed at his mother. "Let me peek at her."

His mother slanted her head at his father's limp face, widening her eyes.

"Freddy, please go in the living room, and don't you wake up Rolf."

He grimaced and tiptoed to the living room, reclining on the rocker, spying on the adults.

"The judge found Nils guilty," said his father in a quiet and tense voice.

Freddy frowned, replaying the word "guilty" in his brain.

"No, Wilhelm; Nils can't be guilty," said his mother.

"The judge threw the book at him; he convicted him of espionage."

"Can't be, that's impossible. He did nothing wrong, he's an innocent man. What proof did they have?"

"I think the judge was afraid Nils might sabotage the Ford plant," Uncle Tomas pointed out in a loud whisper. "I think the judge decided before Nil's walked inside the court room."

"No, he walked into hell," whined Freddy's mother. "Nils couldn't hurt a fly; it's hearsay. Where's the evidence? Damn the person who turned him in; I hope they rot in hell."

Freddy grimaced, glancing at Rolf, touched by a slight tingle in his stomach.

His father's voice sounded strained. "The judge asked Nils if he and Aldo wrote each other. Nils nodded, said he did, but didn't save the letters. It made the judge mad, and he asked Nils why he didn't become a citizen. He told him he loves America but hadn't gotten around to it. Nils's accent bothered the judge. He asked Nils how long he had lived in America. And he was furious when Nils said nine years."

"Nils did nothing on time; it was his nature." Rolf's mother sniveled. "Nils didn't go with me when I swore allegiance to a judge and signed the papers. He always found something else to do."

Freddy's mother's voice sounded sad. "What will happen to Nils?"

"His father said, in a pained voice, "Two court officers led him away in handcuffs. He couldn't raise his head. Tomorrow morning they're taking Nils to a prison in Georgia."

"Honey, for how long?"

"The judge didn't give a date."

Rolf's mother's voice dropped, and she spoke painful words. "How will Rolf and I manage without Nils?"

"Hilda, there's no cause to worry; we're here for you and Rolf."

"Prison!" said Freddy to himself, giving Rolf a wistful gaze.

His mother said, hardening her words. "Oh no, Wilhelm— it can happen to us too."

Freddy's mouth fell open, and he drove his back against the cushion.

"What is it?" his father asked.

"Don't you see it, Wilhelm?" His mother fussed.

"See what?"

"Otto—Otto's fighting for Germany. They might jail you and Tomas, too. From now on, we can't mention Otto's name. If someone finds out who he is, we could be under suspicion. We must be careful; there're spies everywhere."

Freddy covered his ears, agonizing over the adults' words.

Rolf yawned, waking up, then growing still, assessing Freddy. "Is my father back, Freddy?"

* * *

Freddy swallowed his last spoonful of baked beans and licked the spoon clean. Rolf lapped up the mustard on his frankfurter before biting into it.

"Hurry, Rolf; your mother will be here soon, and she'll be mad if food's on your plate. Don't you want a cookie?"

Rolf's lips turned up, and he nodded. "Yes, Mrs. Bauer."

Freddy beamed, delighted at Rolf's smile.

Rolf ate his dinner, and Freddy's mother laid a plate of cookies on the table and walked back to the sink to clean the dirty dishes.

Freddy's eyes widened, catching Rolf slip two cookies into his pocket as he broadcasted a mischievous smile.

Rolf's mother walked in at her usual time, wearing the same black dress and white apron she wore every day.

"Hi, Barbara. Tough day. Hope Rolf behaved himself?"

"He did. Freddy and I love having Rolf around; he's no trouble. Freddy's teaching him English words."

"Good. His father never did. I don't know what we'd do without Saint Paul's."

"Freddy, bring Rolf to the living room and read a book to him," said his mother, pointing a finger, giving him a vigorous nod.

He gave her a fake smile and grabbed Rolf's hand, pulling him into the living room. Rolf couldn't sit still and slid off the sofa, crawling within hearing range of the kitchen, and crossed his index finger over his lips. "Shush!"

Freddy's eyes narrowed on Rolf. The devilish smile on Rolf's face raised Freddy's cheeks, and he inched toward him.

"Barbara, look at my knuckles. Bitch made me scrub pots with the cook the complete day. She threw a party yesterday, and every damn one of them was full of crud. The bitch is entertaining people Saturday. Can you watch Rolf for me?"

"Sure I can, Hilda. Freddy loves having Rolf here."

Rolf stared at Freddy. "Mrs. Bitch is a meanie."

Freddy slapped his hand over his mouth.

"Hilda, have you heard from Nils? He doesn't answer our letters."

"I did, but his letters never change."

"What do you mean?"

"They're never different—asks me how Rolf's doing and tells me he doesn't know how long he'll be in prison and nothing else."

"It must be hard on him being cooped up in a prison."

"I miss Nils. Mrs. Bitch won't give me have three days off. I take an entire day to reach the prison. She doesn't know Nils is in prison. Rolf doesn't understand; he never stops asking when his father is coming home and cries for him at bedtime."

Rolf dragged himself back to the sofa. Freddy cuddled up beside him, saying with a note of softness in his voice, "Rolf, your father loves you; he'll come back."

Rolf slumped, sniffing, and faced the wall, sticking his hands inside his pockets. Freddy's eyes glowed as he noticed the kitchen door open. And he sprung from the sofa to the kitchen, jumping into his father's arms and kissing him.

"I'm glad to see you too," said his father, lifting his cheeks.

* * *

"Mam, the coat fits the boy," said the dapper junior clerk, beaming at his mother, uncrossing his arms.

His mother frowned, pulling on the coat's shoulders. "I'm not sure; what do you think, Wilhelm?"

Freddy's father tugged on his blue six-buttoned coat's shoulders and yanked on the sleeves.

"It's big, but he'll grow into it. Freddy, do you want the coat?"

"Yes. Blue's my favorite color; I want it."

"Good, we'll take it; that solves one problem." Freddy's mother rejoiced, speaking in a pleasant voice, tilting her eyes at Rolf. "Now we need to find one for this boy."

"I want a blue coat too, the same as Freddy," squawked Rolf, furrowing his brows and stomping his feet.

The clerk scratched his head, peering at Rolf. "I don't understand what he said."

Freddy's eyes furrowed, and he stepped closer to the man whose hair color resembled the mustard at the German Club. "Mr. Rolf only speaks German; he wants a coat that looks the same as mine."

"Oh, why is it he's the only one that doesn't speak English?"

"His parents don't speak English at home."

"What a shame, lady; he should speak English if he's living in America," said the clerk with a note of contempt in his voice. "How old is the boy?"

"Rolf's seven."

The clerk searched three coat racks and disappeared behind a door.

"Rolf, the nice young man's trying to find you a blue coat that's the same as Freddy's."

Rolf's feet bounced, and he beamed, catching the clerk coming from the back room with coats.

"Lady, one of these coats I found in the backroom should fit the boy."

His mother gave the clerk an adoring gaze. "It fits. Thank you. Wilhelm, please pay the nice man."

Once they crossed into Germantown, his father turned onto Mullett and went along the peaceful street.

"Wilhelm, the boys must be hungry. Weren't the stores crowded?"

"Yes. I'm glad we didn't waste the entire day looking for coats; I've other things to do."

"Me too. Thank God we got the boys' coats. I wasn't looking forward to shopping at Hudson's or Kern's. Since the war started, I'm afraid to walk outside Germantown."

Freddy picked up shouting coming from Karl and Gunter's house. His father, wearing a long face, stopped to listen.

"Barbara, Heinrich's cursing at the boys." Said his father, giving his mother a dazed look. "I wonder what's happening."

"He's always yelling at Karl and Gunter; let's go eat lunch."

"You're right—let's eat lunch."

Mrs. Schmidt flew out the front door. The shapeless old woman dripped tears, saying, "Wilhelm, help me. Heinrich's screaming at the boys and might hurt them."

"Emma, what's wrong?"

Mrs. Schmid bared her teeth, breathing hard. "It's the boys; Karl and Gunter enlisted in the army with their friends. Heinrich lost his temper and threw a chair at Karl. He told the boys they'd get themselves killed."

Rolf shivered and hugged himself.

Mrs. Schmidt tilted her head at Freddy's mother. "Barbara, they're too young to fight in a war."

Freddy's father rocked in place, glancing at the house. "Let me talk to Heinrich; he might listen to me."

"Stay here with us; Heinrich is a powerful man."

"I'll be okay, Barbara; we've always gotten along with each other."

Freddy frowned, watching his father disappear inside the noisy house. He gazed at his mother, visualizing Mr. Schmidt's huge muscles.

"Emma, is Wilhelm safe in the house?"

Mrs. Schmidt looked his mother in the eye. "He should be; Heinrich isn't mad at him."

Freddy detected a baseball bat leaning against the fence. And a smile crossed his lips as it called to mind, playing baseball with Karl and Gunter. His eyes sparkled. He thought back to the time Karl nicknamed him "slugger" after he walloped his pitch over his head.

"Heinrich stopped yelling," said his mother, raising her vocal pitch.

Rolf buried his head in Freddy's mother's stomach.

Freddy squeezed his lips, scrutinizing the empty doorframe, and gasped as he spotted his father walk out grinning with a beer.

"Emma, you can go back inside; Heinrich and the boys are drinking a beer."

"Barbara's a lucky woman to possess such a wonderful husband," said Karl and Gunter's mother with a radiant face.

His mother's cheeks turned pink as she caressed Rolf.

"Papa, what's 'enlisted' mean?"

His father gulped a mouthful of beer from the amber bottle. "It means you want to be a soldier."

"Papa, isn't it good to be a soldier?"

His father took another gulp, staring into space. "You'll never be a soldier if I can help it."

Freddy pouted, gazing up at his mother, who rubbed the back of his neck. "I can fight. Karl taught me—jab twice and unload the haymaker."

His father smiled, "Freddy, I bet you can."

His mother gasped, placing her hand over her heart. "Wilhelm, Emma's right—I'm married to a wonderful man. What did you say to Heinrich to calm him?"

"Nothing. It was easy; pulled out four beers from the ice-box and put them on the table, smiling at Heinrich."

As she grinned widely, his mother's cheeks blushed, and she squeezed his father's hand.

* * *

Rolf's mother hugged herself and coughed, wandering inside the kitchen with Rolf. "Barbara, I might carry a cold. Hope Rolf doesn't get it; he never leaves me alone since Nils went away. Rolf's coat is good and warm. He needed one. Let me pay for it?" asked Hilda.

Freddy's mother frowned, planting her hands on her hips. "Hilda, we've gone over this before. Save your money; you might need it one day."

Rolf's mother had a pleasant edge to her voice. "Thank you, Barbara. Must run—don't want Mrs. Johnson to cut my wages for being a minute late."

Rolf's mother threw a white scarf around her neck and kissed the top of Rolf's head. "I love you; be good for Mrs. Bauer."

Freddy scrunched his eyes. "What does 'cut my wages' mean? Mama, do you need a scissor to do it?"

"Not now, Freddy. Get ready for school; I don't want Sister Emily sending you home with a note for me."

Freddy and Rolf put on their new blue coats, red scarfs, and mittens and headed off for Saint Paul's. Dicky and Gus shivered the other side of Russell Street, chilled from the cold, waiting for them. Gus and Dicky kicked a can up Gratiot Avenue.

Gus picked up the can, staring at Rolf poking his cheek with his tongue. "Rolf, is your father still in jail?"

Dicky narrowed his eyes on Rolf. "If he's in jail, he killed someone."

Rolf dropped his head.

Freddy's gaze moved between Gus and Dicky. "Rolf's father killed no one. My mother told me he did nothing wrong," said Freddy, squinting at Dicky.

Dicky's head tilted, and he scrunched his lips. "He killed someone; that's why he's in jail."

Rolf wiped away snot from under his nose with a finger. "Don't say that."

"I won't stop, and you can't make me." Dicky scowled at Rolf.

"I can." Freddy whacked Dicky in the stomach, making his mouth fly open.

Unable to speak, Dicky sucked in air through his trembling lips and ran up ahead.

Gus tagged behind Rolf and Freddy. Rolf stopped and bobbed at the curb, noticing two white-booted horses exhaling clouds of smoke, pulling a wagon full of beer barrels.

A pudgy man who sat alongside the driver raised his cheeks and waved at Rolf.

"Freddy, when I'm big, I want to do that."

"You can't, Rolf. My father said you can't buy beer anymore; that's why he keeps it in the cellar and we can't use the punching bag."

Rolf's eyes moistened. He shook his head and faced Freddy with raised brows, opening and closing his mouth, speechless.

Chapter Six

1918 and 1919: Two Dark Years

Whack, whack, screech, whack. Sister Emily's chalk struck the blackboard as she wrote words with her long strokes, sending shivers up Freddy's spine. He shifted his head, avoiding Rolf's cowlick for a better look at what the tight-lipped nun was writing. The skinny woman with a prominent chin faced the class with her brows twitching, spotting Dicky napping. Her lips crinkled, and she slithered toward Dicky and slapped her hands together hard above his head. Dicky's mouth flung open, and he trembled at the sight of the nun's icy glare. Sister Emily's white knuckles beat down on Dicky's desk. Her face reddened, and she and said, raising her voice, "Dicky Sturm, go stand in the corner."

At the last bell, Freddy rose, scrutinizing an image of a cross on a white wall, and gazed outside, blinking, seeing the bright sun behind the church steeple.

Rolf tugged on his sleeve, smiling. "It's Friday; can we go see the horses?"

"My mother will be mad at us if we come home late."

"Freddy, please, can we go? I promise we won't stay long."

He gave Rolf a quick nod. "Okay, but not long."

Rolf's face glowed, and he bounced on his feet.

Freddy and Rolf raced across an old wood-planked railroad bridge and flew to the bottom of its stairs, heading for a stable with weathered gray wood. Freddy's nostrils flickered, catching the odorous scent of horseshit.

"Chester's here; let's go pet him," said Rolf in a loud voice.

"Want to give Chester an apple?" said a silvery-voiced stable hand, offering Rolf an apple.

Rolf lifted his chin and danced on his toes, feeding Chester the apple.

"We better head home; my mother might be angry if we're late."

Rolf swatted at a horsefly. "Please—one more minute?"

He swayed, concentrating on Rolf, rubbing the back of his neck. "One more minute, then we should go home."

Rolf ignored him, petting Chester with a wide grin.

With restless legs Freddy said to Rolf, drawing his brows together, "We better run home; my mother is going to be mad at us."

Rolf's face lit up as they approached the bridge's steps. "I'll be eight March fourteenth. My mother's making a chocolate cake for me; are you coming to my house?"

Freddy displayed a dimpled grin. "Yes, my mother bought you a present at Kern's."

Rolf moved back and forth, swinging his arms, smiling his delight. "Kern's—the present must cost lots of money?"

The boys frolicked on the creaky bridge, spotting three boys coming the other way. One, who stood inches above the others, positioned himself in front of Freddy and lowered his head, flaring his nostrils. "Where are you going, punks?"

"Home," said Freddy, speaking in a hushed tone.

"I've never seen you guys before; where do you go to school?"

Freddy stepped back and turned, pointing at Saint Paul's, saying, "That's our school, over there."

The tall boy eyed Saint Paul's and cranked his head slow toward Freddy, squinting. "Are you boys German?"

Freddy elevated his chin, giving the boy a quick nod. "Yes, I am."

The boy rubbed the inside of his cheek with his tongue before speaking with an inquisitive voice. "Is he German too?"

His voice cracked, and he slumped his shoulders. "Yes, but he can't speak English."

"I hate Germans," said the boy, drawing air, releasing it in Freddy's face. Freddy's jaw dropped; he stepped back, focusing on the boy. The bully gathered saliva in his mouth and discharged spit in Freddy's face through his puckered lips.

His eyes bulged, and he wiped the boy's drool off his face, which was turning white. "Why did you do that?"

"Are you dumb? I told you I hate Germans; my uncle's fighting them in France."

The angry boy unloaded another round of saliva at Freddy's face and punched him hard in the stomach. He buckled, releasing wind. And the bully punched him in the mouth, knocking him to the deck. And he cried, rubbing blood off his bleeding lip.

One of the other boys pinned back Rolf's arms, and another slugged him in the mouth. Rolf wailed, bloody lipped, "Freddddy, help me." Freddy caught his breath and got to his feet. The big boy laughed and shoved him to the ground, listening to Rolf's cries. "Freddddy, Freddddy, help me."

His heart pounded, and he stayed on his keister, breathing hard.

"Bobby, he's bleeding; hit the crybaby again," said the tall boy, tilting his head at Rolf.

Bobby did, again and again, and Freddy wept, looking over Rolf's bloodied face.

"Hey, boys, stop fighting," screamed a man running toward him. The boys scrambled the other way, heading for the street.

65

The man, wearing a soiled coat, grabbed Freddy's shoulders and shook them. "It's too dangerous to fight up here; you're lucky one of you didn't fall off the bridge and get killed."

Freddy puffed hard, collecting his thoughts. "They started it," he said, pointing to the other end of the bridge.

Rolf cried, shaking his head, weeping, and he bolted for the stairs. Freddy yanked away from the man and trailed behind him. Rolf descended the stairs and ran into the street in front of a fast-moving cable car. Freddy screamed, "Rolf!" covering his face, hearing a loud thump, crying. "Rolf, Rolf!" And he backed away, slowly shaking his head before falling to his knees, sobbing. "Rolf!" He wept, picking up somber voices from a crowd. His eyes bulged as he saw a young-looking man placing his coat over Rolf. A loud police siren rung in his ears. His knees knocked together. He spotted a blue suit pull back the coat hiding Rolf. A youthful woman wrapped Freddy in her coat, giving his hand a soft squeeze.

"Freddy, Freddy," screamed his mother, dragging her fingers down her cheek as she arrived at the scene. "Where's Rolf?"

He stood on weak legs, sobbing with shortness of breath and tears blurring his vision, angling his head toward the crowd. "Mama, it's my fault."

His devastated mother spun around screaming, "No, no, it can't be; he's a young boy."

Freddy's lips trembled, and he cried, seeing his hysterical mother slap her sides, weeping. "He a young boy!"

His mother hurried back, sticking her quivering chin in his back. Haunted by what had happened, he sobbed, and said, "Mother, I should have stopped Rolf."

* * *

Freddy gave a glassy stare to the drab brown painted walls and curtains inside Pohl's funeral home. And with his father beside him, he wept, feeling nauseous, with his mind growing dull. His father sniveled and held his hand, tightening his fingers around it.

"It's my fault Rolf's dead," said Freddy, bawling, letting tears drip off his chin.

"Rolf, I love you," screamed Rolf's mother.

Freddy closed his eyes, plagued by her hysterical cries. He glanced up at his father, noticing his welled-up eyes. "Why can't Rolf's father be here?" He wept, shaking his head.

His father bowed his head and softened his tone to convey his thoughts. "Freddy, the prison has its rules, and letting Rolf's father go to the funeral isn't one of them." His father drew his brows together and slumped, saying to him, "It's not right, but maybe one day they'll come to their senses."

Freddy stood up, wearing a somber expression, and dragged himself toward the closed wooden box. His knees poked the padded kneeler, and he wiped a booger off his nose, laying eyes on white flowers placed behind Rolf's coffin. His cheeks burned red, and he shut his eyes, performing the sign of the cross. *Please God, forgive me; I needed to stop Rolf.*

Depressed, he hung his head and walked away heavy-legged to the darkest corner of the room. For him, the dials on the clock never moved. His deadpan expression never left him. He caught Father Schultz beside Rolf's casket. The slim priest with salt-and-pepper hair brought his hands together and prayed for Rolf's soul. Freddy rocked, imagining Rolf at school, the stable, the German Club—then the haunting thud made by the cable car.

He headed home in the frigid weather with his father, crossing quiet streets, aware of blackened houses lined up in rows with his father's fingers tightening their grip often. He used the sleeve of his blue coat to wipe his nose. "Papa, he didn't listen to me."

And kneeling, his father pulled him inside his arms, letting out a heavy sigh, before saying, "Son, you're not to blame; Rolf wanted to see the horses. God will watch over him."

The organist played somber music, bringing tears to Freddy's eyes. Rolf's mother bawled and rose, facing the back of the church. Freddy sighed and cupped his mouth with his hands, spotting his father, uncle, and two other men edge inside the church with Rolf's casket. A wave of heat covered him, seeing the pallbearers place Rolf's body on a stand ringed with flickering candlesticks. When Father Schultz read the liturgy, Freddy sat expressionless, dwelling on what had happened to Rolf.

Afterwards, standing in front of Rolf's grave, he shivered and shut his eyes, preyed upon by images of Rolf's last moments. And his eyes opened; hearing the footsteps of two strangers carrying white flowers on the other side of Rolf's the coffin. Rolf's mother screamed, "My baby." Freddy bawled and buried his face in his father's coat, catching Rolf's mother cry out, "R-Rolf, I love you."

* * *

On a warm July day, while she was reading to Freddy, sweat beaded on his mother's forehead. Freddy's eyes opened wide, aware of the racket Mr. Schmidt's black coal truck made skidding around the corner. It spewed a trail of black smoke, speeding to a screeching halt in front of Karl and Gunter's house. Big muscled Mr. Schmidt bolted from the truck and scrambled inside the house, leaving the door open behind him. Freddy's mother wrinkled her nose and scratched her head.

A few minutes passed and a black automobile pulled behind the coal truck. The people inside the vehicle abandoned it and ran inside the house through the opened door.

"Um, I hope Mrs. Schmidt's not sick." His mother shrugged, grimacing.

A short time later, he spotted two old women hurrying up the street.

His mother stood up, leaning over the porch railing. "Irma, is everything okay?"

A skinny woman stopped and glanced at his mother with a deadpan expression. "No, no it's not."

His mother's brows wrinkled, and she rubbed her thumb over a page in the book. "Is Emma sick? I just saw Heinrich run into the house."

"It's not Emma; she's fine. It's the boys, Karl and Gunter."

His mother swallowed, blinking hard at the woman. "Are the boys okay?" she asked, with Irma lowering her brows, giving her head a quick shake. "Irma, please tell me they're okay."

Irma's voice shook as she dipped her head. "Barbara, Emma got a telegram telling her Karl and Gunter died in France."

"Both boys? Oh my God, not both boys," she said in a disbelieving voice, sagging into the chair, placing her head in her hands.

Freddy pictured Karl and Gunter smiling in their uniforms. His eyes welled up, clouding his vision and lining his quivering cheeks. Freddy agonized over Karl and Gunter, recalling their mother's words the day he bought his blue coat. "Heinrich told them they'd get themselves killed." His eyes filled with tears. *Why didn't you listen to your father?*

His mother picked up her head, looking into space. "They're too young to die; they're just babies."

* * *

Frowning, Freddy monitored Rolf's empty chair, feeling his heart grow heavier. A hard line crossed his tight lips, and his body shivered as he bored his eyes into Sister Gertrude's long face. And he swallowed hard, focusing on the date September 8, 1919, written on the blackboard—he'd spend the entire year with the strict nun missing Rolf. His limp posture perked up, and he let out a sigh when the bell rang, ending his first day.

And while walking along Gratiot Avenue, he spotted Chester, reminding him of the time Rolf fed him an apple. He gazed at Dicky and Gus, trying to understand why they never brought up Rolf's name. He grimaced at a poster stuck to a window with an angry German soldier stabbing a baby with his bayonet.

Gus shuddered, covering his eyes. "Freddy, it scares me."

Open-mouthed, Dicky kept his eyes glued to it.

Freddy closed his eyes, bowing his head, figuring the world had gone mad, swaying his body, reviving images of the mob outside Saint Paul's and the awful day on the bridge with Rolf.

Dicky's boisterous voice snapped him out of his trance. "I want to buy candy; my mother gave me pennies for sweets."

"I got two pennies to buy sweets," said Gus in a bubbly voice, shifting his weight between feet.

"Okay," said Freddy. And he chased after Dicky and Gus till they reached a corner candy store. Dicky and Gus rushed inside, and Gus walked back and forth, viewing glass jars filled with different sweets. Gus pointed to licorice drops and showed a smiling youthful woman dressed in white two pennies.

"That's not enough money; you need two more pennies."

Gus stared at Freddy with a quizzical brow over his right eye. "Freddy, what did she say?"

The woman tilted her head toward him, dropping her smile, saying to him, "Oh dear, he doesn't understand what I said, does he?"

He made unwavering eye contact with her. "No, he doesn't, but I do."

Gus settled for a peppermint stick.

"Do you want some candy?" the woman asked, smiling at Freddy.

Freddy let out a heavy sigh. "Everything. But have no money."

Dicky bought six lemon drops. "Freddy, too bad you've no money."

Freddy stepped outside the sweet shop, noticing six boys wearing head caps and blue overalls glaring at them.

One, a freckled-faced boy with red hair peaking under his cap, roared at them, "Hey punks, give me your candy." The boy edged closer, wetting his lips, and said with anger, "Did you hear me? I want your candy."

Dicky and Gus stared at each other, with the corners of their mouths sliding downward.

Dicky pulled on Freddy's coat. "Why's he mad?"

The boy sneered. "Heh, what d'you say to him? I don't know those words; do you go to Saint Paul's? Are you Germans?"

Dicky raised his brows with delight in his voice. "Saint Paul's, *ja*, Saint Paul's."

The boy huffed, glaring at Dicky.

Freddy tugged on Dicky's arm, grimacing at him. "Run, Dicky."

His lips trembled, and he scooted from the bullies, with Dicky and Gus following him. One boy screamed, "Stop, you fucking blockheads."

Freddy ran faster. Gus fell behind, short-winded.

"I hope the army kills every German in the world," screamed one boy.

Gus looked back and tripped, releasing his lunch box and books to brace himself.

"Freddddy, help me," wept Gus, bloody-kneed, holding onto a broken piece of his peppermint stick.

He stayed with Gus, observing Dicky dashing up the street with a lunch box in one hand and tied books swinging in the other. The gang moved in on Freddy and Gus, laughing.

The ring leader stomped hard on Gus's lunch box a few times. "Tee hee, did the little blockhead get a booboo?"

A short beefy boy with a catlike grin said in hurried speech, "Johnny, let's slug them."

Freddy's heart pounded as he scrutinized the gang, hearing Gus cry. His lips curled, yanking Gus to his feet. Gus's hand shook as he picked up his books.

A plump butcher wearing a bloodied apron and frowning checked out the gang. "What's going on here?"

Johnny gave him a pained stare. "Go away, fatso; they're fucking blockheads."

"Boy, if I were your mother, I'd wash your mouth with Ivory soap." Freddy's mouth opened wide; he gawked at glossy-lipped woman with a weak chin. He took a deep breath, sweeping his eyes over the gang.

Anger roared through the leader's lips. "Lady, they're Germans; we're going to punch them."

Speechless, he assessed a space between the short boy and his skinny friend, who paid attention to the leader. Freddy grabbed Gus's hand and charged through the opening.

"If I catch you, you'll be sorry."

And he hyperventilated, fixating on the threat. "Ouch!" Hit in the head with something hard, Freddy stumbled a step.

Gwuf, gwuf, gwuf. loud footsteps ran through his ears. He passed onlookers maneuvering through a crowd. The footsteps quieted, but Freddy continued running, gripping Gus' hand.

"Stop, what's your hurry," said a smiling police officer, standing in Freddy's way. Freddy dropped to the ground, catching his breath, and rubbed the back of his head, noticing blood on his hand. Gus hunkered alongside Freddy, shaking.

The officer narrowed his gaze on Freddy's head. "Nasty cut—how did you get it?"

He eyed him, speechless.

"Young man, the cat didn't get your tongue too?" he asked, wrinkling his nose with a smile in his eyes.

"Freddy, what did he say?"

"Ah, you speak German," beamed the blue suit, nodding, creasing his forehead.

Freddy blew air through round lips. "I speak English."

"That's good." The officer nodded, pulling out a handkerchief. "Here, give me your hand, hold it there; this should stop the bleeding. Better hurry home and let your mother take care of it."

His face whitened as he tried to figure out what he'd say to his mother. He cringed and shivered. *Might Mama be mad? I'll never walk on Gratiot Avenue again.*

* * *

Chimneys erratically spewed black smoke on a raw, windy November day. Freddy waved goodbye to Dicky and Gus. "See you tomorrow." And he crossed the street, ambushed by gusts of wind. Heartened by the warm kitchen, Freddy planted his lunchbox and books on the table. He smiled at his mother, stuffing his mittens inside his blue coat, flinging the coat on a chair.

His mother took a noticeable breath with a lopsided curl to her mouth. "No, you don't, Freddy Bauer—hang up your coat this moment."

"Yes, Mama. Can I get a glass of warm Ovaltine first?"

His mother's lips straightened, and she tapped her foot. "No. Hang up your coat."

He sneered and dropped his head, sounding somber. "Yes, Mama."

His eyes twinkled as he hung up his coat, detecting a spoon clink against a glass. He burst into the kitchen, eyeing a warm glass of Ovaltine on the table, seeing a warm smile on his mother's face.

"Freddy, when you finish do your homework."

Freddy warmed his fingers around the glass of Ovaltine, saying to her, flashing a smile, "Yes, Mama."

His mother crossed her arms, giving him an intense stare. "Um, Freddy, it's been a while since Father Vogel last wrote me a letter."

He lowered the glass of Ovaltine, staring at his mother's wrinkled nose.

"I hope he's not sick."

Freddy shrugged, concentrating on his mother.

"That's it—he must not be feeling well; he always writes," said his mother, tapping her fingers.

His mother glanced up at the ceiling for a few seconds. She sprung to her feet, pointing her head toward the living room. "Finish your Ovaltine; let me see if mail came."

He took a gulp of cooled Ovaltine.

His mother flopped back in her seat, picking through the mail. "Aha, got one, a letter from home," she said in a gloating tone, drawing his attention. And she opened the letter and mumbled the words she read. She stopped reading and covered her mouth in an instant. Freddy perked up, stiff-necked. His mother gave him an opened-mouthed stare before jumping to her feet, her voice shaking. "I'll be back soon; do your homework." She studied Freddy, wrapping a coat over her shoulders. "Be right back, Freddy."

His mother returned later than expected with Aunt Andrea and his cousins.

"Freddy, please play with Charlotte," said his mother, raising her eyebrows.

He seized Charlotte's hand and sat beside her on the cushy sofa. Charlotte dozed off, and he tiptoed over to the tufted chair to spy on his mother and aunt.

"Do you want me to tell them?" Aunt Andrea asked.

"I should do it; Father Vogel wrote me the letter."

Freddy picked up sobs and a few loud sniffles. "It will crush them when they find out Otto's dead," said Aunt Andrea.

He blinked fast and bit his bottom lip, shedding a tear, reckoning death had marked his soul one more time. The noisy kitchen door opened and shut. Freddy leaned back, tilting his head to the side.

"Wilhelm, please sit. I've something to tell you; its unpleasant news," said his mother, weeping. "Wilhelm, Otto's dead."

Freddy's shoulders slumped, and he let out a long breath.

"How, when, where did it happen?" his father questioned in a weary tone of voice.

"He died during a French artillery fire barrage, in France; honey, they didn't find Otto's body."

"There got to be a body!"

Her voice cracked. "Wilhelm, Father Volker wrote his regiment suffered heavy losses."

"I'm sorry," Aunt Andrea sniffled.

His father whined, "Mother, how can she handle this?"

The squeaky kitchen door opened again, and he heard Uncle Tomas say in a puzzled voice, "Hi, everyone. Came right over when I saw Andrea's note; what's wrong?"

"Tomas, Otto died in France," said Aunt Andrea, whimpering in small bursts.

"What?"

The voices in the kitchen hushed.

"How will Mother and Father cope? Without Otto, they won't be able to run the farm. Thank God Father Vogel got them help. Poor Michael. Otto's son's too young to grow up without a father," said Uncle Tomas in a shaky voice. "Huh, Otto thought he'd be a hero fighting for the kaiser. No one could change his mind once he decided on something. What did it get him, medals he'll never see?"

Freddy trembled, hearing grieving voices and occasional snivels, registering the sound of footsteps pacing back and forth.

"Oh no," screamed Freddy's mother.

"What's wrong, Barbara?" said his father, sounding anxious.

His mother's voice grew caustic. "Wilhelm, the letter was open; do you know what that means?"

"Someone read grim news," Aunt Andrea said in a shrill tone.

"No, oh no, they might watch us. Father Vogel complained I don't write enough, but I do. Are the authorities reading my letters? Do they think I'm a spy because I know Nils Keller?"

"Barbara, why should they; did you forget we're citizens?"

His mother raised her voice, complaining, "That means nothing, Wilhelm. We're in a war; the country hates Germans. Look what happened to Nils; is that something we imagined? I'm scared maybe someone turned us in too." His mother paused, and a sudden tone of anxiety came to her voice. "Wilhelm and Tomas, watch what you say at the plant—someone could spy on you."

A quiet spell gripped the kitchen. Tight-lipped, Freddy mulled over what had happened to Rolf's father and its consequences. His breaths quickened, and he rocked in place, chewing over what could happen to his parents and aunt and uncle, teary-eyed.

* * *

Freddy's head hung as he relived Sister Gertrude's words from that eventful day. "The war's over! The war is over!" And recalled assessing her wide smile and top teeth for the first time. "We won the war," announced the nun, nodding. "The war ended on the eleventh minute of the eleventh hour of the eleventh month," she proclaimed, stomping her foot, hanging her mouth open.

A wild pink color flushed his cheeks; he awaited a doorbell ring from Rolf's parents. *It's my fault Rolf's dead.* His muscles froze, recalling what his father had said the night he met Rolf's father at the station. "Barbara, he insisted we go to Rolf's grave and fell to his knees crying in front of it."

Freddy's mind filled with what ifs, and he pinched his lips a few times. His eyes welled up, and he poked his tongue into his cheek, glaring at the Christmas tree, its majesty giving him no joy. Footsteps thumped on the porch's wood planks. His eyes bulged, and he held his breath, expecting his world to unravel. His head jerked when the new Sears doorbell that his father had installed ding-donged. And his stomach tightened a notch while he pushed back against the cushy cushion in the chair.

"Freddy, go answer the door."

His chest deflated, and he blew air out of his swollen cheeks, making out Uncle Tomas's loud voice on the other side of the door.

And he opened the door, exposing a slight smile, finding Aunt Andrea holding presents with Charlotte pulling on her coat. His uncle grinned, holding Maria's hand.

"Freddy, you grow more handsome every day," cheered Aunt Andrea, nodding.

"Mama, they're here."

"Who's here?"

"Barbara, it's us—Andrea and Tomas."

"Good. Make yourselves at home. I'm stirring gravy, and Wilhelm's mashing potatoes. Freddy, take their coats and put them on your bed."

He peeked outside his bedroom door, letting let out an enormous sigh, relieved to see no one stood on the porch. Freddy flopped back in the chair, catching Aunt Andrea place presents under the tree and join his uncle and cousins on the sofa.

"It's four days till Christmas, Freddy; I bet you're excited?" said his aunt, exposing gums under her lips.

Scared of facing Rolf's father, he nodded at her, displaying a fake smile.

"Barbara, what smells good? Can I help you?" said Aunt Andrea in a warm voice, smiling.

"No thanks, Andrea. The roast's done; I made it for Nils," sang Freddy's mother. "Hilda told me it's his favorite and gave me her recipe."

Balanced on the edge of his chair with a contrived smile, he endured idle chitchat, glancing at the door now and then.

A slow smile built on Uncle Tomas's lips as he pondered Freddy. "What do you want Santa to bring you for Christmas?"

Freddy shrugged, dull-eyed, convinced Santa Claus didn't exist. Uncle Tomas asked him again, but the doorbell rang, distracting him, and he glanced at it, widening the gap between his lips.

His father raised his voice from the kitchen. "Freddy, see who's at the door."

He froze for seconds, puffing hard. And his hand trembled while he inched toward the door. His eyes closed. He turned the doorknob and tugged on it. His lashes sprung up. He found Rolf's mother grinning, balancing presents wrapped in green paper and thick red ribbons.

"Hello, Freddy," she nodded, "you're looking very handsome today."

The plump woman entered, sidestepping past him. Freddy stuck his head out the door, catching Rolf's father flick his cigarette off the porch. Rolf's father handed Freddy his oversized coat and removed his hat, revealing thick gray hair, and bared his yellow-stained teeth. Rolf's mother smiled, handing him her coat. He brought the coats to his bedroom, wanting to hide in the closet.

Freddy ate dinner crammed between his father and uncle. He spied on Rolf's father. The frail man caught him looking once and hung his head. *Did Rolf's father blame him?* His stomach did somersaults, and he squirmed in his seat.

"Nils, you haven't touched the roast," said his mother, stroking her temple.

Nils Keller glared at the meat and stuffed a chunk in his mouth, chewing it, moving his eyes sideways.

Freddy was breathless. The space between his brows creased, and his throat constricted as his brain toyed with an idea. *Were the joyful times at the German Club gone forever?* He stared at Rolf's father, letting out a heavy sigh, aware his sweet-sounding voice had switched to raspy sounds.

He leaned back in his seat, catching Maria crawl. The grown-ups laughed at her. She neared the sad man wringing his hands, who had lost his whoopee. Rolf's father's cheeks raised up for a second but collapsed, with the corners of his mouth falling. He rose and stepped outside into the chilly air, staring at the starlit sky, coatless. Freddy peeked through the lace curtain, catching him firing a cigarette.

"Hilda, I'm sorry; I thought dinner with friends might cheer him. I don't enjoy seeing him this way," said Freddy's mother, wrapping herself in her arms.

Mrs. Keller dragged her fingers along her cheeks. "He doesn't talk to me and sleeps on the floor in Rolf's room. The entire house stinks from cigarette smoke."

Uncle Tomas's face saddened as he looked at Hilda. "He needs time to sort things out; I can't imagine what he's thinking."

Freddy sneaked into his bedroom and threw on a coat. He slipped out the kitchen door, heading for the porch. And he crept over the creaky floor, weak-kneed, staring at Rolf's father with a gaping mouth. The man blew a white cloud into the starlit night before he flicked his cigarette on the lawn. He crept toward him, arriving with welled-up eyes. Freddy gave him a deadpan face and a sigh.

Rolf's father pulled out a green tin with a red circle and snagged a cigarette from it. He placed it between his lips and stared up at the starlit sky without lighting it.

"I'm sorry," wailed Freddy.

Rolf's father sniffled, and his head flinched hard, freeing the cigarette from his lips.

"I'm sorry; it was my fault Rolf died."

Rolf's father's eyelids grew heavy.

"I told him not to go." Freddy sobbed. "I miss Rolf every day."

"Me too." Rolf's father whimpered, rubbing his chest with a shaky hand. He dropped to his knees and hugged him. "It's not your fault, Freddy; don't blame yourself."

Freddy exhaled, welcoming Rolf's father's tight embrace.

Freddy often visited Rolf's grave at the end of school. There, once he finished his prayers, he counted cigarette butts, reckoning the more there were, the longer Rolf's father had stayed. Freddy's eyes teared, and he gazed at the heavens, his heart thumps keeping pace with his heavy breaths. *Please, God, bring back Rolf's father's enticing voice.*

Chapter Seven

Detroit, 1920: More Agony

Nerves crept into Uncle Tomas's voice at the German Club as he darted his eyes between Rolf's and Freddy's parents. "We're going back to Germany; it's been on our mind ever since Otto died. It was a hard decision because we love you and will miss you."

A pained expression covered his mother's face. Freddy's eyes watered, drawing a small breath. *Maybe I'll never see my aunt and uncle or cousins again.*

Freddy's father glared at his uncle and lifted his head, anger in his words. "Goddammit, Tomas, why didn't you talk to me before deciding on it?"

His tone startled Charlotte, and she cried. Aunt Andrea gave her a biscuit, quieting her.

"Wilhelm, if we had said something to you and Barbara earlier, you would have tried to change our minds."

"You're right, and I think you're making an enormous mistake," Wilhelm replied.

"Listen to me—when Otto died, everything changed. I'm the oldest son now, and it's my responsibility to take care of the farm for Mother and Father. Who else will do it? They can't always rely on Dieter's and Manfred's kindness; it's a big farm to manage."

"They might want to sell the farm," said Rolf's father, lighting a cigarette.

"Who'll take care of them if the farm's sold?" Uncle Tomas frowned, running his hands through his hair.

Freddy's mother leaned in, making strong eye contact with Uncle Tomas. "We could make room for them in our home."

"No, that won't work out," said Uncle Tomas, narrowing his eyes. "Their entire life's the farm; they'd never leave it. I might save the farm, returning home."

"Think of Andrea and the girls," said Freddy's mother with a downcast expression. "Living on the farm might be too hard on them. Andrea's a city girl; she doesn't know how to farm. I can't picture her working the fields or dirtying her hands in muck."

Aunt Andrea's lips twisted. "Don't worry for me, Barbara Bauer. I'm a healthy woman and can handle hard work."

"Andrea won't be in the fields," said his uncle, brightening his gaze. "I've saved enough money. I'll buy another horse and better plow. She will tend to the animals, do the cooking, and mind the girls. Besides, she'd be an enormous help to mother, and the girls won't grow up in a country that doesn't want them."

Freddy's father frowned at him. "It won't be that way forever."

Uncle Tomas blinked hard, with his voice taking a bitter tone. "And what if you're wrong?"

His mother pinched her lips. "What of the girls' schooling?"

Uncle Tomas's lips contorted and dropped his shoulders. "Barbara, they're girls—when they're old enough, they'll get married and raise a family, just as you did."

Freddy's mother slumped and snatched the German Club's gravy-stained menu and forced laughter from browsing over it. His father chewed on his bottom lip, fixating on his folded hands.

* * *

The March fourteenth date on the calendar sent chills through Freddy's body. He sniveled and placed his palm over his trembling lips. *Rolf would have been ten today.*

Freddy slumped on his bed with a heart that hurt.

"Are you dressed for church, Freddy?" asked his mother, tapping on the door.

Having finished tying his shoes, he checked himself in the mirror. And he elevated his brows, surprised by a loud knock on the door. He edged over to the door and peeked out, recognizing Nils Keller's choir director.

"Wilhelm, drop everything and come with me," said a man, huffing and puffing. "I'll explain everything to you on the way."

"What, what is it?" sputtered his father, using a high-pitched tone.

The man tugged on his father's arm, saying in a breathy voice, "Wilhelm, tell Barbara you'll be back."

"Um, Augie, can't it wait? We're getting ready for church."

"It can't. Come with me right now."

Freddy's mother walked in, shooting glances at the choir director. "What's the fuss, Augie?"

The gape in the choir director's mouth widened, and his small shoulders slumped.

"Barbara, Wilhelm will be back. He'll explain everything when he returns; plan ongoing to a late mass."

An old woman with a conspicuous pin stuck into her enormous hat returned with his father and gave Freddy an insincere smile. She took notice of his mother. And she puckered her lips and limped toward her with solemnness etched in her face.

"Barbara, let me take you into the bedroom. I got unpleasant news." The black-hatted woman sniveled.

Seconds later Freddy winced, picking up his mother's loud scream. Not long after, she walked into the room crying, holding a handkerchief over her nose with a shaky hand. His father handed her a coat, and they eased out of the house. He inspected the old lady, burrowed in the sofa, focusing on the smudged rouge on her cheeks.

* * *

Dazed and confused, catching a whiff of coffee in the air and a spoon clinking against a cup, Freddy entered the kitchen with a slack expression on his face. "Papa, it's Monday; why are you home?"

"I know it is. I'm not working today," said his father in a somber tone, attempting to smile.

"Morning, Mama."

"M-morning Freddy," she said, turning her red eyes sideways.

A slack expression appeared on his face as he heaped Wheaties in a bowl and oozed milk on top of them. He munched on his Wheaties, squinting at his father, catching his mother's snivels at the sink. And he finished his last bite of Wheaties in a spooky silence. He took a gratifying sigh and reached for the newspaper, but his father snapped it up. His brain stopped working, and he gave his father an incredulous stare.

"Freddy, I don't want you to read the paper!" said his father, hardening his words, placing the paper beside him, giving Freddy a painful stare. "Hurry, get dressed for school."

He pulled a long face, scrutinizing his father.

"Better get a move on, Freddy; Dicky and Gus are waiting for you," said his mother with a woe in her voice.

He exhaled, wrinkling his nose at her. "Uh, yes, Mama."

She let out a sigh and gave him a feeble hug. "Bundle up—its chilly."

* * *

"Mama, where's Papa?" asked Freddy dressed in his coat, tightening his grip on his hat, expecting to say goodbye to him before heading to school.

"He's busy; don't forget your scarf."

His smile vanished as he left the house, but it came back to him as soon as he caught a glance of Gus and Dicky shivering on the other side of Russell Street, waiting for him.

"Hi, Freddy," said Dicky, swinging his strapped books.

Gus tilted his head and stepped closer to Freddy, scrunching his eyes. "Freddy, is hanging in the basement from a rope bad? I do it sometimes from a tree in the yard. My mother cried when my father told her Rolf's father did it."

Dull-eyed, rooted to the ground, he stood still with his mouth falling open, unable to control the thoughts racing through his mind. His heart sank, gawking at Dicky with his lips trembling around empty words. His head cranked back and forth fast, snapping his eyes shut, whimpering. "Noooo!"

And he tasted bits of breakfast, pulling back from Dicky. With a whitened face, struggling for air, he backpedaled, opening and closing his mouth. "No! No! He didn't?"

And he crashed through the door, burying his head in his wide-eyed mother's apron, repeating Gus's words.

"Oh no, Freddy, I'm sorry you heard it," said his mother, tightening her arms around him.

And Mrs. Schmidt cared for him the night his parents visited Pohl's.

One day, sitting at the kitchen table, his mother sobbed, dropping her head and shoulders. "Freddy, I've terrible news—Rolf's mother moved to Milwaukee to be with her sister."

School ended, and Freddy threw a scarf around his neck, displaying to Dicky and Gus' sad eyes. "It's Wednesday; I'm going to the cemetery."

He crept the scant distance to Saint Paul's Cemetery, taking little breaths, wanting to be by himself. In mournful silence, he ended his journey at the foot of Rolf's and Nils Keller's gravestones, weeping, mindful of what had happened to them. In silence, sad thoughts came and went. He gazed at the grassless plot where Rolf's father rested, minding his heartbeat. And he turned his head, scrutinizing the numbers 1910–1918 chiseled into Rolf's headstone, picturing Rolf's smile catching the ball. With tears falling off his cheeks, he whispered, "Rolf, I love you."

And he remembered his mother's quiet words: "Freddy, they're in God's hands."

Freddy stared into space, reckoning Rolf's father took his life to be with his son in heaven. He focused on Rolf's marker, dry-washing his hands with moistened eyes, blurring his vision. His head shook, and he blinked away tears, concentrating on thoughts circling in his brain. *When I die, will I go to heaven? Will I be with Rolf and his father? What's in heaven? No one ever tells me.* His body shuddered, and he closed his eyes, wishing to see when they opened Rolf's father's cigarette butts on the ground. He pivoted, staring at a mound of dirt in front of a hole, agonizing over where Karl and Gunter rested.

Chapter Eight

1922–1924: Hate and Prejudice

A nd dropping the ankle-length black gown over his shoulders, letting it fall in place, twelve-year-old Friedrich Bauer finished dressing, with a miniature white robe dropping to his knees.

"Herman Stein, get rid of that gum," seethed the slim priest with salt-and-pepper hair.

"And as for you, Friedrich Bauer, how many times must I tell you altar boys arrive fifteen minutes before mass starts, not five?"

Freddy ducked his chin, feeling a tingle in his chest, thinking Father Schultz was not himself today.

Walter Frick's lips trembled, and the candlelighter bobbed in his hand.

Herman and Walter moved from the vestibule holding brass candlelighters. Freddy followed behind, and his heart leaped as he marveled at the enormous space that unfolded ahead of him. He exhaled and let out a low moan, glancing at it, curious how it held together without the ceiling falling. He fired the altar candles and blew out the lighter with a faint breath. And he tiptoed back into the vestibule. Lined up ahead of Herman and Walter, holding a sparkling gold cross, he waited for Father Schultz. "I'm ready, Friedrich."

He unlocked his ankles and set off for the altar. And he rested the cross on a stand facing parishioners. Father Schultz made the sign of the cross at the altar. "Amen."

He repeated the word, reflecting on Father Schultz's unusual behavior.

At the time Father Schultz finished his homily, he pressed his lips together, and he ran his eyes over the congregation.

"Harrumph, I ask myself if it will ever end and pray to God someday it will," said Father Schultz, pouting, taking a step back. "As you know, last week, on the Fourth of July, they burned a cross fronting Saint Raphael's Church, and they could fire one up on our own lawn. And on that very day last week, a hundred thousand Klansmen marched eighty miles from where we stand against us. And if you ask me why, I will say nothing. But we don't standalone; those who throw stones at us throw them at negroes and Jews too. And if you ask me what they've done to deserve it, I will answer 'nothing' once more.

"But why mark us if we did nothing? The only answer I can give is they fear our numbers, and nothing more. We're not American enough for them; that's why they curse us. Our ways scare them; we teach our children in a foreign language, the same as Jews do, and it bothers them. We're Roman Catholics, and they dislike it. Our numbers multiply; that frightens them. They're afraid that one day we'll overtake them and change the faith of the nation to ours, and the law of the land as well. They come out at night and sneak around doing horrible things, and they hold hate rallies in front of a burning cross telling falsehoods to anyone who will listen. And they say we must change our separatist ways. And even spread falsehoods the pope will leave Rome and build a great cathedral in Washington, DC."

"They're cloaked in white robes but no longer hide their identities when they flaunt themselves, displaying their arrogant nature. But what can we do? We must be vigilant and confront their evil minds with truths. Confront politicians, police, or anyone else that wants to do us harm or pay a heavy price if we don't. They don't frighten us; we've rights, and we must guard them against this new evil." Father Schultz paused and parted his lips, assessing the crowd.

Freddy glanced over at his still parents, whose eyes were on Father Schultz.

"Ahem!" Father Schultz coughed. "Remember, to get through this, we must stand together as one. And never forget to ask for God's help."

After mass, his parents chatted briefly with usual acquaintances before he headed toward the German Club with them in quietness.

His father's smile wavered, and he concentrated on his mother. "What's on your mind, Barbara? Are you still bothered at what Father Shultz said in church?"

"Yes, I am. It crossed my mind our world changed when that German submarine attacked the Lusitania. We can't win—first the war, now they dislike the way we teach our children or preach our religion. If they had their way, they'd put us on a boat and ship us back to Germany." Her pace slowed, and she nodded. "Thank God Andrea and Tomas won't witness the insanity."

"Barbara, we got through the war, and we'll make it through this."

"How can you be sure? They hate Catholics, coloreds, and Jews." His mother stopped walking, rubbing her arm. "And now that Henry Ford bought the Dearborn newspaper, he's speaking out against Jews."

Tight-lipped, he stared at his worried mother with a question on his mind.

"Father Schultz calls Henry Ford the king of Dearborn. What does he mean by that?" Freddy asked, scratching his head.

Her head jerked back, and she said to him, "I'll tell you what it means. It means he owns everything in Dearborn and gets his way when he wants it."

His mother's cheeks moved up and down, and she raised her brows, eyeing a brightly colored dress in a store window.

"Wilhelm, it's charming; will it look good on me?"

His father nodded with a smile in his voice. "Nothing could look awful on you, Barbara."

She blushed and bowed her head.

* * *

Freddy leaned back at the kitchen table with warmth spreading across his face. *I'm thirteen, and each day that passes, I'm treated as if I'm older.* His eyes filled with an inner glow as he caught his father's grin.

"Barbara, the first time I met Clarence, we both had trouble understanding each other." His father's smile changed into a grimace. "Do you think my accent's terrible? Sometimes Clarence looks confused when I speak."

"When you speak English, I understand you. Freddy, what do you think?"

"He has a slight accent, but I can clearly understand him," he said, squinting, tilting his head at his father, using a curious tone of voice. "Father, who's Clarence?"

His father said, pinching his chin. "Clarence grew up the same way I did, a poor farmer. And as I did, wanting a better life for his family, moving to Detroit. He has big muscles from working in the plants foundry."

"Um, Father, what's a foundry?"

A hint of a frown appeared on his father's face. "It's a fiery place where red-hot metal's poured into molds to make automobile parts."

Freddy's voice firmed, and he tilted his head at his father. "Papa, isn't that dangerous?"

"Freddy Bauer, let your father eat his dinner."

He crossed his arms, giving his mother a fake smile.

* * *

Almost a year after first hearing Clarence Johnson's name, Freddy tapped his foot on the curb, waiting for traffic to ease alongside his parents, and flinched, picking up a husky man's voice behind him. "Howdy, Wilhelm."

His father spun around, flashing his teeth at a brawny black man. "Thought that was you, Clarence."

The black man's eyes twinkled, and he thrust out his chest. "Afternoon, folks. I'm Clarence Johnson, and this here is my wife, Ida, and the girls are Athena and Chalice. Athena will be five next month, and Chalice is three."

Both his daughters giggled and curtsied.

Freddy's grin widened as he eyed a muscular man in a straw hat, a skinny woman wearing a white dress, and two beaming adolescent girls, each dressed the same, in sable dresses and hats.

Creases dug into his father's face. "Clarence, meet my wife, Barbara, and son, Friedrich."

"Pleased to meet you," he said, beaming, making strong eye contact with Freddy and his mother.

Freddy tilted his head at the powerful man, blinking, sorting out Clarence Johnson's unusual dialect.

"Wilhelm, we've been out looking for a house, but there ain't none," he said with an unexpected change of tone. And he swallowed hard, circling his eyes. "People tell us ain't none for sale, but we keep looking."

"Clarence, it was nice to meet you and Ida and your lovely daughters," said his mother, nodding, with a warm tone in her voice. "Wilhelm's mentioned you often; you must come for dinner."

"Thank you; that'd be nice," said Clarence, grinning.

Speechless, his wife froze, flashing two rows of ivory.

"Well, it's nice meeting you. We're going to go; we got more time to look," said Clarence, seizing his daughters' hands, heading toward a traffic light.

"You never mentioned he was black," said his mother, grimacing.

His father winced. "Does it matter?"

"No, certainly not. I was just surprised he was."

* * *

Freddy salivated, eyeing the meatloaf and potatoes on the table.

Wet with sweat, his mother wiped her face with her apron and collapsed in the chair.

His father's expression changed to a radiant glow. "Barbara, guess what? Clarence told me he found a house. I can't say I blame him for wanting to move. He said he lives in Black Bottom."

His mother's jaw dropped. "Wilhelm, Black Bottom?"

"I suspected he did but felt funny asking him; he's a proud man. He said his roof leaked in the other house and it was drafty in winter. And jazz clubs played all night with prostitutes and drunks walking the streets."

"Wilhelm, be careful your sons here."

Freddy sneered, securing his eyes on his mother. *I'm not stupid—if I don't know a word, I'll check it in the dictionary.*

His father wore a bleak expression, and he stared at his hands. "Barbara, his son caught pneumonia and died."

"So sad; it must have been hard on him and his family."

His father's head lifted. "I'm glad Clarence is staying in Detroit. Ida wanted to move to Inkster where other blacks at the plant were settling."

"Can he afford to move out of Black Bottom?"

"Why can't he? Ford pays blacks the same wages as whites."

"Well, then he should buy it."

"Yes, he should," said his father, raising his cheeks. "I'm starved. Let's eat."

Freddy's father unhinged a latch on a white picket fence in front of Clarence Johnson's new home on a warm Sunday afternoon in 1923. The door swung open, and Clarence stood inside, smiling, unmasking white teeth with raised-up cheeks. The brawny man, who overshadowed his lean wife and small daughters, belly laughed. "Please come in; we're happy y'all could come."

Freddy noticed Clarence's daughters' spacious bedroom and glanced at the ceiling, convinced his family would no longer fear the rain.

Ida Johnson's voice took on an excited tone, and she spread her lips wide enough that Freddy could count every tooth in her mouth. "Pleased y'all could come for dinner with us."

At five o'clock sharp, Ida Johnson served dinner. Freddy dined on sliced ham and a few items he never tasted and grinned, dipping a biscuit into a tasty brown gravy that puddled in the middle of a thick white substance that Ida Johnson called grits. Finished with a helping of sweet potato pie, he joined the men on the porch while his mother helped Ida Johnson clean up and Athena and Chalice colored with crayons on the floor. Clarence and his father plopped on the folding chairs they carried with them outside, and Freddy squatted on the top step of the porch and quenched his thirst with sips of lemonade. Two boys with devilish smiles walked back and forth, and one stopped, rubbing his head, gawping at Clarence. "Who lives here?"

Clarence jumped up, grinning and nodding. "I do—my name's Clarence Johnson; pleased to meet y'all." The two boys eyed each other, wearing frowns, and ran away.

No longer than ten minutes passed before three big-eyed men inched their way past the house. A brief time later, a group of men and women formed on the opposite side of the white picket fence in front of Clarence's house. A tall young man roared, shaking his fist. "We don't want niggers here." The crowd pumped fists in the air; crying bitter words. "Niggers get out. Nigger's get out, go somewhere else."

His body shaking, Freddy followed the men inside the house. His mother and Ida cuddled with the girls. Clarence peaked out from one of the inside windows, "There's two men telling them what to say," whimpered Clarence, his chest heaving.

The crowd's angry racial slurs grew louder.

"There's more of them," said Clarence, shutting his eyes. "We can't go anywhere."

Clarence dashed to the basement, bringing back with him a double-barreled shotgun, panting.

"I bought this house; I won't leave it," Clarence shrieked with beads of sweat on his forehead.

A rock crashed through a window, hitting the floor with a thud. Freddy's eyes bulged, and his heart raced. Clarence's mouth fell open and his lips curled back. Ida and the girls screamed. Freddy peeked in on them, finding his mother comforting them.

The veins in Mr. Johnson's neck jutted out, and he shouted, "Wilhelm, git out my way," and went through the door.

Clarence faced the screaming mob with the shotgun barrel pointing to the floor. And for a moment glanced back at Freddy's father with white surrounding his brown irises.

"Go away; please, let us be," he shouted. "This is my house. I bought it. We mean you no harm; we're God-fearing people like you."

Clarence ducked to avoid a rock hurled at his head. Freddy caught a pubescent boy yanking the front gate off its hinges and other youths ripping pickets off the fence and passing them around to the crowd.

"Please go home; my wife and daughters inside—y'all scaring them."

Another rock missed Clarence's head and bounced off a brown painted wall. He raised the gun to the sky and pulled the trigger. The crowd stopped for an instant, then continued screaming at him. He loaded the gun again with cartridges he had tugged from his pants pocket and fired into the sky once more. Freddy's father burst through the door, pulling up beside Clarence, gazing at the damaged fence.

"Go home. Look what you did? You should be ashamed of yourselves; leave this family alone," said his father, crinkling his lips and letting his jaw slack.

"Go home," Clarence said, lifting his voice, eyeballing the mob. "I'll shoot if I got to; please let us be."

Freddy picked up a police car siren growing louder and watched the crowd disperse.

Two police officers drove up with guns pulled and edged toward Clarence.

"Drop the shotgun, or we'll shoot," said one officer, giving Clarence an icy stare.

Clarence dropped the shotgun. The two blue suits took Clarence and his shotgun away. Hours later Clarence returned, perspiring, without the gun. Ida fetched him a glass of water. Clarence gulped the water, spilling plenty on himself.

Freddy's father's veins beat in his neck, and the words coming out of his mouth shook. "Wh-what happened, Clarence?"

Clarence slumped and hung his head. "Said we should move, will watch the house tonight. Who knows what tomorrow brings Wilhelm, take your family home?"

His father's voice deepened. "Clarence, if there's more trouble, let the police take you to my home; I'll write my street and house number. Clarence, let Barbara and Friedrich take Ida and the girls to my house; I can stay with you."

"Me and the girls staying with Clarence," cried Ida.

"We'll be fine, Wilhelm. Police said they will watch the house."

* * *

A loud *puh-puh-puh* came from someone pounding on the kitchen door, waking Freddy. He jumped out of bed and hurried into the kitchen, catching his father peeking through the green curtains. His father opened the door and stepped back, letting Clarence Johnson and his family wander into the kitchen. Clarence gripped his groggy girls, and Ida trembled, shedding tears. His mother emerged wearing her blue robe. She cupped her mouth, seeing Clarence with his family. "Clarence, what's wrong?"

"Sorry to be a bother. People been driving past the house calling us names, scaring Ida, Athena, and Chalice. Police only came once, got worried, I took everyone here. Snuck out but dropped the piece of paper you gave me. Walked many streets in Germantown before finding somebody who knows y'all."

Freddy's parents frowned at each other.

Athena and Chalice slept in his bed. Way past Freddy's bedtime, Clarence Johnson finished a third glass of water. "Must go now; my house isn't safe without me there."

"Don't go; you'll be alone," said Ida Johnson, nerves shaking her voice.

"Ida, it's safer here."

The brawny man rose, attempting a smile, and eased out the door. "Thanks, y'all."

* * *

Wilhelm arrived home holding his lunch box, noticing Ida Johnson and Barbara preparing dinner. He kissed his wife's cheek. "Freddy read Athena and Chalice a story from an old Bunny Brown book he kept on his bookshelf."

"Hello, Ida; where's Clarence? I didn't see him in the cable car. Did he stay at home?"

Dull-eyed, lowering her head, Mrs. Johnson dropped the potato in her hand.

"Wasn't Clarence with you?" Ida backed off, blinking hard. "I should go home."

His father's smile wavered. "Ida, maybe's he home; I'm sure he'll come by for you soon."

One hour passed, and Clarence never appeared. Ida never ate her dinner. Another hour passed, and Mrs. Johnson sat with the girls, a worried look on her face.

"Ida, I'm sure Clarence knows what he's doing. I bet he's hungry. Barbara, fill a plate with your pot roast; Freddy and I'll walk it over to him."

Freddy stopped with his father at the curb of Clarence Johnson's home. Only two posts remained from the white picket fence. And he trailed behind his father, noticing chards of glass stuck in the broken window and chipped paint and dents on the painted wood behind where Clarence Johnson had stood. His father's brows wrinkled, staring at him. He knocked on the door, and when no one answered, he whacked it hard.

His father raised his voice, examining the house. "Clarence, it's Wilhelm." His lips crinkled and yelled louder. "Clarence, can you hear me? Are you in there?"

He followed his father off the porch steps and raced to the back of the house, discovering the kitchen door hanging from one hinge and the screen door ripped off its jamb and tossed aside. He walked into the eerie space with chairs thrown around and a broken table with two legs missing and blood smeared across the floor. His father expelled air through ballooned cheeks till they deflated.

His father's lips pressed into a grimace and began tapping his foot. "Freddy, wait for me at the curb."

Freddy licked his lips, looking through a space a door had once blocked.

Lips puckered, his father fled the house trembling and yanked him to the front of the house.

"Freddy, I'm scared something's wrong; I can't find Clarence anywhere. Come with me. I can't let you go home and tell everyone what you saw," Freddy's father asserted, pulling his brows together without blinking.

His father drew a long breath, arriving at the police station ahead of sunset. He wiped sweat off his brows and hurried inside to the front desk. Once he had explained what had happened, two police officers drove him and Freddy back to Clarence's house in a shiny four door black automobile. They waited inside the car while the two men holding flashlights searched the house.

"There's blood everywhere," said one officer, shaking his head. "Come back with us; we need to file a report."

After they finished interrogating his father, the two blue suits took him and his father home, swerving on the way to avoid a dog that ran in front of them. On the way Freddy prayed, "God help Mr. Johnson."

The moment the police car appeared in front of the house, Ida Johnson bolted out the door and started beating on the window, when she discovered only Freddy and his father in the back seat. Freddy's father burst out the car door and wrapped his arms around the hysterical woman. From the other side, Freddy swallowed, noticing Ida's lips had curled back. "Wilhelm, where's Clarence, where's Clarence? Tell me he ain't dead."

Freddy's mother held Chalice in her arms while Athena cried, pulling on her dress. Mrs. Johnson fell to her knees, beating on her chest. "Clarence!"

* * *

"Mother, it says here in the paper a farmer named Samuel Brewster and his son Luke were herding cows into a meadow and found a black man hanging from a tree with a sack over his head."

His mother yanked the paper from his hand and sat back, recoiling her head, staring at it.

"Pray God it's not Clarence; hide the paper before Mrs. Johnson sees it. It's likely someone else. We'll tell your father when he comes home."

Freddy ran to the basement and hid the newspaper behind his father's wood toolbox. And he came back up searching for Mrs. Johnson, finding her hunkered on the porch, fanning herself while her daughters browsed through pictures in the *Saturday Evening Post.*

He had never forgotten the horror on Mrs. Johnson's face when the police car pulled up without Clarence inside it.

When he was older, his father brought up what had happened to Clarence Johnson on that terrible day. He told him the police drove him to the morgue, speculating the body found hanging from a tree on the Brewster farm might be Clarence Johnson. Sad faced, his father never explained what happened inside the morgue.

At the train station, Mrs. Johnson fought back tears, returning to Georgia with Clarence's body. She gave Barbara's hand a squeeze with grin lines slashing her cheeks. "I'll miss you all."

Freddy stood in silence, with a down-turned mouth, gazing at Mrs. Johnson and her daughters. His stomach knotted and he let out a heavy sigh, concluding hatred had destroyed a loving family.

Clarence Johnson's name never came up anymore at dinner. And they never brought his killers before a judge. While eating dinner, there were times his father looked sad, with his mind going somewhere else. When it did, Freddy and his mother's faces became somber, and they gave each other understanding nods.

* * *

The purple-robed priest took two swipes with his finger, placing a black cross on Freddy's forehead. He settled in a pew beside his marked mother.

"I hope your father gave up something for Lent."

"I'm sure he did; doesn't he always?"

"He's had lots on his mind this morning; I hope he remembers to go to church after work."

"Mother, how could he forget? He'll see people with ashes on their heads."

"Stupid me, what was I thinking?" said his mother, fidgeting with her hands.

On their way home, speaking German to his mother, two silent dirty-clothed men passed by them. One shouted from behind them. "Wipe that shit off your heads and go back to Germany where you belong; we don't want any of you fuckers living here."

His mother covered her mouth. Freddy seized her elbow and directed her inside a nearby store. Close to tears, she wrapped her arms around him, tightening them. "You're my hero; thank you for protecting me."

Freddy sighed, staring at his father's empty chair. His quiet mother pushed food around her plate with her fork.

"Something wrong," said Freddy, wrinkling his brows.

His mother dropped her fork. "I've lots on my mind."

Freddy cleaned off his dish and settled in his seat, doing his math homework. Time went by fast as he worked out equations.

"Freddy, it's getting late. Your father's dinner's no longer warm; I must reheat it."

"Mother, don't worry; he could've run into someone at church getting ashes. I hope it wasn't Father Schultz. If he did, you know how he can get when he gets your ear."

His mother gulped air. "Yes, you're right, that's it."

At nine o'clock, with still no sign of Freddy's father, his mother began tapping on the table. Another hour passed, and she said to him, rubbing her fingertips against her pale cheeks, "Freddy, he should be home; there's something wrong."

"Where is Wilhelm?" she asked, sobbing, when the clock hands approached eleven, peeking out the curtains.

In an instant she yanked open the living room door coatless and dashed outside into the biting air without closing it. Freddy looked out the opened door, spotting her pounding on the Schmidt's door and disappearing inside the house.

He waited on the sofa, covered in a blanket, for her to come back. Wrapped in a shawl, his mother came back trembling, bringing along Karl and Gunter's heavily whiskered father and bundled-up mother.

"Freddy, Mrs. Schmidt will take care of you till I come back," she said teary-eyed, changing into a green coat, shaking.

Freddy frowned, glaring at her, feeling a flush of heat in his face. "I'm going with you, and don't try stopping me."

Mr. Schmidt's face softened. "Barbara, Freddy's fourteen; bring him along. Emma can watch over the house, and if Wilhelm shows up, she'll tell him where we've gone."

Freddy squeezed inside the dirty coal truck with his mother. Mr. Schmidt ground the gears, and the truck lurched forward. And a short time later, Freddy stepped inside the red-brick police station with a head full of awful memories. His mother's eyes gave the place a darting gaze before she dashed up to a blue suit sleeping at the front desk.

Mr. Schmidt nudged the man, and he opened his eyes.

"Sorry to wake you; this woman's worried her husband hasn't come home."

"What did you say?"

Mr. Schmidt's voice firmed; he glared at the officer. "I said, this lady's husband hasn't come home."

"Oh! Sorry to hear it. How long since he's been missing?"

Heavily breathing, his mother pulled on her hair, giving a quick glance over the room. "For six hours; he's never been out this late."

The officer's lips twisted, and he shook his head, saying in an unsympathetic voice, "Six hours isn't a long time for him to be missing, lady, if you ask me. Maybe he stopped for drinks with friends."

His mother's voice held a tremor. "He'd never do that."

"Yeah, that's what he told you, but lady, I still think he's at a speakeasy drinking with friends."

Mr. Schmidt's voice boomed. "Listen to me, shithead, the lady's right—I know her husband, and he's not the kind to visit a speakeasy for drinks. Now get off your ass and help us."

"Okay, what's your husband's full name? I'll check around to see if he's turned up someplace else."

She turned an eye on the bleak man, draining color from her face. "Wilhelm Bauer. He works for Ford."

"Ford, huh? Lady, he's out with a friend having a pleasurable time at a speakeasy."

"Not him," barked Mr. Schmidt, "I told you he'd never do that."

"Okay, why don't you both go home and wait for Mr. Bauer? I'm sure he'll turn up."

"No, I can't. I know something's happened to him; please let me stay here with my son."

"Have it your way, lady, but I'll bet you he's home by now."

With a slight grimace, Mr. Schmidt softened his tone. "Barbara, stay here with Friedrich. I'll run back home and see if Wilhelm turned up. Did you leave a note?"

His mother pressed her lips, giving him a feeble head-shake.

Mr. Schmidt returned a short while later, lowering his head. His mother jumped up, whimpering. "Something's happened to Wilhelm!"

She fell back into her seat, covering her face. Mr. Schmidt brought her a glass of water, handing it to her. Freddy noticed his dirty fingernails. She sipped the water, keeping a wary eye on the contrary officer dozing on and off behind the desk.

Freddy's eyes opened, and he caught a loud, shrill voice. "Your nuts; who ya calling drunk?"

Two police officers held up the grungy man, walking him out of sight behind thick metal bars. His fingers touched his parted lips, and he noticed the wall clocks black dials showed it was close to three in the morning. His mother continued to spy on the blue suit. The telephone rang, and his mother's eyes widened. The officer pulled the wired receiver off the phone and placed it against his ear, whispering into a cylinder attached to a black stick he held in his hand. He shrugged, shook his head twice, and glanced at his mother, hanging up the phone. The man sighed and rose and advanced toward his mother. Freddy's stomach made somersaults; he heeded his mother's rasping breaths.

"Mrs. Bauer, your husband's at Detroit General; someone found him hurt in an alley near Saint Paul's."

Mr. Schmidt's tires screeched, pulling away from the station, heading for the hospital.

His mother jumped from the truck the instant it stopped and ran into the hospital, with Freddy and Mr. Schmidt chasing after her. And Freddy waited outside revolving doors with his mother and Mr. Schmidt for a doctor. His body shook, and he monitored the ticking clock while his mind conjured up what ifs. At one point, anxiety got the better of him, and he paced the hall, hoping to relieve his building tension.

A doctor with a stethoscope hanging from his neck swung open the doors, startling his mother. Freddy poked Mr. Schmidt with his elbow and squeezed his mother's hand.

"Mrs. Bauer, I presume? I'm Dr. Foster."

His mother's voice lost its energy. "Is Wilhelm okay?"

With brows pulling down in concentration, the doctor squeezed her hand. "Your husband's resting. Whoever did it hurt him bad. They brought him in, drifting in and out of consciousness. I'm afraid he's got a severe concussion. He's lost blood and has lots of bruises and a few nasty cuts I stitched. He's lucky someone found him."

She sobbed, wringing her hands. "Doctor, when can I see him?"

"He needs rest right now, Mrs. Bauer. I don't want him disturbed till we're sure he's fine. Get some sleep, Mrs. Bauer. I'll take excellent care of your husband."

Freddy's father mended at home for weeks. And his mother loved having the grouch at home with her. A detective dropped in one day with questions his father couldn't answer. He could recall an angry word. "Catholic."

The day his father returned to the Ford plant, he complained to his mother, that his back still bothered him. On that day, in the late afternoon, Freddy was doing his homework, and his mother stared out the kitchen window, daydreaming. Freddy's eyebrows drew together; he guessed she missed his father, recalling her warm, doting voice when he mended at home. And he remembered she never left his father's side, and more than once he had caught them kissing. Trips to the German Club ended, and when he asked why, his mother's voice cracked as she stared down at her hands. "Too many terrible memories."

His stomach fluttered; he sensed things had changed forever.

* * *

It was a hot summer day. His mother rushed into the kitchen holding a letter from Aunt Andrea. She ripped open the envelope and read the letter. Freddy leaned back in his chair, content to occupy his time observing the smiling woman's head move through the lines. While she was reading the first page, her eyes bulged. "Oh! No, it can't be true?"

Clueless, with a quizzical expression, Freddy locked eyes on the hushed-up woman.

"Grandma Bauer's very sick; what will I tell your father when he comes home?" said his mother, nibbling on her lip.

In time Freddy's father walked into a still room, widening his eyes. "What, no kiss?"

Wilhelm gave his wife a fake smile. "Barbara, you sick? Is something wrong?"

He spotted the letter on the table and eased himself into his chair.

"Okay, Barbara, what is it? What's wrong?"

"Wilhelm, your mother has cancer," she said, shedding tears.

His father was dull-eyed, and his shoulders slumped.

"I'm sorry, Wilhelm. Andrea wrote—she has a lump on her breast, and the doctor didn't give her much hope."

Freddy's father wept.

* * *

With a longing gaze, bound for Germany somewhere in the choppy North Atlantic, feeling the ship's motion under his feet, Freddy grasped the railing with his fingers. And he caught a whiff of salt air with a whimsical fall wind ruffling his hair, mesmerized by the sunset's grandeur. "Hmm." His throat thickened, and he looked inward, believing he'd never sleep again in the house and city that had filled his life with memories. A sudden chill flew up his spine, reminded he headed for a world filled with new mysteries. His eyes moistened as he glanced at glimmering stars with an unfocused gaze. *Will Germany be nice?*

Chapter Nine

October 1, 1928

icktock. Ticktock. "Stop!" whimpered Freddy, raising his head off the pillow, canvassing a colorless space ringed with darkened objects in distinct shapes and sizes protruding from gray walls, with the only conspicuous light the glowing dials from the bothersome ticker. *Ticktock.* He snatched the irritating timekeeper and brought it closer. It read half past six. His chest caved in, tormented with more *ticktock.* He stroked the iron hammer resting between the two brass bells on the clock, wanting to move time. He cursed the clock and shoved it under the pillow.

Tired, he lifted his gaze across the room, begging for a ray of light to pass through the curtains. His stomach rumbled, and he wiped off his clammy palms on his bedsheet. Not long after he dragged his fingers over his cheeks, observing light through the curtains. He gasped for a breath, fuzzy-minded, picking up a gentle knock on the door. *"It's him."*

"Morning, Father!"

"Freddy, can I come into the room?"

"Yes."

The door squeaked open, with a beam of light preceding his father. Freddy watched him push aside the curtains, letting light soak the room, and open the window. With his hands resting on the windowsill, he checked over the quiet street below him.

"Ah, Freddy, nothing soothes the mind more than fresh air in the morning."

After his father elbowed shut the door, he hunkered on a chair brought from Freddy's desk. Freddy's eyes widened and his gut tightened.

His father was bleary-eyed, and his voice trembled. "Your mother and I got little sleep; you worried us."

Freddy forced a smile. "Sorry I worried you. First day jitters, I guess; I'll get through it. I always do, don't I? Father, I hope mother looks better than you do."

His father smiled at a thought, singing his words. "Your mother always looks gorgeous."

His father's calloused hand brushed back his hair. There was a sheen in his eyes, and his cheeks rose. Freddy's throat thickened as he recalled his father's blissful expression when he pleased him; he could never get enough of it.

"Freddy, I wanted to wish you luck before heading to work."

A relaxed smile crossed Freddy's face as he scrutinized the genuine man. And his voice weakened, bringing a shaky hand to his forehead. "Father, I'm scared. My stomach's in knots. How will I get through the day?"

"Nonsense. You'll get through it; nothing stops you," said his father, firming his voice, questioning Freddy's words. "I want to hear how your day went when I come home." He rose, giving him a sympathetic glance. "You can do whatever you set your mind to; one day you'll be a brilliant lawyer."

"I'll try," Freddy said with a warm smile.

His father sat, lightening his voice. "There's something you should know. After you were born, the doctor told us we couldn't have more children. His words shattered our hopes and dreams. Your mother had a tough time getting over it."

His father's Adam's apple bobbed.

"After one of Father Schultz's sermons, your mother hatched up a scheme. She jumped up, letting out a gasp. 'Wilhelm, God has enlightened me. Pay attention; it's important. Freddy needs an inner voice, something to guarantee him a good life. I'll call it the three-legged stool.'"

"You remember that? It was a long time ago," said Freddy, scratching his head.

"Son, I will never forget it."

Freddy's forehead creased, and he glanced up at the ceiling, minding his mother's words when she fussed over the three-legged stool. "Freddy, it's a simple plan to follow, with only three legs. God, family, and education—combined they will put your life on a rewarding path. Loving God and obeying his commandments will ensure a place in heaven for you. The next leg is your family; never lose sight of the fact that they give you unconditional love and give you strength. And the last leg, education, is necessary; it comes from books and teachers and gives you intelligence. It will empower you to make the right choices."

"I love you, son. Tell me how your day went tonight."

The conversation with his father comforted him, and warmth filled his chest.

Lured by the aroma of coffee, Freddy shaved in a flash without nicking himself and whisked into the kitchen. He glared at his usual breakfast of hard-boiled eggs, liverwurst, and rolls.

His mother made strong eye contact with him, swallowing hard. "Is something wrong?"

"No, Mother, everything's fine."

"Good, eat; you didn't touch your dinner last night. Did you sleep last night? Your eyes are puffy."

Freddy's limbs tingled, and he forced a smile. "No."

He sipped coffee, noticing his mother sneak a peek at him. And he finished the meal, observing a half-hearted smile on her lips and her wrapping her hands around herself. "Guess you were hungry?"

Dressed in his new gray tweed suit, he pulled a handkerchief from the top dresser drawer and stuffed it into his slanted coat pocket, leaving just enough exposed. Joy warmed him from within as he brushed his wavy blond hair back and correcting his blue tie.

He stepped inside the kitchen, catching his mother wiping an eye with her apron. Her lips started trembling, and she rushed over, wrapping her arms around him.

"Mother, we knew this day would come, didn't we? I know it's hard letting go of me, but you did a splendid job raising me. Take comfort in that; I won't disappoint you."

"You can't disappoint me," she said, sniffing, with a glimmer in her eyes.

She shed tears and placed her moist lips against his cheek.

The corners of his lips rose. "Mother, I should get going. If I stay any longer, you'll have to wring your apron."

Her hand rested over her heart. "Freddy, I'm proud of you; I love you."

His bright blue eyes sparkled. "I love you too. And don't you worry—you'll see I can take care of myself."

Freddy left her and stepped outside the apartment, worshipping the blue sky, and traveled toward the university with a spring in his steps.

Fifteen minutes passed before the university gates came into sight. And he rushed through them, meandering down a cobblestoned path, heading toward the law building. He reached the law building, admiring the massive columns on the gray stone building. And he dashed up the steps and ran his fingers over chiseled lines on one of the long pillars.

Freddy stepped through one of the enormous bronze doors and choked with burning eyes in a large smoke-filled room cluttered with students. He plowed through the crowd till he reached a reception desk. "I'm looking for Professor Karp's room."

The overweight woman with pinned gray hair scrunched her eyes at him. "Room number fourteen. Next, please."

Freddy grimaced and with a sense of direction, walked away and wandered through long passageways lined with giant windows, dark-wood doors, and clocks on every wall. He arrived early and found a place in front of a sunlit window. The warm sunlight penetrating the glass made him sleepy, and his eyelids bobbed.

He glanced across the hall, paying close attention to students grouped around the door. One of them, with brown hair and prominent forehead, standing much taller than the rest, kept checking his watch. A slender man standing beside him with slicked-back black hair puffed on a cigarette. He concentrated on a youthful man with uncombed hair reading a thin book, leaning against the wall, ignoring traffic passing him. Curious, he kept monitoring him.

At five minutes to eight, a hall bell placed between two doors detonated. He glared at it, picking up the ear-piercing noise from its hammer. The students huddled in front of the door rushed inside the room. The youthful man who had caught his attention rose and threw on his coat, leaving his shirt untucked, moving his fingers through his strawberry blond hair twice, and walked into the classroom. Freddy moved away from the warm rays, tightening his eyes as he entered the room. The large, open space lacked the intimacy of the smaller rooms at the gymnasium. Freddy found a seat beside the oversized man he had seen earlier. He caught sight of a dark-brown wood podium placed close to the first row. And he twirled his fountain pen, keeping his eyes on the door.

The hall bell rang again, at nine, and a well-groomed man entered the room wearing a tiny knotted tie lost between the two points of a large white collar. He gasped—the black-haired man with a receding hairline differed from the beer-bellied fossil he had expected. His tongue rubbed against his inside cheek, and stopped fumbling with his pen, concentrating on the silent man who strummed through a stack of papers, rearranging a few on top.

"Good morning, students, my name's Professor Doctor Stefan Karp," said the man, thrusting out his chest with delight laced in his voice. "I consider it an honor to welcome you to the university's law school. It's my hope that when you finish my class, you will command a basic understanding of the Weimar Republic's laws. May I assume everyone's in the right room? If not, please leave."

No one budged. Professor Karp eyed the untidy student. The student read a book. Professor Karp's curious stare grew into anger, and he raised his voice, using a harsh tone. "Whatever your name is, are you in the right room?"

The student paid no attention to him and kept reading. Professor Karp sneered and crossed his arms. "Is this your room?" he asked again, his voice rising to almost a scream. The person seated alongside the inattentive man elbowed him. His head shook, and he lurched back. Professor Karp repeated himself.

The student's voice wobbled. "Yes, Herr Professor Karp, I'm in the right place."

Professor Karp's mouth twisted. In a loud voice, he said, "Tell me—what's so important that you can't pay attention to me?" He sucked in a breath, letting it out fast. "You ignored me while I spoke. I'd stood here a minute without you looking at me. Whatever it was, that's unacceptable and inappropriate behavior, isn't it? What was so damn important? Tell me. I'm interested."

"Herr Professor Karp, I don't want to. I apologize for my offensive behavior. It won't happen again—I promise you."

Angered, the academic bared his teeth. "You're correct, Herr. What's your name?"

"It's Herr Leo Herzfeld, Professor."

"Well, Herr Herzfeld, what's that you're reading?"

"Herr Professor, must I? I'm sorry I wasted your time; it won't happen again."

Professor Karp lifted his voice, squinting at him. "Herr Herzfeld, not so fast—answer my question. What are you reading?"

"It's...it's...it's just a pamphlet," said Herzfeld stuttering his words, resting his chin on his chest.

Professor Karp's brows came close together. "Not good enough; what is it?"

Bug-eyed Herzfeld rocked, straining his voice. "No, I can't."

The professor's head flinched, and he flared his nostrils.

Herzfeld let out a sigh and hung his head. "Uh, Herr Professor, it's *The Communist Manifesto*."

Professor Karp's face reddened. The only noise came from his fingers tapping the podium. A student with wavy coal-black hair nudged the person huddled alongside him. He said in the blond-haired man's ear, "Herzfeld's the Jew Communist I warned you was a troublemaker."

The light-haired man's head nodded. With a crack between his lips, Freddy ran his fingers through his blond hair, stunned at what he had overheard. Professor Karp considered Leo Herzfeld for a moment.

"Ahem, you're studying law—it might be the most important decisions you'll make in your life," said Professor Karp, examining the class with large, endearing eyes. "May I assume you were of sound mind when you made it? And it interests me why you did. Will each of you stand up and introduce yourself and oblige me by revealing to me your reasons."

Freddy picked up loud moans and heard stomps on the floor. Professor Karp gave Leo Herzfeld a vile stare.

"Uh, Herr Herzfeld, you're excused from speaking," said Professor Karp, widening his stance. "You've better things to do with your time, don't you?"

"Yes, Herr Professor," said Leo Herzfeld, appearing freaked out.

Professor Karp directed his eyes to a light-haired student in the first row, and he rose, declaring his reasons in a shaky voice. Freddy pulled back in his seat in disgust. *He's terrible! He's not answering the question.*

An idea percolated in his brain as he agonized over the speaker's unoriginal thoughts. Energized, he opened his book to a blank page and scribbled good, average, and thoughtless across the top of it. Each speaker he graded by placing a check mark under one of the three columns. Breathless, he watched the dark-haired classmate who warned another about Leo Herzfeld rise to speak.

"Herr Professor and classmates, my name is Rudolf von Krieg. I'm the grandson of Heinrich Jung, one of the acclaimed judges seated at the Court of Appeals for Berlin. I'm sure you're aware of him and his distinguished colleagues. He has presided over important judicial cases, and his written opinions are renowned in Germany."

Freddy detected aloofness in the faceless man's voice.

When the student hesitated, he pictured an arrogant expression on his face.

"I come from a titled Prussian family with grandfathers that were prominent judges. I cherish these men and want to follow them; that's why I chose law," bragged the presumptuous man.

Freddy cursed him under his breath and added a fourth column. In bold letters he jotted "PA" next to the third column and underlined it twice. And his jaw stiffened as he put a gigantic mark under it. The king-sized man who had caught onto Freddy tapped on the letters with his pencil. And Freddy's lips curved into a smile, writing "pompous ass" above the "PA." The onlooker gave him a vigorous nod. "Yes, yes," he said, whispering, exposing a space between his front teeth.

When Freddy's time came, his stomach quivered, and he rose, pulling back his shoulders, gazing at his teacher with an impassive expression on his face.

"Herr Professor and classmates, I'm Friedrich Bauer, from Berlin. Until three years ago, I lived in America. There the First World War brought misery to German Americans. Many doubted their allegiance to the country. A judge sent my best friend's father to prison. He wrongly accused him of spying for Germany. Prejudice and bigotry affected my life growing up. So I decided to study law because I wanted people to be treated fairly." His tight lips drew into a slight grimace as he observed Professor Karp. "I came back to a bitter country divided by political dissension and from its defeat in World War I. The kaiser left, and a democratic republic arose. But there were political factions that wished to abolish it. And before the new government declared a constitution, Communists rebelled."

Rudolf von Krieg jumped up, waving his fist at Leo Herzfeld. "Traitors. They should shoot every one of you."

More students left their seats, cursing Communists. Leo Herzfeld sprung up, saying, "Sit, Nazi pigs."

Pucker-lipped, Professor Karp moved his finger from Krieg to Herzfeld. "Sit. You're both out of order." And the man's lips parted, exposing his teeth; he whacked the podium, sending papers flying. Tight-lipped, wide-eyed, students glance at each other. Professor Karp's nostrils twitched. He moved his head slowly across the hushed room, and his loud breaths sped up.

117

"The next time it happens, you can explain to Rector Vogt why it did." The instructor lashed out, crossing his arms.

Professor Karp bent to pick up the papers. Rudolf von Krieg's nameless blond-haired friend shouted, "Jew pig."

Professor Karp bounced up and faced the class, scrunching papers in his hand. The speechless man's lips twisted, and he inspected the quiet room. "Who said that?" he demanded, stepping back, wide-eyed. His face reddening; he threw the papers in his hand at the class. And with a pained stare, he hurried back behind the lectern, moving his eyes slowly over the class.

"God dammit, who said it? Say it to my face!"

The blond-haired student shrugged his shoulders and cast a glance over the room. The oversized man said, knocking his leg into Freddy, "I want to kill him."

Professor Karp fumed, shaking his fist. "Which one of you said it?"

The room hushed. Professor Karp assumed a pensive look. And Freddy couldn't imagine what crossed his mind, replaying the two despicable words.

The teacher darted his eyes between the corners of the room. "Whoever you are, you're a coward."

Professor Karp locked eyes on Freddy, stroking his throat. "Herr Bauer, do you know who it was?"

Freddy's heart thumped in his chest. "No, Herr Professor, I don't."

Professor Karp slammed his fist on the podium, coloring his ears red. "Good God, where's your sense of decency?"

And he rested his elbows on the lectern, bringing his hands together as if praying. Freddy's body stiffened, and he sucked in his cheeks.

Professor Karp calmed his voice, glaring at Freddy. "Herr Bauer, please continue."

Freddy wet his lips, pulling his thoughts together. And he began speaking where he had left off, directing his sight at Professor Karp.

"Autocrats and right-wing fanatics attempted to overthrow the government too."

Picking up a few groans, he assessed Professor Karp's wry face

"Herr Bauer, I didn't ask you for a history lesson; hurry, please tell me why are you're here."

He bowed his head. "Sorry, Herr Professor. I'll get right to the point."

Karp's face hardened. "Hurry, Herr Bauer, or sit down."

"Uh, t-the Weimar Constitution for the first time gave every German free speech, religious freedom, and equality under the law."

"Herr Bauer, to the point," said the professor, crossing his arms and tensing his tone of voice.

"Yes, professor, uh, I want to defend the Constitution from power-hungry politicians with selfish purposes, and I hope one day I'll stand beside many other lawyers eager to protect it from the scoundrels seeking to exploit it."

The professor's cheeks lifted.

The oversized man's leg brushed against his as he rose and cleared his throat. "My name is Albert Hass. I'm from Aachen, Germany, a city near the Belgium and Netherlands border. I chose law because a gymnasium professor told me I should be a lawyer because I like to quarrel."

Freddy's jaw dropped, listening to Albert; he judged him thoughtless. At the end of class, he tallied the marks, grinding his teeth. He counted forty from a class of forty-two, leaving out Herzfeld and himself. He graded five students good, five average, and the rest were thoughtless, except for Rudolf von Krieg's eye-catching check mark.

After class ended, he sat still, his mind revisiting what happened earlier. He picked up heavy footsteps and caught Leo Herzfeld hurrying toward Professor Karp. "Herr Professor Karp, excuse me. I wish to apologize. The last thing I wanted was to anger you and cause trouble," said Herzfeld, flapping his hand against his sides.

"But you did, and see what happened?" remarked Professor Karp, lifting his neck to give his collar a tug.

Freddy faced Herzfeld's back, noticing his fingers tightening into fists.

"Jew pig," Karp whined. "I'll take those two words with me to my grave."

"But Herr Professor, you're a Jew—those words aren't new to you."

"I never expected to hear them from a student in my room."

The dark-eyed man's lids closed, and he gave his head a few quick shakes.

"Herr Herzfeld, those words turn my stomach."

Professor Karp's straightened his head, mumbling words that were inaudible. Freddy wrapped his arms around himself, figuring they were the same two words that had tormented him.

"I'm sorry, professor," he said, slumping. "I caused that trouble."

Leo Herzfeld's grimace lingered as he marched up the steps.

"Herr Bauer, may I speak with you?"

Freddy looked at him, dazed. "Yes, Herr Professor, right away."

Professor Karp grew still, observing Freddy. "Herr Bauer, were you waiting to speak to me?"

"No, professor. I was looking over what you wrote on the blackboard," he replied, speaking in a flat voice, leery of his gaze.

"Oh," he said, uncrossing his arms. "Herr Bauer, I peeked at your entrance exams. I do it every time before a fresh class starts. Yours was noteworthy, one of the highest I've seen in a long time. It was curious at the time why you favored law over medicine, physics, engineering, where you'd make more money. But you convinced me where your heart was when you said, 'defend the Constitution from power-hungry politicians with selfish purposes.'

The professor's eyes widened, and he pulled in a breath. "Herr Bauer, law's a passion that comes from the heart. I'm glad you selected law and look forward to our conversations."

Happiness bloomed inside Freddy, overwhelmed by the kind words. "Thank you, Herr Professor. I won't forget what you said to me." And he walked away from Professor Karp, sticking out his chest, sensing his body felt lighter.

"Herr Bauer, when you have the time, please see me," said the professor, raising his voice a notch. Freddy spun around, prompted by Karp's firm voice. "I'm interested in what happened to you in America."

With a juiced-up state of mind, he felt his body warm. And he stopped at the door, catching the professor staring at the ceiling. His cheeks lifted, imagining he had met a unique man.

A few steps into the hall, he spotted Herzfeld standing beside the window he had been standing at earlier. The sun's rays disappeared. The Communist headed his way.

"What happened, Friedrich? I heard Professor Karp call your name. What did he want? Is he mad at you too? What did you do?"

"I did nothing wrong, and it's my business what he said."

His loud voice startled the Red, and he stepped back.

"I'm sorry; we got off to a terrible start. My name's Leo Herzfeld."

"I know who you are."

Leo Herzfeld bowed his head. "Yeah, guess you do. Who doesn't? I made a mistake and paid for it. How can I blame Professor Karp for getting pissed at me? I deserved it. So now the entire class knows I'm a Communist. But your speech didn't help matters, did it?" Leo blew air in Freddy's face. "I bet you're a fucking nationalist, aren't you?"

Freddy stabbed him in the chest with his finger. "I'm a constitutionalist, not an extremist bent on taking over the world. Didn't you pay attention to me in class?"

Herzfeld pointed his finger at him, saying, "You're a fucking dreamer, Friedrich, that's what you are. Save that shit for Professor Karp's class; I'm sure he'll jump for joy when he hears it."

"Ha-ha, I'm impressed at least you remembered my name."

The young Communist scowled, rocking on his feet, "Don't be an asshole; it wasn't hard. My uncle's named Friedrich, and I hate him."

"Hmm, let me guess, I bet he's not a Communist."

"Not funny, shithead."

"I'd bet money you're a Red Front fighter—are you?" said Freddy, narrowing his eyes on Leo.

A crooked smile showed on Leo Herzfeld's lips. "You'd win the bet. Brownshirts don't intimidate us."

Freddy frowned at him. "From what I read in the papers, you're losing more of your comrades than they are."

With flared nostrils and wrinkled lips, Leo made an obscene gesture with his middle finger, sticking it in Freddy's face before he walked away. Stunned, he froze and tracked the hotheaded Red till he dropped out of sight.

* * *

A fleshy woman stirring gravy sneered at Freddy, waiting for him to decide what he wanted.

"Hurry, I don't have the entire day," the white aproned woman shouted, convulsing her nostrils. "Do you want it or not?"

He nodded, and the testy woman slopped a ladle full of meat and gravy on his plate, spattering droplets on his coat sleeve. Freddy left the line, searching for a place to sit. Once he spotted Rudolf von Krieg and the blond-haired trouble-maker, he headed for tables in the other direction.

"Friedrich, over here," said a screaming voice, stopping him in his tracks.

"Over here, we're over here, Friedrich."

He laid eyes on the gap-toothed man, motioning him his way. And he arrived smiling, noticing the greasy-haired hair man who had been with him earlier take his last drag from a cigarette.

"Hey, Friedrich, pull up a chair and join us. Your name's Friedrich, right?"

Freddy maintained eye contact with him, laying down his tray and planting himself in a chair.

The giant-sized man's voice firmed, and he shook his head. "Good thing Professor Karp handled it. If he didn't, I can't imagine what might have happened. I wanted to kill the bastard who said it."

Still smiling, Freddy uncrossed his arms. "I can't blame you, but I didn't catch his name."

The other student scratched his lubricated hair. "Erich Wagner is his name."

The gap-toothed man lowered his eyebrows, saying, mindful of the name, "I won't forget it."

"I'm Albert Haas, and the student with the Rudolf Valentino haircuts, Curt Krause. Curt and I met this morning."

"I know; I saw you hanging close by the door before Professor Karp's class started."

"That's right, Friedrich, you couldn't miss Albert, could you?"

Albert Haas wrinkled his nose, scratching the back of his neck. "It made sense what you said in class, but you could have caused a riot." Albert's smile faded. "Words have consequences, and the ones you chose pissed off many people. If I were to grade your speech, the best I could do was rate it average, and I would be too generous giving you that high mark." Albert gasped and bounced in his seat, changing his straight lips into a grin. "Hah! fooled you; if only you could see your face."

Curt Krause smirked. "Don't mind him, Friedrich; he thinks that's funny."

"It was funny," said the large man, nodding.

Curt chuckled, widening his eyes. "You could've fooled me."

Albert forced a smile, nudging him. "Ha-ha."

"Friedrich, I told Curt what you were doing in Professor Karp's class. He agreed with your assessment of von Krieg. Uh, what grade did you give me?"

"It was good," Freddy lied, scratching his arm.

Curt made unwavering eye contact with him. "I guess your grading method needs improvement, doesn't it?"

Freddy grimaced with a pink flush edging over his cheeks. "It's a pity what happened to Leo Herzfeld in class."

"It is," said Albert, softening his tone. "I pity him."

"Not me—he deserves what he got," said Curt, seething.

Albert slumped in his seat, rubbing his ample forehead. "Curt, show sympathy for the poor bastard."

"You should," said Freddy, sticking a fork in a piece of meat and putting it into his mouth.

Contempt crept into Curt's voice. "It angers me what he did."

Albert's eyebrows slanted, and he pinched his chin, shrugging his shoulders and dilating his pupils. "I think we should be friends. If we don't share a laugh, this place could be dismal."

Albert's eyes darted between Curt and Freddy. "There's only one condition, and I should explain it to you."

Curt laughed, throwing his head back, "Just one—that's hard to swallow. What is it?"

"We must be honest with each other; I've no tolerance for hypocrites," said Albert, uncurling his immense body.

Curt chuckled and slapped the table, saying, "Wow, never expected that shit coming out of your mouth."

"How can you be friends if you're not honest with each other?" said Freddy, lifting his chin.

He straightened up, gazing at the giant. "Albert, there's something bothering me," he said, pulling the skin on his neck.

"Yeah, what's that?"

"Your speech bored me; I put a check under the 'thought-less' column," said Freddy, narrowing his eyes.

Albert Haas's mouth opened, and it stayed that way till an unexpected smile unfolded on his lips.

"Huh, that's terrible," said Albert, with one brow curved higher than the other. "At least you were being honest with me."

"Thank God you're not pissed at him," Curt Krause said, eyeing Albert. "I'd hate to be in his shoes if you were."

Albert's eyes danced between Curt and Freddy. "I've something to confess, and it can't wait."

Freddy leaned in, drawing his brows together.

"You're in the wrong place; you need a priest," said Curt, grinning.

Albert's face became stern; he pursed his lips. "Listen up, it's important, our friendship depends on it."

125

Freddy tapped his foot on the floor, tilting his head at Albert. "Okay. Tell me what it is."

"I hate the Nazis—if you're one, we'll never be friends," said Albert with an air of intolerance in his voice.

Curt giggled at him, saying, "That's it? I thought you had something real important to tell us."

Freddy scrutinized Albert, pulling back his shoulders. "Don't worry over a bunch of street brawlers wearing brown shirts and jackboots. They won a handful of seats last election. That makes them irrelevant in my mind. They're just a bunch of thugs with no future."

"Hope you're right, Friedrich, but don't forget they held a colossal rally last year in Nuremberg; it might be a mistake for you to overlook them."

Curt attacked a sausage with a knife and fork and chewed a piece, swallowing it with water.

"What's in this? It tastes awful—mustard and sauerkraut can't help it," he complained, licking a drop of mustard off his lips.

Albert smirked. "Don't ask; you might throw up. The beef's no better—if it's beef, could be horsemeat."

Students sung, setting a tempo by stomping the floor with their shoes. Freddy edged around, catching sight of a two tables lined on both sides with red-capped fraternity brothers singing. Nearby Rudolf von Krieg and Erich Wagner gave him fraudulent smiles.

Albert shrugged, concentrating on Freddy. "Um, is something wrong?"

"I'm fine; why are you asking?"

"Your cheeks flushed, and you looked sad."

"How much of that shit did you eat?" said Curt Krause, taking notice of Freddy's plate.

"I'm okay; there's nothing wrong with me."

Albert's eyes brightened, and he straightened up, saying, "Friedrich, walk with us to Professor Rath's class. I heard the fat man's got a terrible temper."

Freddy swallowed, playing with his cuffs. "Who told you that?"

"Dirk Krug did this morning."

Curt Krause flinched and asked, stuttering, "W-whose Dirk Krug?"

"A third-year student who drank coffee with me at breakfast. He asked me a bunch of questions, and when I mentioned Rath's name, he shook his head hard, saying, 'You're fucked. He got Professor Rath his first year and urged me not to piss him off and said if I did, I'd live to regret it."

"Albert, I think he was kidding you," said Freddy, smirking at him.

"No, I don't think so. He grimaced when he said it."

Curt watched Albert lean back and look up. "What else did he tell you, Albert?"

"That Professor Rath's a tough marker."

Lines crossed Freddy's forehead, and he blew air expressively, imagining Krieg and Wagner still spying on him. He was eager for another peek at them. Three winks later, he shot a glance their way, detecting a burn in his gut, spotting the poker-faced men approaching. Erich Wagner split from Krieg, positioning himself inches away from Curt, lowering his eyes on him. Curt glanced up at him, jabbing his elbows into his sides, and hunched his shoulder, expressionless.

Wagner clapped his hands. "Curt, it's good to see you again—you haven't changed," Wagner said, giving Curt a playful nudge.

Curt's eyes evaded Wagner, and he said in a shaky tone, "It's been a while, hasn't it, Erich?"

The well-developed man hunched over Curt, reminding Freddy of a cat preparing to pounce on a mouse. And Erich

Wagner said to him, curving his lips into a sly smile, "Curt, I'm sorry, I hope I'm not interrupting you and your friends."

Curt lifted his head, blinking hard, turning pale. "Uh, uh, no, you're not."

Erich's body straightened, and with a coy smile plastered on his face, he said, "Curt, you never said hello to me in Professor Karp's class; you hurt my feelings." Snickering, Wagner tilted his head to the side, sighing.

Albert sneered at him, adding a crimson color to his cheeks, saying, "I hated what you said to Professor Karp—you do it again, and you'll answer to me."

Erich Wagner displayed a fiendish expression on his face and crossed his arms, bobbing them against his chest. "Oh, is that right?"

"I meant what I said," said Albert, narrowing his eyes, hardening his words.

Rudolf von Krieg straightened up, pulling back his shoulders. "Relax. It's our first day; we're jittery," huffed Rudolf, glaring at Albert. "Eric told me he was sorry for what he did."

Freddy leaned back, widening his eyes. *Does he think I'm stupid?*

Albert stretched, tightening his lips. Erich stayed on his feet, gloating over Curt.

Albert's nostrils spread, drawing air, and his head pulled back in disgust. "Dammit, step back, give him room to breathe."

"Sorry, Curt and I are old friends," said Erich, bringing his wide grin to a squint.

Freddy's face tightened; he grew suspicious of him.

"Yes, Curt and I are old friends," said Erich, facing Albert with a sly smile. "My name's Erich Wagner."

"I'm sure you remember my name from Professor Karp's class," said Rudolf, thrusting out his chest with a cheeky expression on his face.

Albert's voice oozed contempt as he concentrated on the cocky man. "How could I forget it? Judge Jung is your grandfather; I was speechless when you said it."

Rudolf's body tensed and he wheezed, glaring at Albert.

Rudolf's pressed lips curved into a smile, and he moved closer to Freddy, saying in English, "My favorite team's the New York Yankees. Whose yours?"

Wide-eyed, Freddy spoke English, "The Detroit Tigers."

"Um, the Detroit Tigers—why them?" asked von Krieg, twisting his mouth sideways.

With a wary face, his gut constricted, and he said, "I grew up in Detroit. Ty Cobb's my hero; he's the best ball player that ever lived."

Rudolf looked down his nose, saying, "You can't be serious. Babe Ruth is the best, ask anyone." And with a condescending smile, giving him a dismissive nod, he said, "Ty Cobb hasn't played ball for the Detroit Tigers in two years."

Freddy's eyes glazed over; he wished he could be somewhere else.

The arrogant man's voice hardened. "This time the Cardinals won't win every game from the Yankees like they did in the Twenty-Six World Series. What happened to the Tigers?"

"It's simple—you can't win if your pitching gives up more runs than you score," he replied, wrinkling his nose.

"How long have you known these two students?" asked Rudolf, giving Albert a sideways glance.

"Just met them. Why?" he said, crossing his arms, pondering the question.

"Paul Bunyan's a troublemaker, and Erich says Curt's a coward. Next time you should eat lunch with us."

With cold eyes, Freddy pinched his lips shut.

"It would be a mistake not to—you decide," said Krieg, giving him a dirty look.

"Speak German, please. I can't understand you," said Albert, glaring at Rudolf, stressing his voice and tone.

Freddy released a pent-up breath, loosening his tense muscles.

Rudolf fixed his eyes on Albert, gritting his teeth. And he glanced at Freddy with a hard smile. "See you in Professor Rath's class. My grandfather says he's an excellent professor."

"I'll save you a seat," said Albert in a jeering tone, leaning back with a sheen of sweat on his forehead.

Krieg gave him an intense stare. And spun around and walked away, with Wagner whispering in his ear.

Albert's voice took a harsh tone, and he glared at Rudolf. "Pompous ass."

Krieg stopped, yanking at Wagner's sleeve, speaking into his ear. Erich Wagner tilted his head at Albert, showing him a hostile gaze. For a second time, he questioned Albert's wisdom. And his throat constricted, agonizing over the large man's words till Krieg and Wagner vanished from sight.

Albert studied him with an unpleasant expression on his face. "I see you made a new friend."

A deep frown formed on his face. "God, I hope not."

Albert gave him a sharp nod, bringing a smile to his lips.

Curt's expression darkened, and he dragged his finger's down his cheeks.

Freddy leaned in, squinting. "Curt, what's wrong?"

"It depressed me to hear Erich Wagner was here. He's dangerous—don't trust him." And with a shaking hand, he grabbed hold of a half-filled glass of water and gulped it fast.

Curt's eyes tightened. "It's worse than I thought; if Rudolf and Erich think alike, we're in trouble."

Freddy squinted, circling his lips. "When did you meet Erich Wagner?"

Curt closed his eyes, cranking his head sideways slowly. "We met at a scout outing three years ago, but a year later he quit to join the Hitler Youth. He talked me into attending one of their meetings. At the meeting Brownshirts told us we were the future of Germany and it was our patriotic duty to join up, so I did." With a bleak expression on his face, remorse crept into Curt's voice. "I know what you're thinking; give me a chance to explain."

Albert scowled in disgust without blinking.

"We played games, and Erich was an excellent boxer," said Curt, fidgeting with his watch, slanting his eyes toward Albert. "We marched and sang patriotic songs; it was fun. The Brownshirts held meetings inside a brewhouse near the town hall. Erich's father, dressed in his brown uniform, led the meetings. He was a fanatical nationalist, wanting Germany to reclaim the land it lost from the war. Most Germans wanted their land back, didn't they? What's wrong with that?" Curt's face flushed, and he looked to the side. "Erich's father forced us to read out loud parts of *Mein Kampf*, and he often shouted these words: 'One day German's will rise and take back what's theirs. And must end the Treaty of Versailles and the Jew socialists who betrayed her during the war.'"

Albert took an audible breath. "My mother's a Jew."

Curt's lips trembled, and he hung his head.

Freddy captured a lungful of air. "Curt, is there more?"

"Yes, there is. His father's madness changed Erich. He once pulled a knife on another scout. It pleased the heartless bastard to pick on weaker scouts."

Curt's eyes focused on the empty glass of water. "I wasn't like him. I never could be."

Freddy leaned in, making strong eye contact with Curt. "What else happened?"

"It's not your concern, I don't want to discuss it."

Albert frowned and squinted at Curt, rocking in his chair. "It must have been awful."

Curt's shoulders curled, and he dropped his head.

Freddy stabbed a chunk of meat, leaving the fork standing up in it.

Albert's cheeks dimpled. "Not as good as home, is it?"

"I've lost my appetite," he replied, concentrating on Curt's words.

"Huh, second time I caught him staring at us," said Albert, building a slow smile.

Curt shot a glance at him. "Who?"

"Over there next to the pole, its Leo Herzfeld; he's seated behind two white-capped fraternity brothers."

Freddy turned his head, noting the Red's gaze.

"See, I told you," said Albert, nodding.

* * *

Freddy tagged along with Albert and Curt toward Professor Rath's class, doubting the second half of his day could be better than the first.

"Call me Freddy; my friends do."

And seconds after the hall bell ran out of juice, Freddy led Albert and Curt into a spacious room, his eyes widening as he spotted Krieg and Wagner in the first row. A beefy man he figured must be Professor Rath, sat displaying, he thought, a fake smile.

Albert's voice took a hard edge. "Oh no, the man looks much worse than I thought." And Albert checked out the room, saying, "There are two places to sit, in the first row or in the back of the room."

"If it's in the first row, you won't be sitting with me," said Freddy, glaring at Albert.

Albert eyed the front row. "Oh! I see what you mean."

Curt gave Freddy a playful nudge, lifting a cheek. "Flip a coin to see who sits next to Goliath."

Albert shook his head at them, wearing a crooked smile.

The heavy-set professor frowned, checking the time. And he lifted his head, smiling when the last bell rung and rose, legging it to the lectern. "Let me congratulate you for being accepted into the university law program. I'm Herr Professor Doctor Siegfried Rath," said the big-eyed man, scouring the class. He gripped the sides of the lectern and glanced up at the door, hearing it open, and he stepped back. Distinct footsteps approached and ceased behind Freddy. He heard huffing and puffing.

"And you are?" said the instructor, giving the person a wicked stare, "You"—he shot his finger in Freddy's direction—"the person who interrupted me while I was speaking." Rath rocked, his face riddled with anger. "Stand up," he said, drawing his brows together.

Freddy picked up a gasp from behind him and feet hitting the floor.

"I'm sorry I interrupted you, Herr Professor. By mistake, I went to the wrong room." Freddy's jaw dropped, recognizing Leo Herzfeld's voice.

"I didn't ask you for an excuse; I asked for your name," said Rath, breathing loud.

Herzfeld's eyes bulged, gulping for air. "S-sorry, H-Herr Professor; Herr Herzfeld, Herr Leo Herzfeld is my name."

Rubbing his chin, Rath spoke with an angry note in his voice. "Herzfeld—that's your last name?

"Ye-ye-yes, Herr Professor."

Professor Rath checked the time, moving his head side to side, saying, "Well, Herr Herzfeld, you wasted enough of my time. Sit!"

"Yes, sorry, Herr Professor, it was careless of me," said Herzfeld, with a slight tremor in his voice.

"Herr Herzfeld, I told you to sit!"

With quivering lips, Freddy gazed at Rath, recalling what the student had told Albert.

* * *

Pleased Rath's class had ended, Freddy exhaled, and followed Albert and Curt into the hall, aware Leo Herzfeld was darting toward him.

"Excuse me, Friedrich, do you have time? It's important."

Albert and Curt eyed each other, shrugged their shoulders, and walked away.

Freddy swallowed, making eye contact with Leo Herzfeld. "What's on your mind?"

"I'm sorry I lost my temper and cursed at you. Can we put aside our political differences and be friends? I could use one after what just happened to me today."

Freddy's eyes widened, with nerves rippling through his stomach. And it occurred to him his improbable day was ending with a Communist seeking friendship. His gaze intensified, and he spit into the palm of his right hand, extending it to the Red.

"What are you doing?" said Leo, squishing his eyebrows together.

"My grandfather said it's not a bargain until two men spit in their hands, look each other in the eye, and shake on it."

"I can do that," said Herzfeld, lifting his cheeks high.

And he made unwavering eye contact with Leo. "Wait, there's one more thing."

"Yeah, what is it?"

"If one of us blinks, the deal's not completed."

Herzfeld spit into the palm of his hand and shook hands without blinking.

Freddy smirked. "Oh, before I forget, the next time you wave your middle finger at me, the deal's off for good."

Herzfeld's lips curled, wagging his head. "Freddy, there's something I should tell you."

"Oh, what?"

"I caught you talking with Rudolf von Krieg. He's dangerous—avoid him. Whoever was with him, I'd stay far away from him too."

"What?"

"I attended Ludwig Gymnasium with Rudolf von Krieg. He and other nationalists picked fights with Communists, Social Democrats, and Jews. No one ate lunch alone. I saw him lose his temper and try to crack a chair over a friend's head. Lucky for Jopie, he blocked it with his arm. We complained to the headmaster, but he didn't interfere. When we wanted to go to someone else, he warned us not to, said it'd be a mistake if we involved Judge Jung."

"What, Judge Jung?" said Freddy, perplexed.

"Judge Jung heads the Ludwig Gymnasium school board."

"Oh, what else do you know about Rudolf?"

"Girls fancied his looks; there was always one hanging around waiting for him after classes."

* * *

Freddy thought of his strange day, and his fingers fumbled with the key before he found the hole and turned it, opening the door. Tired and hungry, he stepped into the kitchen, finding four focused eyes staring at him. A pleasant odor lured him to a black pot, and he peeked inside it. He smacked his lips and eased a beef stew onto a plate.

His mother stopped tapping the table, giving his father a quick glance. "Well, Freddy, are you going to tell us what happened at the university or not?"

"Not at all what I expected. I'll tell you what happened after I eat."

135

"No, answer me now! How was your day, and don't you dare leave something out? I've been a nervous wreck worrying over you the whole day."

"All right, Mother, I'll tell you."

"Drop your fork," his mother said, twisting on her ring.

"Okay, I'll tell you."

She frowned, crossing her arms. "Hurry!"

Freddy hashed over what had happened to Leo Herzfeld. He mystified Freddy, so he decided not to divulge he was a Communist. He saved his rage for Rudolf von Krieg and Erich Wagner. At the end, her lips spread apart, and she gave him a long, cold stare.

Her voice hardened. "Freddy, stay away from both of them—their trouble."

His father tilted his head toward Freddy. "She's right."

She cut her eyes toward his father. "Wilhelm, can a person be a Jew and a Communist?"

"Think so."

Father Vogel disapproves of what Hitler thinks of Jews. He writes a religious man couldn't behave that way."

"Huh, come to think of it, I didn't know many Jews till we moved to Berlin."

"I knew a Jew at the Ford Plant but he left after Henry Ford started publishing articles against them in his newspaper."

His father dipped his head. "Once, Clarence told me he overheard men call Jews terrible names, but it made little sense to him why they did. He asked Ida why, and she told him to pay no attention to them. She said the preacher told her they were God-fearing people too."

"Wilhelm, do you recall the Jewish butcher beaten to death outside his store?"

"I remember him; why do you ask?"

"Well, I used to notice his wife in church before it happened, but now I don't."

The man spoke, adding astonishment to his voice. "She's not Jewish?"

His mother's voice stiffened. "How could she be if she goes to church on Sunday? Well, the store never reopened, and Anna Drass told me her husband thinks Nazis killed him. She made me promise to keep it to myself and tell no one."

His lips pursed, and he gave his head a quick shake. "That didn't work, did it?"

"Honey, you're my husband; I know you won't tell anybody." She stroked her chin, lifting her pupils to her eyelids. "Wilhelm, how many Jews do you know in Berlin?"

"Herr Klein?"

"Humph, only the shopkeeper?"

With a devilish smile on her face, his mother turned her eyes on him. "Is there more on Leo Herzfeld?"

He ate fast, not surprised by the question, convinced his eyes had given him away, expecting more inquiries.

"No, don't think so."

She squinted at him. "Freddy, are you sure?"

Panic held his thoughts captive, and his blue pupils danced. Afflicted with shame, he no longer could keep her in sight. "Hm, Leo Herzfeld's a Communist."

"What! He told you that?" she said with venom in her voice.

"Yes and no."

"What does that mean?" she shouted.

"Professor Karp caught him reading *The Communist Manifesto*."

"What! keep away from him; I won't say it again. You don't want to be friends with his kind. He's probably an atheist, a damn heathen. Chaos and revolution, is what's on his mind; his loyalty's to Moscow, not Germany."

His agitated mother elbowed his father, catching his eyes close.

He threw out Judge Jung's name to get her mind off Leo Herzfeld.

Her brows jumped up. "Judge Jung's Rudolf von Krieg's grandfather?"

"He is."

She frowned. "He's a nationalist."

His father cocked his head. "Barbara, you don't know that."

"Yes, honey, he must be. It makes sense. If his grandson's a Nazi, then he's got to be one too. I'll ask friends if they have heard he is."

Upset, his father sneered and boosted his voice. "No you don't. People gossip—don't stick your nose where it doesn't belong; keep your mouth shut and mind your business."

Freddy's mother flinched, pursing her lips. "Wil-Wilhelm, don't raise your voice to me."

Rattled, Freddy's breaths quickened. "I'm tired, let me get some sleep; tomorrow's another day."

Freddy dragged himself into his bedroom with a haunted expression and drew the curtains closed before he fell into bed, losing consciousness.

Chapter Ten

First Year at University

His overworked brain begged for mercy as he mulled over countless facts and figures in the book. Light-headed, with a churning stomach, Freddy's breathing sped up. His eyelids sprang up, hearing loud footsteps and an eerie screech that sent shivers through him, and frowned at the hefty librarian dragging a ladder across the floor. The woman, whom he dubbed "The Thumper," never worried over the racket she made. He watched her climb up the ladder, amazed the rungs held together under her enormous weight.

A lump appeared in his throat as he leaned back, recognizing Rudolf von Krieg easing toward him, saying to himself, *No.*

"I thought it was you, Friedrich," said Rudolf, studying him, speaking English in a hushed tone, a concerned look on his face. "I just finished a cigarette; I needed a break. The Jew professor hands out excessive work. While I checked out the library, I noticed you." And his mouth gave a slight twist as he said, "It's hard studying law. My grandfather warned me it was difficult."

"He's right—if you're not committed, you'll fail at it."

Rudolf stooped, wrinkling his brows. "Friedrich, I hope I'm not disturbing you."

Freddy closed his book, smiling politely.

"Good!" said Rudolf, widening his eyes, pitching his voice higher. "It stunned me when I read the Yankees swept the Cardinals in the World Series and Ruth hit three home runs in the last game. Imagine that, Babe Ruth hitting three four baggers in one game?"

Freddy tapped his foot, forcing a smile. "I was too busy to follow the series."

"Friedrich, for God's sake, enjoy yourself. Why don't we go for beers at the Boar's Den; you shoot darts, don't you?"

The corners of his mouth dropped; he gave Rudolf a stony stare. "I don't have the time."

Rudolf smirked, placing his hands on the back of the chair. "Friedrich, we can drink beers with a desirable woman rubbing against us."

Freddy wagged his head. "No, thank you, I'll leave the debauchery to you; I'll bet you're good at it. What might Judge Jung think?"

Krieg exposed a wide grin. "Ha, you've got a sense of humor."

Rudolf sat, mooring his elbows to the desk. "Friedrich, you never told me where you learned to speak English; was it in Detroit?" In an instant Rudolf's brows rose, and he gave Freddy a toothy smile. "Ah, that's it. I got it, that's why you favor the Tigers."

He gave Rudolf a sarcastic taunt. "Wow! You're a genius."

Rudolf's chest inflated with a satisfied smile. "Friedrich, I learned English in America too; a nanny taught me at a young age. My father was a diplomat in Washington, DC, before the war ended."

"Lucky you," said Freddy, developing a slight headache raising his eyebrows at the self-important man.

With an arrogant pride in his words, Rudolf said, "Friedrich, there's a long list of distinguished military officers in my family. Some had even fought against Napoleon at Waterloo."

Freddy smirked at the radiant man, recalling an obnoxious parrot at the zoo.

"Friedrich, my grandfather's library is full of medals and swords, even Roman antiquities dating back centuries."

Freddy's mouth twisted into a wry smile, adding a hint of sarcasm to his voice. "Wow, that's impressive; save the rest for your next family reunion."

Rudolf's jaw dropped, and he raised his voice a notch. "Friedrich, might you boast if you came from a rich, influential family?"

His fists clenched, and his gut tightened, catching Rudolf leaning closer.

Rudolf's gaze intensified, and he said, "Are you and Leo Herzfeld acquainted? I saw you talking."

Freddy's head moved back, and he rubbed his arm. "Why do you care whom I talk to?"

Rudolf glared at him, deepening his tone. "Friedrich, you need to choose sides, for your protection. Can't you tell I want to be your friend and look after you?"

Freddy flinched, darkening his expression. "No thanks. I have enough friends."

Rudolf's eyes tightened, and he crossed his arms. "Be careful who your seen with. You don't want to give people the wrong idea, do you? Impressions matter. If I were you, I'd stay away far away from Leo Herzfeld."

His face reddened, and he tilted his head from Rudolf, his gut tightening more, saying in a taut voice, "I can pick my friends; I don't need help."

Krieg's lips puckered, and his eyes glittered with anger. "Do...do you want classmates to see you talking with Leo Herzfeld? If I were you, I'd stay away from the Communist troublemaker. We knew how to handle him in Ludwig Gymnasium."

"W-w we—who's we?"

"Nationalist students who want Germany to rearm and burn the Constitution that protects the backstabbing Jews and other traitors."

"So you lied when you said Erich misspoke when he called Professor Karp those despicable words?"

Rudolf gave Freddy a dirty look. "It was because of them Germany lost the war and forced to disarm."

"Huh, it was better when Germany owned a powerful army and soldiers fought for land, killing innocent people who got in their way doing it? Do you see victors inflating their chests with the stench of death in the air? Did they smile, hearing voices cry out in pain?" With a downturned mouth, he spoke in a sardonic tone. "What do you see? No, don't answer, I'm sure it will be lies. I see fatherless children, widows without hope, girls without lovers, my world's far different from yours."

Rudolf's face drained of color, and he rose, giving him an angry stare.

Freddy's shoulders curved over his chest, with his voice holding a bitter note. "Sit, I'm not finished!"

With a brittle laugh, Rudolf fell into the chair.

Freddy grimaced, feeling a flush of heat in his face. "Three of my uncles fought in the war. One's missing legs, and another suffers from shell shock, and the last, no one knows where he fell, or if he died in one piece." Freddy's nostrils flared, and he gawked at Rudolf, running his hands through his thick blond hair. "Hatred, suspicions, and false-hoods blacken your world; mine lives on love, decency, and justice."

Rudolf bared his teeth, coloring his ears red, and jumped up, knocking against his chair. And he stood erect, trusting out his chin, saying in a voice with a savage edge to it, "You can go to hell. What are you? A pacifist or fucking coward?"

Freddy surrounded his blue pupils in a sea of white. "I'm no coward. If I must fight for my country, I will, but I hope it's not for your sick ideology."

"You're wrong," said Rudolf, "only the fit survive."

Freddy's head recoiled as he widened his eyes with a shudder, shaking his body.

Rudolf examined him, inflating his chest with a pro-longed, audible breath. "Germany must rearm and project strength or it will cower to the whims of stronger countries. Did you forget what you told the class on your first day? I didn't." Rudolf ran his hands through his hair. "Did you for-get the Reds tried to overthrow the government? They'll try it again if they're not stopped. They will cause less damage if they're put in prisons."

Freddy raised his chin, crinkling his brows. "They found the Communist Rosa Luxemburg's body in a canal before they could give her a fair trial."

Rudolf displayed a scornful expression, dry-washing his hands. "Friedrich, be careful whom you choose as friends; there could be consequences if you make the wrong choice. The offer still stands. You can meet at the Boar's Den any-time for beers."

Rudolf's lips pinched together, and he shook his head before spinning around and walking away.

Freddy chewed his lip, sickened by the thought of Rudolf von Krieg's notions.

* * *

Freddy's jaw stiffened, and he gave an intense stare to the obstinate alarm clock. He climbed out of bed and wiped gunk from the corner of one eye and turned off the irritable timekeeper. And ignoring breakfast, he plowed through the apartment door and became captive to a November chill. Invigorated by crisp air, he buttoned his coat and threw a scarf around his neck, deciding to walk instead of pedaling to the university. And traveling to school, he applied his mind to answers on Professor Karp's exam.

Hungry, he stopped in front of a quaint café across from the university's enormous gates. He entered the eatery, finding a seat by a window, which faced a noisy truck coughing black smoke. He shrugged, checking the time, determining he had ample time until class started. An impatient truck driver cursed and honked his horn. When the truck moved on, he spotted Rudolf von Krieg and Erich Wagner, on the other side of the boulevard, gabbing with a bunch of fraternity brothers in front of the university gates.

"Cup of coffee, sir?"

He glanced up at a middle-aged woman flashing a smile before giving her a decisive nod. "Yes, thank you, coffee's fine."

And he glanced across the street again, seeing Rudolf and Erich alone lighting up cigarettes, and went back to hashing over answers on Professor Karp's exam that worried him.

"Sir, something to eat?"

"Yes, Braunschweiger and bread will do."

He glanced outside, discovering a man wearing a wrinkled gray coat and black worker's cap pass by him with a stylish woman wearing a black coat and matching hat. The couple stopped at the corner with the man's head blocking the woman's face. She pulled an envelope from her purse and gave it to the man, who stuffed it inside his coat. The two strangers hugged goodbye, and the lady crossed the street and stopped, pointing her head at Krieg and Wagner, pulling on a piece of hair hanging below her hat. Freddy tried focusing on the woman's face, but she stepped back and a lamppost obstructed his view. Freddy grimaced and directed his eyes where her head pointed, but only found Krieg and Wagner. A youthful girl rushed up to Rudolf, throwing her arms around his neck, kissing him. The well-dressed woman shook her head and walked away, disappearing into the crowd. Freddy slanted his head to the corner, discovering the rumpled man still there. The man reached into his coat pocket, drew change, and leaned over, dropping it in a tin cup, a legless beggar dressed in a tattered army uniform held out. His cheeks rose, and he straightened up in the chair, eyeing the charitable man. When the stranger turned, Freddy's jaw dropped; he dug his eyes into Leo Herzfeld's face. And he followed Herzfeld across the busy street, noticing Rudolf, Erich, and the affectionate girl had vanished.

"Here we go, sir—Braunschweiger and bread. Can I get you something else?"

"No, that'll do."

The server removed a pencil lodged between a white bandana and her salt-and-pepper hair and wrote out a check. Freddy took a sip of coffee, smeared Braunschweiger on the bread, took a large bite and chewed it, pondering his exam.

* * *

Freddy was on edge, and a wave of heat crossed his face, and his breaths sped up as he searched for his grade on the board hung outside the classroom. He stumbled back, wiping his sweaty palms against his pants with a knot in his stomach, appearing haunted, giving Albert and Curt a harsh gaze. "I don't understand, there's no grade beside my name." Professor Karp had jotted instead, "See me after class." And with a cheerful expression, his gaze shifted to Albert and Curt. "Well done, you both passed."

Inside Professor Karp's classroom, cowering in his seat, he plunged into despair. Curt nudged his elbow, saying in a sympathetic tone of voice, "Why don't you take a big breath, and release it slowly. That helps me when I'm nervous."

His throat thickened, and he said, "Won't help the way I'm feeling right now."

"It never fails; it works for me every time." said Curt, leaning in, nodding.

Freddy shrugged, staring at Curt with a lump in his throat.

"Do it, Freddy. What's there to lose?"

He inhaled, releasing air through his lips at a slow rate, noticing his body relaxing.

Curt's brows lifted. "See—it works, doesn't it?"

He eased back in his chair, calming from Curt's technique. "It might work?"

"Freddy, do it again."

"You windbags are nuts. The exam's over; you don't see me sweating over it," said Albert, making a face.

Curt laughed a little. "No, you wouldn't, because you're a fucking idiot and should be ashamed you just passed."

Albert's head pulled back in disgust. "Shut up!"

Curt winced and swallowed hard and tilted his head sideways.

Albert's lips loosened, and he pulled on his collar, concentrating on Curt. And in a flash, he exposed a funny face, and his lips vibrated a loud *brrrrrr*, making Curt's eyes brighten with indignation. Rudolf and Erich snapped around, giving him a dirty look.

"Is there something wrong?" asked Albert with sarcasm in his voice, forcing a smile.

Rudolf wagged his head at Albert and faced the podium. It angered Albert, and he let out a more intense *brrrrrr*.

Erich gave him a fevered stare, making an animalistic growl in his throat. "Enough! Shut your fucking mouth," said Wagner, in a ferocious voice, silencing the room. Albert bared the gap between his teeth, lengthening his lips, and rose to his feet, dwarfing Erich Wagner.

"Who you telling to shut his fucking mouth?"

Freddy's heartbeat sped up; he was aware the class was eyeballing Albert and Erich.

Skin wrinkled under Albert's eyes, and he shook his fist in Erich's face, wanting to provoke a fight with him. "Now's your chance to show us how brave you are, or are you a coward? It's your choice—which one?"

Curt gasped, edging away from Albert.

Erich blushed, breathing hard, and pulled back his right shoulder and threw a straight punch at Albert's stomach. Albert deflected the blow with his left hand, looking amused, saying to Erich with hard irony in his voice, "That's the best you can do?"

Outraged by Albert's arrogance, Rudolf sneered, saying to Erich, "Don't stop, hit him!"

Erich barred his teeth and threw another punch at him, but Albert blocked that, too.

Erich's fist trembled, and he darted his eyes.

Freddy's lips pressed into a slight grimace as he studied Erich. *Had he lost his nerve?*

Albert gave Erich a dirty look, bringing color to his cheeks.

Professor Karp came inside the room and stopped drawing, a quizzical expression on his face as he inspected the room. "Why the silence? Did I miss something?"

At the end of class, the professor squinted at Freddy, saying to him, "Ah! Yes, Herr Bauer, don't forget to visit me. We can discuss your exam in my office."

Devastated, feeling numb all over, Freddy examined Professor Karp, expecting the worse when they met in his room.

"Yes, Herr Professor, I'll be there," he said, squeezing his fingers on the corners of the desk.

Dry-mouthed, he shifted his eyes from side to side, sensing classmates staring at him. His pulse slowed, feeling time had slowed down. With his vision clouding, he glanced at Albert and Curt without a solution to his dilemma.

After class ended and Professor Karp walked off the floor, Albert stood and let out a *brrrrrr* at Rudolf and Erich, watching them move up the steps.

"Fuck you, asshole," said Rudolf von Krieg, pivoting, jabbing his finger at Albert.

Albert narrowed his eyes on them till they disappeared from sight.

* * *

Freddy's pulse raced as he hurried over shiny floors brightened by overhead lights hanging above them. And he turned a corner, taking quick steps along a wide corridor with paintings of old men placed inside gold frames hung on the walls. His stomach quivered as he reached a lengthy corridor lined with faculty offices. And short-winded, he stopped, finding a brass plate with Professor Karp's name on it screwed to a door. Stressed, his mind raced through different scenarios, one worse than the other, but he mustered enough courage to strike the door with his knuckles.

"Who's there?" a loud voice asked, causing his head to shake.

His body stiffened as he beheld the brass plate. "Herr Professor Karp, it's Herr Bauer; you wanted to see me this afternoon."

Professor Karp's tone softened. "Good, I was expecting you, Herr Bauer; please come in."

He entered a dimmed room with its only source of light, a lamp resting on an old wooden desk. He stopped for a second to check out the room before placing himself beside a chair in front of Professor Karp's desk. In plain sight Freddy spotted a lighter with a white cameo of a nude woman fixed on it, resting on top of an exam. He gave it a second look, eyeballing his name.

A flush deepened on Professor Karp's cheeks, and he pointed a finger at the exam. "Take it, it's yours."

Freddy lowered himself in the chair, resting his briefcase against his leg, keeping Professor Karp in sight. He could not stay still; his knees shook, and with Curt's advice on his mind, he drew a big breath, releasing it piecemeal through a slight crack in his mouth. His fingers touched his parted lips; he caught a smile on Professor Karp's face, before he pressed his lips into a slight grimace, seizing it.

"Thank you, Herr Professor," said Freddy, tightening his jaw, confused by Professor Karp's upturned face.

With an empty feeling in the pit of his stomach, expressionless, Freddy secured the exam in his hand and jumped to his feet and headed for the door.

"Wait, don't you want to see your grade?"

"Herr Professor, I'd like to look it over at home, if you don't mind," he said in a voice lacking emotion.

Professor Karp's face glowed, boosting his tone of voice. "Nonsense, Herr Bauer. Open it—I want to see your face when you see the high mark."

Freddy gasped, freeing his mind of its concerns.

Karp's mouth curved into a smile. "Herr Bauer, please sit and open the exam."

He tucked himself in the chair and placed his briefcase on his lap, and set the exam on top of it. The professor's eyes sparkled. Freddy licked his lips, and his fingers shook, peeling back the cover. He let out a gasp, spotting a 1.0 with three check marks placed beside it.

Professor Karp's entire face perked up. "Herr Bauer, I'm proud of you. It's rarely I see an excellent exam from a first-year student. Your arguments were profound, logical, and to the point."

He eyed Professor Karp, feeling euphoric. "Thank you for your kind words. I'll remember them."

Professor Karp narrowed his eyes at him. "Herr Bauer, is Rudolf von Krieg a colleague of yours?"

Freddy shrugged, widening his eyes. "Professor, I'm not sure what you mean."

With his mouth twisting to one side, Karp spoke more loudly. "It was a simple question, Herr Bauer—are you a friend of Rudolf von Krieg's?"

He shrugged, giving his head a soft shake. "No, but why are you interested?"

The professor pulled back in his chair, crossing his arms. "It surprised me to see you talking with him in the library."

"Oh! We were… he spotted me there and came over to talk."

Professor Karp released a pent-up breath, widening his eyes.

Freddy pushed his shoulders forward and rubbed the back of his neck. "Rudolf bragged about his ancestors, mostly."

The professor tilted his head sideways, scratching his forehead. "Um, mostly?"

Freddy's mouth opened and closed; he decided not to air his differences with Rudolf von Krieg. And he lowered his brows, saying in a placating tone, "It wasn't important; we discussed American baseball. Oh, there was one other thing—we both speak English."

With an odd smile on his face, Professor Karp reached in and seized his brown pipe, keeping Freddy in sight. With a knot in his belly, he disclosed a fake smile, figuring something bothered him.

"Herr Bauer, where were your parents from in Germany?"

A light feeling gripped Freddy; a slow smile came to his mouth. "From a small village in the east no one knows exists."

While eyeing Freddy, Karp squinted. "And where did you live in America?"

"Detroit."

"Ha, I never expected you'd say Detroit, more like New York or Philadelphia."

"Lots of Germans live there. We lived in Germantown; my father worked at the Ford automobile plant."

Karp's eyes opened wide. "Ah! he puts together cars?"

He cracked a smile. "No, he doesn't, makes parts for them."

"Oh, makes parts. He must be good with his hands? I'll bet his fingernails are always dirty?" He gave Freddy a gummy smile. "Your father could teach me a thing or two, couldn't he?"

"Think so."

Professor Karp's smug look vanished. "But my wife won't let me fix things at home. I over tightened a screw, once, and broke it inside a hole. She never lets me forget it." Professor Karp paused with uplifted cheeks. "Maybe she's right."

Freddy's cheeks flushed; he admired Professor Karp's folksy sense of humor.

Professor Karp spoke in a light tone. "Your parents must be proud of you, Herr Bauer."

"They are. Life wasn't easy for them, but I grew up loved. My mother made sure I was well read. Only God and family mattered more to her."

"Well, Herr Bauer, from where I sit, she's done a splendid job."

The professor moved his head to the side and blew air out of his fat cheeks. "Can I tell you something?"

"Why, yes, professor, you can."

He faced Freddy and closed his eyes. "Hitler's twisted ideas frighten me. How could he fool so many people?" And with his chin quivering, he asked, "Herr Bauer, what's your opinion of the rat catcher?"

"Uh, the rat catcher?" said Freddy, wincing.

"Hitler, the Rat Catcher of Hamlin, the piper with the magic flute who led the children away, him." Karp whined in anger.

"Oh, him, sorry."

Professor Karp's chin dipped, touching his chest.

"Sorry I asked, Herr Bauer; I should respect your privacy. I meant no harm."

"Professor, I don't feel threatened by street brawlers with a few seats in the Reichstag."

Professor Karp rested his pipe.

"You and synagogue elders overlook that Adolf Hitler's dogmatic ideology inspires people."

Freddy shifted in the chair, feeling a slight chill, and dipped his chin, assessing Professor Karp's words, taking a few slow breaths. "Professor, is there something else?"

"The court's assault on the rule of law keeps me up most nights. Nationalistic judges sidestep justice to pass out unjust verdicts. The price paid for committing a crime depends on party affiliation or religious beliefs. Sympathetic judges interpret laws to favor Nazis or other right-wing fanatics. Patriotism is the means they apply to justify their crimes," said Karp. "And you ask, is there something else? Colleagues I've known a long time now shun me and at most give me a nod. I hear a student call me a Jew pig; am I to forget it?"

"Herr Bauer, I'm sure you've discussed proportional representation at the gymnasium."

"I remember it," Freddy said, uncrossing his arms.

"Memorizing facts and figures does not guarantee you understand what it means."

Freddy rocked in his seat. "It doesn't?"

Professor Karp hardened his gaze. "Friedrich, you won't see democracy in Germany till the government mirrors the will of the of the people. What I see is a proportional government hampered by too many political parties. Each wheeling and dealing to help themselves."

Professor Karp eyed his pipe.

"I'll tell you what keeps me up nights. A close friend who studied law at Heidelberg with me recounted a recent case of his. His client, an elderly Jewish woman, whose husband died on the Western Front, tried to evict a tenant. The Spanish man called her a 'German asshole.' After enduring more abuse, she asked my friend to help her evict the foreigner. My friend agreed and took her to petty court, and it ruled against her."

Freddy dug his eyes into Professor Karp's face.

"Herr Bauer, does this upset you?"

Freddy swallowed hard, strengthening his gaze.

With a hopeless expression, Professor Karp sagged back, saying, "Never mind. I'll tell you why the court ruled against her. She wasn't German enough. You heard me. The court said she was not German enough. Can you imagine being told that, despite your husband's sacrifice for his country?"

Freddy's mind clouded, and he gave a hard look at the despondent man. Professor Karp opened the window to let in air. And he parked himself in his seat, puffing on his pipe.

"Sorry. That was selfish of me; I shouldn't trouble you with this."

Freddy swallowed, shifting in his chair.

With unpredicted movement, the corners of Karp's mouth lifted. "Tell me, Herr Bauer, what do you do with your spare time? Assuming you have any."

"Before school started, I read and played chess with my father from time to time."

"Oh, so do I. What authors do you prefer?"

"Jack London, Mark Twain, and James Fenimore Cooper come to mind, but there's more. I bought a copy of Hemingway's *Fiesta* but can't find the time to read it. I'll have a chance this summer. Professor, did you read it?"

"Yes, but never tell my wife. She didn't approve of it. She thinks Hemingway's an anti-Semite. Me, I'm not so sure. I enjoy his style; he doesn't bore me with long, complicated sentences."

Professor Karp's words eased Freddy's jitters.

"Chess, chess's my passion," said the professor in a monotone voice. "I don't play anymore. Nessa complained it took up too much of my time."

"Sorry, Herr Professor."

"We should play someday."

"Yes, that'd be good."

* * *

"Ahem!" Freddy's head jumped, startled by the unexpected sound. And he glanced up, widening his eyes on Leo Herzfeld.

"I like this spot," said Leo, curving his lips into a smirk. "It's an excellent place to hide from the police."

"I bet you're good at that, aren't you?" Freddy snorted.

"Ha ha. Was that supposed to be a joke?" said Leo, grinning. "Didn't you know Communists are good at robbing unsuspecting people? Aren't you reading right-wing newspapers?"

Freddy made a face, folding his arms across his chest. "Hah, thanks for reminding me to read Joseph Goebbels's current article in *The Attack*. Isn't he brilliant? He makes convincing arguments on what's wrong with Germany, I'd say."

"Ha, not funny, no more talk of the rat-faced, club footed Nazi dwarf; he disgusts me. Do you mind if I sit?" asked Leo, sitting before he could answer him.

"Guess not."

"I went to see Professor Rath to complain over my low grade on the exam. I just passed."

"Noticed when Rath posted grades."

"Thought you might. You don't miss a thing, do you? Even Rudolf von Shit did well. I bet you remember everyone's grade."

"Leo, study hard, even on weekends; see what it did for my grade?"

"You can't keep up that pace; one day your mind will explode. You need to unwind."

"Huh, heard those words before. I'll wait till I finish law school."

"What! Are you insane? That's a long time from now. What about your girlfriend?"

"I've no girlfriend."

"What! No girlfriend? Why, you're handsome and could have many girlfriends. Do you know what you're missing? You better find one before you lose your hair or worse, your fucking mind. Remember, time doesn't stand still."

"Thanks for your concern, but I figure I've got plenty of time to find the right girl."

"Find yourself a whore, it's impossible to go without sex unless you're crazy."

Freddy squirmed with a dash of red coloring on his cheeks and dipped his chin.

Leo examined Freddy and leaned in, offering him a small smile. "I'm sorry. I should've shut my mouth. Forgive my impertinence. You know what, my girlfriend, Sara, has lots of girlfriends; she could find you a gorgeous one. What kind of girl interests you? No, don't tell me, let me guess. Yes! I know. A big-breasted woman with long blond hair, right?"

"Stop, I don't need your help or that of a Communist girlfriend that's plotting to overthrow the world. I appreciate your concern, but I'll be fine."

Leo stared at Freddy, drawing his brows together. "That wasn't funny. I was trying to help."

Freddy scratched his neck, auditing Leo's face. "Why me? Are you hungry for recruits?"

Leo lifted his brows, baring his teeth. "Not funny. Forget politics; can't you see I appreciate you?"

A relaxed smile appeared on his face, and he sighed, recalling the girl with Leo outside the university gates. "Sara wears nice clothes; does she come from money?"

"What?" said Leo, frowning.

"I saw you embracing a girl outside the corner café across from the university gates."

Laugh lines showed in the corners of Leo's eyes; he gave Freddy a toothy smile. "That wasn't Sara. It was my twin sister, Jette; isn't she gorgeous?"

Dumbfounded, Freddy gave him a decisive nod. "I'm sure she is, but I didn't see her face."

A warm smile appeared on Leo's face. "Believe me, she is, but she's very choosy." Leo's smile wavered, and he dipped his head. "Jette gives me money to live on; my father disowned me."

"Was it because you're a Communist?"

Leo struggled to make eye contact, ducking his chin, he said in a subdued voice, "No, he knew that, but when I told him I didn't believe in God, he cried and told me to leave."

"Y-you did what?"

"Freddy, from the day I was born, I worshipped his God, and under his conditions, he did not give me a choice. I told him there wasn't room in my heart to glorify two gods.

I chose the Communist Party; they're my church and religion now."

Freddy dropped his head and shut his eyes. "Leo, when we're young, we make mistakes; time changes minds."

"He never wants to see me again."

"Where did you go?"

"I sleep at party headquarters, as long as I sweep the place. And Jette's money pays for my meals."

Freddy's pupils dilated, and he fixed his eyes on the complicated man who lived a complex life.

"Leo, tell me, what happened in Professor Rath's office?"

"The fat bastard gave me an angry stare and tapped his foot when I brought up my exam. Then Rudolf burst into the office without knocking, and Professor Rath asked me to wait outside in the hall. I detected loud laughter in the room. Twenty minutes passed by, and Rath called me back into his office. Rudolf bumped into me, leaving with an evil expression on his face.

"He refused to go over the exam," said Leo, pressing his palms against his cheeks. "He told me if I studied harder, I'd get a better grade. I spotted an old picture of him looking fit in uniform. Shows you what fifty pounds of ugly shit will do to you. Freddy, I can't let him get away with it; it's not right." Leo's cheeks blew out, and he concentrated on Freddy. "What should I do?"

"Not sure; he worries me."

"What worries you?"

"His relationship with Rudolf. He might be a superpatriot who hates Jews and Communists. If it happens again, take it up with the student council."

* * *

"I love you, my little *schnucki*," confessed a man with a shaky voice.

A woman's voice softened. "Shh! Lutz." Freddy picked up a loud bang outside the window, identifying a woman's voice. "Ouch!"

He gazed out the window, staring at a woman parked on her butt alongside a garbage can. With an unbuttoned black coat and blue dress draped above her knees, her head bobbed, looking dopy. The man swayed on his feet, gazing at her. Amusement slashed the intoxicated woman's cheeks.

"*Schnucki*, are you okay?" the man asked, slurring his words.

The seated women cackled loudly, moving her head back and forth.

Lutz took a drink from a brown bottle and slurred his words. "Shh, sweetie, keep quiet, we don't want to wake everybody." Lutz rocked on his feet, offering the woman a hand, giggling. "Shh, be quiet, people might think we're drunk."

Then the euphoric couple gripped each other, gargling words, and zigzagged over the street.

He headed for his bed, narrowing his vision on the light in the space under the door. Groggy, he entered the kitchen, finding his father idling with a bleak expression; he figured something was bothering him. His eyes furrowed, and he yawned, concentrating on his father. "Didn't expect to find you up this late; is there something wrong?"

His father rounded his shoulders and bowed his head. "I tiptoed past your room. Did I wake you?"

"You didn't, but the racket outside my window did. Did the noise wake you too?"

"No, I didn't notice it."

"Why are you up this late? Is everything okay?" asked Freddy, squinting.

His father's smile wavered, and he made eye contact with him, without blinking. "A couple things happened at work today that upset me."

"Oh! Sounds serious. What happened?" said Freddy, making strong eye contact with his father.

"It's okay, you've enough on your mind; I didn't want to do is burden you with my problems."

His father crossed and uncrossed his arms, keeping his puffy eyes on Freddy.

Freddy scrubbed his bottom lip against his upper teeth. "Tell me what happened. I can see it's troubling you. You're not good at keeping things from me. So, why do it now?"

His father's eyelids closed, and he exhaled a slow stream of air between his puckered lips.

"Guess you're right. But keep it from your mother; she'd worry."

"I promise. What is it?"

"The plant supervisor fired Conrad Sauer and Fritz Wurst. Should've expected it when sales declined. Fritz's wife's seven months pregnant. I'll never forget his face after he learned they had fired him. Bernt Frank, the man that fired them, doubted shipments would recover. He blamed it on the American Depression and thought Conrad and Fritz would have a tough time finding jobs."

"Sorry, for them, but you'll be okay, right? You've been working there longer than anyone; that must count for something."

"Maybe. I prayed for Conrad and Fritz at church. Father Graf told me it troubled him that many parishioners were out of work and the Nazis were taking advantage of their difficulties. He said he scrubbed a Nazi poster preying on the unemployed off the front door. It angered him they did it."

Freddy sighed, wishing he could ease his father's pain. And with a watery gaze clasped his hands together, feeling weighed down with his father's dilemma. Appreciating his father, his face brightened. "I love you. Get some sleep; try not to let it bother you."

* * *

The door handle moved, but it didn't open, and his mother spoke, muting her voice. "Freddy, are you awake?"

"I am, was getting ready for school."

"Can I come in? I promise it won't take long."

"Yes."

She entered, walking lazily, and idled on his bed, drawing her lips into a thin line and bowing her head.

Freddy pulled his chair closer, sensing something bothered her. "Mother, what is it?

"I'm worried."

His wavering smile changed to a grimace as he prepared himself to find out what tormented her.

"Freddy, it's Saturday night; you should be out enjoying yourself with friends."

"I don't want to get drunk and pick up tramps."

"Shame on you—you know what I meant. I want you to find a delightful girl and take her to the cinema."

"I can't make the time; it's more important to finish law school with honors. There'll be plenty of time for girls after I finish law school."

"There won't be many single girls your age."

Freddy gave her a pained stare and strengthened his voice. "Then I'll find an eighteen-year-old girl who likes older men." And displaying a wide grin said, "Hmm, mother, that might be worth the wait."

"Stop it. Can't you see it upsets me?" she said, sniffling, wiping off a tear, trying to find words. "Freddy, I made you this way. I'm sorry; it was selfish of me."

He nodded, lighting his eyes and softening his words. "Mother, you're too hard on yourself; you did what you believed was right because you loved me. I have no regrets. The three-legged stool was a splendid idea."

She dropped her smile, saying to him, "It hurts me to think what I did to you."

With a sense of despair, he recalled the conversation with Leo Herzfeld about his not having a girlfriend.

His throat tightened as he stared at the sniffling woman. And he sat alongside her. "Mother, look at me." She lifted her head and fixed her eyes on him. "I'll try to make time, but it's difficult with my schedule."

Her jaw slackened. "Nonsense, Freddy, a few hours a week won't hurt your grades. You need to do other things; you can't study the entire day."

"Maybe you're right," conceded Freddy, mulling over the idea.

She smiled, regaining her composure. "Marlene Bach told me her daughter Heidi has a crush on you."

"I know. She stares at me in church."

With an upturned face, she gazed at him. "She's an appealing girl, isn't she?"

Tongue-tied, Freddy stared at her, wanting to be somewhere else.

"Freddy it's settled, I'll tell Marlene you're interested in Heidi."

"No, don't, let me consider it."

"Good." She nodded and slowly smiled. "That makes me happy."

Freddy blinked, pressing his lips into a grimace.

"I'm worried. I ran into Bettie Wurst in front of Kleins, and she told me her husband is unemployed and can't find work. She's pregnant and blames the government for their troubles. Bettie and Fritz want to join the Nazi Party. Your father never told me they fired Fritz Wurst; he doesn't keep things from me."

"I'm sure he kept it quiet because he didn't want to worry you."

"Freddy, do you tell me everything?"

"Yes. Why wouldn't I?"

Her lips twisted, and she scrutinized him. "Are you sure?"

* * *

Two creases stood upright between Freddy's brows as he lingered near the law building, daydreaming. *I don't care what others believe. I see good in Leo Herzfeld.*

Albert dipped his head and scratched the back of his neck. "Are you sure he was there?"

Freddy glanced at the marble steps. "Albert, nothing could keep him away."

Curt kept his head still, eying Albert and Freddy. "People died. I hope Leo wasn't one of them."

Albert's cheeks bobbed. "Me too. I'm fond of the Red; never dreamed I'd say that."

Curt reached into his coat pocket and pulled out a green pack of cigarettes.

Freddy frowned at Curt. "Must you?"

"It relaxes me."

With trembling fingers Curt put a cigarette in his mouth and dug into a pocket for matches and fired the cigarette up, discharging a cloud of smoke in Freddy's face. Freddy frowned, fanning the smoke away. "Dammit, Curt, blow the smoke the other way."

"Sorry, wasn't using my head."

Albert rubbed his hand against his jacket. "It shattered Millie, and she closed the Pig for two days."

Freddy let out a heavy sigh before speaking in a somber voice. "My mother kept me away from the door. She was a nervous wreck when a neighbor told her what had happened. She was on edge for days and jumped up every time she detected sirens or loud noises."

"Who could blame her?" conceded Curt, blowing smoke through his nose and gazing at the sky.

Albert's tight lips opened, and he cranked his head slowly from side to side. "The dead might be alive if they had stayed home. The police warned them not to march."

Sarcasm crept into Freddy's voice. "They won't be content till they rule the world."

Curt's voice firmed after he finished a puff from his cigarette. "Why don't you both light up one of my cigarettes? It might calm your nerves."

"Beer's better," said Albert, waving him away with a mocking grin.

Freddy gave Curt a stony stare. "It made me sick when I tried it."

"Give it up; your breath stinks," said Albert with a smirk, giving Curt a playful shove.

Curt snorted, shifting his weight to his other leg. "I don't care if it does."

Freddy's heart raced as he saw Leo and Isaak were heading up the steps; he noticed blackened circles around the whiskered men's eyes.

"What happened to you?" asked Freddy, focusing on Leo.

Leo bared his teeth, angling creases from his nose to the corners of his mouth. "It was a peaceful march till we approached the baths. The police blocked our path. Some comrades threw stones and bottles at them. I asked them to stop, but they didn't listen to me. It got out of control, and they fired water cannons at us. And the police charged, beating anyone on their way with clubs. I ran from them, hearing gunshots behind me."

Albert crossed and uncrossed his arms, shaking his head. "Is that it?"

"No, it's not, there's more," said Isaak, making strong eye contact with Leo.

"Isaak, stop," said Leo, rubbing the whiskers on his chin. "Let me tell them."

Isaak gave Leo a brief nod, slumping his shoulders. "Okay."

"My best friend, Josef, ran alongside me holding a red flag. Josef fell, and three police officers clubbed him. Isaak and I left him when three more came at us." Leo stopped, catching Isaak's sniffle. "Josef's dead; the fucking police murdered him." His lips trembled, and his voice cracked. "I'll never forget what I saw. One day they'll pay for it."

Isaak's voice stiffened, and he inspected Leo. "Every one of them."

"We manned barricades and stayed up nights," said Leo, fretting, glaring at Freddy. "How can you sleep fired on by the police?" Red-eyed, Leo blinked hard, quivering his lips around the words. "I should've never left Josef."

Freddy swallowed the lump that gathered in his throat. He spoke using a soft tone, giving Leo an understanding nod. "I lost my best friend too; it hurts."

Leo caught Albert shaking his head. "Albert, we marched to defend worker's rights; we never expected it to end this way."

"If you had stayed home, Josef would still be alive," fumed Albert, rolling his eyes. "It was for nothing."

Red stung Leo's cheeks as he gave Albert an incredulous stare. Isaak shook his head.

Curt pulled the cigarette out of his mouth, tossing it, and checked out the time. "Shit, we better get going. Professor Karp's class starts in five minutes."

Albert glanced at Freddy. "Relax, he won't complain if we're a minute or two late because genius is with us."

Freddy frowned at him, shaking his head before stepping back open-mouthed, discovering Rudolf with other Nazi students heading his way. Leo glared at them cross-eyed, his cheeks and forehead lined. Albert grunted, moving in front of Leo, clenching his fists. "Is there something wrong?"

Rudolf glared at him. "No." And he walked away, saying to Freddy in English as he passed, "I wish the police had killed him."

Freddy's stomach hardened and his eyes widened.

Albert's voice took a harsh tone. "What did he say to you?"

"It wasn't important," said Freddy, displaying a pensive smile.

Chapter Eleven

A Place to Unwind

Dark gray clouds filled the sky, pushed by the gentle wind. And Freddy beamed at his recently made friends, mindful of their uniqueness.

Albert glanced up at the dreary sky. "It won't rain. I'm heading to the Slippery Pig for a beer; make up your minds."

Freddy's voice took an amused tone, and he elevated his brows. "Albert, you just want to see Karla."

Albert nodded, turning his flat lips into a smile. "That's a lie; I want a beer too."

Freddy's smile wavered as he cranked his head skyward. "Hm, are you sure you want to do it? It's chilly, and the sky's black."

"Who cares? I need a beer too," said Curt. "Professor Karp's exam was difficult; I barely finished it. What did you think of it, Freddy?"

The corners of Albert's lips dipped, and his voice hardened, discharging sarcastic words. "Stupid, you don't ask the class genius for his opinion. He'd say to you, 'Oh, Curt, it wasn't too hard, but it surprised me when Professor Karp didn't ask us to write articles sixty-eight through seventy-six in section five on the constitution.' That's what he'd tell you."

He snorted at him. "Albert, you missed one—there are seventy-seven articles in section five."

"Ha ha, Freddy, you're incorrigible."

Curt glanced at Freddy, constricting his eyes. "Are you coming, yes or no?"

He put his hands inside his coat and gazed at the sky. "Are you sure you want to go?"

Albert flashed a lopsided grin at Freddy and bared his teeth. "Freddy, take a chance, not everything adds up."

"That's a big surprise!" he said, dimpling his cheeks.

"I was making a point, shithead, but you contradicted me," said Albert in a taut voice, reddening his face. "Sometimes, Freddy, you're a fucking PA. Make sense out of that, and shove it up your ass."

Surprised by Albert's words, he stepped back. "I'm sorry. I didn't want to upset you."

A smile grew on Albert's lips; he nodded at Freddy. "Are you coming, yes or no?"

Curt said in a blunt voice, rubbing his hands together, "I'm thirsty."

Freddy shrugged, cranking his head sideways slow. "Okay, I'll risk it,"

"Curt, Freddy's taking a risk; there might be hope for him," Albert said, poking Freddy. "I'm glad you're coming; let's go."

Touched by a raindrop on the cheek, Freddy stopped outside the university gates. "It's raining. Maybe we should turn back?"

Albert's tone stiffened, and he twitched his nose. "Freddy, you worry too much."

"Albert, suppose it doesn't stop?" said Freddy, warming his hands in his pockets.

"I'm beat, Freddy. Run ahead if you're worried, but you better have beers waiting for us."

"Freddy, who wouldn't after spending the night with Karla," said Curt, chuckling, tapping Albert's shoulder.

Albert gave Curt a hard smile. "You're jealous because you can't find someone who wants to sleep with you; try the zoo."

"Albert, you're amazing. How did you do it?" asked Curt. "We just started at the university, and you've found a waitress at the Slippery Pig to sleep with, but aren't you afraid Millie will catch you?"

Albert grinned, producing laugh lines at the fringes of his eyes. "Karla sneaks out at night to my place after Millie goes to bed."

Freddy frowned, bringing a touch of pink to his cheeks.

Albert inspected the sky and said, "We better walk."

"Freddy, run ahead. I'll keep Don Juan company; don't forget the beers."

"Have it your way. I'm starving, and don't want to chance the rain. I'll meet you there."

Freddy frowned and sped away. At the end of a street, two blocks from where he had left Albert and Curt, he caught sight of posters stuck to store windows. One grabbed his attention, and he stepped closer to read it. A Nazi flag covered the top half, with a swastika displayed in the middle; beneath the flag, sad men and women stood. And he swallowed, fixing his eyes on a woman who resembled his mother. Across its bottom, it advertised a meeting for Saturday, the next day, and offered injured veterans and unemployed workers half-price admission. Three bold red lettered words drafted below it shocked him: "JEWS NOT ADMITTED." Freddy closed his eyes, revisiting Rudolf's angry words.

A fine rain fell. Fearing it might pick up, he fled, minding the three words. Images of Rolf and Clarence Johnson flashed through his mind. The rain picked up; puddles grew larger. Freddy raced over the street and stopped at a corner across from the Slippery Pig, waiting for a creeping beer truck. He picked out a youthful woman slumped, clutching a tarnished metal cup, wrapped in a black shawl, shaking under a building's archway. A bundled baby nested between her legs, with a wet baby carriage nearby. He sighed, reached for loose coins in his pocket, and edged under the archway to drop the coins into the metal cup, picking up clinking noises. The woman blushed, looking up at Freddy. "Thank you."

With a long face, observing the crying baby, he squeezed its tiny fingers, quieting the fussing infant. And a relaxed smile crossed the mother's face. "Lina likes that." And his lips quivered as a falling raindrop hit him.

His cheeks rose while he observed the woman. "Will you be okay?"

The destitute woman's lips parted, and she nodded, exposing a missing front tooth. "Yes, my husband's coming for us." Her voice broke up, and she closed her eyes. "He's out looking for a work."

Freddy dodged a truck and hurried inside the Slippery Pig.

"You're wet; let me take your coat," said Millie, in a soothing voice. "Helga, get Freddy a napkin to dry his hair."

Helga hurried back with a handful of napkins, grinning, watching him dry his hair.

Karla balanced five beers as she left the bar, heading for customers. "Where's Albert and Curt?"

"They're coming."

Millie closed the cash register with her stomach and eased her short, chubby body to the window. And after Karla dropped off beers, she joined her.

Millie slumped, glancing out the window. "Curt's soaked, but where's Albert?"

"I see him," said Karla, looking annoyed. "He's right behind the other idiot, dripping wet."

Freddy swallowed, facing the space where the woman and child were.

When Albert and Curt burst inside, Millie scolded them. "Shitheads, you'll be sick by morning."

* * *

Freddy caught Helga spying on him. And she covered her face with a newspaper, realizing he had discovered her. His arms folded across his chest, and he hid half his blue eyes under his lids. *Why does she do that?*

Albert asked him, using a curious tone of voice, "Is something bothering you?"

"Nope, why do you ask?"

Albert shot a quick gaze to Curt. "Uh, you looked annoyed."

Freddy gave him a hard smile, mindful of Helga's angelic face, striking figure, and sheepish grin, which could be intoxicating.

Albert's voice startled him. "Freddy, when you close your eyes, where ever your mind travels, it puts a smile on your face."

Freddy bent his spine, producing a sly smile. "I was contemplating something in the Constitution."

"Freddy, you never get a second chance." Albert grinned, shaking his head. "Have fun while you're young enough to enjoy what life offers."

Freddy mulled over Helga, reckoning the simple-minded girl could never appeal to him.

His eyes drifted across the room, seeing a middle-aged woman with raised cheeks viewing him. He had caught that smile on women's faces many times. He gave her a timid glance, gathering his pleasant looks appealed to the woman, reckoning women made him anxious. It occurred to him, shifting in his seat, at fifteen his body changed, and his interest in women too; he recalled erotic pictures passed around in class. Now at eighteen, and still a virgin, he bared his teeth, mindful he was living when a significant number of woman rejected virtue.

Freddy bared a wide grin, capturing Karla Dietz pushing a chunk of sausage in her mouth. Her full cheeks and circling lips mimicked a monkey eating a banana at the zoo. Ren, the gray-mustachioed bartender, seized an empty mug with his right hand, flaunting the old sailor's tattoo on his forearm. Ren steadied the mug under a shiny tap before he pulled back its handle, watching a gold-colored liquid gush out of it. Having finished pouring the last beer, Ren headed for regulars at the other end of the bar. Albert Haas blew air through his pressed lips, catching Freddy in the face with its drift. His face flushed, and he glared at Karla.

Albert whacked the table with his fist. "Shit. I can't take it much longer."

He hadn't picked up Freddy's hard stare. Freddy looked toward the bar, spotting Karla chatting with Helga. And his head flinched as he heard a loud noise and saw Albert's palms flat on the table.

Albert clenched his teeth together, moving his lips. "Shit!"

"Um, what's wrong?" said Curt, blinking at Albert.

Albert ignored him, tightening his eyes. Curt nudged him, shrugging.

Albert's finger tapping grew louder.

"God dammit, Karla, what's taking you so long, move your fat ass. I don't have the entire day," screamed Albert, gawking at Karla, bulging his eyes.

Albert's outburst reached the corners of the room. Customers' eyes widened; two shook their heads.

Karla faced Albert, giving him an ugly stare.

"Right away; be patient. They're coming, Albert," she screamed, swaying her body.

"Albert, you disgust me," said Millie, sticking her face inches from Albert's. "Better behave or out you go; do you understand?" Millie straightened up, canvassing customers. "Huh, don't know what Karla sees in you; she must be nuts."

The buxom server placed three beers on the table, each overflowing with foam. Freddy recalled the brawny woman carrying over ten beers on a busy day. Tight-lipped, Karla grunted and crossed her arms. "Albert, why don't you stick them up your ass," seethed the red-faced woman, "one at a time."

Freddy grinned, saying to Karla in a whimsical tone, "Why do you put up with the big ox?"

"Because she loves me, that's why," interrupted Albert with a coy smile. "Don't you, my little sweetie?"

Karla's face softened, and she quieted her breathing.

Curt focused on Albert, elevating his brows. "Ha ha, stop before I heave; your little sweetie's out of her mind if she loves you." And he guzzled beer releasing a long burp."

And Freddy shut his eyes a moment, guessing Karla and Albert's fling might end, reckoning Karla's body might be the only thing Albert wanted from her.

Helga's cheerful voice raised his cheeks. "Freddy, can I get something for you to eat?"

"I'm fine. Thank you, Helga."

Curt bitched, swallowing hard. "Helga, you didn't ask me. Don't I count?"

"Sorry, Curt, didn't know you wanted anything. Your glass was half-full."

Curt checked his beer. "Helga, I'll chug it before you return with another."

Helga backed up next to her sister. Taller than Karla but better looking than her muscular sister, Helga lacked her older sister's social graces. Most times, the timid woman parked herself in front of the bar, waiting for customers.

Albert guzzled the rest of beer and belched, waving his empty glass in the air with a smile, eyeing Helga. "Helga, get me another beer."

Karla's head recoiled, and she barked at him, "Shit-face, say please."

Albert made noises, inhaling through his flared nostrils. "I won't say please. Helga, get the beers."

Freddy covered his mug with his hand when Helga inspected his glass. "No more for me."

Albert fussed. "Nonsense, Freddy, drink one more beer."

"I don't need one; my stomach's full."

Albert gave Freddy a bitter smile. "Okay, see if I give a shit. Helga, get the beers, and hurry back with them."

Helga's voice and hands shook. "Freddy, sure you don't want one more?"

Albert gave Helga a dirty glance, cording his neck. "Dammit, what'd I say? Get the fucking beers."

Helga flinched and pivoted so fast her dangling pigtails swung, and she rushed for the bar.

Millie tiptoed behind Albert and smacked him on the head with a newspaper. Albert's mouth popped open, and he pivoted to see who had hit him.

Millie greeted his inquiring eyes with quivering lips and a sour expression. "You got what you deserved. Last chance. Next time I'll hit you harder and won't let you in the tavern. Try me. I'm not bluffing." This time Millie's loud voice opened customers' eyes.

Agitated, Karla lashed out at him. "Albert, you're a bully; tell Helga you're sorry when she returns with the beers."

Albert crossed his arms, giving his noggin a few fast shakes. "That won't happen."

Millie slammed her newspaper against Albert's cheek, leaving a red mark on it. "Albert, you make me sick. Where are your manners? Apologize to Helga."

"Dammit, I said no."

Albert ducked to avoid Millie's blow, and on his way up, snatched the newspaper out of her hand.

Millie raised her voice two notches. "I'll bring a club the next time; it's your last chance to apologize to Helga."

Millie's brows wrinkled, and she pivoted to check on regular customers seated at the other side of the room. She looked back, with color flushing her cheeks, before heading over to their table. Freddy tilted his head at her, suspecting she wanted to explain to the curious onlookers what had happened.

Freddy glared at Albert, pitching his voice too near a scream, saying, "What's wrong with you? Where are your manners? Sometimes I wish I never laid eyes on you."

And he shifted in his chair, chewing over Albert's heartless words. "Albert, do you remember what you told us the first day we met?"

"I don't remember; it was months ago."

Freddy pulled back, staring at Albert, resting his palms on the table. "You said friendship depends on honesty. Well, listen up, Albert, I'm sick and tired of seeing you make a fool of yourself. I expect more from a child. Your temper tantrums are unbearable; I want to strangle you when they occur. You wanted honesty? Well, I just gave it to you; do what you want with it."

"Freddy, good for you." Curt Krause agreed. "The big jerk deserved it. He wanted honesty? Well, he got a plate full, and I hope he chokes on it."

Albert's cheeks blushed, and he shot a gaze past Curt and Freddy, resting it on Karla, speechless.

"You're right, I'm sorry; let my temper get the better of me," whined Albert, cringing and crouching. "I made an ass of myself, didn't I?"

Freddy crossed his arms, dropping the sides of his mouth. "Albert, don't apologize unless you mean it."

Albert eyed Freddy, speaking in a gentle voice. "Yes, you're right. I should tell her I'm sorry."

"Albert, you're an asshole," bitched Karla, stroking her pigtail.

Helga's hand trembled; she placed a dripping beer on the table and wiped her wet hands with her apron.

Albert rocked in his chair, scrutinizing Helga and bringing a slow smile to his lips. "Uh, Helga, I'm sorry I upset you. I promise never to do it again."

Karla's voice hardened. "Say it to her again, Albert!"

Albert exhaled loudly and bowed his head. "I'm sorry, Helga."

Helga's voice wheezed, and she stepped back, holding her hand over her lips. Her soft voice held a tremor. "I-I forgive you, Albert."

"Helga, you should've cursed at him," said Curt, sneering.

Tongue-tied, Helga dug her eyes into Albert.

Karla's voice showed her thoughts. "Helga, thanks to Freddy, the big jerk came to his senses; it's a shame he embarrassed himself before he did."

Helga's eyes found Freddy, and she gave him a wide smile. Freddy nodded, returning her smile. Helga held her smile, and her braids bounced as she quick stepped to her station at the bar near Ren. The slender woman grabbed a drink of water and smiled, catching Freddy staring at her. Freddy glanced the other way, pressing his lips together, afraid he had given her the wrong impression.

A pleasing aroma spewed from the kitchen, triggering a fond memory at the German Club in Detroit. With welled-up eyes, he sighed, picturing Rolf licking mustard off his pretzel with a sheepish smile when his mother gave him the evil eye.

Albert made a funny expression while observing Freddy. "Not again! Freddy, snap out of it. If I catch you daydreaming again, I'll take you to a psychiatrist."

Freddy wiped the smug smile off his lips, opening his eyes, clearing his mind.

"Albert, that's funny." Curt jeered. "He must have a girlfriend."

"Do you?" Albert beamed at him. "If so, I only want to hear seedy details."

Amused, Freddy snorted. "There's no hope for you, Albert."

* * *

And with a hard smile, Freddy stared at the page, rubbing his weary eyes. He hunched over the opened book, harassed by a relentless headache, battling hunger pains in his gut. With a strong mental focus, he nodded and closed the book and fled the library. Outside in the bitingly frigid air, he stopped under oversized light fixtures, nudged by the wind, and buttoned his coat before descending stone stairs, hurrying over a graveled pathway leading to the university gates. And on his way, lampposts lit his path, a few flickering, with wind stirring up leaves ahead of him. The noise from honking horns grew louder with each step taken, and he made his way through the iron gates, aware city light conquered darkness and loud helter-skelter noises prevailed. A whiff of something pleasant in the air passed under his nose. He stepped off the curb but jumped back at the sound of a clinking bicycle bell. He scooted across the street and passed a tacky fraternity bar with two white-capped brothers holding up a third upchucking gunk. A few prostitutes stood in doorways to keep warm, bolder ones flaunting their wares curbside.

Closing in on the Slippery Pig, he picked up a piercing screech from the tavern's wavering sign. And he shuddered, slipping past two middle-aged prostitutes wearing similar hats and fur collared coats, taking drags from cigarettes. His mouth fell open as he noticed one steadying herself on a peg leg. The one-legged woman licked her lips and jabbered with a strange accent, "Hey, handsome, where are you going?" The woman widened her eyes. "Haven't I seen you here another time? Never forget handsome men. Want to give Gertie a go? I'll put a smile on your sour puss. And for you, cause you're so handsome, I'll charge you less."

Her plump accomplice displayed an impish smile, holding on to Gertie's other crutch, speaking with a similar accent. "Come on, handsome. You can't beat Gertie's price; give her a go."

Spooked, refusing a second look, he bolted inside the tavern, bumping into Millie coming through the door. "Huh, Freddy, I never expected to see you this late."

"Hi, Millie, couldn't study any longer, was hungry."

"Albert and Curt came with a friend."

"A friend?"

He pivoted, seeing Leo Herzfeld seated at the table with Albert and Curt. Freddy meandered across the creaking floor and fell into a chair. Karla made room for beers without spilling a drop and clanked two empty mugs, plucking them off the table.

"Karla, can you get me something to eat?" he begged, loud enough to turn her head, hungry, feeling his stomach gurgle.

"Are sausages and potatoes okay, Freddy?"

Albert sat up, eyeing her. "Is there a choice?"

"Karla, anything will do; I'm hungry."

Albert checked Karla, lifting his brows. "Karla, be sure it's dead; someone complained his wiggled till he stabbed it four times with his fork."

A hint of sarcasm echoed in Karla's voice. "Not funny, Albert, the sausages taste good."

"Karla, don't forget Freddy's beer—he'll need it after tasting the sausages," said Albert, watching her head for the kitchen.

Karla spun around, giving Albert a pained stare.

Freddy sized up Leo Herzfeld's discolored eye. "Why are you here?"

Albert leaned in, making eye contact with Freddy. "We bumped into him outside the library; someone got the better of him. He won't tell us who and asked for money to eat. I told him I'd buy dinner, as long as he doesn't bring up any Communist Party bullshit, politics, or the economy,"—Albert grinned—"but Nazis weren't off limits, and if he ate too much, I'd make him pay me back."

Freddy smirked. "That's generous of you."

"Yes, it was, wasn't it?" said Albert, bright eyed, puffing up his chest.

"How come you're broke?" asked Freddy, rubbing his chin. "Doesn't Jette give you money?"

Leo closed his eyes. "Tomorrows Jette's birthday. I spent my money to buy her a gift."

"Um, Jette, who's that?" asked Albert with a curious expression.

"Um, must be Leo's girlfriend." Said Curt, brushing the sides of his slick hair.

Freddy smirked, pulling his body near the table. "She's not his girlfriend, she's his twin sister."

"Uh, how come you know that? asked Albert.

179

"Leo told me."

"Oh, he did, did he?" said Albert. "Hope they don't look alike. What a pity if she resembles him, but can't imagine God could be that cruel."

Leo's head bobbed with a smirk on his face. "You're not funny?" Leo frowned, moving in his chair, "Well she doesn't, asshole."

"J-Jette's glamorous," said Freddy, twisting his watch.

Albert tapped his fingers hard. "How do you know that? Did the Red tell you that too?"

"Yes, no."

Albert and Curt looked at each other and shrugged their shoulders. Albert turned an eye on Freddy. "Is she or isn't she? It's a simple question."

His mouth opened and closed.

"There are two choices, Freddy—she is or isn't glamorous. Make up your fucking mind," said Albert, straightening his spine.

He stared at Albert with a slight grimace. "I didn't see her face; her back faced me as she walked past the café."

Albert's gaze clouded, and he pinched his forehead. "Stop, enough. You're making me nuts with this yes, no, she is, she isn't. I'll take Leo's word for it; Jette's a glamorous girl."

With a nervous smile on his face, Freddy shook his head, checking the messy table, grimacing at empty beer glasses, books, food crumbs, and a couple of cigarette butts. "I can see you've been studying very hard."

Leo pulled back his shoulders, squinting at Freddy. "We've been studying hard; we needed a break."

Freddy gave Leo an incredulous stare, focusing on his bruised eye. "What happened to your eye?"

Leo's shoulders hunched and dropped his chin. "It's nothing; I was in a fight."

"I can see that, but didn't anyone teach you how to duck?"

Curt glanced at Albert and moved his chair closer to Leo. "Why won't you tell us what happened? Was it Brownshirts? Were you in a fight with them?"

Leo's nostrils flared, and he said to Curt loudly, "No, it wasn't with any of them!"

Freddy's voice steadied as he focused on Leo. "Tell us what happened; you're with friends."

"Friends is okay with me—but never call me comrade; I couldn't bear it," said Albert, glaring at Leo. "If you do, you'll get another black eye to go along with the other."

Freddy narrowed his eyes, glancing at Albert, speaking in a tight voice. "For once, can't you be serious?"

"Okay, I'll tell you, Benjamin Gruner sucker punched me during an argument at the Communist student council meeting."

Albert inspected Leo, inflaming his words. "Who the hell's Benjamin? What's his last name?"

"Gruner's a Bolshevik who wants a revolution to overthrow the government. I argued they tried that before, reminded him what occurred with Rosa Luxemburg; remember the militia shot her in the head and dumped her body in a canal?" Leo paused, widening his eyes, and glanced at the ceiling. "I argued a nonviolent solution by exploited workers might achieve that end without shedding blood. He got pissed, called me a coward and an idealist, and hit me. I hit him back and might have broken his nose."

"Wow, that makes me feel better," said Freddy, with a mocking grin on his face, refocusing on the messy table.

Albert wiggled and squirmed in his seat, examining Freddy. "We're prepared for Rath's exam. The Red know his stuff."

Freddy winked at Leo.

"How can anyone learn from a big-headed blabbermouth?" said Leo. "What a pity he's not Professor Karp."

Curt brought a lopsided curl to his mouth, eyeballing Freddy. "I'll bet you Rudolf does well on Rath's exam."

Freddy blinked hard, giving him a surprised gaze, saying in a tremulous voice, "What! Why should he do well?"

"I've seen them together many times. Last week Rudolf came out of Rath's office laughing, and I heard Rath ask him to come back later."

"Where was Wagner?"

"Don't know, but I heard that the bartender at the Boar's Den called him a beer-guzzling skirt-chaser that owes him money."

"If Erich's not doing well in Professor Bergmann's class and flunked Professor Karp's last exam, he's in trouble."

Leo lowered his brows, calming his voice. "Freddy, do you think Professor Karp knows it was Erich?"

His lips twitched and gave Leo a decisive nod. "He's not stupid."

Freddy crossed and uncrossed his arms and shut his eyes, agonizing over a thought. *Huh, Professor Rath might just be a right-wing fanatic, he's praised Judge Jung often?*

Albert focused on him with a tight-lipped smile. "Freddy, is there something wrong? Are you okay?"

"Yes, I'm fine," replied Freddy, licking his bottom lip.

Albert made strong eye contact with him, tapering his eyes. "You worried me; your face turned white."

"He's fine; he just needs a beer," said Curt, angling his body at Freddy.

Karla showed up with a smile, shaking her head. "Freddy, here are your sausages and cabbage. Sorry, no more potatoes in the kitchen."

"Look at him—he doesn't need potatoes; he needs a beer," said Albert, glowing.

With a wide grin, Helga arrived gripping a dripping beer, wiping foam off it before setting it on the table.

"Thanks, Helga, I could use it right now," said Freddy, and he swallowed his beer, catching sight of Karla and Helga returning to the bar from the corner of his eye.

Curt's mouth opened, and he pulled back his lips, looking stupid. "Ha ha, Gertie and her friends flapping their arms."

"She is persistent, I'll give her that," said Albert, tilting his head to gaze outside the window. "It's too chilly outside for her regulars. Never could figure why crippled veterans bothered with the peg-legged whore. There are plenty of prostitutes in Berlin more attractive with none of their parts missing. Her girlfriend's got a better chance at snagging a customer than she does. Hey! Curt, maybe she'll pity you and lower her price?"

Curt gave him a pained stare, broadening his nostrils.

Freddy leaned back, hardening his gut, considering six sinister men across the room, reminded of prostitutes, pickpockets and street gangs wandered the streets.

He flinched, hearing Karla's loud voice. "Freddy, want more to eat?"

"No thank you, Karla. I'm full. My stomach's queasy—must have eaten too fast."

Albert tore a page, slamming his palms against his book, grinning. "Told you not to eat that shit. Someone claimed his sausage wiggled."

"Shut up, stupid," said Karla, and she took an audible breath, glaring at Albert. "Can't you see Freddy's not feeling well?"

"I'm okay. It's not serious; I just need more time to digest my meal," said Freddy, rubbing his stomach.

"I'll fetch a glass of bitters from Ren; that always works," said Karla.

Albert's voice took a cheerful edge. "Carry back more beers while you're at it, my little dumpling."

Angered, Karla's brows dropped. "Kiss my ass, you pile of shit."

"How can you study? It's too noisy here," said Freddy, fixating on them.

Albert stiffened, grabbing the table's edge. "We ask each other questions. Besides, it's too chilly to run back to the library."

"Keep it up and you'll find yourself similar to Erich Wagner."

Albert's puckered mouth changed to a grin; he added amusement to his voice. "At least he's enjoying himself at the Boar's Den."

"Not funny, Albert," said Freddy, pulling back his lips in disgust.

And Karla appeared, smiling with the bitters, placing the half-filled glass in front of Freddy.

"Call me if you need more bitters."

"Thanks, Karla; this should settle my stomach."

He sniffed a baffling aroma emitted from the black liquid under his nose. He lifted the glass and eased the bitter sweet liquid through his lips, reminded of medicine his mother gave him when he was ill.

"Get out! I don't want your kind in here!" Startled, Freddy cast a glance sideways, spotting Millie facing Gertie. The prostitute lowered her head, squeezing her brows together before joining them with a crease, and pivoted on her peg leg, limping for the door.

"You can go to hell; I wanted a drink to warm up. It's freezing outside, bitch."

Karla scrambled back, speaking with a short-winded voice. "Did you hear that?"

Leo leaned forward with a hint of a frown on his face. "How could we have missed it?"

Karla's eyes bulged, and she said in a harsh voice, "Gertie makes me sick. Millie caught her in the alley once with a crippled vet and tossed a bottle at her. Gertie's customer dropped his crutches and fell to the ground."

Freddy shut his eyes, bringing a relaxed smile across his lips, feeling the bitters work their magic.

"Freddy, need one more bitter?" said Karla, uncrossing her arms with a warm smile on her face. "Are you feeling better?"

He closed his eyes with a slow headshake. "My stomach's still queasy. I better head home." And he picked himself up, preparing to leave, catching Leo's voice.

"Hey, Freddy, wait. I'm finished studying. I'll join you. You don't want to be by yourself this late." Freddy and Leo walked against an icy wind arriving on a bustling boulevard and went different ways after giving each other genuine smiles and shaking hands.

* * *

Freddy always suspected Curt worshipped Helga, but lacked courage to do anything about it. His head tilted to the side and laughed faintly, imagining what might happen when Helga arrived with Curt's beer. He put his elbows on the table, resting his head in his hands, hoping Curt might perform his odd routine. Curt didn't disappoint him. He started the second Helga appeared. Curt removed reading glasses from a pocket, wiped off the lenses, sneaking a peek at Helga's long legs, and after putting them back smoothed the right side of his slick black hair, ending up clearing his throat two times, never three. His eyes darted between Curt and Helga, reminded of a Shakespearian tragedy which never ended well.

A bit later, Freddy rubbed an eye, conscious of Karla whispering into Albert's ear. Albert's head lurched back, and he widened his gaze, glancing at him with an odd look on his face. Freddy's lips puckered, concentrating on him. Karla did it again, baffling Freddy. And Albert's cheeks burned red, listening to her. "Karla, it's not my concern; ask Freddy yourself."

Karla pulled on her pigtail. "Albert, you ask him. All Helga wants to know if he likes her."

Curt's jaw dropped, his face saddened. Speechless, he picked himself up and limped to the bathroom.

Albert's firm voice sorted out his thoughts. "Freddy, answer her; she won't stop pestering me till you do."

Freddy's brows raised up, and his voice softened. "Helga's a nice girl, but I won't be looking for a girlfriend until I've finished law school."

Karla bared her teeth and shook her head hard, saying to him, "What, you're not interested in, Helga? She's a gorgeous girl. What, are you a fucking faggot?"

Freddy's mouth sprung open with her words ringing in his ears.

"Stop!" shouted Albert, giving her an unbelieving stare. "Enough of this shit; he's doesn't like Helga. What don't you understand? Don't you get it? Freddy's no faggot. Never call him that; you'd better apologize to him right now."

Karla's face whitened, and she dropped her head, lowering her voice. "I'm sorry, Freddy, I didn't mean it."

* * *

Freddy stopped to wipe sweat off a brow and unbutton his collar. He smiled, noting shade on the other side of the street, and crossed over to it and stepped faster toward the Slippery Pig. His arms swayed when he arrived on a sun-drenched corner opposite the tavern, waiting on traffic. Rackety machines beeping their horns passed in front of him, and he detected gaseous odors spit out from a standing truck's exhaust pipes. A truck full of rowdy Brownshirts stopped for traffic, blocking his view. One of them jumped up with his back to Freddy, yelling to someone he couldn't see, "Hey! Sweetie, give me a kiss."

His chin lifted, and he sighed when the truck moved away. And he dashed across the street, catching sight of a stylish girl dressed in a green-colored print dress and a white hat pacing back and forth. It crossed his mind the Brownshirt had harassed the girl. The gorgeous girl flashed a smile, exposing white teeth between her red lips.

A flush crossed his cheeks, and he dipped his chin, easing himself in front of the tavern door, tugging on its dull handle and walking inside the place.

"Freddy, stop. I need your opinion," said Millie, sounding confused.

"My opinion on what?"

Millie brought her lips inside her mouth, pointing outside at the girl Freddy had passed standing alongside a lamppost. "The girl wearing a green dress," said Millie in a voice laced with concern, "do you think she's a prostitute? She parades in front of the lamppost, checking the time; she could expect a customer to arrive."

Karla shrugged, arriving, her voice firm. "What's the matter?"

Millie raised her voice, gazing out the window. "That floozy standing by the lamppost—I wonder if she's a prostitute," shrieked Millie, glaring at Karla.

After Karla inspected the woman, she faced Millie, smiling. "If she is, she makes good money and dresses nice; wish I could afford her clothes. Do you think I should give it a go? I could always use the extra money, if it's okay with you, Millie."

Millie flinched, inhaling a quick breath. "Stop joking."

The girl displayed a pensive smile, aware people were watching her, and faced the other way. Freddy's fingers touched his lips, finding Leo Herzfeld rushing into the elegant girl's open arms. They embraced, spoke a few words, and walked toward the door. Baffled, Freddy abandoned Karla and Millie and scampered across the creaky floor, flinging himself into a chair at the table, surprising Albert and Curt. Leo brought the girl with an alluring smile to the table, followed by Karla.

"Uh, pleasant afternoon," said Leo, fumbling with his shirtsleeve, nodding and grimacing. "I forgot to tell you I was coming and bringing someone with me."

Albert burst out laughing, before he said, "No one cares about you; who's the nice-looking girl with you?"

Leo boosted his voice, getting the giggles. "Everyone, meet my twin sister, Jette."

Karla raised her voice, darting her eyes between Leo and Jette, keeping her head still. "Leo, she's your sister?"

"Yes, she is; she works for my father. She was visiting customers close by and wanted to meet you."

Freddy pulled up a chair for Jette.

Albert gawked at Leo as he sat. "Um, Leo, what did you tell her?"

"Nothing awful. She was curious and asked lots of questions." Leo grimaced and stiffened his body.

Albert burst out laughing, spraying beer on himself. He eyed Jette, grinning. "Hope you brought cotton and bandages with you; no one taught your brother to duck."

"That's nonsense! Don't believe him, Jette, I can handle myself in a fight."

Albert mocked Leo with a hint of sarcasm in his voice. "No, you can't. Run away before you get punched."

Leo frowned, shaking his head. "Jette, if you laugh, you'll encourage him."

Curt said, "Leo, is she a Red too?"

Jette glared at him. "She's not a Communist."

"I didn't think so," said Albert, crossing his arms. "She wears nice clothes and smells nice, not liked she lives in the sewer."

Leo flinched, letting out a heavy sigh. "Albert, stop. Jette can't stay the entire day to listen to your lousy sense of humor."

Freddy fidgeted with a shirt button, casting his blue eyes on the mysterious woman, saying to her, "Jette, Albert needs an audience; he'll stop if you ignore him."

Jette's red lips flashed a smile.

"We get along, because we agree never to bring up politics, economics, world conquest, or social conditions in Germany."

"Hm, what's left?" said Jette, assessing Leo.

Jette turned toward Freddy with a wide grin, twirling a long curl of hair that fell from under her fashionable helmet hat. "And you must be Freddy Bauer?"

Freddy's voice sounded fragile as he audited Jette's face. "Um, h-how did you know who I was?"

"Leo said you were handsome," said Jette, giving Freddy a warm smile.

Albert squinted, inspecting Jette. "Did he mention me? If he did, I bet it wasn't good, was it?"

Jette delivered Albert a dismissive glance.

Albert pulled his shoulders back and wagged his head. "You don't want to poke fun at me."

Jette gave Albert a devious smile. "Oh dear, you're scaring me," she said with a hint of mockery in her voice.

Curt leaned back, laughing.

Jette made a face at Curt. "What's so funny? Wait till I tell you what he said of you."

Curt's jaw dropped, and he focused on Jette.

Leo's chest bounced from laughing.

Jette teased, grinning at him. "Curt, I'm not sure you can handle it, can you?"

Curt stuck out his chest. "Sure I can."

"Uh oh," said Jette before lowering her voice and vaulting up her eyebrows, "hope I didn't get myself into trouble."

Curt inspected everyone, gasping.

Jette's lips tensed, giving Curt the evil eye. "Gotcha, Curt."

Grin lines dug into Freddy's cheeks.

Albert checked out Jette, then Leo, with a mischievous smile. "It's impossible, Leo, she can't be your twin sister; she's not ugly."

Leo's lips turned into an angry scowl, and he crossed his arms.

Freddy's cheeks inflated; he puckered his lips, holding in a laugh.

While tapping her foot, Karla cleared her throat. "Jette, I'm Karla; can I fetch you something to eat from the kitchen?"

"Yes, you can, thank you, Karla; what do you suggest?"

"You can't go wrong with the sausage plate—everyone likes that."

Jette looked up at her. "Do you serve fresh fish?"

"We got fish, but Millie's mother's the cook, and her sausages taste better."

Jette eyed Karla, pursing her lips. "I'm sorry, Karla, can't eat sausage; the fish will do."

"You'll be sorry, Jette; don't say I didn't warn you," said Karla in a nagging voice, shaking her head.

Jette's voice warmed. "I'm sorry; let me explain myself. At home I eat kosher food, but away I bend the rules sometimes."

Karla scratched her head, raised one eye above the other, and crinkled her lips. "Kosher, what the hell's that?"

"Jews follow laws that tell us what we can or cannot eat."

"Why? I wouldn't want that," said Karla, fidgeting with her pigtail, baring her teeth.

Jette's head seesawed, and she spoke in a consoling voice, eyeing Karla with a half-smile. "Jews have fewer choices than you do."

Karla's voice fired up, and she cranked her head back and forth hard. "Who'd do that?" She scrutinizes Leo. "He eats sausage. I've seen him do it. He can't be a Jew, right?"

Freddy assessed Leo, remembering he had renounced God for Communism.

Jette flashed her white teeth. "Jews don't have to eat kosher; it's up to them if they do."

Karla poked her cheek with her tongue. "Um, you do, you don't—I'm mixed up. I can't handle any more shit. It's fish for Jette and sausage plates for the rest of you, whatever you are."

On Karla's way to the kitchen, Freddy caught sight of Helga giving him a chilling stare. His head detoured; he spotted Curt gazing at Albert with a puzzled expression on his face. "Albert, do you know what eating kosher is? Your mother's Jewish."

Leo's mouth shot open, and his voice softened as his words took a curious tone. "Your mother's a Jew?"

"She is, but my family's not religious; we value God but don't practice any faith."

"How sad," proclaimed Jette, looking at Leo. "Everyone needs a place to pray."

Albert blew out a quick burst of air. "Don't anyone shed any tears for me; I'm no charlatan."

"Charlatan!" Jette flinched, hearing the word, dropping her jaw.

"Yes, a charlatan. I don't profess to be something I'm not. At least I'm being honest with myself and am not a phony. I worship God in my way. I don't go to church or a synagogue to prove what's in my heart. If holy days are the only time you're self-righteous is hypocritical, don't you agree?"

Quieted by Albert's candor, Freddy gave his head a slight shake, focusing on Helga's sour stare. And stuffed a chunk of meat in his mouth.

Jette tilted her head at Freddy. "Freddy, be careful, you might choke on it; didn't your mother teach you to chew your food?"

"Jette, he doesn't because he never makes mistakes, he's perfect," said Albert, spitting bits of food from his mouth, speaking fast.

Freddy ignored him, squinting at Helga now and then. Jette picked up on it, twisting her mouth.

"Is she your girlfriend?"

Albert rubbed his chin, blinking at Jette. "Is who Freddy's girlfriend?"

"The charming girl standing in front of the bar," said Jette in a quiet, tense voice.

"She's not, she's Karla's sister," said Albert, giggling.

Jette eyed Freddy, bringing a slow smile to her shiny red lips, teasing him with her fluttering eyelashes while she stroked a dangling curl.

Curt by chance interrupted one of Jette and Freddy's flirty moments. "Jette, did Leo say you were visiting customers?"

"Potential customers, our sales slowed. I was out drumming up new business."

"Sorry. What do you sell?"

"Fabrics."

Albert rounded his shoulders with a notable inflection to his voice. "Huh! Fabrics."

She tilted her head at Freddy, bringing a smile to her face.

"Freddy, Leo tells me exams start next month," inquired Jette. "Guess you'll be busy studying."

"Yes, I'll be living in hell till I finish exams."

"Don't cry over him," said Albert, firming his voice. "When exams finish, he'll have done the best."

She placed a hand over her chest, eyeing Freddy. "I'm sure you're right; Leo told me he does well."

"Professor Karp found his prodigy a summer job interning at Adler and Beiner, a prestigious law firm," said Curt, forcing a laugh.

"Freddy, that's marvelous news." She grinned. "Where's their office?"

"Near the Reichstag building."

Albert nudged Freddy, shaking his head at him. "Hurry, Freddy, we can't be late for Professor Rath's class. He'll scream at Leo if he's late one more time."

Freddy frowned, displeased Albert had tapped him. "Albert, give me a minute."

"Can't," said Albert, yanking on his sleeve. "Say goodbye. If we show up late for Rath's class, the fat bastard will explode."

Freddy shrugged, exposing a nervous smile. "Sorry, Jette, must run; I hope we'll meet again."

Her face glowed, and she said in a soft voice, "I hope so."

Chapter Twelve

The Summer of 1929

Freddy squinted, angling his head away from the morning sun's bright rays. A relaxed smile crossed his face; he was fancying a soft breeze sweeping through his hair as he waited for a black automobile to pass before mounting his black bike. Freddy peddled hard through puddled streets for ten minutes, putting on the brakes on a boulevard on the other side of the Reichstag building. He slid his bottom off the smooth leather seat, gripping the handlebar with one hand, and stayed put a moment to catch his breath and fan his face. He trekked up Wilhelm Street, gasping at the sound of a women's voice calling out his name.

"Freddy, Freddy Bauer; it can't be. I don't believe it—it's you," hollered a bouncing, coquettish girl.

He stopped mid-stride, facing gleaming teeth and eyes. He glowed inside, admiring the radiant woman's short, wavy strawberry blond hair. "Good morning, Jette, what a surprise to see you." The wind nuzzled her dress, outlining her long legs, and his eyes examined them.

Jette's eyes sparkled as she bounced from foot to foot. "Well, are you happy to see me?"

Embarrassed, his heart sped up. "What? Uh…uh, yes, sorry, didn't recognize you for a moment without your hat."

"Huh," she said, swinging her arms, moving closer. "Well, do you like what you see?"

"Uh…uh, yes, I do, you look lovely," said Freddy, widening his eyes.

"Did you know I waved at you and you ignored me? Your mind was somewhere else." She wagged her head, unable to contain her smile. "Silly boy, what were you thinking? You must be careful, or you'll get hurt. You don't want to get run over, do you?" Jette moved closer, observing Freddy. "Curt said you were interning near the Reichstag building. That's good, now you can meet me after work; I know a nice café near here. Meet there at six thirty, is that okay?"

He froze, stunned by Jette's bluntness.

She raised an eyebrow and tapped a foot. "Is there something wrong?"

He gave her a nervous smile. "Um, six thirty's fine."

While she jotted the café's location, his eyes probed her long legs. A relaxed smile crossed her face. "Naughty boy—I guess I'll take that as a compliment."

She checked the time and slumped. "Damn it, I'm late. It's a pity I can't stay for more naughty looks." Her eyes widened, and she flashed her white teeth. "Herr Bauer, don't you be late."

Jette shifted her gorgeous body away from him and strutted away. Freddy captured every movement her sensuous body made. She spun on her heels, capturing Freddy's admiring glances. And she crept up to him, enlarging her eyes, catching him with her warm breath. "You must stop doing that; it might cause you trouble."

A rosy tinge fanned out on his face. And Jette snagged a piece of Freddy's blond hair that dangled below his hairline and brushed it back with her fingers until it stayed in place.

"Darling, you need a woman's touch, to start the day." She let go of her black bag, stood up, and kissed him on the cheek, leaving a whiff of sweet vanilla in the air. Dazed, his hand lost its grip on the bicycle. He picked it up, examining her seductive legs.

Jette's face turned skyward, and she spoke in a whimsical voice. "Clumsy boy, caught you again. You're too obvious; learn to be more discreet." Her lips twisted into a wry smile, and she stood erect. "Don't be late; it's not nice to keep a girl waiting." And she sashayed off, her curvy hips never missing a beat, and raised her right arm in the air, twirling her index finger.

Freddy stroked his chin, having in mind Jette's kiss.

With an unrestrained smile on his lips, he parked his bicycle outside Adler and Beiner and burst through the door, welcomed with bright eyes by Berta Koch. He smiled, nodding at the wide-hipped receptionist with thick gray hair. His smiled vanished as he recalled her husband had left her for a younger woman many years ago, leaving her with a disabled son.

Agnes Peters, the heartless office manager, whom Berta helped, dropped a file on Berta's desk and walked away.

"Friedrich, I need you to come here," said Hugo Hahn, a hotheaded lawyer. Freddy scrutinized his thin mustache, envisioning a sinister actor in a silent movie. "Hurry, I need you to fact-check a brief for me."

Jan Meier, the other despicable lawyer, raised his voice, shaking his head. "No you don't, Hugo; he worked Friday and Saturday for you. Herr Beiner just asked me to go over his brief. He told me to grab Friedrich if I needed help. It's his defense papers for the Arnold Schuster treason trial. That's his number-one priority right now."

Hugo rubbed the back of his neck. "Why can't Agnes handle it?"

"Impossible," said Jan Meier, running his fingers through thick, wavy brown hair. "She's overwhelmed; Herr Adler dumped a stack of papers on her desk."

He examined Hugo and Jan with a slight smile creeping across his lips. *Three more weeks to put up with their petty grudges and Hugo's temper.*

Whenever something went wrong, Hugo lost control of himself and released his anger on him. This day was no different. Adler's secretary had given Hugo a file with a note attached to it. He caught Hugo's face reddening as he read the note. Freddy wet his lips, expecting Hugo's boiling rage.

Hugo pointed his finger at Freddy. "I asked you to check the Hoehner abortion papers," said Hugo, raising his voice to a shout. "Herr Adler found two mistakes."

He swallowed, unable to look Hugo in the eye. "I never checked the brief."

Hugo ran his hand through his black hair. "But I told you to."

He gave his head a quick shake. "Herr Hahn, you didn't."

"Y-y yes, I did," said Hugo, forming a tight circle with his lips before protruding them. "And don't you dare contradict me. If I said I did, I did, do you understand me?"

Freddy was dull-eyed; his voice shook. "Yes, I do, more than you know."

Hugo crossed his arms, tightening his lips. "You're an impertinent bastard. Who do you think you're talking to? I ought to report your wisecrack to Herr Adler and Herr Beiner," snapped Hugo, spraying saliva. "Let me tell you something. It's my opinion you'll never be a lawyer. If Herr Beiner or Herr Adler should ask, I'd tell them to find someone else."

Freddy looked away. *If I tell the bully off, I won't show up here next summer.* His face warmed, catching people staring. Berta's cheeks rose, and she gave him an understanding nod.

Herr Meier shouted, drawing his brows together, "You can't speak to him that way. You owe him an apology."

"I don't owe him shit; he's just a wretched intern."

"We'll see what Herr Beiner thinks of it," said Jan Meier, breathing heavy. "When he comes back from lunch with Herr Adler, you can repeat what you said to Friedrich. I'm sure Herr Beiner might want to know Professor Karp was wrong on Friedrich. I'll ask Ada if Herr Beiner can meet with us this afternoon."

"No, wait, don't do that. I misspoke," said Hugo, softening his tone.

"You owe Friedrich an apology," hollered Herr Meier, bulging his eyes.

Close-lipped, Hugo shook his head, saying, "Never," and walked away.

Freddy switched on the fan, glad Herr Meier had diffused his predicament. Freddy's smile faded, and he shifted his sight, debating Herr Meier's intentions. *Is it possible he hates Hugo Hahn more than me?* Freddy shook his head, picking up a smile on Berta's face.

* * *

Freddy spotted Jette tucked into a remote corner at a lakeside café in the Berlin Zoo. She had changed into a yellow chiffon dress with a matching hat wrapped in green ribbon. He straightened, arching his neck, admiring her dazzling face.

"You're on time," she said, drawing air between her white teeth. "Isn't the lake amazing? I love coming here; it's my favorite place in the whole wide world."

"Oh, have you brought other men here?"

Her smile faded. "Could that matter to you?"

"No, why should it? You're a free woman; do whatever you want," he said, wincing, wishing he could take back his insensitive words, seeing her bow her head and look at her hands.

A slow smile appeared on his lips when the female server arrived. "Drinks?"

"Riesling, please," said Jette, lifting her head, expressionless.

Moments later, the server reappeared, placing a glass of Riesling and a beer on the table. He gave her a sheepish grin and moved his head sideways, running his eyes over the lake's sparkling water, ending on the other side, where tall grasses and green trees swayed, directed by the gentle wind. And he shifted his eyes back, discovering once more happiness bloomed on Jette's face, beholding him. Her red lips shined, and she toyed with a strand of hair that peeked below her hat.

"Jette, you're right; the view's impressive."

"More than me?" she said with a faint flush tinging her cheeks, batting her broad eyelashes.

"No, not more than you."

"Freddy, wait till sunset." Jette beamed, leaning in toward him.

And he felt an effusion of warmth; his cheeks flushed as he assessed her.

"Leo said you don't have a girlfriend. Why?"

"Oh, the big mouth did, did he?"

Her eyes zipped back and forth, refusing to concentrate on him. "Don't blame Leo. I was curious and pestered him till he answered me," she confessed, hanging her head.

It flattered him; his cheeks dimpled.

The server appeared with the bill. Jette smiled at the person and started opening her bag. "I can afford to pick it up," he said with a slight frown.

"Are you sure, interns don't make any money," said Jette, blinking.

"I'll have you know Adler and Beiner pay their interns," said Freddy, knowing the bill could take a chunk from his meager wages.

Jette spotted two lovers drifting in a rowboat and faced Freddy, smiling. And she snapped her hands together as if praying, bouncing in her seat, acting childish.

"Freddy, please, can we?" begged Jette excitedly. "Please, please, I've always wanted to do it."

And moments later he paddled away from the dock with Jette having no direction in mind. He smiled at Jette's glowing face. The boat moved along the shoreline at a measured pace, with the water mirroring white clouds above, while nature filled the air with music. Freddy stopped rowing now and then to take in the sights of nesting birds or to gaze at multicolored ducks leaving ripples of water behind, or the majesty of a white swan splashing water while flapping its wings. A black iron bridge caught his attention. He paddled toward it. Jette smiled, and her eyes twinkled. She removed her hat and ran her fingers through her lucent hair, firing emotions new to him. Freddy stopped paddling, worshipping Jette's alluring features. From where the boat rested, the evening sun ignited Jette's strawberry blond hair and cast a golden glow over the water beneath it and lit up the trees and high grasses that faced it. At that moment, he understood Jette had left his heart defenseless.

Her mouth twitched. "There you go again. This time, it was too obvious. Well! Freddy Bauer, are you pleased with what you see?"

"Must I answer?"

Jette's eyes twinkled; she laughed. "Weren't you taught not to answer a question with a question? Let me make it simple for you, Freddy Bauer—yes or no?"

He blinked, feeling his arm muscles twitch. "Uh, yes."

She wore a wistful smile. "Freddy, hold me."

Careful not to rock the boat, he settled alongside her. And she kissed his cheek before putting her lips against his mouth. When she finished, Freddy smiled, touching his lips, savoring the smell of her sweet-smelling perfume.

"Is this what they teach you in law school?"

"Teach what?"

Jette stroked her arm, smiling with an inward gaze. "To avoid the inevitable."

Speechless, his vision narrowed on the rising corners of her mouth. She looked pleased with a sense of contentment. Her face beamed as she put her lips to his mouth. Her eyes brightened; she lowered her head, whispering, "See what you missed."

He grinned, breathing a slow, steady breath, sensing his body warm.

And when light faded, she shivered, and he wrapped her with his coat and paddled to the other side of the iron-fenced footpath and moored the boat near patches of tall grasses. Shades of orange and red crossed the horizon, and an ominous cloud flickered the fading sun. Bewitched, gazing at the brilliance of the sunset, Freddy kissed Jette.

"Isn't twilight breathtaking," she said, grinning at Freddy. "Each sunsets more amazing than the last; this one is special because it's with you."

Freddy's eyes found Jette bathing her red lips with her tongue. The fading sun fired them. The sight intoxicated Freddy, and he wanted them. Driven by passion, he took hold of her hair. And she relaxed and shut her eyes. Their lips touched. Jette's free spirit excited him; her playful innocence and passion for life put him under her spell. He pressed his lips against hers and held them there, catching her body quiver. Guided by the café lights, Freddy used one oar to wander toward the dock. His body tingled with delight; he caught happiness on Jette's face. Jette sighed, closing her eyes. And he smiled, steering the boat to a point where moonlight lit up her face. She opened her eyes, catching Freddy admiring her. She giggled, dipping her head. "There's hope for you, Freddy Bauer."

They eased over a footbridge and inched toward a tree-lined gravel path, taking time to caress and press their lips together on their way. Close to the park's gate, Jette and Freddy settled on a weathered bench. Freddy breathed in, gazing into Jette's moonlit eyes. His lips trembled as he explored her. He wanted her lips and kissed them, carried to a world new to him.

"Freddy, I will never forget what happened tonight," said Jette, glowing, cherishing the moment. And with happiness blooming inside her, she gave him a peck on his lips. "My head's spinning. Is this what you do to girls? Will I see you again? Will you add my name to your list of broken hearts?"

The uncertainty coming from the secure woman surprised him. "If you look at me, you'll have your answer." His thumb caressed the top of her hand, and he made unwavering eye contact with her. "I want to be with you."

Her eyes darkened, and she bowed her head.

"Can we keep what happened between us a secret?"

Freddy's mouth slackened. "What, why?" he asked with her words fixated in his mind, triggering memories of his parents' covert affair and the pain it caused them.

Jette whimpered and cried, with a tear marking one cheek. Freddy wiped it dry with a finger while his mind struggled to make sense out of it.

"I need time; our feelings toward each other will concern other people."

"I don't give a damn what people think and neither should you."

"Freddy, please don't be mad. I wish it were simple; it's not. I must consider my family and what it'll do to them."

His cheeks burned with anger, and nerves shook his voice. "What's wrong? I'm not good enough for your family? That's it, right?"

His rant spooked her, and her lips quivered. He considered leaving, but while assessing the inconsolable woman, concluded he couldn't. Jette sensed his despair and grabbed hold of his hands, and he shoved them away, staring at her with fire in his eyes.

"Freddy, that's not true. Please trust me," she said, her eyes moist. "Give me time to sort things out; my mother's not well, and it's upsetting my father. Since Leo left, I'm the only one at home to console him. I'll tell my parents when my mother feels better."

"What if our feelings change?" said Freddy, taking a breath to sooth his frazzled nerves.

Jette's face wilted, and she exhaled, trembling. "Mightn't they? We just met."

"I hope not," he answered, pressing his lips into a slight grimace, unable to concentrate.

Close to tears, she gazed into his eyes without blinking.

* * *

"Come in, Friedrich." Freddy entered Herr Beiner's office, sniffing cigar smoke. He frowned, waiting for Beiner to turn away from the opened window. The telephone rang, and Herr Beiner answered it. Freddy bared his neck, breathing a whiff of fresh air from the open window. Through the vacated windows, he assessed inky clouds above the Reichstag's dome. Beiner hunkered down in his tufted brown leather chair and picked up the telephone's chrome receiver off its black base to answer the call.

"Hello. Herr Beiner speaking." His pleasant voice changed to anger. "Guilty, that's what I said—you heard me, guilty… Heinrich Jung, that's who."

Freddy's mouth fell open, and he pushed back in his seat, whispering weakly, "Heinrich Jung, Rudolf's grandfather?"

"I'll call you back. Herr Bauer's here with me."

A slight shiver came over Freddy, suspecting something was wrong hearing Judge Jung's name in Herr Beiner's conversation.

The thick-spectacled-man smirked at him. "Herr Bauer, just finished talking with Professor Karp. He's in Munich vacationing with his daughter; did you know that?"

Freddy shifted in his seat, having on his mind Judge Jung. "I did, Herr Beiner; he told me he'd be there this summer."

"Professor Karp told me you were intelligent and would make an excellent lawyer. He pleaded with me to hire you for the summer, said I'd be making a mistake if I didn't, so I did," spoke the thick mustached man, crinkling his lips and shaking his head. "Don't disappoint me. I just received the judge's written opinion in the Arnold Schuster treason case. They backed the Ministry of Justice and found Herr Schuster guilty of treason and sentenced him to six months in prison."

Freddy gave him a flat gaze. "He didn't commit a crime?"

Alfred Beiner ground his teeth. "Right but wrong, Herr Bauer."

"Right, but wrong. That makes no sense. Herr Schuster reported irrefutable facts in his newspaper? The truck overturned, and six of the ten soldiers killed were volunteers."

"Morality has clouded your judgment," said Herr Beiner, making unwavering eye contact with Freddy.

Freddy loosened his collar. "What do you mean, Herr Beiner?"

"The judges reached their verdict to save Germany's honor. And it had nothing to do with justice. When Schuster's newspaper published the volunteer soldiers' names, he revealed to the world Germany had violated a term written in the

Treaty of Versailles. It forbade Germany from mustering a volunteer army. That's the reason Chief Judge Heinrich Jung and his cronies sided with the Ministry of Defense and not Schuster."

Herr Beiner slammed the desk hard enough that it knocked his unlit cigar off its perch.

"Friedrich, acknowledge it—justice is not always fair, even when evidence looks unquestionable," stressed Beiner, using a somber tone of voice.

Freddy audited Herr Beiner's face with a thought. *Judge Jung and his grandson think alike.* He dropped his head and scratched the back of his neck. *Practicing law will be more formidable than I thought.*

* * *

Jette wiggled her hips and stretched, admiring the blue sky above her. She sat up, untying a black scarf wrapped round her head, letting it fall off her fingers. Grin lines slashed her cheeks, and she beamed at Freddy, combing her gold and copper hair. And once she finished, her body twisted and fell beside him, pressing her lips against his, cuddling in his arms.

She whispered, catching him with warm breaths, "I love you, Freddy Bauer; say you love me?"

With a sense of weightlessness, he gave her a yearning look, saying in a soft tone, "I do, I love you."

Sunlight colored hers cheeks, glowing on her wet lips. He touched her soft lips with a finger, looking deep into her eyes. Obsessed with their majesty, he tasted them. And moments later her eyes shut, with her breaths easing, and she drifted off to asleep. He grinned while fingering one of Jette's curls and kissed her forehead. And while she slept, he ran his eyes over her listless body, leaving no part in it unchallenged.

The curvature and fullness of her breasts pleased him. He carried his eyes over her flawless long legs. Aroused with an inventive imagination, he pictured her without her purple swimsuit.

And his cheeks dimpled as he detected children's voices and watched them playing along the lakeshore and others splashing each other in the water. He collected the warm bottle of Riesling and stashed it in cool water between high blades of grass. And he idled on the blanket with his blue pupils appearing larger, admiring Jette. He leaned forward, wrapping his arms around his bent knees, wanting to touch her. She stirred, wiggling her body and stretching before opening her eyes. She giggled, delighted to see him chewing her bottom lip. Freddy sighed, catching his heart race.

"Caught you, didn't I?" said Jette, giving Freddy a playful nudge. "Have you been a naughty boy?"

"Guilty, how could I resist the temptation." professed Freddy, nodding with a childish grin.

Freddy lay beside her, smiling at nothing. Jette turned on her side, saying in a quiet voice, "I love you." And she placed her head on his chest, confessing, "Did you know you stole my heart at the Slippery Pig? You were everything Leo said you were, and more. I have to tell you something. It's important. I don't want there to be secrets between us. I was waiting for you near the Reichstag building, wanting to see you, because I knew you were working for Adler and Beiner."

Surprised, he released a sigh, fixating on the event with happiness blooming inside him.

"I'm glad you did. I missed you," said Freddy with an upturned face.

Moments later, he gave her a pained gaze, deepening his voice. "It's been two weeks since we started seeing each other. I've kept it a secret. Have you?"

Jette's voice strained, dropping her head. "Yes, no, I told Ester Weitz—she's my best friend; she covers for me when I'm not home."

"What? Can she keep a secret?"

Jette grimaced, tensing her words. "Yes, she can. Why are you asking me that?"

"Our cloak-and-dagger affair frustrates me. Someone might discover us. It's not what I expected after our first date. We can't keep it up; one day we'll get caught, and it'll make things worse than they are. I lied to my mother last night, told her Adler and Beiner needed me today and I'd go to an early mass," said Freddy, looking away.

"I lie too. Told my father I'm meeting Ester at the Jewish shelter," said Jette with a wince.

"What happens at the shelter?" asked Freddy, examining her.

"We take prostitutes off the streets, offer them clean quarters, and teach them a trade. Ester and I meet them at the train station and try to persuade them to come with us to the shelter. Their pimps beat the women."

"That sounds like dangerous work. Are you crazy? You shouldn't spend your nights talking to prostitutes."

"We're careful; we stay away from dangerous places. There was only one problem the whole time we've been doing it."

"Yeah, what happened?"

"One girl warned us of a pimp named Vladimir. She said he was violent and wore a black patch over a missing eye with a nasty scar under it. Another girl told us a Cossack stabbed him in the eye during a fight in the Ukraine."

"Jette, it's risky; odds are you'll run into Vladimir again. Find another way to help people."

"We did. He threatened us, but he ran after spotting two police officers."

"Quit! It's not safe. I've enough on my mind without worrying over you."

"Freddy, it will be fine. We gave the shelter a month's notice."

"Did you tell Leo?"

Jette dry-washed her hands, auditing him. "He lost his temper, said he wanted to kill him, but he calmed when I told him Ester and I were quitting."

"Jette, until you do, I'll be a nervous wreck." The skin under Freddy's eyes bunched, and he struggled with his thoughts. "Jette, when you're finished working at the shelter, we should tell Leo. The longer you wait, the harder it will be."

She nodded and sniffed, shedding tears. Freddy leaned in, wiping them off her cheeks, apologizing. "I'm sorry; I didn't mean to upset you."

"Freddy, my mother's health's deteriorating?"

He grimaced and held out his hands, saying to her in a voice that softened a little, "Let's go for a walk; it'll be good for you."

He stood up, grabbing hold of Jette's hands and helping her to her feet. And he squeezed her hand, guiding Jette along the water's edge, consoling her, stopping to pull the wine out of the water and yank out the cork, offering her a drink.

* * *

Freddy headed north and zigzagged through traffic on rain-slicked roads and crossed over the River Spree on a street bridge and jumped a curve, stopping in front of an apartment building on Oranienburger Street on the other side of a wonderful park. He opened the building's glass-paneled door and headed inside; he checked the wall directory till he found the name he wanted. And he lugged his bicycle to the second floor and walked till he came to a door numbered four. There was a strange object nailed to the upper part of the doorjamb. Freddy rested his bicycle against the wall and pushed the white-buttoned bell. Footsteps thumped toward the door. It opened, and a pear-shaped woman in a white cotton dress with wavy black hair parted in the middle of her head smiled at him.

"You must be Herr Bauer. Please come in, Professor Karp's expecting you. I'm Frau Karp, his wife."

Frau Karp led Freddy through a hall with a whiff of tobacco smoke toward two stained-glass pocket doors. She tapped on a glass panel and slid the door open.

"Stefan, Herr Bauer's here to see you."

"Good! Please show him in."

He entered a spacious room that reeked of pipe smoke and stayed on his feet. Standing holding onto a pipe in front of a brown leather chair with a book placed on it, Professor Karp greeted him with a smile. The book-filled room some-what reminded Freddy of his cubbyhole at the library.

"It's good to see you, Herr Bauer; hope you could find the apartment."

"No problem finding it, professor."

Professor Karp pointed to a seat in front of his cluttered desk. "Please, Herr Bauer, make yourself comfortable. I hope you're hungry. Frau Karp's a splendid cook and has prepared a roast duck just for you." The contented man kissed his fingers. "Um, wait till you taste her almond pockets—best in Berlin if I say so myself."

Professor Karp sprawled in a chair behind the desk and leaned back.

"Herr Bauer, how was working at Adler and Beiner? Did you get to work with Alfred Beiner? He a tough man, but

fair. I'm having lunch with him on Tuesday. Tell me everything because if you don't, I'll find out from Albert Beiner."

His breath caught a hitch; It surprised him at his direct
question.

"Ahem!" He cleared his throat. "I…I'll try, professor. I
spent most of the day poring over law codes, reading long,
drawn-out judges' opinions, and searching through library
archives. There were times I thought my brain might
explode trying to remember everything. I helped Herr Meier
with the Schuster trial. One day, he dumped two boxes on
my desk concerning the trial and told me not to go home
until I finished going over them. Herr Meier never smiled,
but was easy to figure out. If I finished my work on time, he
left me alone. Herr Hahn was ruthless and treated me badly,
but I took it. Twice I wanted to hit him, but I learned from
him and want to go back next summer if they'll have me.
But I'm worried because Herr Hahn dislikes me and might
say something to Herr Beiner against me." Freddy's eyes
narrowed. "I assisted him on an abortion case, but it never
satisfied him. When the judges reached their verdict, I mem-
orized paragraph two-eighteen of the penal code. Afraid of
losing her job a young chambermaid let the hotel manager
exploit her. She got pregnant, and the married manager
insisted she abort the baby. Ashamed and under duress from
the manager, she aborted the baby. Now she's in prison for
doing it." He paused. "Professor, she is being convicted for
the same crime twice."

"Twice, Friedrich?"

"Yes, twice. The Catholic Church excommunicated her
for violating canon law." And he licked his lips, keeping
Professor Karp in sight. "Both the state and church have
sentenced her for the same mistake."

"Herr Bauer, it's not a perfect world. You're different
from most students; hate and injustice touch your soul,

more. You're a principled man with a unique perspective, a noble trait. You can make your life important, pursue your dreams, don't give up hope, aim to be the best damn lawyer you can be."

Gratified by Professor Karp's response, Freddy smiled.

"Herr Bauer, I know what you think of Herr Hahn and Herr Meier, but what's your opinion of Herr Adler and Herr Beiner?"

"I spent no time with Herr Adler. I only saw him coming and going. Herr Beiner asked my opinion on cases."

"He did?" Karp squinted, scrunching his nose at him. "That's not like him. I expected to hear intolerable, deplorable," said Professor Karp, snorting. "You impressed him."

At the dinner table, Frau Karp glanced at him, growing a smile. "Herr Bauer, do you have a girlfriend?"

"Nessa, stop your meddling; leave Friedrich alone," said Professor Karp in a taut voice, making Freddy's lashes jump.

Freddy mimicked her smile, replying to her question. "Yes, I do, Frau Karp. I started seeing someone in July."

"Oh! You did. How nice."

"Good! Thank God he does. Now you can stop interfering in his business. Ruth and Paula should find someone else for their plain daughters."

Nessa shook her head and gave her husband an evil eye. "Stefan, how could you speak of the girls that way; they're both adorable."

Professor Karp shook his head, puckering his lips. "Nessa, get your eyes checked."

Frau Karp wore a cheeky smile. "Herr Bauer, what's her name?"

The professor's lips crinkled, and he tilted his head at his wife. "Whose name?"

"Stefan, Herr Bauer's girlfriend's name, who else?"

"Oh! Her."

Freddy lifted his chin. "Jette. Jette, that's her name."

Frau Karp wrinkled her nose at Freddy. "Jette, huh? Where does she live?"

"Prenzlauerberg."

Frau Karp's eyes lit up, and a finger crossed her bottom lip. "Prenzlauerberg—Jette's Jewish?"

"Nessa, please, no more questions. Bring coffee and more almond pockets," barked Professor Karp, narrowing his eyes on his wife.

Relieved, Freddy released a pent-up breath.

Chapter Thirteen

Tell Me It's Not True

Color ebbed onto Freddy's cheeks, seeing Karla arriving with four beers, placing them on the table. And with a wide grin, lifting one up in the air, she shed happy tears. "Cheers! Life's wonderful, isn't it, especially if you see it through a full glass of beer with friends."

"Amen to that," said Albert, and the mugs clinked together, spilling foam.

Millie arrived, her voice wavering. "What's this? You're toasting without me? Helga, fetch me a beer."

Millie's voice bubbled when Helga arrived with the beer. "I wish you all a wonderful new year at the university." And her lips flattened, giving Albert a hard stare. "You too, you oversized buffoon."

Everyone laughed, and five beer mugs clanked with the contents of two or three spilling. Karla leaned over and kissed Albert's cheek.

Albert's mouth twisted into a smile. "Sweetie pie, what did I do to deserve that?"

A girlish smile came on Karla's face. "Albert, I missed you."

Freddy's eyes lit up, and he concentrated on Albert and Karla. *I might be wrong. There could be more than sex holding them together.*

"Freddy, what's your excuse for not answering my letters?" said Curt, hardening his words, crashing into Freddy's thoughts.

"I wrote you back."

"Yeah, you did—you answered the letter I sent you at the end of July. Did you read any of my others?"

He flinched, covering his mouth without blinking, recalling stashing Curt's letters inside his desk drawer, forgetting to read them.

"I did. I'm sorry I didn't write back. I worked day and night at Adler and Beiner."

Curt's mouth slackened, eyeing Freddy. "Well, if you read them, did I mention Erich Wagner's name?"

"Uh, don't remember reading that one," said Freddy, lying, shifting in his chair, "Must be the one I didn't read. What happened to Erich Wagner?"

"He flunked out of law school."

"I'm not surprised; he spent most of his time in the Boar's Den rather than studying law," said Freddy, nodding at Curt.

Albert's cheeks blushed with pleasure. "That's one less Nazi shithead to consider. He was failing Karp's and Bergmann's classes; only Rath gave him a passing grade. Wonder if Karp found out he was the one who called him a Jew pig?"

Freddy shrugged, his gaze clouding. "Uh, he never mentioned it to me."

Curt leaned forward, saying, "A friend ran across Erich handing out Nazi propaganda before Hitler's Munich speech last month."

"Curt, Professor Karp told me Hitler was there visiting his daughter in Munich."

Albert swallowed his beer, banging the mug on the table.

"Hitler spoke to a crowd near my home," shrieked Albert, pulling back, looking detached and sad. "Friends of my father went to Cologne to hear him speak. My mother cried hearing them agree with Hitler on the Jews." Albert's tongue pushed forward as he clenched his fists. "The shits didn't know she was Jewish."

"I'm sorry she went through that," said Curt, narrowing his eyes on Albert, giving him an understanding nod.

Freddy leaned in, softening his face, squeezing Albert's shoulder.

And minutes later he leaned back, humming to himself, dreaming of Jette with a catlike stretch.

"A pfennig for your thoughts," said Albert, grinning. "Whatever was on your mind, you looked happy."

He brought a warm smile to his lips, thinking of Jette, and nodded.

Curt slid his chair forward. "Want to tell us why you're smiling?"

Albert's cheekbones lifted. "Come on, Freddy, tell us; we need terrific news."

With a slight grimace, he dipped his chin. "Albert, it's nothing."

And his mouth sprung open as someone tapped on his shoulder; he heard Helga's silvery voice. "Freddy, someone's here to see you. She didn't tell me her name, said it's important. She's waiting for you up front."

He lowered his brows, edging around toward the bar. Between it and where Millie perched, a woman dressed in black kept her eyes on him. Baffled, he headed toward the somber woman, curious. The mysterious woman's gaze grew more intense.

"Freddy, I'm Ester, Jette's friend; she wanted you to know her mother passed yesterday and is being buried today."

He was speechless and wore a downcast expression; his heart slowed as he worried over Jette. "Ester, what should I do? How can I help her?"

Teary-eyed, with an inward-facing gaze, her mouth slackened, Ester said, "She needs time to mourn; she has to help Leo and her father get through it. She told me to tell you she'll reach out to you once shiva's finished."

"Shiva?"

"When seven days of mourning end. I'm sorry, can't stay longer, must get back to Jette. It was nice meeting you." Ester offered him a half smile and squeezed his hand and headed for the door. He monitored the petite woman until she vanished into the street. And kept his eyes on the door, agonizing over his circumstances, finding his complicated world made worse with the death of Jette's mother.

Albert tapped his shoulder, arching his brows. "What's wrong? Who was that woman?"

Freddy glanced at Albert, trying to speak, the words caught in his throat.

"Freddy, what is it?"

"It's nothing, I'm okay."

"No, you're not. Your face tells me there's something wrong. Can I help?"

The edges of Freddy's lips twitched, sorting out Albert's proposal.

"Albert, there's something bothering me; it's tearing me apart. I'm in love and promised her I'd keep it a secret. But it's troubling me because it meant lying to my parents and keeping it from you and Curt."

Albert examined him, pursing his lips. "Is she married? Are you involved with a married woman?"

Freddy stood still, widening his blue eyes. "No, Albert, no."

"Freddy, follow me; we need to talk." At the bar Albert pulled out change and slapped it on the counter. "Ren, two beers—and make it fast."

Ren walked away from two customers, giving Albert a sour look.

Karla arrived with a fake smile, tilting her head at Albert. "Um, is something wrong?"

"Yes, but it doesn't concern you; tell Curt we'll be over shortly?"

Ren poured two beers and picked up the change, exposing a skull placed over an anchor on his arm just below his rolled-up sleeve. Albert drank some beer and placed the glass on the table, eyeing Freddy.

"Now talk to me."

Freddy swallowed hard, his face drained of color.

"Freddy, say something."

"Um, where do I start? It's complicated."

Albert's tongue peaked out, and he leaned forward. "The beginning is a start."

"Yes, when it began, okay."

"Fine, now we're getting somewhere," said Albert, growing still. "When did you meet her?"

Freddy burped, finishing swallowing a mouthful of beer. "Not that long ago."

Albert gulped his beer, swiping foam off his upper lip with his tongue, and slammed the empty mug on the bar, holding a puzzled look on his face. "Was it the girl that just left?"

"No, it's not her, she's Leo's sister's best friend."

Albert's eyes brightened, putting together the pieces of the mystery. "Her!" And with his facial muscles slackening, he said, "What's her name? I forgot it. How long you been seeing her?"

Freddy blinked hard, tightening his chest. "Her name's Jette. Five weeks."

"Ah, Jette, I remember her; you've been seeing her for five weeks. No wonder you didn't answer Curt's letters. Did you get her pregnant?"

"No, she's not pregnant. I told you it's complicated."

Albert made strong eye contact with Freddy, wrinkling his nose. "Talk to me."

Freddy's eyes widened, and he gazed up, recollecting memories. "I ran into Jette on my way to Adler and Beiner. She's gorgeous. Her quick-witted humor captivated me. She was different; she lived in a world where she set the tempo. It began at the zoo's lakeside café. We laughed; we—"

"Stop, I got it. You fell in love. Save the mushy stuff for Jette. Stick to the complicated part."

Freddy gave Albert a decisive nod.

"Jette's mother's been sick; Ester told me she died yesterday. I can't imagine Jette's pain. She couldn't tell her parents about us until her mother was better. I wanted to tell Leo, but she said it could wait. And while her mother was sick, Leo and his father were talking. Now with her mother's passing, everything's a mess. M-my world's filled with can't dos." Freddy dropped his head, rubbing the back of his neck, mirroring his thoughts in a hushed tone of voice. "I can't see Jette till shiva's over, and I can't tell Leo about us because it's too soon after her mother's death, and I can't tell my parents I've been lying to them. Complicated, huh? Need I say more?"

With Albert's eyes pinned on him, Freddy's mind weighed terrible outcomes.

"Freddy, give it a week or two and you'll see things differently," said Albert with a flickering grin.

"And what if I don't?"

"Stop! It's not the end of the world. You're just frustrated. There's always a bright side. I can help with Jewish customs; I've sat shiva with my mother many times."

"Freddy, drink up—you're glass isn't empty," said Albert, snorting. "I'm buying two more beers; they might help us sort things out."

Freddy examined Albert, mustering a smile, thankful he had talked with him, then chugged the rest of his beer, hearing Albert yell, "Two more beers, Ren, and hurry."

"Two beers coming up, big spender." Ren snorted.

* * *

Freddy trailed behind his parents on the hard ground until he came upon the stout priest adorned in a green robe. Father Graf's words were just audible: "The body of Christ." He placed a wafer on Freddy's tongue. Freddy shut his eyes, bowing his head. "Amen." He made the sign of the cross, inching toward Father Schwan, who was standing with a gold cup of red wine. "The blood of Christ," he said, and handed Freddy the cup for a sip. Freddy sighed, freed from pardonable sins, and inched back to his seat from the soft padded kneeler. He had contrition on his mind. When finished, he pondered the aches and pain death caused. He wished he could help Jette. He bowed his head, growing still, whispering to himself, "Please, God, see her through it."

From the pulpit, the plump old priest with black circles under his eyes scrutinized his flock. He pulled back his thin lips, displaying his teeth.

"Ahem, many parishioners are jobless, and it troubles me the numbers growing. Some children go to sleep hungry," lamented Father Graf, slumping. "Those with jobs, I beg you, please give what you can; if you can't give money, food will do. The rectory never closes. Not one among you should go to sleep on an empty stomach under my watch. Those without jobs, pray to God, ask for his help, but don't abandon him during the time you need him the most. It's easy to do when you imagine life's hopeless and believe no one cares. God loves you, without conditions, and we should treat each other the same way. Whatever you do, don't let false prophets lead you to Satan's door. The Nazis are not a solution, unless you inhabit their world—it's not God's; it's one filled with savage violence, and bigotry and intolerance are its commandments. I know them well; I followed the schemers for many years. And I was a priest in Munich at the time Hitler declared publicly the party's goals; they turned my stomach," warned Father Graf, darting his sunken eyes sideways. "Consider this—he's capable of anything, even murder."

With a frightening expression on his face, Father Graf waved his finger at the gathering.

"I warn you, better take my advice while you can."

Father Graf sighed and vacated the pulpit. Freddy frowned, assessing in his mind the holy man's words added to his heavy burden. He pictured Jette following an elderly couple through Saint Jutta's stained-glass vestibule and out through the church's massive arched doors. In the chilly air, Freddy stood with his parents. His mother turned, concentrating on a crying baby.

"Bettie Wurst!" his excited mother screamed and dashed over to a thin woman wearing a dowdy brown coat cradling a cranky baby. "Bettie, was that your baby making that noise in church?"

The woman, with a clump of brown hair hanging from under her black knit hat, grabbed his mother's hand, and nodded. "Afraid so, Barbara. Carly's a handful; she's always fussing."

His mother placed her hands over her chest, smiling at Bettie. "Carly—a girl. I like the name. Let me see her face."

Bettie Wurst exposed her sobbing baby's face.

"Oh, Bettie, she's adorable. Please, please let me hold her," said Freddy's mother, bobbing her head.

Bettie Wurst flashed her teeth and handed her whining child to his mother. She rocked Carly, and the baby stopped crying.

His mother blinked happy tears. "Bettie, I'll never get over the feeling of holding a newborn baby."

With an upturned face, he watched his pleased mother.

"Fritz, any luck finding a job?" said Freddy's father, pursing his lips.

"It's hopeless, Wilhelm; no one has surfaced since they sacked me. I've used up my benefits, and I'm running out of money," said Fritz, sagging his head.

"Cheer up, Fritz; things will get better."

Fritz shifted his weight to the other leg. "Yeah, easy for you to say; you have a job and money to feed your family."

Freddy's father clenched and unclenched his hands, speaking in a soft voice, narrowing his eyes on the hopeless man. "Fritz, don't forget what Father Graf said—if you need help, the rectory's open."

Frau Wurst gave his father a pained stare, anger in her tone. "Fritz doesn't need charity; he needs a job and won't beg for food. To hell with Father Graf and his handouts. We joined the Nazi Party yesterday; they're fighting to find jobs for us. Politicians squabble and build alliances to protect their fat asses while people suffer. We need results, not promises."

His father straightened, glancing at his mother, who stopped rocking Carly.

With cringed lips, Freddy's father said to him, "Fritz, you're not thinking straight. Don't do something you'll regret. Swallow your pride; go see Father Graf."

Fritz's chin lifted, and his puckered lips parted. "Sorry, Wilhelm, I can't. I've decided. I won't live off handouts. Father Graf's not right. The Nazis offer me hope and a chance to get back my pride."

And his father reached into his pants and pulled out a wad of money held in a shiny clip. "Here, Fritz, take the money; it'll hold you over for a spell."

Fritz shook his head, saying to him, "No, I can't, Wilhelm."

With a pained expression on his face, his father said, firming his words, "Fritz, don't be foolish. Think of Carly. Consider it a loan—you can pay me back when you're on your feet." Fritz blinked, observing his wife's nod, and seized the money.

"Thank you, Wilhelm. I'll never forget this. I'll pay you back first chance I get."

The corners of Freddy's father's lips and cheeks lifted. "I don't doubt it."

His mother's face softened, and she handed back Carly to Bettie Wurst. Freddy walked home in silence until his mother stopped and faced his father, struggling to get words off her mind. "Wilhelm, there's something bothering me."

"Yeah, Barbara, what is it?"

"Was it a mistake leaving America?"

With a grim expression, his father gave his head a soft shake. "Dunno, Barbara; it bothers me sometimes."

* * *

"What!" Albert said in a fit of rage, throwing the paper on the table.

"What's going on?" asked Curt, leaning forward in his chair, drawing in his lips.

"The headlines say Thuringia appointed a fucking Nazi as interior minister."

Curt's vision clouded, and he said, softening his voice, "Can't be true."

Albert's palms whacked the table. "Dammit! It is true."

Curious, Freddy seized the paper and edged it toward him. Albert drove his right hand over it, pinning the paper to the table. "Don't waste your time reading it; it'll anger you."

"Stop it, Albert; let go of the paper."

Albert's hand slipped off the paper, allowing Freddy to nudge it closer until he could make out the headline. He read Thuringia Appoints Nazi Minister in big, black, bold letters. His eyes searched for a date, finding one under the morning paper's name. It read Friday, January 24, 1930, four days ago. Appalled, he rummaged through the article and when he finished, faced Albert, pulling back in disgust.

Albert bared his teeth. "I warned you not to read it."

"Keep quiet!"

And his eyelids closed with anger burning inside him, and his mind swallowed its pride. *Stupid me, I underestimated the Nazis; Adolf Hitler tried to overthrow the government and went to jail for it.* And he imagined his outraged gymnasium teacher saying to the class, "Hitler spent less than a year in jail for such a severe crime." His skin tingling, he said with astonishment tinging his tone, "It's seven years later, and the Nazis now hold an important government office."

Startled by Curt's loud voice, his eyes sprung open. "Karla, three more beers, please," said Curt, disrupting Freddy's thoughts

"The beers are coming, Curt," screamed Karla, pulling away from the bar with full beer glasses, hurrying toward two elderly men with empty mugs in front of them; Freddy guessed they might be pensioners killing time at the tavern.

"Karla, I'll get Curt's beers," said Helga, heading for Georg.

Helga's hand trembled as she placed a beer in front of Albert. And she blushed while putting a beer beside Freddy.

"Thank you, Helga," said Freddy, seesawing his head, tight-lipped, afraid a smile could give her the wrong impression.

*   *   *

Albert made unwavering eye contact with Freddy. "You just missed her."

"Missed who?"

"Jette's friend Ester. She was unwell but wanted to drop off a letter from Jette," said Albert, grinning, sniffing it. "Ah, I smell perfume."

Karla frowned at him. "Jerk, give him the letter."

Freddy yanked the envelope from Albert's hand and opened it. Albert and Karla beamed, watching him read it.

Albert looked at him with a quizzical expression on his face. "Pleasant news, I hope?"

"Yes," he said, beaming, shaking Albert's hand.

The next day, warmer than usual for a November night, a few weeks past Jette's mother's burial, Freddy roamed a quiet street on which most shops were closed until he found the place mentioned in Jette's letter. Beneath its red and white awning, Freddy stood behind a curbside menu and peeked inside the café. Jette sat in a secluded corner, wearing black, toying with the top of her wineglass. A candle flickered, and its light danced on her somber face and the weathered bricks behind her. He took slow breaths, observing her till she caught him. And he opened the door, hearing a tingling bell, finding Jette facing him, weeping.

Her shiny eyes searched his face, and she cried her words. "Freddy, I miss her. I'm lost without her."

"I'm sorry for your loss," said Freddy, struggling to figure out the right words to tell her.

He held her tight, sat her down and stroked her back, catching her heavy sighs. Candlelight found the trails left behind from her tears when a short, plump old woman interrupted, wearing a soiled apron.

"Sir, can I get you something to drink?"

He said, lifting his cheeks a bit, glancing at Jette's wine. "I'll take the same."

His eyes caught Jette sipping wine with an unsteady hand, and he wished the gold liquid could lessen her pain.

"Freddy, what's on your mind?" Jette sniveled.

"It hurts me to see you in pain."

"Freddy, I love you," proclaimed Jette, edging a smile across her trembling lips.

Freddy's mind let go of its concerns.

"Jette, I will never stop loving you," Freddy professed, kissing Jette's wet lips while closing his eyes.

Jette assumed a pensive look.

"Freddy, I miss my mother. She was thirty-nine, twenty years older than I am, and will never see her grandchildren or hug them." Jette sniffed, regaining her composure. "Life's too short and unpredictable; we never know when it will end. Will it be today, tomorrow, or next year? But we can be sure it will. Oh Freddy, when my time comes, I don't want any regrets or to have missed a heartbeat. Before I die, I want to know I lived a full life and lived it with you."

Freddy needed to touch her and inched closer, detecting a rapid heartbeat. And she shivered and closed her wet eyes, surrendering her lips to him.

"Freddy, I want to lie beside you, stroking your face after we've made love—that's what I want from life."

And tingling with pleasure, he caressed her cheek and put his lips on hers, giving to her what she wanted from him, commitment.

The door opened, tinkling the overhead bell, and a man and woman stepped inside, ending their romantic moment. They hurried outside with yearning looks and roamed the chilly streets, using every chance to kiss and embrace. And they inched along a moonlit river, discovering a red-brick bridge, and eased over it, listening to waves made by a boat underneath them. Freddy steered Jette to a secluded dark spot between ornate statues on the bridge whose iron lamps had lost their soul. Caught up in the moment, he touched his lips to hers. And she unbuttoned her black coat and carried his hands to her breasts. His trembling finger caressed them. She sensed his nervousness and squeezed his hand. With his imagination fired up by her moans and breaths, she controlled his fingers. Her chest heaved, and she panted hard, wetting her lips. "Freddy, don't stop."

The sounds of the night returned after her last whimper. They walked off the bridge arm in arm, and they stopped briefly with beaming expressions to glance at the place where there blissful encounter occurred. And they gazed into each other's eyes before their mouths touched. At a busy corner, wishing the night would never end, Freddy hailed a taxi. He kissed Jette good night and helped her into a rumbling taxi, keeping tabs on it until its lights disappeared into the darkness behind buildings.

* * *

Days later, Freddy yawned and fluffed his soft pillow, thinking of Jette. He stretched, bringing a smile to his lips, welcoming the sun's light bursting through the opened curtains. In the comfort of his bed, he felt content, remembering the time spent with Jette. He finished breakfast and whistled, dressing in a tweed jacket before kissing his mother good-bye and within an hour bumped into Curt standing outside Professor Karp's classroom. "Where's Albert?"

"Leo's friends wanted to talk to him, alone; he won't be long."

"Um, that's odd, Curt."

Curt lifted and dropped his brows. "Yeah, that's what I thought."

Freddy checked out the time on the wall clock. "We should go inside before the bells ring."

Settled inside Professor Karp's lecture room, Freddy drew his lips into a straight line, seeing empty seats the Communists filled.

"Uh, I wonder if something's wrong. Leo's missing."

"You worry too much."

"Didn't you say one of Leo's friends grabbed Albert?"

"Maybe he wanted to borrow money from him."

Freddy heard the door slam and watched Professor Karp head to the podium. Loud footsteps pounded the floor behind him. His head cartwheeled, and his jaw dropped, as he discovered Albert huffing and puffing.

Expressionless, Albert tugged on his coat sleeve. "Freddy, come with me."

"What, why? What's going on, Albert?" he said, parting his lips, inspecting the room with adrenaline speeding through his veins.

Albert gripped his coat, pulling him. "I'll explain it to you outside the room."

Freddy's eyes assessed the room, stopping at Professor Karp.

Professor Karp frowned, pinching his chin. "Herr Hass, you're disturbing the class."

"Sorry, Herr Professor, but Herr Bauer must leave with me. It's urgent; don't ask me to explain why."

Professor Karp released the lump in his throat and pressed his lips together.

Albert yanked Freddy off his seat and dragged him up the steps before pulling him through the door.

"Albert, what's wrong? You embarrassed me in class," shrieked Freddy.

Albert's voice broke up, and he dragged his fingers along his cheeks. "I can't say it."

"Albert, say it."

Albert had a grave expression, and his head swept back and forth. "Freddy, Jette's dead."

Freddy stumbled back, with his muscles weakening, struggling to breathe, shaking his head slowly at him. "What?"

"Freddy, she's gone. They found her in an alley near the train station early this morning."

Freddy closed his lids, whimpering in darkness. "Albert, you're wrong. It's not her; it's someone else."

Albert gripped him tightly, whispering in his ear, "Freddy, she's gone. I wish it wasn't true. I know how much she meant to you."

His world having disintegrated in seconds, Freddy shuddered, feeling his body chill, replaying Albert's words. Alley, train station, dead. And he cried, saying, "It can't be. No— it's a mistake!"

Held in Albert's powerful arms, he stood on shaky legs, shedding tears from eyes darkened with pain. Devastated, he pulled away from Albert, taking rapid breaths, closing his fingers into fists, and he lifted his chin. "No, Albert, you're wrong; she's alive." His muscles convulsed from grief with eyes watering beholding the gray sky, he muttered, "Jette, I love you; you can't leave me."

Albert's head dropped, and his immense body withered. "Freddy, I'm sorry."

He sniveled and said to him, wiping his nose, in a distant voice, "Albert, I want to be alone."

"I understand. You can find me in the library if you need me," said Albert in a quiet tone, raising his cheeks faintly.

Freddy sucked in the crisp air, walking the university grounds with a stabbing pain in his chest, wanting to touch Jette. Red-eyed, he crumpled on a secluded bench, pushing pebbles underneath him with his foot, crying often. And he bowed his head and shut his eyes, praying for Jette. Mindful of crunching footsteps approaching, his eyes opened; he sniffed smoke and gazed up, holding back tears, minding Professor Karp's gaze as he smoked his pipe.

"Freddy, it's too chilly out here. Come with me to my office and warm up; we can talk."

In a mental fog, tormented by irrational thoughts and his loss, Freddy fought back tears, trying to explain to Professor Karp what had happened.

* * *

The next day, covered by thick black clouds, he grieved, hiding behind dense trees on dirt surrendered to dark green ivy. The veiny plant's creeping tentacles attached themselves to weathered gravestones, and trees conquering the ground. Freddy shed tears, seeing a crowd grieving for Jette. Women screamed, and other mourners comforted them. The pallbearers lowered Jette's shrouded casket into a grave lined with aged headstones on either side of it. He sobbed on shaky legs, catching sight of people praying alongside the grave. A bearded man wearing a black fedora wiped away tears with an unsteady hand as he approached a mound of dirt placed alongside Jette's grave. The man drew a shovel from it and scooped up dirt with his shaking hands and dropped it into the abyss where Jette rested. He kept his sight on a black-suited man till he finished staring in the hole. The mourner looked at the disturbed ground beside Jette's grave, holding his gaze on it.

Leo approached, holding a shovel of dirt, keeping his emotions in check. A woman screamed Jette's name at the same time Leo placed dirt in his sister's grave. Freddy turned an eye to two old women consoling Ester.

Later, in strange silence, Freddy gathered enough strength to leave his hiding place. He migrated through the cunning ivy that conquered the ground, inching to the front of Jette's grave. Heartbroken, he glanced up at the heavens, angry with God for taking Jette.

* * *

That evening a black taxi pulled up to an apartment building on the north side of the River Spree. And the vehicle's curbside door sprung open, with Freddy following Professor Karp out of it, each man wearing a black skullcap. Freddy froze, picking up his name. Ester Weitz hurried over to him, crying, and hugged him.

Ester's eyes misted with tears. "Freddy, what will I do without her?"

Freddy's mind recycled his pain. And his tongue tasted salty tears. "Ester, what happened?"

"Oh, Freddy, I begged her not to go, but she didn't want to stay home. She said it saddened her watching her father grieve." And Ester scratched her cheeks without breathing or blinking. "I was sick. She shouldn't have gone alone; she said it was her last time. It's my fault she's dead; she'd be alive if I wasn't sick."

Freddy sighed, twitching his nostrils, struggling to hold his emotions intact. "Ester, don't blame yourself; it's not your fault. How could she be in an alley?" lamented Freddy. "Why was she there?"

"I told the police Vladimir threatened us; they think he caught Jette talking to one of his girls and snapped. They believe he followed Jette and dragged her into an alley and killed her. Oh, Freddy, it could have been different if I were with her," said Ester, crying, blotting tears.

Freddy's fingers tightened into fists. *If I could find him, I'd kill Vladimir with my bare hands.*

Ester showed Freddy and Professor Karp up a white marble staircase, leading them to a dark-wood door with a water pitcher beside it. Professor Karp glimpsed at him, lowering his voice. "Freddy, wash your hands."

Ester gasped, flinching, and grabbed Freddy's hand. "Freddy, you were there, at the cemetery?" Freddy let out a sigh, nodding.

She sealed her eyes, bowing her head. "Please follow me."

And she kept her head low, inching inside a candlelit room filled with grievers sitting on boxes. Freddy's eyes teared hearing her introduce him to Jette's red-eyed father. Freddy's arm muscles tensed as he shook his hand. He offered his condolences, not wanting to let go of his hand, feeling a bond with him.

Freddy's eyes clouded, searching for Leo, paying attention to foreign words.

Leo appeared, pale-faced, picking through the mourners, stopping once to glance at a crying woman. He blinked hard, and his lips trembled. A youthful woman cried and rested her head against Leo's chest. Dead-eyed and breathless, Leo wrapped his arms around the weeping woman. Freddy assessed the woman. *She must be Sara.*

When Leo spotted Freddy and Professor Karp, his chin touched his chest. Freddy and Professor Karp rose, and Leo limped over to greet them. Freddy's face mirrored his sorrow. He understood his despair, walked with him in anger, and lived his heartache, but couldn't tell him why.

Leo gave him a feeble handshake, lowering his eyes.

"Thank you for coming," he said, before taking a seat beside his father and the mourners that gathered near him.

With a blackening expression and a breath lodged in his throat, Freddy played back Jette's commitment to always love him. And he pulled out a handkerchief, pretending to blow his nose, wiping off tears that built up in the corner of an eye, seeing Ester staring at him. Leo came back and sat alongside Freddy, rubbing an eye. Leo mumbled something Freddy didn't pick up. The second time Freddy understood him. "Jette, an eye for an eye."

On Friday Albert showed up at Professor Karp's room with a newspaper, and his fingers fumbled through it until he found the right page and handed it to Freddy. Freddy held his breath, reading through it. He reeled back, gawking at Albert. "Vladimir's dead, his battered body found floating in the River Spree. Police think he was the victim of a rival pimp." Freddy covered his mouth with his fist, thinking back to Leo's words.

Chapter Fourteen

Coping

With Jette on his mind, streams of tears ran off Freddy's cheeks, puddling on the desk. His insides quivered; he made the drops disappear little by little under slow circular motions of his index finger. *Why didn't I stop her?* The nagging question gnawed at his insides, and his eyes closed, hoping he could find a part of his mind less traveled, but he never did. His eyes opened wide, picking up an enticing drawing of a bare-breasted angel sleeping on the cover of Hemingway's *A Farewell to Arms*. He grasped, beholding the captivating woman's picture that love had escaped him and he would never see or touch Jette again. He dwelled on the man alongside the sleeping angel, thinking that he'd never share the ultimate state of pleasure with Jette. A knock on the door freed his tormented mind from its demons. The knocker tapped harder when he didn't reply.

"Freddy, did you hear me?" asked his father, pitching his voice higher. "We're leaving for church in an hour."

Freddy brought a shaky hand to his forehead. "Sorry, Father, I'm not well—staying home."

"What's wrong? You missed dinner last night. Your mother's worried, thinks you're studying too hard, and couldn't remember the last time we ate dinner together."

"My stomach's queasy, must have caught something that's going around the university."

"Hum, can I come in the room?"

"Maybe you shouldn't; you might catch it. Wait till tomorrow. I'm sure I'll be better by then."

And his fingers pressed into fists; he reacted to noise from the twisting door hand. He gave his father a nervous smile, watching him enter and inspect the room before sitting on the bed.

"Freddy? You've been acting strange, lately."

Freddy's posture sagged, and he glanced sideways. "Strange?"

"Stop, you're not fooling me. What's wrong?"

Freddy blinked hard, distorting his lips, and dropped his head.

"Freddy, talk to me."

"I-I want to be alone," stressed Freddy, bowing his head, envisioning Jette.

His father sucked in air through his nostrils, releasing it at a slow rate through folded lips.

"Freddy, look at me."

With a weighed-down feeling, taking unhurried breaths, Freddy kept his head bent.

"Look at me, Freddy."

His head drifted up.

"I've always been here for you. Why is it different this time?"

Freddy shuddered, unable to control his thoughts. "I-I can't. Please leave me alone."

"I'm not leaving till you tell me what's wrong."

A tap on the door made Freddy's head flinch. And when the handle moved, he cringed.

"Wilhelm, is everything okay? Can I come in?"

Freddy's lips spread wider, and he said, with panic in his voice, "Father, please, no."

"Barbara, not now; go to church alone."

"What's wrong, Wilhelm? Is Freddy sick?"

"No, he's not," said his father, tilting his head, making strong eye contact with Freddy. "Barbara, it's important Freddy and I talk."

"Okay, but what will I tell Father Graf if he asks where you and Freddy are?"

Freddy's father paused and narrowed his eyes. "Think of something in case he asks."

His father's head moved side to side. "Now, tell me what's bothering you."

Freddy's cheeks burned with shame, and he crumpled in the chair, staring at nothing. "I'm not the person you think I am. You deserve a better son. I'm a fraud, a coward who kept the truth from you by lying."

"Freddy, I don't understand."

"I made the wrong choices—the worst was deceiving you by telling lies."

"Freddy, you're scaring me. What did you do?"

Freddy let out a heavy sigh. "I fell in love."

Inconsolable, he told the truth, beginning with Jette at the Slippery Pig. Attentive, his father gave him understanding nods while he explained. And after he finished, his father moved off the bed, embracing him with a shine to his eyes. "I'm sorry you went through this."

Freddy wept, touched by his father's tight grasp.

And following mass his mother knocked, peeking in, squinting. "Wilhelm, what's wrong? I lied to Father Graf, told him you and Freddy were sick."

His father's lips pressed into a slight grimace.

"Wilhelm, what are you hiding from me?"

"Barbara, not now. Leave us alone; I'll tell you later."

"Huh!" said his mother, shutting the door; they heard her loud footsteps as she walked away.

Late that night Freddy heard the door nudge open and saw his mother's face through the crack, sensing she had found sympathy in her heart for him.

* * *

Freddy sped up worn steps, needing a fresh coat of shellac to the second floor and made a sharp right traveling through a congested corridor heading for Professor Rath's class. On the way he encountered Leo and his Red buddy Max and stopped to chat. Leo offered him a half-hearted smile, struggling to hold eye contact with him. "Hi, Freddy. Excuse me—I've something to do before class begins."

"Better be in the room on time."

"Fuck Rath," said Leo.

"M-Max, how's he doing?"

"Not good, he's lost without Jette. As if Josef wasn't enough for Leo, now he's lost his mother and sister too. He was close with Jette. She was fun to be with, made me laugh. Leo will never get over it. How could anyone? Spends Saturdays visiting their graves."

Freddy was weak-kneed, in a state of acute anxiety; his heart raced.

"Freddy, are you sick? Your face turned pale."

"I'm okay—maybe ate something that didn't agree with me at the corner café."

And motioning with his hand, Max shouted, "Isaak, over here."

Isaak pivoted, smiling. "Good morning. Sorry I was late, did errands. Where's Leo?"

"Gone. Said he'd meet us in class. Hey, Freddy," said Max, smirking, "walk with us, unless you're afraid Rudolf might see you."

"I don't care what Rudolf thinks. I'm meeting Albert and Curt under the wall clock. And I'll leave you there."

Freddy snaked through crowds with the two Reds until he discovered Albert and Curt standing idle underneath the brass-ringed time keeper.

Albert caught sight of him and nudged Curt with his elbow. Skin bunched around Albert's eyes as he glared at Freddy. "Can't decide what's less good, getting my head chopped off in prison or listening to one of Rath's high and mighty lectures. I cringe and want to strangle him every time he praises Hitler."

Curt swallowed, moving closer. "Freddy, it's not the same at the pub without you."

Albert squeezed Freddy's shoulder. "Curt's right. It's god-awful drinking without you. Millie and Karla ask when you're coming back; they miss you."

"Albert, the place brings back sad memories."

"You're wrong, Freddy; they were grand memories," answered Albert, tweaking his cheeks. "You met Jette there."

* * *

Soft knocks roused Freddy from sleep.

"Freddy, it's ten o'clock," said his mother in a quiet voice.

With his mind struggling to find sensibility, he wiped gunk from an eye.

"I'm up, Mother."

In blue pajamas, he sat in the kitchen gulping his milk.

"You were thirsty?" she said, softening her voice a little.

He gave her a nervous smile, furrowing his brows, expecting questions. "I was; where's father?"

"Out doing chores."

"Mother, is everything okay at work?"

"Freddy, I don't want to discuss it."

"You're worrying me; answer the question," said Freddy, waiting for her answer with a watery gaze.

She hung her head, breathing a few rasping breaths. "Your father's worried; he's afraid he might lose his job."

"Mother, don't worry yourself—he'd be the last sacked. He has lots of experience."

His mother's deadpan face adopted a cheerful expression. "Yes, you're right, he's a capable machinist. If they sacked him he'd find a job."

Freddy's vision blurred, and he hung his head with images of Jette dashing through his brain.

"Freddy, what is it?"

His head crept up with the corners of his mouth flickering; he could not hold a smile. "It's nothing, Mother. I'm just tired."

He picked at his food, sighing at the noise his mother made while turning the pages.

"Freddy, aren't you hungry?"

With a pained expression on his face, his shoulders fell. "I'm not that hungry, Mother."

"Freddy, we don't talk anymore. I miss it," she said, examining him with shimmering eyes.

He stared at his empty hands, with guilt blooming in his gut. "I guess we don't."

When he looked up, she offered him a polite expression. He focused on a teardrop in the corner of one eye. "Freddy, she must have been incredible to catch your eye."

His mouth cracked; he audited his mother's softened features.

With her blue eyes glimmering, her faced flushed, and she lost strength in her voice. "We can talk another time if it's too painful for you."

A slight chill shook his body, and he leaned back. "It's okay. I can't run from it forever."

His mother whimpered, wiping stray tears from her blue eyes. "Freddy, I'm sorry Jette's gone."

Freddy leaned in, seizing her trembling hand with downcast eyes. "I adored her. No one could take her place. My heart skipped faster when we were together."

Freddy's cheeks burned, and he inhaled to calm himself. "Jette's Leo Herzfeld's twin sister; he doesn't know we were together."

"We visited Professor Karp; he told us what he knew."

And with a sad demeanor, Freddy pulled his head back. "Then you know everything?"

His mother sighed, rubbing her fingertips slow over the coffee cup's handle.

Freddy's chin trembled; he spoke in a reluctant tone of voice. "I'm sorry I disregarded your warning, but I believe Leo Herzfeld is a decent person who lost his way and might change. Please try to understand?"

She gave him a warm smile.

He bit on his bottom lip, gazing at his hands. "Mother, she made it easy to love her. She was different—she challenged me, was full of contradictions. She could tease yet flatter or be daring yet cautious." Freddy's eyes clouded. "Mother, am I confusing you?"

"No, you're not," she said, sniveling, with eyes focusing inward.

Freddy's brain struggled to pull together illusive thoughts, and he wept, burying his head in his hands. "She wanted to live a complete life and love me doing it." He raised his head, dripping tears, causing his words to tremble. "I felt alive the first time I met Jette and empty inside when she left," said Freddy, closing his eyes. "Am I making sense?"

Her eyes closed. "Yes, you are."

"She wanted to keep our relationship a secret. I promised I could until she was ready." He wept, broken-hearted.

"I should tell Leo everything; it's not right to keep it from him any longer."

Speechless, she bowed her head, wiping a finger across her dripping nose.

* * *

Gravel crunched under Freddy's feet as he navigated through the city of the dead. He inched ahead, fighting demons that infiltrated his mind. Freddy stopped twice and spun around both times, but changed his mind and continued fighting his war. He swallowed, approaching a man's shadow, and his chin trembled as he eased closer. The mourner edged up detecting footstep, and said with a tremor in his voice, "It's you, isn't it?"

Speechless, Freddy wept and hung his head, catching leaves skip from a gust of wind.

"It is, isn't it?" said Leo, softly, keeping his head still. "She got through my mother's death because of you. Thank you. We never kept secrets from each other." Leo whimpered, cranking his head slowly. "She kept you a mystery; she said when I asked her, 'I'll tell you at the right time.'"

"It was complicated; it conflicted her."

Leo flinched and stepped back, gazing up at the gray sky. "You! I recognize your voice. Fr-Freddy, Freddy Bauer."

Leo pivoted, his legs shook, and he blew out nervous breaths through his pursed lips, concentrating on his face. "Fr-Freddy, Freddy Bauer, it's you." And he stepped back with a flat gaze. "Did you love her?"

Freddy's lips trembled, and he shut his eyes, squeezing teardrops from them. "Yes, she meant everything to me. I don't know how to carry on without her."

Leo gave him a vacant stare. "I miss her every day."

Freddy let out a heavy sigh. "I do too."

"Huh! Should've guessed it was you; she was interested in you."

Leo moved closer. Freddy was on the verge of tears; his vision clouded, and color rushed into his cheeks. "I should have stopped Jette. Why did I let her go?

"Freddy, it wasn't your fault." said Leo, hanging his head. "I'm glad you were in her life."

Freddy's eyes welled up, and he slumped, feeling his body grow heavy.

"Shiva must have been difficult for you."

And Freddy took audible breaths, wiping tears from his eyes with a shaking hand. "Jette's funeral was worse."

Leo faced him, spilling tears on each the side of his nose.

And both men cried, embracing each other.

* * *

Freddy sniffed, and his eyes darkened with pain as he focused on a book. In small print he recognized Ernest Hemingway's name on its spine, followed with bold letters placed one on top of the other, reading, "Fiesta." His shaky hand grabbed hold of the book and brought it toward him. He blew dust off the cover and detected particles floating in the air, caught by the lamp's light. A portrayal of a couple sitting at a café reminded Freddy of magical moments spent with Jette. He opened the book where a green marker lived and strummed the unread pages, imagining Jette from time to time. He snickered, picking up cries from whipped-up voters and honking horns. A few times, he jumped up to catch sight of the commotion outside his window. Once, a truckload of high-booted Brownshirts beating hard on drums and waving flags passed under the window urging voters to vote Nazi Party. At another time a group of Social Democrats paraded demanding labor reform while boys ran haywire up the street, passing out leaflets to anyone who'd take one.

The front door shut, waking his dreamy mind, and he placed back the bookmark. Freddy's brain filled with questions, and he pulled up a chair in the kitchen.

"Well, how did voting go?"

His mother glanced at him, exhaling a heavy sigh. "Freddy, it's a madhouse out there. People shoved handouts in our faces and begged us to vote for the Social Democrats Otto Wels, the Communist Ernst Thalmann and Adolf Hitler. An adolescent boy, maybe ten, pestered your father till he took a leaflet from him for Alfred Hugenberg."

"I believe you. I heard the racket outside my window."

His father's eyes brightened as he admired his wife.

Her cheeks brightened a rosy color, and she blinked. "Stop that, Wilhelm."

An image of Jette flashed in Freddy's mind. He frowned.

"Is something wrong, Freddy?"

"No, nothing's wrong," he said with a fake smile. "Why do you ask?"

"For a moment you looked sad."

"I'm okay; is there more?"

"Yes, while I waited to vote, I bumped into churchwomen without their husbands. There's no excuse for it; the Centre Party relies on the Catholic vote. Father Vogel could not stand for it back home, and Father Graf reminded everyone to vote last Sunday."

"Mother, maybe their husbands are minding the children, or were busy doing something else and will vote later."

"Huh! You could be right. It's a pity, Freddy, you're not yet twenty; the party could've used your vote."

Freddy pondered his political choices, having on his mind he'd never consider a right-wing party.

"Mother, why are you convinced I'll vote Centre Party? I could vote for the Social Democrats, the largest party."

"What! Nonsense, where's this talk coming from, the university? Freddy, your sense of loyalties to the church... the Centre Party's the only one that takes care of Catholics. What could I tell Father Graf or Father Vogel if you voted another way?"

"Nothing. It's my decision, not theirs."

"Wilhelm, is this what he's taught at the university?"

His father squeezed her hand. "There's no reason to get upset. Freddy's giving himself elbow room. I'm sure he'll see things your way by the time he votes."

With her eyes locked on him, Freddy's mother frowned. "Ugh! Freddy Bauer, what should I do with you?"

He spoke with a gleam in his eyes. "Nothing, Mother. I'm perfect; don't you agree?"

* * *

"Friedrich, promise not to keep you long. You must be hungry. But I want to give you something."

With a smile, Karp drew a book from his desk.

"I've just finished this novel and enjoyed reading it."

"Last month my sister, who lives in New York, sent me a copy of Ernest Hemingway's newest. I read it in my office. Here, it's yours to keep, takes up too much space in the desk. Besides, Nessa will be mad if I bring it home. I told you she doesn't approve of Hemingway, didn't I?"

"Thank you, professor. Promise you I'll read it," said Freddy, glowing. "Oh, *A Farewell to Arms.* Huh! It's written in English?"

"What's wrong with that?" said Professor Karp, sneering. "You know how to read English?"

"Herr Bauer, there's lots you don't know of me."

Freddy slanted his head away from him. "Ahem, what's in the book?"

"War and love, topics that interest young men. And with two Ernest Hemingway novels to read, you'll be busy this summer."

Freddy could not contain his smile.

He arrived at the Slippery Pig, blowing air on his icy fingers. Karla spotted him and hurried to him with a cool beer.

"Thanks, Karla, you're a mind reader."

"You're welcome, Freddy. I'll gather something in the kitchen for you to eat."

"God, it's chilly outside. Can't find my gloves; must've left them in Professor Karp's office," concluded Freddy, blinking hard, gazing at Albert and Curt.

"Why did Professor Karp want to see his prize student?" asked Albert, sneering, speaking in a sarcastic tone.

"He gave me a book written in English."

Curt's brows lifted. "In English?"

"English?" said Albert with a disbelieving stare.

"Yes, English; he surprised me. It was the first time we had spoken in English."

"Who wrote the book?" asked Albert, shifting his eyes to Freddy.

"Ernest Hemingway."

"I've heard his name; he's a famous writer."

Curt tilted his head to the side. "Freddy, what's it about?"

"War and love, Professor Karp said."

Curt gripped Freddy's shoulders, squinting at him. "Can I see the book?"

"Sure." Freddy angled his body to reach inside his briefcase for the book.

Karla showed a cheeky smile, reaching the table with Freddy's beer. "Sausages coming, Freddy, be out in a minute."

"It took him fifteen minutes to give you a book?" said Albert, scrunching his eyes.

"Yes, it did."

Freddy sipped the crisp beer and snorted, wiping foam off his nose. "Hum, why is it the first sip of beer tastes better than the second?" His smile disappeared as he picked up a loud, angry voice.

"Heh, bitch! We've waited long enough; move your fat ass and bring the beers," a man screamed out.

And Freddy caught another laughing out loud. "That's telling her, Gerhard—she better move her fat ass if she knows what's good for her." Albert's eyes bulged, and he banged his hands against the table, making empty beer glasses jump. He sneered, tilting his head at the noise, drumming his fingers on the table.

A man's voice neared a scream. "Hurry, bitch, bring the beers before I get mad."

Albert's jaw thrust forward. Freddy's head pivoted, locating angry Brownshirts wearing black military boots, waiting for Helga to bring their beers. Helga stood still, waiting for Ren to finish pouring the beer. Millie confronted them, hardening her tone. "Pay up and get out. I don't need your money."

A storm trooper rose, giving Millie a hard smile. "Fuck you, bitch. I'll do what pleases me; no fat woman's telling me what to do."

Millie's face reddened; she gave him a pained stare. "That's it—get out before I get the police."

"You heard her—get out; you're not welcomed here anymore," said Karla, pushing her head in his face.

He laughed at her and shoved her hard, sending her tripping to the floor. Albert jumped up, spilling beers, knocking his long legs against the table, and charged the Brownshirt. The man's lips flattened, and he threw a right-handed punch at Albert's head that missed. Albert delivered a stiff right to the smaller opponent's jaw, dropping him to the floor. Helga screamed and rushed into Ren's arms. Millie's mother popped out of the kitchen door, looking confused, mumbling something. Millie screamed, "Police, police," fleeing out the door with a few customers. Five Brownshirts left their table, cursing, heading for Albert. He spread his legs and shot a straight right to the stomach of one. He grunted and curled up on the floor, holding his stomach. Two men leaped on Albert, and he threw them off him. Karla sprang up, biting one's hand. "Ouch," he cried and seized Karla's pigtails, swinging her to the floor.

Freddy rolled his fingers into fists and headed toward two Brownshirts, eyeing a target. He moved in on him, throwing a hard right in his face, sending the big-eyed man earthward. The second threw a punch with his right hand that Freddy deflected with his left elbow, and he discharged an uppercut against his jaw, catching his teeth click together. The instigator got to his feet and whacked Curt on his chin, dropping him with a dazed expression on his face. Freddy sidestepped two of his blows and connected with a left to the mouth, dropping him unconscious beside Curt, who was bleeding.

"Hope you killed the bastard, Freddy," yelled Karla with a fevered stare, staying on the floor.

A Brownshirt picked himself up, throwing punches at Freddy with both hands. He deflected the blows with his arms and ducked to avoid one more before bloodying the Brownshirt's face with hard jabs. The man swayed on his feet, and he held him up with his left hand and angled his right arm, preparing to deliver the haymaker, but reconsidered, listening to the defeated man whimper, "No more."

Freddy's lips curled. He released his grip, and the Brownshirt dashed for the door without glancing back. "Coward, next time you won't be so lucky," said Freddy, pounding his fist.

"You broke my nose." And Freddy pivoted, finding a Brownshirt on the floor with blood spilling from his nose.

Albert held another in a headlock, bloodying his face with punches. Masked in blood, the man's legs no longer could support him; he dropped, lifeless. Three Brownshirts dragged a friend out the door, leaving a trail of blood.

"This isn't the end of it!" one said, screaming, heading for the door.

"Come back, you'll walk funny the rest of your life," said Albert, wiping blood off his lip with his sleeve.

"Albert, you okay?" asked Freddy, studying Albert's cut lip.

"There were only six. Back home, I'm used to an even dozen," said Albert, nudging Freddy with a genuine smile, enlarging his eyes. "Hey, Freddy, who taught you to fight? I liked your style."

Freddy lifted his chin, imagining Karl and Gunter's approving glances.

Karla applied a wet towel against Curt's forehead, snapping him out of his trance. "Helga, get more ice from Ren." When Helga returned, she added more ice in the towel and held it against Curt's head.

"Ouch, that hurts," screamed Curt, pushing her hand away. "What happened?"

Karla smirked, reapplying the ice to his head.

"I can do it myself," squealed Curt, grabbing the towel.

"Curt, don't be a jerk; let me hold it on your head," seethed Karla, baring her teeth at him.

"I'm fine, Karla. I don't need your help."

"Shut up; let her help you!" said Albert, glaring at him.

And while Curt made a face, Millie rushed inside, panting, with two black-booted blue jacket police officers wearing leather hats. Wide eyed, each officer sized up the room.

One said to the other matter-of-factly, "I see minor damage, Herman."

"You'll never catch them standing there," said Karla, frowning, with her hands on her hips.

The taller of the two men gave Karla an icy glare. "Uh, we know how to handle it; file a complaint at police head-quarters."

"They'll get away," said Albert, grimacing, staring down his nose at them.

The second officer stiffened, speaking with contempt in his voice. "Berlin's an immense city; where do you suggest we look for a few bloodied Brownshirts in it?"

"You can start by following their blood trail; I'm sure that's not too difficult for you." Albert said mockingly, smirking at him. Millie flopped in a chair once the indifferent officers departed, widening her eyes, exhaling hard through her nostrils, and inspected the room, before narrowing her focus on Curt. She lowered her voice a notch above a whisper. "How's your head, Curt? Should we get you a doctor?"

Curt removed the ice pack. "I'm less dizzy and don't need a damn doctor."

Millie gave Curt a stony stare and faced the bar, speaking in a breathy voice. "Ren, three beers and a glass of water for Curt."

"I don't want water; get me a beer," said Curt.

Albert narrowed his eyes at him. "You'll drink water."

Karla brought over the beers and water. Millie grabbed a beer and chugged half of it, belching. Freddy's blue eyes widened as he believed she never drank beer.

Pale-faced, Helga froze, standing alongside Ren. Curt's fingers tapped the table. Freddy worried he had suffered more than a head wound. Curt's fingers stopped, and he mumbled something. Seconds later, loud, abrupt words shot out of Curt's mouth. "Shit, Brownshirts are everywhere; I hate them."

Curt moved his head in circles. Freddy moved closer to examine his eyes. "Curt, are you okay?"

With glazed eyes, he sat speechless. "Say something, Curt; you're scaring me," said Freddy, with uneasiness stirring his stomach.

"The blow to his head made him dizzy. I know how it feels. He'll live," said Albert, squeezing Curt's shoulder.

Curt remained speechless, moving his head from side to side. Freddy hyper-focused on Curt, moving closer to him.

Albert released a hard sigh. "What's wrong? Why do you hate Brownshirts?"

"Stop! Albert, he's not himself," said Freddy, with his tongue peeking out between his lips.

Curt's right hand shook as he finished a sip of water. "I'm fine. Leave me alone; it's personal."

Karla and Millie eyed each other before walking away. And a relaxed smile crossed Curt's face when he saw them leave.

"Curt, what is it? Why can't you tell us?" asked Freddy, with a quizzical brow arched above his right eye.

Curt's fingers made red streaks on his face as he dragged them against his cheeks.

"We're friends, remember, we said we'd be honest with each other?" said Freddy, gulping a lungful of air.

And Curt cringed, dropping his head. "It's awful."

Albert gave him a hard smile and said, with his temper erupting, "Dammit, Curt, what is it?"

"Albert, it's my hell, not yours."

"Bullshit. What is it?" said Albert, glaring at Curt. "I'll get you to tell me—do you understand?"

"Okay, I'll tell you," said Curt, shiny-eyed, in a harsh tone. "The Brownshirts did horrible things at the Hitler Youth camp."

Albert glanced over at Freddy. "Wasn't it fun and games?"

"No, it wasn't," snapped Curt, touching his chest with his chin. "I caught two Brownshirts sodomizing a boy in the woods. I-I-I thought they saw me. It made me sick, and I quit the Hitler Youth. At daybreak I sneaked out my tent and hiked home." Curt squeezed his eyes shut. "I shook and jumped off the road each time I spotted a car or truck coming. When I arrived home, I told my parents what happened, and my mother cried."

With an ache in his throat, fastening his eyes on Curt, Freddy said, "How dreadful that was."

"They visited my home, wondering where I was. My father told them I wasn't coming back to the scouts."

Freddy pinched his chin, doubting Curt would ever shake the demons that had bored into his mind that horrible day.

* * *

Freddy sat up, flexing the fingers on his sore right hand, refocusing his pupils on sunlight bursting through the window. He checked the time and noted the date on the calendar: Saturday, March 1, 1930. Hungry, he dressed and hurried inside the kitchen smiling, "Good morning, Mother."

She looked happy, glancing at him and continued whipping the contents of a bowl. "Good morning, Freddy; you slept late."

His father dropped the morning newspaper, studying him. "I'm glad you slept late. I worry you're not catching enough sleep."

And Freddy sniffed, wiggling his toes. "Mother, what smells good?"

"Sugar cake; that ought to delight you and your father."

He flashed his white teeth, jiggling the coffee pot, figuring there was a full cup in it. "Great! How old's the coffee?"

"Made it half an hour ago, surprised any's left. Your father likes his morning coffee with the paper."

Freddy snatched a cup and emptied the pot into it, with enough room for milk, and settled in a chair, grinning, noticing his father's head shifted back and forth, traveling from one line to another in the paper.

"Remember me? I'm your son, Freddy," he teased, minding his father.

The man's wrinkled lips spread into a grin, and he rested the paper on the table.

"Sorry, got caught up with something. The Nazis are holding a parade for Horst Wessel today."

"Horst Wessel?"

"He's the Brownshirt two Communists shot in January. He died a week ago."

"I know his name; it comes up often at the university."

"Goebbels is giving the eulogy at his burial."

Freddy's forehead wrinkled, knotting his stomach. "Think they'll be trouble when he gives it?"

"You never can tell; it didn't please the Communists."

His mother turned around and cocked her head to one side. "It worries me; can we talk of something else?"

Freddy sipped his coffee, feeling that he was being watched.

"Freddy, what happened to your knuckles?" asked his father, engrossed in his swollen knuckles.

"What! Let me see." And Freddy detected a spoon drop behind him with his mother seizing his hand, paying attention to it. "What happened? Were you in a fight?"

"No, banged it on a desk."

Her voice softened, pressing on a knuckle. "Does this hurt?"

"A little."

"You should be more careful; you're lucky it's not broken."

A relaxed smile crossed his face; he guessed they had bought his lie when she went back to beating the contents of the bowl and his father continued reading the paper.

"Oh my, Wilhelm. I'm short on sugar; can you run to Klein's and get me more?"

A pinched expression appeared on his father's face. "Why are you always short on sugar?"

"You know I don't keep too much sugar in the kitchen; it attracts cockroaches."

Freddy finished a sip of coffee. "I'll go, Mother. I don't mind; I need a whiff of fresh air. I'll eat when I return."

And he rushed out the apartment door and raced for two blocks, finding himself at Klein's grocery. He entered, detecting a metallic chime from an overhead bell. Herr Klein peeked through the curtains, looking delighted, and he pushed them aside, hurrying behind the counter.

"Herr Bauer, it's you?" cheered the heavy man with a thick gray walrus mustache, "My, my, how big you are. Your mother tells me you're studying to be a lawyer; that's a wonderful thing to be if you ask me. Right?" Still smiling, Herr Klein leaned on the counter. "What can I get you?"

"A pound of sugar will do."

Herr Klein bared his gums, filling the bag with a large measurer from a metal bin on the counter. Herr Klein's lips curled; gazing over Freddy's shoulder. Freddy twisted his head, giving a quick glance to a crowd waiting for a cable car on the corner. Herr Klein's face turned pale, and he shut his eyes.

"Herr Klein, what's wrong?"

The storekeeper opened his eyes, shaking his head slow. "Sorry, Herr Bauer, look at the gathering waiting for a streetcar. Someone said the crowd headed for the Street of the Jews near Saint Nicolas to attend Horst Wessel's funeral procession. Imagine that, paying homage to a street thug and listening to Joseph Goebbels bigoted words. What's this world coming to?" Herr Klein sobbed, blinking hard. "I installed the bell to stop thieves from robbing my store."

He paid Herr Klein and stepped into the street, becoming aware men were screaming. And he spun around, sizing up a truckload of Nazi's spewing antisemitic phrases. His eyes zeroed in on one of them, circling his lips. *No, it's the Brownshirt who begged for mercy at the Slippery Pig.*

Freddy stopped, expecting to find Albert and Curt in their usual spot, standing under the clock. He shrugged and continued walking till he stood under the timepiece, exhaling with a *pfft* sound, lowering his voice below a whisper. "Huh, late again." An uncontrollable shutter swept through his body as he recalled the Brownshirts' words while leaving the Slippery Pig. His head recoiled, widening the space between his lips, and he redirected his thoughts after catching loud cries nearing him. Petie, a red capped fraternity brother spoke in a gruff voice. "We must punish the Communists who murdered Horst Wessel."

Petie's voice inflected his tone. "They should lose their heads in Plotzensee Prison." Freddy's gut tightened, and he expelled air through his nose, examining the gruesome scar on Petie's right cheek. He cringed, closing his eyes, thinking of others with the same disfigurement. *How could anyone believe a grotesque scar from a dueling match is a badge of honor?*

Freddy suppressed a shutter, seeing Rudolf and his cronies meeting with fraternity brothers. He tilted his head toward them, detecting anger in their voices. And edged away, taking a few fast breaths, feeling his stomach tighten. Rudolf spotted him and sneered, folding his arms across his chest. Freddy returned a nervous smile, backing away, noticing a tingle in his chest. His lips sprung open, and his breaths quickened, noticing Leo, Max, and Isaak with a stranger, sensing trouble. Rudolf's and Petie's faces reddened, and they locked eyes on them. Rudolf stepped in front of Leo, shouting in his face, "One of your pimp degenerates killed Horst Wessel."

Leo flinched and stepped back, drawing his brows together, glaring at Rudolf.

Petie breathed hard through stretched nostrils. "The Red should have his head chopped off in Plotzensee Prison."

Max bared his gums, keeping Petie in sight. "He was a worthless shit who slept with and pimped for a whore."

Rudolf's smirk grew larger as he sized up the outnumbered Communists. Freddy's legs spread apart, and he drew his lips together in a snarl. Leo's eyes narrowed; he ballooned his cheeks before blowing out air. Rudolf gave Leo a stony gaze, inhaling through his nostrils. They bumped chests, staring into each other's eyes. Rudolf shoved Leo back, using the space between them to punch Leo in the face. Leo's head rocked back from the blow and blood dripped from his nose, but he stayed on his feet and delivered a punch to the side of Rudolf's head. Leo grabbed onto Rudolf, forcing him downward.

Petie dropped his fraternity colors, cursing Max, and charged him, throwing a straight right punch, which bounced off his left arm. Isaak and the stranger backed up, approached by five-right-wing students. One of them threw a punch at Isaak, and he moved his head aside to avoid it. Isaak scowled, tightening his fingers into fists, placing his hands in front of his mouth. Smaller than Isaak, the unknown man's chest bounced as he breathed through his nose, and his neck disappeared, raising his hands to protect himself.

Freddy's face went red, and joined Isaak and the stranger, hearing his heart beat in his ears. His pupils enlarged, and he exposed his gums with adrenaline speeding through his veins. His arm pushed aside a left-handed jab thrown by a tall student, and he bent before springing up, striking him hard with a right hook to his side, making him grunt and corkscrew in pain while he headed for the floor. He sucked in his cheeks, assessing the aggressors with narrowed eyes, and started banging his fist into his palm. "Who's next?" A red-capped bully stepped back in horror, followed by the others. Freddy's lips formed a circle; he blew a long breath through them. "Fight, fight—there's a fight!" A voice screamed.

Students flooded the halls when the bell rang, ending the fight.

Unmarked, Petie and Max rose, panting, keeping each other in sight.

Rudolf rolled on top of Leo and kneed his belly, anchoring his weight with his other leg. Freddy yanked him off Leo, fearing he might hurt him. "Rudolf, that's enough."

Flushed, Rudolf rose, giving Freddy a fevered stare, and walked up to him, directing a foul breath in his face before filling his words with hatred. "One day I'll kill you."

Freddy's skin bunched around his eyes, and he shoved him, quieting his tone. "And how will you kill me? Hit a chair over my head when I'm not looking?"

Rudolf's lips shook with a vein pulsating in his neck.

He crossed his arms, digging his eyes into Rudolf, firming his voice. "It wasn't a fair fight. Is that how the von Kriegs earned their medals?"

Rudolf's voice took on a malicious tone. "Your time on Earth has an early end date; I'll make sure of it."

He was hypervigilant; his breathing sped up, and he monitored Rudolf till he disappeared inside a classroom.

"Freddy, thanks for helping us." Freddy turned, discovering Leo grinning with a drop of blood falling from a nostril.

* * *

Freddy flinched, observing the Slippery Pig's front door missing. Saliva collected in his mouth as he ran his eyes over bits of glass stuck in the frame where the oversized window once sat. He passed through the charred doorjamb and caught sight of Millie standing at the bar speaking to Albert and Curt, and spotted Ren seated with Millie's mother alone at the next table. His eyes roamed the room, and he saw Karla and Helga sweeping up bits of glass. Dull-eyed, he eased himself over the floor. "What happened?"

Millie fussed, shedding tears. "Four Brownshirts tried to burn the place while we were sleeping."

"How do you know it was four Brownshirts?"

Millie said, "Two strangers saw them jump off a truck. One spilled petrol on the door and lit it, and the others threw bricks through the window. They laughed and hopped back on the truck, and it sped away. The strangers put out the fire with their coats."

"Lucky they came by," says Freddy, inhaling fast and releasing a quick burst of air out his mouth, "I hate to think what could've happened if they didn't."

Helga finished sweeping up the last pieces of glass in a dustpan. And with glazed eyes, Karla picked up a brick and handed it to Albert with a trembling hand, saying, "The noise woke me up. A voice yelled, 'Fire, fire, fire.' I'll never forget it. I shook Helga and bumped into Millie coming from her mother's room. We hurried downstairs, smelling smoke, noticing broken glass from the front window spread over the floor. My eyes burned, and I stepped on a piece of glass, cutting my foot."

"Why, why'd they do this?" said Millie, crying, pressing her hands against her chest.

"For revenge," said Albert in a scathing tone.

"But Albert, I didn't hurt them."

"No, you didn't, but we did. They want to get even with us for the whipping we gave them," answered Freddy, widening his eyes, lining his forehead.

Fear covered Millie's face. "Oh no," she said, and she covered her mouth with the palm of her trembling hand.

Freddy pulled up a chair for Millie. "Sit. You need to be off your feet. Karla, get Millie water."

It saddened him to behold the wet-eyed woman with a colorless face, distressed.

Her hand trembled as she took a drink of water. Then she looked at Freddy, widening her eyes. "What should I do?"

With a hopeless feeling, his belly knotted, he said to her, softening his voice, "Millie, I don't know."

"I do," Albert's tempered voice spouted. "She should sell the place before it's too late; it's not safe to live here anymore."

"I can't sell it; the place is full of memories with my late husband, Peppi."

Curt let out a heavy sigh. "Did the police come?"

Millie breathed shallowly, and her head slumped. "Yes, two, asking questions and said they'd be back."

Albert's neck corded, and he tensed his words. "Millie, don't bet on it."

Karla's head shook hard as she glared at Alberts. "Goddamn you, Albert, keep quiet."

Helga dropped her broom and dustpan and sat with Ren and Millie's mother.

Albert wore a sheepish smirk on his face, spotting two police officers and a heavy-set man wearing a fedora and thick belted black coat walking through the door.

In a deep voice, the beefy man said, "I'm Detective Kowalsky. Um, where can I find Millie Wurfel? I'm here to investigate the firebombing."

Her words drained of emotion, Millie said, "That's me. I'm Millie Wurfel."

Detective Kowalsky's eyes brightened, and he tilted his head at Karla. "And you must be Karla Dietz, right?"

"Yes, I'm Karla Dietz."

Kowalsky focused on a table in the corner. "Ladies, tell me what happened over there."

After the detective and the police officers left, Albert frowned, examining Millie. "What did he say?"

"Detective Kowalsky said it's easier to find a needle in a haystack than the Brownshirts who did it," said Millie, shivering, gazing at her hands.

"Tell him to buy a magnet!" said Albert in a rage, running his hand through his hair. "I'll bet you he's knows who they are?"

Karla's head shook. "Stop it, Albert, you're scaring me."

"The evil bastards won't stop till they burn the place," fretted Albert, stretching the tendons in his neck.

Millie shook, huffing and puffing. "No, they can't, it's all I have."

"We'll figure something out," said Freddy, squeezing Millie's hand.

For a short time, Albert, Curt, and Ren rotated nights at the tavern until the women relaxed. And Millie offered Albert free lodging if he'd move in to the tavern.

Albert said, "Free beer, food, and bed—can you beat that?"

A smile came to Freddy's lips as he pictured Karla tiptoeing to meet Albert late at night.

* * *

Freddy frowned, catching a whiff of unpleasant tobacco smoke in the air. Professor Karp extinguished his pipe and pointed to the newspaper below him.

"Well! Herr Bauer, what's your opinion of the insignificant street brawlers now? Six million people voted for them. Now the Nazis are the second largest party in the Reichstag."

Professor Karp's nose sucked in air, blowing it from his mouth. "But I must confess the election results didn't shock me. Nessa and I vacationed with my daughter Miriam and her husband, Johan, at their home in Munich last month."

"Yes, I remember you mentioned it."

"Well, as it was, days before Hitler's speech, Nazis organized rallies, handed out leaflets, and stuck posters all over the city. A friend of Johan's, a Jew no less, visited the Circus Crown to listen to him. Hitler promised he'd put people back to work, restore German glory, and take care of the Jews." Karp scratched his head. "Hitler was everywhere. Every time I picked up a paper, he was giving a speech somewhere in front of enormous crowds. Traveling by plane made it easy for him." Professor Karp's lips twisted into a grimace. "When I visited the New Synagogue on Oranienburger street, the election results had stunned the elders; now Hitler's no longer a joke."

Freddy slumped, and his voice shook. "The outcome caught me by surprise too."

With tight lips, Professor Karp eyed him and shrugged. "Germany has enough problems, now she must contend with this right-wing extremist. It bothers me what can happen to the country if Hitler succeeds."

"Herr Professor, can't the courts stop Hitler?" Freddy swallowed, struggling to hold his eyes on him.

The professor shut his eyes. "Herr Bauer, I wish I knew the answer."

Freddy could not draw a breath. His throat constricted; he feared his world might crumble.

Professor Karp coughed, focusing on him. "Tell me how it went at Adler and Beiner."

"Hard work, same faces, but this year Herr Beiner spent more time with me," said Freddy, bringing a slow smile to his face. "Huh, Hugo Hahn never blew his stack; that was unusual."

A faint smile appeared on Professor Karp's lips, and he raised his thick eyebrows. Freddy guessed he had told Beiner that Hahn had bullied him.

"My grandfather died."

"I heard; Alfred mentioned it to me. My condolences to you and your family."

Freddy sighed, fixing his eyes on a unique brass dog-shaped pipe holder resting on one corner of the professor's desk. *Jette, now my grandfather.* "Herr Beiner patted me on the back and gave me time to attend his funeral. He was a proud man who smiled when I caught him peeking at me. I loved him but didn't know him; I didn't visit the farm often. Does that make sense to you?"

The attentive man dipped his chin. "It does."

Freddy gave him a vacant stare, noticing him fondling a blue stone on his cuff link.

"Jette's always on my mind. At night I can't sleep—demons prey on me till first light." Freddy sobbed, his voice weakened. "I don't know what to do; I can't live without her."

Professor Karp leaned in, nodding. "It'll take time for your heart to mend."

Freddy covered his face for moments, minding his words.

"I surprised Leo when I turned up at Jette's grave; it went better than I imagined."

"Friedrich, it's a good thing you did; now you can get peace of mind."

"Dinner's ready, Stefan," said Nessa, tapping on the door.

"Good, I'm starving. Friedrich, Nessa's cooked up something special just for you and warmed plenty of almond pockets for you to take home with you."

Professor Ziegelberg appeared in the room, limping, striking the floor with even beats of his cane. The thin gray-haired man wore a mustache that curled at both ends and a pointed beard, with creases folded under his eyes. He stood in his usual spot on the floor, supporting his weak right leg with the cane. Ziegelberg never stood for over five minutes. Freddy overheard a student state a horse fell on his leg and fractured it somewhere in Belgium during the war.

The class moved along without incident until Ziegelberg put forth his arguments for supporting the League of Nations.

"And class, it's my opinion," said Ziegelberg, pulling on his beard, "that world order will never come until there's a place for nations to air their differences. Ahem, without the league aggressive nations could go unchecked."

Rudolf von Krieg rose, raising his fist at Ziegelberg. He shook his head hard and raised his voice. "That's nonsense, Herr Doctor. You're wrong. It's the right of every country to decide its destiny, and not the leagues members living well in Switzerland. No, Herr Doctor, I don't buy your argument. The league's part of a shitty scheme to make sure Germany pays off its war debt and renegotiates the terms when she can't. Herr Doctor, does the league give a shit about Germany? Tell unemployed workers and their families they care."

Professor Ziegelberg glared at Rudolf and bashed the floor with his cane. "Stop! Sit, Herr Krieg. Germany, and Austro-Hungary must pay damages because they started the war."

Rudolf raised his voice, waving a finger at him. "No, I'm not finished, Professor Ziegelberg. The Freedom Law made it a crime for officials to collect money to pay them. Herr Doctor, you're mistaken if you think the treaty's worth the paper it's written on. Germany should never apologize for causing the war, nor should she pay one fucking reichsmark in restitution for it. Your kind are nothing but fucking traitors."

Right-wing students rose, pumping their fists in the air, saying, "Traitor, traitor, traitor," stomping in cadence hard on the floor.

Ziegelberg's face blushed red, and he screamed, "Stop it, or I'll give your names to the rector."

Rudolf's supporters' voices quieted.

Rudolf rocked and gave him a pained stare. "You are an insignificant old man whose time has passed," raged Rudolf, lifting his chin with an evil smile. "Go see Rector Vogt; I have rights."

And Rudolf stood taller and lifted his chin.

"Sit. Your behavior sickens me," Albert screamed, standing up, facing Rudolf.

"Idiot! Sit!" said Isaak, glaring at Rudolf. The rest of the class rose and shouted at Rudolf and his supporters to sit.

Whack, whack, whack. Ziegelberg clobbered the desk with his cane. "Enough, sit. It's your last chance before I give the rector your names and demand you're booted from the class. He might disagree with my position on the law, but I'm sure he'll agree with me that your behavior was inappropriate."

Rudolf's nostrils flared; he moved his lips and collapsed in his seat.

"Herr von Krieg, we live in a democracy, and you have every right to express your opinion, and to be frank with you, I welcome it in class," replied the squinty-eyed professor, keeping Rudolf von Krieg in view, "but this is not a forum in which to misbehave and use foul language. I won't stand for it. Hugenberg and Hitler campaigned hard for the Freedom Law, and voters rejected it. Your emotional outburst was out of order and accomplished nothing."

Rudolf rose, sneering. "You're wrong. I showed the class what you are, a leftist traitor."

Nationalist students stood, raising their fists and stomped on the floor, chanting loudly, "Traitor, traitor."

Professor Ziegelberg's eyes lit up with indignation and he slipped back, giving the class a harsh squint. "Stop it!" he screamed, giving Rudolf a harsh look. "I won't tolerate disobedience in my room." And he turned and limped toward the door, giving his head a slow shake.

Freddy combed through rows of angry students leaving class. And Albert sat still with an unfocused stare. "Fuck!"

Freddy nudged Curt, motioning his head toward Albert.

Albert's face blushed. He clenched his fingers into fists, and he barreled up the stairs, pushing aside two right-wing students in his way.

"Hey, watch who you're shoving," griped one, refusing to break eye contact with him.

Albert aired his teeth and punched him in the stomach, sending him crashing into the arms of the other man. Freddy chased after Albert, keeping his fingers crossed he didn't cause more problems. He imagined Albert assaulting others. He caught Albert outside the room as he shoved Rudolf against a wall. Rudolf's face flushed as he struggled to remove Albert's large fingers from his throat. He drove up his left hand, freeing himself from Albert's grip. Albert whacked him, and blood gushed from his nose. In a dazed state, Rudolf drew a nervous breath. Albert smiled, holding a clenched fist. Rudolf's companions urged him to continue. A middle-aged professor wearing horn-rimmed glassed picked up the fuss and came between Albert and Rudolf. "What's going on here?" said the black-haired professor, using a harsh tone laced with concern.

Big-eyed, with his brown pupils surrounded in white, Albert gulped for air. "Nothing."

The professor frowned and shook his head, eyeing Rudolf's nose, saying, "If it's nothing, then why is his nose bleeding?"

Albert crossed his arms. "I don't know why, professor. Ask him."

The angry man turned to Rudolf. "What happened to you?"

"It's a nosebleed."

The middle-aged professor glared at Albert and Rudolf. "Move on, but go different ways."

"Albert, you'll regret this happened," huffed Rudolf, noticing the professor out of earshot.

"Oh yeah, can't you see I'm shaking?"

Rudolf's lips hardened as he glared at Albert. "We'll meet again; the next time it will be under my conditions."

Freddy's face lined and his throat constricted; he gathered right-wing students had tipped the scales of justice at the university in their favor.

Chapter Fifteen

Never a Dull Moment

I t thrilled Freddy achieving high third-year grades; a smile creased his face as he pedaled his two-wheeler harder, weaving through traffic, speeding toward Adler and Beiner. At one point he raced past a truck, ignoring the crossing guard, who blew his whistle loudly at him. Heavy traffic forced Freddy off his wheels in front of the Reichstag building. His smile faded as he focused on the spot where he had met Jette two years ago. His head and shoulders sagged, and he steered the two-wheeler, taking slow steps the rest of the way.

And released a pent-up breath as he edged inside Adler and Beiner's door. Berta's face glowed, and she rose and took quick steps to embrace him.

"Friedrich, I've missed you; it so good to see you again," she said, wrapping her arms around Freddy.

"I've missed you too; how's Arnie doing?"

Berta fidgeted with a button on her dress. "No better no worse, but thank God I've someone to take care of him while I'm at work."

How can she smile with an invalid son harassed by Agnes Peters?

"Herr Hahn will be right back; he's meeting with Fräulein Peters and Herr Meier is in the conference room."

The front door opened, and Hugo Hahn penetrated the room, stopping in front of him, exposing a wry smile. "Good morning, Friedrich; we were expecting you. Hope your year at the university went well?"

Freddy put a fake smile on his face for the self-absorbed man. "Good morning, Hugo; it did. We've plenty to discuss, don't we?"

Hugo Hahn stared at him, nodding. "Oh, Herr Beiner wants you to attend a meeting in the conference room at one thirty."

Freddy shrugged. "I'll be there. Why the meeting?"

Hugo displayed a hard smile. "You'll find out when you come; I don't have to discuss it with you."

Freddy eyed Hugo till he disappeared on the other side of the conference room's door. He tilted his head at Berta, releasing air from his puffed-up cheeks. "Berta, do you know what's happening?"

Berta checked out the conference door, filling her lungs with air. "Nazis killed a Communist."

"A Communist?"

"Yes, they attacked them in daylight."

Freddy's mouth sprung open. "What!"

Berta pulled in her shoulders and crossed her finger over her mouth, "Shh."

The conference room door slam shut, and bony Agnes Peters appeared clutching a file, bolting toward Berta and Freddy. The insensitive redhead's face burned shades lighter than her hair. Freddy figured she displayed a bogus smile. "Good morning, Friedrich. Good to see you again," said Agnes, shifting her meager weight to the other foot. "Herr Hahn's driving me nuts. Here Berta, put this in the Fischer file, and bring into the conference room what I asked you to do yesterday."

The tight-lipped woman glanced at him, saying, "Excuse me, I must head back."

He giggled, echoing Agnes Peters' voice. "Good morning, Herr Bauer, good to see you again."

A smile danced on Berta's lips, and she clapped her hands.

"Berta, are Herr Beiner and Herr Adler here?"

"No, Herr Beiner's out and will be back after lunch. Herr Adler's not been well and seldom visits the office."

Berta's smile turned into a frown, and she pulled out a folder from her desk drawer. "I forgot Agnes needs this in the conference room."

Freddy finished a quick bite at a corner sausage cart and hurried back. He stepped through the door, finding five men dressed in black pants with rolled-up sleeves on their blue shirts; one wore an arm cast.

"Friedrich, Herr Beiner's been looking for you," said Tillie, arriving, Herr Beiner's middle-aged secretary with salt-and-pepper hair.

Albert Beiner's lips danced, settling into a grin. "Friedrich, welcome back," he said, gazing at Tillie. "I was telling Tillie how much I miss you."

Tillie focused on him, giving a polite smile. "Everyone did, Friedrich, but Berta has never stopped grinning since she heard you were coming."

Herr Beiner paused and ran his eyes over him, pinching his thick mustache, shaking his head. "Friedrich, you haven't changed one bit."

Beiner cranked his head toward the standing woman. "Thank you, Tillie; you can go."

And he sat up straight, pointing at a chair with his cigar-bearing hand.

A frown clouded Freddy's face as he fell into a seat in the smelly room.

"Friedrich, I wanted to speak with you before the meeting starts. I talked with Herr Karp before he left; did you know he's visiting his sister in New York?"

"I did."

"Talked with him Saturday, glad you're doing great at the university. I decided it was time you took part in meetings with clients. Oh, one more thing,"—Albert Beiner beamed—"I asked Agnes to give you a twenty-five-mark-a-week raise; you'll earn it, and it should get Herr Karp off my back."

His cheeks dimpled as he audited Herr Beiner's cheery face. "Thank you, Herr Beiner. I won't disappoint you, and I will show you I deserve it."

Alfred Beiner lifted his chin, fingering his bushy black mustache. "I'm sure you will."

Freddy followed Beiner inside the conference room, his chest beating, his fists clenching and unclenching.

Beiner hunkered down at one end of a long table and parked his unlit cigar in a glass ashtray, and motioned him to sit. Albert Beiner's thick brows wrinkled, and he stared at Hugo and Jan. "Are you ready?"

Hugo and Jan said, "Yes."

Alfred Beiner's voice firmed. "Good. Impress everyone with what you know."

Red-faced, Hugo's lips turned into a lopsided grin.

Alfred Beiner hardened his words. "Herr Bauer, ask Frau Koch to bring in the gentlemen."

"Yes, Herr Beiner, right away."

Berta entered the room with the five men Freddy had spotted earlier, seating them across the table.

Herr Beiner brought a slight smile to his tight lips, inspecting the Communists. "I'm Attorney Beiner. Who is Karl Fischer?"

A scrawny man of average height with thinning black hair rose and sneered, revealing he was missing a front tooth. "I'm Karl Fischer."

"Herr Fischer, please sit."

The man lowered himself into a chair.

"It says here that the state has charged Karl Fischer, Paul Becker, Gunther Schwartz, Leon Roth, and Wolf Busch," read Herr Beiner catching a nod from each man named, "and that you breached the peace and you,"—pointing his finger at Karl Fischer—"started it, causing Arnold Roth to lose his life."

Karl Fischer's chin bounced up and down, and he jumped to his feet, hardening his gaze. "That's a damn lie. We're the victims, not them; they attacked us."

The men eyeballed each other, shaking their heads. Leon Roth walloped the table with the palm of his uninjured hand. "We did nothing wrong, we're innocent, and Karl didn't cause my brother's death."

Alfred Beiner spoke, darting his eyes at the Communists. "I concur. Who wants to explain to me what happened?"

The defendants conferred with each other and reached a consensus.

"I will," said Karl Fischer, hanging his head, lowering his voice. "I've more to lose than the others."

Alfred Beiner concentrated on Karl Fischer. "Start at the beginning and leave nothing out," then he glanced over the others, forming a straight line with his lips. "If he does, interrupt him and tell me what he omitted."

Fischer bowed, fondling a few strands of his sparse hair and glanced up, drooping his eyelids. "After we walked out of Communist Party headquarters in Berlin-Mitte, it was near six on my watch; we were hungry and headed for a close-by pub for something to eat. We joked with each other, unaware a bunch of Brownshirts were following us. One of them shouted, 'Kill the fucking Reds,' and they attacked us."

Alfred Beiner raised his eyebrows. "Hmm, how many were there?"

"Over ten; it happened so fast." Fischer shrugged and checked to see if any of his comrades doubted the number.

Alfred Beiner fumbled with his unlit cigar. "Huh, over ten, maybe twelve or thirteen Nazis?" He touched his parted lips, using a wistful tone. "Not what I'd call a fair fight, is it?"

Herr Beiner focused on Leon Roth. "Tell me what happened to Arnold."

Leon Roth's voice strained. "A bigger man punched Arnold; that's the last time I saw him alive."

Freddy squeezed his chin, holding air in his lungs. And his belly warmed as he imagined what the Nazis had done to Arnold. He stared at Leon, clenching his teeth. He blinked hard. "How did you get away from Brownshirts?"

Roth shifted his eyes at Freddy, saying, "Who's he?"

Freddy winced, coloring his ears red, expecting to be chastised for his intrusion.

"Herr Bauer's a bright law student studying at the university. He works for Adler and Beiner during summer break and is an asset to the firm. Herr Roth, you can answer him."

Beiner's kind words brought a slow smile to Freddy's lips, and he became energized.

Roth stared at him, letting out a heavy sigh. "Two police officers broke up the fight and held two Brownshirts. The Nazis pinning my shoulders got up and ran off with the others. Arnold's head was bleeding."

Hugo Hahn examined Roth's sling. "How did you break your arm?"

Glossy-eyed, Roth checked the sling. "Didn't notice it till the fight ended."

When the meeting adjourned, Freddy left the room with a head full of doubts and plopped at his desk with a slight quiver in his stomach. He ran his hands through his hair, mulling over the court's malfeasance toward the Reds, recalling what happened to Nils Keller. His lower lip trembled, and he wrapped himself in his arms, recalling what Professor Karp told him kept him up at night.

"Friedrich, is everything okay? You look sick," said Berta, pinching the skin on her neck.

He shuttered, envisioning what had happened. "I'm fine. Too much on my mind. It's been an unusual day."

* * *

Nef Muller placed his hand over his black, yellow, and blue fraternity colors on his chest with an upturned face. "Friedrich, each time the bishop speaks, he fills the auditorium. He never brings notes and speaks his mind." The square-faced man with thick black specs frowned, checking the time. "What's keeping Manny?"

"Manny?"

"Oh, sorry, forgot to mention he's coming; Manny's a frat brother."

Freddy cursed Father Graf under his breath. Sorry he talked him into attending the bishop's speech with Nef Muller. He sighed heavily, studying the bishop.

Bishop Klaus von Rauch smirked, paying attention to the student leader. He rose, releasing his grip on a gold cross attached to a conspicuous chain at the end of his introduction. Dressed in black, wearing a purple skullcap with a radiant face, he sashayed to the podium with the majesty of a king. The gathering rose, smacking their hands together, and cheered the exalted man until he motioned to them with his hands to quiet the crowd. Bishop Rauch beamed, accepting the audience's approval. The holy man brushed back his purple cape and extended his arms to claim the podium. "Thank you, Herr Engel, for your kind words, but they were too short. May I suggest before the next time I speak, you come to see me so I can give you more remarkable things to say of me."

Nef rose, beaming, to make room for a student wearing matching fraternity colors and cap. "Manny, glad you made it, wondered if you changed your mind. Meet Friedrich Bauer."

"Oh, the smart one." The toothy student grinned, shaking Freddy's hand. "Pleased to meet you, Friedrich."

Bishop Rauch cleared his throat, wringing his hands. The room grew quiet, and the bishop's head dipped, making the sign of the cross. "Let us pray. Heavenly father, enlighten us to withstand the blackness and give us the strength to finish our journey. Let us pray. Heavenly father, hear our prayer and offer us righteousness and wisdom to prevail and reject the temptations championed by Satan." Bishop Rauch dropped his head. "Let us pray. Heavenly father, hear our prayer and protect us from evil. In Jesus's name, amen."

The man of God raised his head and seized the hanging cross in his hand and lifted it over his heart. "A proverb says, 'The devil's favorite piece of furniture is the long bench.'"

Bishops Rauch pressed his lips together and lowered his thick black eyebrows, which thinned out as they approached his ears. And his head moved slowly over the onlookers as he let out a heavy sigh. "But what does that mean? It means you better get it right the first time; it might be your only chance." Freddy played with the button on his sleeve, taking to heart the holy man's words.

The solemn man ran his index finger over the crowd, shaking his head. "No, you cannot plead ignorance or make excuses when you are knee deep in wickedness. You will answer to

God for your sins. A heavy burden is placed on your shoulders. If you fall from grace, you will pay the ultimate price."

Bishop Rauch stuck out his chest, nodding. "Many years ago, the Centre Party ascended to preserve the church's autonomy and protect it institutions. Bismarck and Protestants marked us but could not deter us. We are Catholics and support the Holy See, but in affairs of state, I might argue we should be independent. Catholics fought and died for the kaiser in the Grand War and our doubters could no longer question our loyalty to the state. From our party's ranks came prominent politicians and four chancellors."

The bishop's heavy black brows narrowed and pursed his lips. "The far right is disinterested in decency. Oh yes, they're willing to concede ground, if it suits their purpose. But remember, if you cut off the head of a snake, it still can bite."

Slack-jawed, heeding every word said, he kept his eyes riveted on the sage.

"Their chorus preaches hate where ours sings of love and praises the heavens." Bishop Rauch grew still, examining his audience. "Which one of these natures do you choose?"

Nef's breath touched his ear. "Incredible, isn't he?"

Freddy uncrossed his arms, scrutinizing the bishop.

"The right dispenses justice with swords, and we with godliness. I ask you, which virtue do you wish to follow? You have a choice, and you ask yourself, why does this humble servant of God ask me which one I'd choose? I chose the latter one. But are you that sure you won't become Judas Iscariot and betray God for thirty pieces of silver? I acknowledge nationalists accept Christianity but only because it serves their purpose, and you should not judge them from what they say but from what they do. In the New Testament Jesus warned, 'Beware of false prophets, which come to you in sheep's clothing, but inwardly they are raving wolves.'"

Bishop Rauch waved his palms, quieting his audience, except for erratic coughs. A luster appeared on his face. And he lifts his chin, shrinking his eyes. "Yes, I reject German nationalism, its elitist beliefs, its territorial ambitions, and the right-wing politicians of the Centre Party who favor it," he cried out, shaking his head. And he paused, examining the still crowd. His harsh tone softened. "I pray for the soul of Matthias Erzberger, a party leader whom ultranationalists murdered a decade ago because he wanted peace and condemned heartless territorial expansion. The superpatriots want absolute power, to rule with a big stick and limit personal freedom. I choose not to live under that roof, one held up by violence, intolerance, suspicions, and expansionism. But nationalists claim it's for our own good; should we trust them? Tell that to the fallen soldiers buried in foreign fields. Did they die for their own good or the greed and ambitions of others? If you are a staunch believer in God, follow the commandments and reject false promises made by schemers sent by Satan."

Bishop Rauch stood still, panting, inspecting the crowd. He sneered, discharging firm words through his lips. "I declare here and now before God that I renounce nationalism's single-mindedness and the impractical visionaries who lead them through the gates of other sovereignties, plundering their land and wealth."

Tight-lipped, Bishop Rauch made eye contact with the members of the silent crowd and waved his index finger over them. "Many of you may be undecided or just outright reject my arguments. It's written on your lips, in your eyes or the movement on your heads." Bishop Rausch wrapped his arms around himself, and his inflated cheeks discharged air through his puckered lips, and he untied his hands, seizing the podium. "Satan will never renounce sin or quit trying to tempt us. He wears many guises. He lives everywhere; his emissary could be a fellow student, a prominent professor, and yes, I hate to say, even a holy man. But those I fear the most are the evil socialists dressed in brown who dispense justice with fists and clubs. We should assess their godless behavior, never forgetting their failed coup just eight years ago. If you keep God in your heart, you'll realize trickery and treachery won't victimize you. It says in the Bible that Jesus spent forty days and forty nights in the desert fasting after his baptism. Satan thought he was weak and vulnerable and tempted him three times, but Jesus could not accept it and said, 'Away from me, Satan! Worship the lord your God and serve him only.'"

Bishop Rauch stepped back, gazing up a moment. "Our faith in God is what protects us from temptation. A staunch believer follows what's written in the Bible. The Gospel of John says that the Apostle Thomas did not believe Jesus rose from the dead. Jesus showed Thomas his wound and let him touch it. Now you ask yourselves why, why does this matter? It does if you doubt your faith. I ask you to remember that Jesus showed Thomas what the Romans did to him before he ascended into heaven. You should take comfort in knowing that if you give yourself to God and resist temptation, he will never abandon you. A Bible verse from the Corinthians enlightens us: 'That your faith might not rest in the wisdom of men but the power of God.'"

A smile came to Bishop Rauch's face at the end of his speech, and his eyes sparkled as he admired the cheering crowd. And Freddy clapped, contorting his lips, rehashing the bishop's speech. *I wish he didn't spend his last fifteen minutes conversing on the seven deadly sins, with his assessment of lust for the longest part.*

Thirsty, he stood at a bar in a murky room. Manny ordered three beers from a scruffy bearded man wearing a dirty shirt who overfilled three mugs and thumped them on the bar, frowning, waiting for payment. Freddy reached inside his pants and pulled out a handful of coins and slapped them on top of the smelly bar and smirked. "Does that cover it?"

The grungy man left five pfennigs change and waited on a shouting customer.

And Freddy lifted his beer, beaming. "Cheers."

Manny caught sight of four capped students leaving and claimed their space. Freddy sipped his beer, absorbed in Bishop Rauch's cautions.

Nef gazed at him, gripping the table, raising his voice. "Friedrich, were you surprised at Bishop Rauch's candor? It makes him popular with Catholic fraternities."

"I was," said Freddy over the noise, "but I'm sure it's made him many enemies."

"Too many. He could suffer the same fate as Matthias Erzberger, murdered taking a walk," said Manny, baring a mouthful of ivory.

Nef leaned forward. "Do you agree with Manny?"

"I do, but the bishop's bluntness also could find him in court answering to judges."

Manny said, squinting, "Friedrich, what are you studying at the university?"

"Law."

"Huh—pegged you for medicine."

"Why, medicine?"

Nef's cheeks lifted. "You remind me of my doctor."

Freddy elevated his chin, saying to him, "It came to mind before I chose law."

Manny angled his body toward Freddy. "Why did you change your mind?"

"Is this an inquisition? What comes next—a rack with thumbscrews?" he said, crossing his arms, grimacing.

Manny's face blushed; he cleared his throat. "Ugh, sorry, didn't mean to pry."

Freddy placed his hand over his heart. "Can we discus something else?"

Manny squinted, eyeing Nef. "That's fine with me."

Nef raised his eyebrows at him. "Good, Manny. Did you read any of last week's fraternity newspaper?"

Manny frowned. "Didn't get around to it."

"It reported Bishop Rauch and Father Brandt were at odds with each other and weren't talking. The bishop worries Father Brandt spends too much time pandering to the right."

Manny blinked hard. "How can Father Brandt succeed if neither the left nor right will compromise? Bishop Rauch offered to intercede, but Brandt didn't want him interfering in his affairs."

Freddy rubbed his nose and proclaimed, "What's he got to lose if he asks Bishop Rauch for his advice?"

"His pride, that's what," said Nef, leaning toward him.

He gave Nef an empty stare.

Nef bowed his head, giving it a few shakes. "The party's torn between old and new ideas. Bishop Rauch is correct, the right won't budge till they win."

"I bet I know which side you're on, Nef," said Freddy, making a funny face.

"The right one, right?" said Nef, with a relaxed smile crossing his face.

"Huh, the right one? You fooled me; I thought you might favor primitive ideas."

Nef's eyes glowed. "Friedrich, I see you have a sense of humor."

Manny spoke, exposing his oversized teeth, "Friedrich, join our fraternity."

"Manny's right; why don't you?"

"I'm honored you considered me, but I've no time for it."

Manny grinned, leaning forward. "Friedrich, join up with us; you'll be glad you did."

"Sorry, Manny, the answer's still no."

Nef leaned closer to Freddy and took off his glasses, rubbing an eye. "Remember, Bishop Rauch said impressive men came from our ranks."

"I expect to be working for an excellent law firm. I intern at a law firm and get paid for it. They appreciate me; that is worth something."

Manny's face lit up, and he grinned widely. "Friedrich, you can buy us one more beer."

Manny chugged his beer and mopped up his white mustache with swipes of his tongue while checking him out and asked in a reluctant voice, "Uh, uh, bet you enjoy lots of girlfriends?"

A lopsided curl formed on his lips. "Not one."

Manny persisted. "Why not? With your looks you should boast hundreds."

Freddy had an image of Jette on his mind. His bottom lip quivered, and he checked the time. "No more questions. We agreed to end the inquisition."

* * *

With cheeks deflating, Freddy entered Professor Karp's office. He detected a smell of stale tobacco and sneered, fanning his face. Professor Karp squirmed and bared his teeth, easing himself into a chair, lowering his head. Freddy's throat constricted as he eyed him. "Is there something wrong, professor? You wanted to see me?"

Professor Karp rubbed the corner of an eye. "This day can't end soon enough; it's brought nothing but pain."

"Oh, sorry to hear it; something wrong?"

Professor Karp fumbled with his pipe and gazed at him with a sad expression. "Alfred Beiner phoned, said the court ruled against the Communists."

Freddy blinked hard and slumped. "What! They're innocent men; they defended themselves. This can't happen."

Professor Karp's nostrils flared, and he rose, concentrating on Freddy. "The two police officers lied, said it involved only six in the fight, the exact number charged, and they didn't know who started it. Under oath Arnold said to the judge there were at least four more, but he didn't buy it. The six Nazis testified under oath that Karl Fischer threw the first punch and Arnold Roth tripped over a curb and fell on his head. The Nazis insisted Arnold Roth called them faggots. Judge Diehl agreed with the Nazi's lawyer that the Communists were to blame and sentenced Karl Fischer to six months more for starting the fight."

He kept Professor Karp in sight, running his fingers through his hair, realizing there was a slow burn in his gut. "Are Diehl and Jung associates?"

"They are."

And Freddy shut his eyes, shifting his head back and forth more and more slowly. "I wasted my time. There's no rule of law; why didn't I study medicine or a physics? What was I thinking? I was a dreamer, filling my mind with foolish ideas, tricking myself into believing I could change a corrupt world. How could I stomach laws that partisan judges dispense?" Freddy gave Professor Karp a hard stare, blushing a red tone. "Tell me I'm wrong, that I didn't make a mistake."

Freddy waited for an answer.

Professor Karp stroked his chin. "I understand your predicament, but you didn't make a mistake."

Doubtful, his face tightened.

Professor Karp crossed his arms. "Not the reaction I expected from you."

Freddy's voice grew weary; he glanced at his hands. "I'm sorry, I don't know what to think anymore."

Professor Karp moved his head forward, firming his tone. "I believe the Friedrich Bauer I know is a fighter committed to justice. A bad verdict could never deter him. Was he a fraud?"

His chin touched his chest.

Professor Karp's voice turned as hard as steel. "Well, which one are you?"

Freddy sucked in his cheeks, regaining his self-worth, and blew a warm breath against his forehead before giving him a grimacing nod. "I'm not an imposter!"

"That's what I thought," said Professor Karp, growing a smile on his face.

"I'm sorry, don't know what came over me," said Freddy, hardening his stomach.

"I do. You discovered judges can prejudice justice; it won't be the last time. Consider it a learning curve," said Professor Karp, smiling, sounding self-righteous.

And he assessed Professor Karp's words, furrowing his brows. "You might be right."

Professor Karp's smile faded, and he covered a piece of paper with his hand, softening his voice. "Friedrich, Frau Koch's son died, Alfred Beiner gave me her street number; he figured you wanted it."

"Oh, no!"

"Alfred said you and Berta were close."

His lips trembled, and he spoke in a low, pained voice. "Berta's a good person."

Professor Karp bowed his head. "Friedrich, I'm sorry."

Freddy slumped in the chair, thinking of Berta, and rubbed the corners of his eyes. *Berta has a hard life, but she's never bitter.*

Karp shook his head back and forth slowly before gazing at the ceiling and closing his eyes. A few seconds later, he snapped out of his trance.

"Um, where was I?" he said, rubbing his chin. "Oh, dear me, I'm sorry, I've got too much on my mind," Professor Karp conceded, remembering.

He watched the professor wipe his nose. "A bunch of students shouted at me walking here; one hollered 'Jew pig' behind my back. It upset me, and I vented my anger at Nessa over the phone. I must remember to bring her flowers later."

Freddy pulled back in disgust, crossing his arms. "Did you recognize them?"

Professor Karp took in a long, loud sniff of air, lowering his eyes. "No, the smiling faces I'm used to seeing changed into hateful stares. Was it that easy for them to persuade others to dislike me?"

* * *

Freddy's eyes widened as he grasped a faint *rat-a-tat* before swallowing a mouthful of beer.

He spread his lips wider, staring at Albert. "Do you hear that?"

Curt shrugged, catching Freddy's glance.

The *rat-a-tats* grew louder; *ra, ra, ra, ra* blared trumpets. Freddy hurried to the window, picking up the music's beat. The music stopped, and tight-lipped youths wearing black shorts and ties and brown shirts marched in place, accepting money from the crowd.

"Oh, don't they look handsome dressed in their uniforms?" said Karla, standing on a stool overlooking the crowd.

Three boys gripped long poles with Nazi flags swaying in the wind, led by the marchers, with rows of boy musicians marching in step behind them.

"Who's making the racket, a circus band?" asked Albert, approaching.

His smile disappeared, and his temple furrowed as he flicked his eyes over the band. He hurried outside, pushing ahead of onlookers, raising his fists at the boys. On restless legs Freddy frowned, picking up Albert's booming voice. "Boo. Hatred doesn't solve problems; it only angers God. Go home to your mothers."

Curt's chest caved in when Freddy came back, and he lowered his head. "I couldn't watch them. The music brought back dreadful memories."

Tight-lipped, Albert plopped into his seat, grinding his teeth. "The Nazi schemers are poisoning their minds; the boys should be home kicking a soccer ball with friends, not learning to be barbarians."

Freddy covered his face, reminded of what hatred had done to his life. Tears welled up eyes as he considered images of Jette, Clarence Johnson, Rolf, and Rolf's father.

* * *

Freddy shivered standing on the Gorlitz Station platform, delighted to see snow whiten the ground, observing a clouded puff of air fading out of sight.

"Son, a pfennig for your thoughts," asked his mother with a gleam in her eyes, wrapping herself in her arms to keep warm.

"Only one pfennig, that's what I'm worth?"

"It's not snowing hard enough to keep us from reaching Berlin before dark," opined his father, dropping his smile, scratching his head. "I wonder which one's right."

"Which one, father?"

Freddy's father's eyes widened, and he did a double take. "The wall clock or my watch—they differ by five minutes."

And his mind revived thoughts of Jette gazing at a pile of snow-covered railroad ties. *She's been dead two years; I miss her. Why, God, did you take her from me?*

"Um, Freddy what's wrong? Why the sour puss?" asked his mother, examining him.

"I'm tired, got little sleep, and the carriage ride bored me."

And she pouted, fidgeting with her coat button. "We weren't on a sightseeing trip. Uncle Dieter tried his best to get us here on time; the roads were wet."

Freddy caught a long whistle blast from the snow-dusted train pulling into the station. "Father, which one?"

"Which one what?" His mother blinked fast, scrunching her eyes.

"Mother, the time between the station clock and father's watch."

And he helped his mother climb the metal treads and followed her into the warm bowels of the car. Dead tired, Freddy collapsed into a window seat and closed his eyes.

His mother said, sniveling, "Wilhelm, I was on the verge of tears leaving her. The visits are too short."

"It wasn't the same without grandfather," said Freddy, slumping.

"It wasn't, was it?" said his father, tightening his focus.

A moment of silence passed before his mother said with an empty stare, "My mother tired and dipped her head a few times while I spoke to her."

"Huh, wonder why," said his father, nodding, slowly smiling."

Freddy detected an uneven smile on her creased lips. "Wilhelm, I'm worried; it's not a joking matter."

His father's eyes scrunched, and his voice softened. "At her age, I'd expect her to doze off now and then."

"Mother, she's fine."

She blinked hard, gazing at his father. "Between you and me, and don't tell a single person—"

"Not even Freddy?" asked his father.

"Wilhelm, can't you be serious? Gretchen's worried; she says Werner fights with his father and won't listen to his uncles."

"He reminds me of your father," said Freddy's father, crossing his arms.

His mother's lips lined, and she looked away. "My God, Wilhelm, is there a chance he will?"

With a straight face, Freddy said, "Take a breath. He'll change; give him time to mature."

His mother hardened her voice. "Freddy, you never talked back to us."

He leaned in toward his mother. "Werner and I are different; you can't expect us to act in the same way."

His mother fretted in a breathy voice. "I hope he doesn't take after my father now that he's wooing Maria." She made strong eye contact with him. "Please forgive me, Freddy, I shouldn't have said that."

Freddy's smile widened.

The train's whistle tooted three times before the train lurched forward and chugged its way over the tracks. "Train for Berlin, next stop Horka, checking tickets," announced the conductor, his voice booming.

Freddy drifted to sleep, wakened later by the ticket collector's loud voice. "Cottbus next stop."

He opened his eyes, fixating on his father. "How long was I sleeping?"

"I guess an hour," answered his father, nodding.

Freddy yawned and stretched, circling his head. "Wish I had slept longer; did I miss something?"

The corners of his mother's mouth fell. "Your father and I were discussing his job."

"Oh, is there something I should know?"

His mother's face slackened, and she stared at her hands, quieting her voice. "It wasn't important."

"Mother, are you sure? You look upset."

His father rubbed his arm, closing his eyes briefly. "She worries I'll lose my job."

"Um, should she worry, Father?"

His father bowed his head, rubbing the back of his neck. "I'm not sure anymore."

Freddy's lips cracked open, and he gazed into his father's eyes. "That's not what I expected to hear from you."

And he pulled out a book, biting his bottom lip, agonizing over his father's job. The train arrived on time, and Freddy's mother sidestepped into the aisle and edged forward with his father at her heels. Freddy picked up a suitcase, grabbed his book, and hurried. The book slipped through his fingers, and a cheeky youthful girl picked it up and put it back in his hand. Freddy locked eyes with the bewitching girl, displaying white teeth, gathering he'd laid eyes on her another time. "Thank you. Um, do I know you?"

"No, you're mistaking me with someone else," beamed the girl, cocking her head to the side.

"Sorry, I thought I'd seen you before."

Her face lit up. "Don't think so. I'd remember it."

And he eyeballed the sparkling butterfly clip in her hair, easing along the aisle. At the bottom of the steps, waiting on his father, she disappeared into a crowd heading for the station. He let out a hard sigh, shaking his head slowly.

"What's wrong, Freddy?" said his mother. "Did you forget something?"

"No, thought I recognized someone."

"Did you know him?" asked his father, concentrating on Freddy, wanting an answer. "Well, did you?"

His shoulders slumped. "It was a girl; she didn't know me."

"That's odd. Hmm, could be you've seen her at the university."

Freddy nibbled on his bottom lip, convinced he knew the appealing girl from somewhere. "It's her! I'm sure of it."

And he dropped his bag and dashed toward the station, holding his book tight. He burst into the building, huffing and puffing. He checked out the waiting room for the girl, but couldn't find her. An opened-mouthed police officer furrowed his brows, assessing him.

A porter came by, wrinkling his nose. "Uh, sir, can I help you?"

"I'm looking for a lovely blond girl; did you see one?"

"No, sir, I'd remember if I did."

Freddy burst out the door, racing along the street, looking for her. Breathless, he slumped at a street corner, shaking his head. *Did I miss my last chance?*

Chapter Sixteen

1932: Hate and Love

"Wilhelm, it's Sunday, April tenth. I should be home preparing a roast, not voting for a president a second time in less than thirty days."

And catching a slight chill, Freddy buried his hands in his pockets. "What a shame, Mother, President Hindenburg just missed getting reelected, but I wonder at eighty-four if he's capable of doing the job."

His father's slight smile veered into a sneer. "Who would you prefer, the nationalist Adolf Hitler or the Communist Ernst Thalmann? Both men are in their forties."

Freddy's chest caved in, and he bowed his head and said in a low, shaky voice, "No, but I worry at his age President Hindenburg might die in office."

With a mocking grin, his father fixed his eyes on him. "There's no alternative."

He chewed the inside of his cheek, concentrating on his father. "What if President Hindenburg loses?"

A smile pulled his father's mouth to one side. "I expect President Hindenburg to get over fifty percent of the vote this time. My hunch is Hitler might win forty percent, counting the war veteran vote now that their leader, Duesterberg's, withdrew from the election."

Freddy's pupils constricted as he noticed both men and boys chase after pedestrians urging them to vote for

Hindenburg, Hitler, or the Communist Ernst Thalmann. With a sense of dread fluttering in his stomach, he gave his father a dazed look. "Father, is this a typical election day?"

His father looked up at the sky. "No, it's worse today."

With a conspicuous stare, he moved closer to the voting station door, hampered by raucous cries, focusing on a beefy man holding a sign with President Hindenburg's picture, lionizing him.

His mother's lips pulled back in disgust, and she tugged on his father's arm a few times. "Wilhelm, can we go inside? The loud noise is giving me a headache."

His father grabbed hold of his mother's elbow and directed her inside the voting place. Freddy brought a slow smile to his mouth, putting an X in a circle next to Hindenburg's name.

Once they finished voting, his mother gasped, locking eyes at a lady attending to an old woman with drooped shoulders.

"Is that you, Bettie Wurst?" said his mother, bouncing from foot to foot, placing a hand over her mouth.

Bettie Wurst stopped, displaying a half smile before inching toward his mother, gripping an elderly woman's hand. Optimism touched his mother's voice, and she grinned widely. "Bettie Wurst, it's nice seeing you again. Where have you been hiding? We've missed you and Fritz. How is Carly?"

Bettie Wurst's cheeks dimpled, and she pushed out her chest. "She's fine, turned three."

"Bettie, no, she isn't three already?"

"Barbara, meet my mother, Wilma; we've been rooming with her since Fritz lost his job."

Bettie's hunched mother glanced up at Freddy's mother, blinking with a warm smile spreading over her lips.

His father gave Bettie Wurst a sympathetic stare and cranked his head lower, gazing at his hands. "Bettie, how are you and Fritz doing?"

Bettie Wurst's face lacked color. "Fritz is home taking care of Carly while we vote. We survive on odd jobs he's able to find; they pay enough to keep us from starving. But Wilhelm, don't you worry about the money we owe you; we'll pay you back one day."

The edges of his father's mouth fell, and he spoke to her in a lifeless voice, holding Bettie Wurst's hands. "Betty, the money doesn't matter to us, but your family does."

Freddy beamed at him with his kind words percolating in his brain.

* * *

"Friedrich, I believe Rector Hartmann's an excellent choice, but I don't envy him." Professor Karp fretted, leaning back in his chair, rubbing the back of his neck. "Stress killed Rector Vogt; you'd be insane to want his job."

"Herr Professor, was it a close vote?"

Professor Karp uncrossed his arms, glaring at Freddy. "Too close for me; Professor Hartmann won by a few votes. After they totaled the votes, professors Blau, Huber, and Baumgarten stormed out of the room. It still upset them Hitler lost the election to President Hindenburg last week. Now that Professor Hartmann's rector, they're blood must be boiling."

"What! They stormed out of the room?"

"Yes, they did," said Professor Karp, crossing his arms. "But I'm glad I voted for Professor Hartmann; he's fair-minded and easy to get along with, the complete opposite of what you might expect from Professor Rath."

Freddy leaned in, crinkling the corners of his eyes, firming his voice. "Professor Rath will never change."

The professor's head shook, and he uncrossed his arms. "You're right, that's not likely to happen."

Freddy rocked in place.

"Friedrich, some members of the student senate wants to throw a celebration for Rector Hartmann."

"Professor, that's a godsend, isn't it?"

Professor Karp's nose twitched. "No, it's not."

"Why isn't it?"

"Friedrich, right-wing members of the senate could make it difficult to throw a celebration for Rector Hartman, they're still upset the government has banned the Brownshirts."

Freddy's head jerked back as he assessed Professor Karp's words, bulging his eyes, recalling he said he promised Albert and Curt to meet them in front of the library.

Professor Karp pressed his lips into a slight grimace. "Friedrich, is there something wrong?"

"Yes, how did you guess?"

The professor snickered, replying in a light voice, "Call it a sixth sense."

"Sixth sense, professor?"

The teacher's face brightened, and he concentrated on him. "Friedrich, it wasn't hard to do. I could see your mind was somewhere else."

"I must meet friends outside the library in ten minutes."

The professor checked his watch. "You better hurry or you'll be late."

Quickstepping through corridors, Freddy burst out the door, noticing Isaak standing in the middle of a group of noisy students. And walked toward Isaak, wrinkling his nose. "Isaak, what's wrong? Where's Leo?"

"Right-wing students in the senate are against giving Rector Hartmann a torchlight parade unless we agree to march without our red flag. I hope they burn in hell."

Steiner, a socialist, bared his teeth and moved within inches of Freddy's face, releasing a funky breath on him. "It was wrong."

"Yeah," chimed in the other students.

Isaak gave Steiner a pained stare. "Steiner, back off; let me tell Freddy what happened at the meeting."

Steiner stepped back, patting the sides of his legs. Isaak slumped, lowering his black brows, and the line between his lips widened. "Leo, argued it was fair if everyone could march with their flags. Rudolf shook his head and yelled, 'Over my dead body,' and every nationalist rose, shaking their fists at him."

A frown darkened Steiner's face. "Leo and Rudolf screamed at each other." Steiner fretted, swaying. "I've never seen Leo that mad."

"Steiner, did Catholics or the centrists protest?"

"No, they walked out."

"Why didn't you go too?"

"Shut up. Who asked your opinion?" seethed Steiner, bulging his eyes, blinking hard.

"Steiner, keep quiet, he's right," said Isaak, firming his voice, drawing his eyebrows close together.

Freddy let out a sigh, monitoring a black-capped student who had arrived. "Leo's crazy. He headed to the Boar's Den alone."

Isaak's nose creased, and his voice shook with fury. "What! He'll get killed."

"We should go after him," shrieked Freddy, fixing his eyes on Isaak.

Steiner's shoulders slumped, and he tightened his eyes. "Not me. I'm not crazy. The place is full of Nazis."

"Who's coming with me?" said Freddy, picking over blank faces and dropped heads.

"I will," said Isaak, leering at him.

And encountering Albert and Curt, they stopped to explain what had happened.

Anger seared through Albert, and he said in a deep tone, "I'll cripple them if they hurt him."

They found Leo pinching his nose to stop the bleeding, squatted outside the Boar's Den.

"Is your nose broken?" asked Freddy, touching Leo's shoulder.

Leo blinked and wagged his head sideways.

Albert shot a quick glance at the tavern. He sighed. "What were you thinking going there alone?"

Leo spit blood. "Someone needed to stand up to Rudolf."

Freddy gave Leo an icy stare, shrugging. "Why you, and alone—are you stupid?"

Leo's voice tensed, exposing bloodied teeth. "It was foolish to go inside. I thought Rudolf might change his mind if we marched without our flags. Krieg cursed at me and called me names."

"W-what names?" asked Albert, fastening his fingers into fists, glaring at Leo.

Leo cringed, glancing away from Albert, saying, "The usual ones for Jews, and then punched me in the nose."

Freddy gave Leo a blank stare, imagining what had happened to him. "How did you get away from them?"

Leo looked up at Freddy, wiping blood on a finger with a red color stinging his cheeks. "I didn't. Krieg and two others tossed me into the street; they were laughing."

Albert's eyes bulged, and his voice shook with fury. "Leo, they'll pay for what they did to you."

Nerves shook Leo's voice. "Albert, how, they outnumber us."

"Leo, back home in Aachen, that's an even fight." Said Albert with a slight smile playing on his lips.

Curt readjusted his collar with a trembling hand. "Albert, you're crazy; we'd be committing suicide if we went inside."

"Listen to Curt; it'd be a mistake if we entered the tavern," said Isaak, glaring at Albert, cracking his voice, beady-eyed.

"Albert, they might be right," said Freddy, with tightness in his gut, considering the odds.

Albert puffed out his chest, sounding confident, assessing each one. "Pay close attention. If we bust through the door, we'll surprise them. After I smack the first two hard in the face, I'll help you handle the rest."

Curt teetered back and forth with nerves shaking his voice. "Genius, if you're wrong, we'd get ourselves killed."

Albert's face blushed red, and he carried his brows together. His lips widened, putting on view the space between his top choppers. "Trust me—we can do this if we stay together."

Curt and Isaak eyed each other, pursing their lips. Curt glanced at Freddy through the corner of an eye. Freddy figured he wanted no part of it.

"Albert, I'm going with you," replied Leo, electrifying his lips.

Curt's voice shook, and he flashed a facial tic. "Leo, you'll get killed if you go back in again."

Albert lowered his brows, reading faces, and drew a cocky smile.

"Listen up, they're not expecting us; we'll strike them before they can think. Pick out someone and poke him in the head before he realizes what has happened," instructed Albert, nodding in a cool, tempered voice, making strong eye contact with everyone. "Ready on three—we burst into the tavern."

Freddy crept up to the door with a rock-hard stomach, speeding up his soft breaths.

Air burst through Albert's mouth as he scrutinized every-one, and his eyes lit up, slowing the count as he spoke. "One, two, three."

And Albert yanked open the door, barging through it, charging a group of students circled around Rudolf at the bar. The oversized man bashed a Nazi student, using his shoul-der to deliver a straight punch to his face. Freddy frowned, storming a man glaring at him. He ducked his right hand, nailing him with a left jab, and unloaded a right hook to his body, bending him before he buckled to the floor. Arms wrapped around Freddy, and he raised his hands, breaking the stranglehold, and spun around with a quickened heart-beat, catching sight of Rudolf von Krieg. Rudolf threw a stiff right jab at Freddy, which he absorbed with the palm of his left hand. Freddy shot a hard right uppercut to Rudolf's chin. He held tight to the unsteady man by his shirt, setting up a hard blow, but Leo pushed inside, delivering an uppercut to Rudolf's chin, decking him. Freddy's legs spread apart with raised fists, finding Isaak throwing a punch at a student, who covered his face with his hands. One cheek scared a right-wing student missed Curt's head with a left jab but found his stomach with a right hook, sending him to the ground hold-ing his stomach. Freddy moved opposite Curt's attacker, sending a hard right jab to his face, sending him to his knees with a bloody lip. Albert caught a Brownshirt in an iron grip and tossed the crying man over the bar. Bunched together with Isaak and Leo, Freddy gasped, watching the banged-up Hitler loyalist abandon the tavern. Bloodied, Rudolf woke, looking up with lifeless eyes. He took a quick breath, gazing at Freddy with flared nostrils, and picked himself up, stum-bling out the door.

Three seedy women cursed out loud at them. Albert gave them a sarcastic smile and wrapped his arms around

Freddy's and Leo's shoulders and vacated the Boar's Den, followed by Curt and Isaak.

* * *

A slow smile appeared on Freddy's mouth, sniffing the sweet scent released from the linden tree's flowers, picturing summer walks with his parents in Detroit, smelling fragrant flowers.

"Freddy, I'm worried. I think I failed my physics exam," said Nef Muller, removing his glasses to rub an eye.

"Nef, you've said that before and passed."

"Freddy, Professor Ehrlich's a hard marker."

"Study harder, spend less time with your brothers," said Freddy, nudging him, widening his grin.

"Not funny, Freddy."

Freddy's eyes brightened as he discovered a gorgeous girl, fixating on a sparkling butterfly clip, capturing long strands of blond hair falling over a yellow coat. His stomach fluttered, and his jaw dropped, hypnotized by sunlight flickering on the stones of the hair fastener. And he stood still, dropping his arms to his sides, slackening his facial muscles. "It's not possible; it can't be her."

Nef grimaced, putting back on his glasses. "What did you say?"

"It can't be her," said Freddy, rubbing an eye, repeating the words.

"Huh, whose 'her'?"

"The amazing girl standing between Father Graf and the glum nun."

"That's Halina Suzansky, Freddy, isn't she magnificent?"

"Nef, she's sensational," said Freddy, with awe coloring his tone, refusing to take his eyes off the dazzling girl.

Nef sighed. "She is, isn't she?"

"Halina Suzansky, so that's her name? Nef, who is she? She's gorgeous."

"Freddy, where've you been hiding, she's the kindergarten teacher. But forget her; the nun's her aunt and won't let anyone near her."

"What, she won't let anyone near her?"

"Yeah," Nef frowned, "Sister Suzansky never takes her eyes off her."

"How come you know this?"

"A friend tried seeing her, but Sister Suzansky scared him away."

"Oh." Freddy shrieked, noticing a slight quiver in his stomach.

His mother's unexpected voice spooked him. "Freddy, better close your mouth; she might catch you gawking at her. She's lovely, isn't she?"

"Uh, uh, yes, she is," said Freddy.

"Want to meet her?"

"All right," said Freddy, firing up his nerves.

"Then come with me. Father Graf will introduce you."

With a mind full of irrational worries, Freddy loosened his shirt's top button.

"Freddy, better hurry," said Nef, awakening him.

His stomach knotting, Freddy approached Father Graf and the women, heavy-footed, with sweaty palms.

"Splendid morning, Frau Bauer. We were admiring the linden's flowers. Don't you love this time of year?" said Father Graf with a cheerful smile.

Father Graf slumped, eyeing Freddy, furrowing his brows. "Herr Bauer, I've missed you, used to look forward to our conversations after mass. Your mother worries you study too hard."

Freddy scrutinized Halina's face. *Does she remember me?* She closed her eyes, pulling on a curl.

A relaxed smile crossed Father Graf's face, and his voice softened. "Herr Bauer, let me introduce you to Sister Suzansky and her niece Fräulein Halina Suzansky."

Freddy's eyes sparkled, his hopes raised. "I'm honored to meet you."

"Herr Bauer's studying law at the university, and he does nothing else but study."

Halina gave Father Graf an understanding nod. "Father, I'm sure Herr Bauer finds other things to do besides his studies."

"Fräulein Suzansky, I wish you were right," said his mother, frowning with a curt nod. "Freddy worries me, never unwinds and works the summer for a lawyer and tells me it's arduous work."

Halina Suzansky shrugged, tightening her smile. "There must be something else you do besides studying. Do you listen to music or go to the cinema?"

Embarrassed, Freddy cringed, hardening his stomach and dipping his head. "I haven't been to the cinema or listened to music in ages."

"Ah!" Father Graf yelped, enlarging his eyes. "I've a great idea. If you approve, Sister Rosa, Herr Bauer can call on Fräulein Halina."

Sister Rosa gave Father Graf a stony stare. "Father, Herr Bauer told you he was busy."

"Nonsense, sister, it might be enjoyable for him to visit with Frau Halina."

Sister Rosa compressed her lips and shook her head. "But Father, Herr Bauer's very busy."

"Father Graf's right," Freddy's mother said with a smile edged on her lips. "Father Graf, it's a great idea."

Sister Rosa grunted, unwilling to give ground to the priest. "Herr Bauer's busy studying."

His mother gave the nun a curt nod. "Sister Rosa, he should make the time; he needs a break from his studies."

Sister Rosa crossed her arms, adding a bitter note to her voice. "Halina's too busy."

Mindful of the two woman's gazes, the gray-haired priest reasoned, "Herr Bauer, call on Fräulein Suzansky if she has the time?"

Freddy's mother's face softened, and she glanced at the slack-jawed nun.

"Well, Fräulein, can you make time for Herr Bauer?" asked Father Graf, looking inward.

Halina and Freddy exchanged glances.

"Father, Friday's fine," said Halina, beaming, dipping her chin.

Sister Rosa gulped. "Humph."

"Well, Herr Bauer, is Friday satisfactory?"

Freddy's heart beat faster. "Father, Friday's fine with me."

Halina's eyes glowed, and color flamed into her cheeks.

Freddy skirted a footpath with his mother, heading for his father. And his mother gave him a gentle nudge, adding amusement to her voice. "You can thank me."

"What happened?" His father asked, making eye contact, pulling back his shoulders.

Invigorated, his mother puffed out her chest, beaming, "Dear, I'll tell you on the walk home."

Freddy bit his bottom lip, heading for Nef, reckoning he might tangle with the resentful nun.

Nef's lips cracked open, and he widened his brows, shooting creases the length of his forehead. "What happened? The nun never smiled."

Mindful of what had taken place, Freddy pinched his chin, forcing a smile. "She didn't, did she?"

"Why?"

Freddy gave Nef a slight headshake. "I'm seeing Halina Suzansky Friday, but Sister Rosa will be there."

Nef's mouth fell open, gripping his glasses. "What!"

* * *

Freddy sighed. "How do I look, Mother?"

His mother drew air between her teeth, smiling. "Freddy, you look handsome."

Freddy lowered his sight into his mother's hands. "What's in the box?"

"Chocolates. I found out from Father Graf, Fräulein Suzansky has a sweet tooth."

Freddy squinted at her, drawing a fake smile. "Mother, what are you and Father Graf conspiring to do?"

"Nothing, Father Graf mentioned she loves chocolate."

Freddy snorted. "I'm sure he did, Mother."

"You better hurry. You don't want to be late; first impressions matter," warned Freddy's mother, misty-eyed, brushing back his hair with a wide smile.

He quickened his steps, heading for Saint Jutta's convent. His smile came and went, stopping to view the brick building. Nerves knotted in his stomach, and he walked on, slowing his pace, talking to himself. "Maybe I should say, 'Good evening, Fräulein Suzansky,' or 'Hello, I brought you a box of chocolates.' Oh, that sounds awful too."

Freddy's stomach churned as he approached the convent door. He exhaled a quick breath, and his trembling index finger found the white doorbell and pushed it. Fräulein Suzansky opened the door, bright eyed, lifting the ends of her mouth. "Hello, Herr Bauer. You're on time. We were expecting you."

Freddy's glow changed to a cringing grimace. "Uh, we?"

"Yes, Aunt Rosa will sit with us."

"Oh, she will." Freddy's voice tensed, and he tightened his grip on the chocolates.

Halina's face glowed as she examined the chocolates. "Herr Bauer, is that for me?" she asked, giving him a toothy grin.

Freddy gave her an adoring gaze. "Yes. I hope you love chocolate."

"I do. How thoughtful of you. How did you know I loved chocolate?" said Fräulein Suzansky, using a hint of sarcasm in her voice.

Freddy swallowed and looked away. "Guessed."

"Herr Bauer, please come in, we've been waiting for you in the parlor," said Fräulein Suzansky, lifting her cheeks, bringing creases to the edges of her eyes.

Freddy greeted Sister Rosa with a lopsided grin, blinking fast. "Hello, Sister Rosa, it's nice to see you once more."

The nun sat in front of a picture of the pope, and her mouth twisted before she spoke. "Huh, Herr Bauer, wasn't sure you were coming to visit my niece."

Freddy sat alongside Halina, inhaling through his nose, observing the nun's chilling and unnerving eyes digging into him.

"Aunt Rosa, Herr Bauer brought me a box of chocolates." Halina's face glowed as she held out the chocolates to her aunt. "Do you want to taste one?"

Sister Rosa gnashed her teeth, shaking her head with a hint of red appearing on her cheeks.

Halina Suzansky's eyes sparkled, and she faced her aunt, speaking to her in a cheerful voice. "Aunt Rosa, I'll be fine; you can leave us."

"Are you sure?" responded the nun, pursing her lips, eyeing Freddy with what he figured was a fake smile. "Halina, I'll be in the kitchen with Sister Ingrid if you want me."

A tinge of pink crept over Halina's face, and she dipped her head, weakening her tone. "Yes, thank you, Aunt Rosa."

A slow smile came to Freddy's lips, and his muscles relaxed as he watched Sister Rosa leave the room.

Halina frowned, and her voice perked up. "Herr Bauer, please don't get the wrong impression of Aunt Rosa. She has watched over me since my father and stepmother moved to Poland. She warned me to suspect university students, said most chase after girls and drink beer. Is she correct, Herr Bauer?" Halina examined Freddy, flashing a devilish smile at him. "Um, are you up to godless behavior, Herr Bauer?"

Freddy lowered his voice, rubbing his arm, stumbling over his words. "I-I-I'm harmless. You've nothing to fear being with me."

"Are you sure, Herr Bauer?" said Halina, deepening the creases in her cheeks.

Freddy's eyes shined, and he grinned, answering her in a light voice, "Yes, can't you tell by looking at me? I'm a sinister university student that chases after girls and guzzles beers?"

Halina slipped a coy smile onto her face. "Um, Herr Bauer, you've a sense of humor, not what one might expect from a busy law student."

"A sinister law student," said Freddy, widening his grin. "If you want to, you can call me Freddy; may I call you Halina?"

Halina gave Freddy an adoring gaze. "Yes, Freddy, you may call me Halina."

Freddy grimaced, pondering a thought, softening his words. "Uh, Halina, why did they go to Poland, leaving you with Sister Rosa?"

Halina lowered her voice, closing her eyes. "My step-mother inherited a farm there; my father helps her run it.

Thank God she did; my father's a bricklayer and couldn't find work in Berlin."

Halina grabbed phonograph records and handed them to Freddy with an upturned face, making strong eye contact with him. "Freddy, I hope you find something in here you want me to play."

Freddy mirrored her smile, worshipping her adoring face. "Why don't you pick out something. I'd love to hear what you play. I'm sure it will be delightful."

Halina's upper teeth seized her bottom lip, and she tilted her head, flushing her cheeks, saying with girlish enthusiasm, "Oh! Freddy, are you fond of dance music?"

Freddy's stomach fluttered, and he leaned in, brightening his smile. "Only if you are."

"I remember seeing you on the train," said Halina, fumbling with a record.

Freddy's cheeks glowed; he caught the edges of her mouth twitch.

"Which time?" asked Freddy, sensing his body warm.

Halina pitched her voice higher, echoing his words. "Which time?"

Speechless, he grinned, aware his heart was beating faster. "Huh, m-more than once?"

"Yes, there were two times."

"You must be mistaken?" Halina swallowed, touching her parted lip.

"The first time was long ago," he said, leaning forward, auditing her radiant face.

Halina smacked her lips. "Huh, how could I forget it?"

Freddy beamed, recalling her cheeky smile and hand wave at the time the electrified train left the Gorlitz train station.

Halina made a wincing grimace, tensing her tone. "Um, why are you smiling?"

Freddy studied her face with affection in his eyes.

"Please, tell me?" she said, staring at him with intense blue eyes.

Freddy snorted, giving his head a slight shake, and his voice took on an amused tone. "I guess it can wait."

Halina's lips spread apart, and she slapped the floor with her feet, speaking in a voice tinged with curiosity. "No, it can't wait; tell me now, Freddy Bauer."

Freddy flinched, gasping for a breath at the sound of Sister Rosa's thunderous voice coming from the kitchen. "Halina, is everything all right? I heard noises; is something wrong?"

"Sorry we disturbed you, Aunt Rosa. I'm okay," uttered Halina, burying her neck in her shoulders, widening her blue eyes.

"Fine, but call me if you need me," shrieked Sister Rosa before she said inaudible words.

Halina rose, displaying an impish smile, and tiptoed with bewitching grace over to the door, shutting it before she settled back on the sofa. "Freddy, please tell me?"

The edges of Freddy's lips lifted, revealing a slight smile; he recalled what happened. "Do you remember taking a train to Gorlitz?"

Halina closed her eyes for a moment, squeezing her chin and stiffening her voice. "That's no help. I've gone to Gorlitz many times."

"It was Easter week, 1925. Do you remember a blond-haired boy sitting opposite you on the train?"

A slight crease appeared between Halina's brows and a smile blossomed on her lips. She pressed her hands against her chest, beholding Freddy. "It was you. Yes, now I remember."

"I'll never forget it; it was my first trip to the family farm, I haven't seen it since I was a baby."

"When you were a baby?" asked Halina, giving Freddy an incredulous stare.

"Yes, a baby." Freddy felt his cheeks grow warm. "My family were poor farmers; my father brought me and my mother to America hoping to find a better life for us."

With a sympathetic smile on her face, Halina softened her tone. "I reckon it didn't work out for your father in America?"

Freddy's voice weakened, and he dropped his head, staring at his hands. "No, it did not."

Halina offered a deep sigh. "I'm sorry it didn't."

Freddy's lips straightened, and he raised his cheeks, focusing on her magnificent lips.

Halina exposed a nervous smile and lowered her head.

Freddy smirked with bright and glossy eyes, leaning his head closer to her. "Let's go for a walk; this despicable university man needs air."

Halina's cheeks lifted, and a nervous laugh breezed through her lips, "I'd love to go for a walk."

Outside the convent door, Freddy grinned, fixating on a bench, and guided Halina toward it. A tingling sensation gripped the back of his neck, and he edged around, catching Sister Rosa peeking through window curtains. His eyes went to the sky, and he pushed air through his lips, whispering to himself, "Go away; leave us alone."

"Did you say something?" asked Halina, squishing her brows together.

Freddy generated a fake smile. "Just talking to myself."

Grin lines slashed Halina's cheeks. "That's not comforting; you might give people the wrong idea of you."

Freddy shivered, figuring Sister Rosa was still staring at him. "Halina, do you want to sit?"

Halina gave him a pleasant smile. "Yes, that'd be nice."

Serenaded by barking dogs and honking horns, he noted a gentle breeze ruffling Halina's gorgeous blond hair. A whimsical smile came to his lips as he noticed Halina's radiant face illuminated by bright starlight. She blushed, bringing a sheepish smile across her lips. Her soft voice quivered, and she dipped her head. "Are you that busy, you've no time for a girlfriend?"

Freddy's smile slipped from his lips as he pictured Jette. He could not focus on Helena's bewitching face any longer, and his head dropped. His eyes shut; he picked up the sound of Halina's breaths.

"Did I say something wrong?" she asked in a subdued voice.

Freddy sighed and lifted his head, and opened his eyes, seeing an empty stare covering Halina's face.

Halina's lips parted, and her dull blue eyes narrowed till they closed. "Please tell me what's wrong."

Freddy's lips trembled, and he spoke in a voice sapped of strength, "You did nothing wrong."

"Freddy, what is it?"

With Jette's notion of life on his mind, with a faint smile, he lifted his brows. Warmth returned to Freddy's heart, and he beamed at Halina, filled with inner peace, saying to her in a quiet breathy voice, "Can we take a walk?"

Halina's long lashes danced, and her twitching lips parted into a glowing smile. "Yes."

* * *

Karla let out a hard sigh and threw her cards on the blanket. "I give up, Halina; I'll never beat you."

"Karla, please don't give up; you'd be better at it if you played more often."

"Fuck the book," said Albert, slamming a thick green law book shut, rolling on his back, curling his lips. "Freddy, it's possible the Nazis might get more than half the seats in parliament."

"Forget about the damn Nazis. Let's go for a swim," said Karla, glancing over her shoulder.

Albert's eyes shined under the sun, and he sat up smiling. "Yes, let's do it; no more law today."

The bear-sized man picked himself up, seizing Karla's hands with his enormous paws, yanking her up from the blanket. He grinned at Freddy, and said with sarcasm in his voice, "Freddy, I'm guessing you and Halina don't want to join us?"

Freddy's mouth curved into a smile, and he felt his insides warm, holding Halina in view. "Great guess, Albert." His smile remained, dimpling his cheeks; he eyed Karla and Albert dashing toward the lake, laughing.

"We've been seeing each other for months, but it still feels strange when we're alone without Sister Rosa watching over us." Freddy's chest bounced, and he nodded at a funny thought.

Halina lowered her brows, twisting her mouth. "Freddy, what's so funny?"

"I was wondering, does Sister Rosa own a bathing suit?" said Freddy, snorting, looking stupid.

Halina's brows jumped, and her lips twisted; she wagged her head at him. "Freddy Bauer, you possess a sick sense of humor."

"I'll take that as a compliment?" said Freddy in a wistful tone, glowing inside, paying attention to Halina's incredible looks.

Halina's cheeks glowed, and her amazing blue eyes sparkled; she twisted a strand of her lengthy blond hair.

Freddy's heart pounded, lured closer by the quick rhythm of Halina's shallow breaths. He edged closer, tingling with passion, focusing on her sensuous lips, yearning to touch her. Her white teeth caressed her bottom lip as her eyes widened. Warmth filled his chest as he explored her angelic face. Ignited by passion, he leaned in, pressing his lips up against hers. He pulled back, sensing he could float on air, gazing at her twinkling blue eyes, and revisited her warm lips, deepening the kiss. His mouth departed her flickering lips, and he noticed her flamed cheeks. He sighed, flushed, and gave her a silly grin before reaching for her hand. "Why don't we walk along the lake?"

Halina's cheeks rose, shooting lines from the corners of her eyes.

Freddy's palms moistened, and his heart skipped at her approving smile.

Empowered, taking small steps along the water's edge, leaning against her, he guided her to a bench. Charmed by her desirable face, he caressed the back of her hand with his thumb.

Halina gave him a faint smile, and her bright eyes found his. "Oh, Freddy, isn't it a splendid sight?"

She smiled a little, waiting for his answer. Her blue eyes sparkled, and her breath quickened.

Unshackled, he answered, gliding her head toward him. Halina's warm mouth touched his, and when they finished kissing, he pulled back his head, sighing with satisfaction, noticing a faint flush tinged her cheeks. His heart pounded, and he pressed his lips against hers again, hearing her soft moans. Thrilled, he grinned, feeling his entire body tingle, and ran his finger across her lush lips, desiring them once more.

A slight smile spread over his face, and he seized Halina's hand, inching along the shore. He stopped a few times, gazing at her with a foolish smile on his face. Halina's eyes fixed on Freddy, and she relaxed her voice. "Tell me what you're thinking."

Freddy pulled her closer and touched her lush lips with his. His heart fluttered, and his body quivered. And he acknowledged love had found him again; stirring desires once familiar to him. He smiled, and his eyes danced, lured by her seductive red lips, and he tasted them.

Her eyes teared, and she rested her head on his chest, wrapping her hands around his waist. Freddy grinned, admiring distorted images of trees sway on the water. He breathed, invigorated by the fresh air. "Let's go in the water."

Halina lifted her head and let Freddy direct her into the water.

"Freddy, it's cold."

He grinned and nodded.

Halina's breaths intensified, and she beamed at him. Freddy was under her spell; his quivering lips found hers, which were waiting for him. After the warm kiss, he smiled, delighted he had made her happy. His vision blurred, spotting a romantic couple drifting on the lake. And shutting his eyes, he felt his body weaken. Breathless, he recollected falling in love with Jette at the lake; he released his fingers from Halina's hand. Halina pulled his hands around her waist, but he could not hold them there, grieving Jette's loss.

His eyes opened, expressionless, finding her examining him.

Freddy's pulse slowed, his head dropped, and he wiped his eyes.

Halina looked at Freddy, shivering. "Freddy, what's wrong? I've seen that look on your face before." She dropped her head, and her voice took on a quiet, tense tone. "It's Jette, isn't it?"

Freddy gave Halina a flat gaze with his stomach muscles contracting. "Who said Jette's name?"

Halina panted, spilling tears from her welled-up eyes. "I overheard Karla and Albert mention her on the train." With despair etched into her face, Halina shut her eyes. "Do you love her?"

Freddy trembled, and his voice faded. "I loved her."

"Did?" sniveled Halina, with each cry louder than the one before. She gave Freddy a slight headshake while opening and closing her mouth.

"She's dead," said Freddy in a lifeless voice, kicking at the water, envisioning Jette.

Halina flung her hands over her mouth, and her cheeks went pale. "I'm sorry. Please take me home." She assessed Freddy, shedding tears while taking shaky breaths.

Freddy seized her hand, but she dislodged his fingers. He rocked from side to side, drawing breaths, concluding his relationship with Halina had ended. He gazed into her eyes, sensing her pain, and hung his head, letting out a hard sigh. His brittle voice expressed his pain. "When Jette died, part of me went with her." His breathing labored, he felt nerves in his stomach vibrate. "I've lost one woman I loved; I couldn't bare losing another. If you leave me, you'll take my heart with you."

Halina's eyes released tears, and her sniffles calmed. Freddy wiped tears off her warm cheeks, catching a slight smile. Absorbed in a thought, he spoke in a wistful tone. "Halina Suzansky, can't you see I'm lost without you?"

* * *

Freddy sighed and ran his hands over Halina's arms. "The train's ready to leave."

"Say the words once more?" said Halina, holding Freddy in her shiny blue eyes.

Freddy dropped his head, wearing a sheepish smile, saying, "I love you."

Halina shivered from the morning chill. "N-no, you don't, Freddy Bauer; look at me when you say it."

Freddy's eyelids rose, and he cleared his throat. "I wish you weren't going to Poland."

Halina blinked tears, saying in a reluctant voice, "Freddy, I'll miss you."

Freddy brooded, gazing at clouds. "What will I do without you?"

Halina grinned, pulling on his arm, adding amusement to her voice. "Don't let me find out you visited a pub with Curt."

Freddy shot Halina a shy grin, warming his voice. "Halina, I love you,"

Delighted, Halina sighed, flaunting her chalk-white upper teeth. "I love you too."

Sparked by her provocative smile, Freddy kissed her awakened lips. A tear marked her cheek after the kiss, and she stroked Freddy's cheek. "Next time I visit Poland, I'll take you with me. You'll love my parents. I wrote them to tell them I'm in love with a wonderful man."

Freddy placed his cheek on Halina's, whispering into her ear, "I'll worry. I wish your aunt was traveling with you. Be careful. The Berlin police still haven't caught the serial killer prowling the streets."

Halina pulled back her head, giving him a watery gaze. "Don't worry, I'll be in Poland, far from Berlin. Aunt Rosa wanted to go, but Bishop Rauch is coming for Christmas dinner and Father Graf won't be without her."

Freddy bent back, lifting his brows. "Bishop Rauch, head of the Berlin diocese?"

Halina shut her eyes, making a *hmm* noise in her throat. "I never mentioned that Bishop Rauch and Father Graf attended seminary together in Munich?"

Freddy's throat constricted, and he pressed his lips together as he picked up the conductor's loud voice. "All aboard, all aboard, next stop Frankfurt."

The train moved away from the station, with Freddy running alongside the speeding-up passenger car, proclaiming at the top of his voice, "Halina Suzansky, I love you."

Chapter Seventeen

1933: The Devil Becomes King

Professor Karp's shoulders shot back, and he parted his lips as he saw Freddy burst through the door holding a newspaper. Freddy threw the paper on the desk, glaring at him, sweeping his index finger across the headline.

The professor sat up and glanced at the headline before anchoring his brown pupils in Freddy's bleak face.

"Impossible!" said Freddy, removing his finger, turning away.

"Hang up your coat and sit."

Freddy sagged in a seat, pulling back his lips in disgust. "Read it!"

Professor Karp's eyes swept over the page and when he finished reading, placed his palms over the paper, staring at Freddy. And he sat back, looking away saying in a low, pained voice, "Friedrich, it's incredible, yesterday was February Twenty-Seventh and a suspected Communist burns the Reichstag building, and today all Germans wake up stripped of their civil liberties because the government thinks it's part of a Communists plot to overthrow it."

"Professor, it's not the first time the Communists have tried overthrowing the government."

The professor bent his head, rubbing the back of his neck. "It could be one or the other."

"Professor, you're not making sense."

Professor Karp shifted in the seat, giving his head a soft shake. "That the Communists were starting a revolution or Hindenburg suffered a bout of paranoia."

He swallowed hard, perplexed. "Um, what makes you say that?"

"The Communists must scare President Hindenburg, that could be the reason he made Hitler chancellor. It was Hitler who advised him to issue the Reichstag Fire Decree today and take away our rights."

And he pondered the professor's words. The phone rang, and the professor picked up the handset, keeping his eyes on him. "Professor Karp speaking." The professor listened, a concerned look in his eyes, and moments later hung up the phone. "That was Rector Hartmann; he wanted to tell me the police will patrol the university till things calm."

Freddy's mouth opened, and he wondered if he had experienced a terrible dream.

The phone rang a second time, and Karp picked it up on the first ring and listened to the speaker till his eyes widened and his lips curled. "What? That can't happen, say it again, louder." Professor Karp slammed down the receiver, saying to Freddy in a disbelieving voice, "That was Alfred Beiner. The Brownshirts stormed the courthouse, rounding up Jews. Hugo Hahn was one of them; he quit after they threatened him if he returned. Beiner called earlier to let me know police were rounding up Communists." At that moment, seeing a vision of Leo Herzfeld pop into his head, Freddy contorted his face and tensed his words. "What's the odds this ends without bloodshed?"

Karp gave him a bitter stare, shaking his head.

Spooked, his stomach tightened as he recalled the dreadful events in Detroit.

Karp examined him. "Friedrich, are you okay?"

He wiped his dry lips with the back of his hand. "I'm fine."

Freddy flinched, surprised by the telephone's unexpectedly loud ring. Professor Karp put the receiver to his ear. "Hello. Professor Karp speaking." His face flushed with anger as he listened to the caller. "Nessa, stop it, stop crying and pay no attention to Mata. Alfred called; he said the police were picking up Communists, not Jews. Go get yourself and your sister a glass of water."

"Um, professor, are you sure?"

Professor Karp replied with a hint of a frown, "No, but I can't worry her with my opinions."

Freddy nodded. "I guess not."

Karp's forehead wrinkled, and his tone sounded philosophical. "It torments my soul not knowing what's unknown with no way of figuring it out; do you know what I mean?"

He pinched his bottom lip, assessing Karp's words. "I think so."

Karp's phone rang again. He let it ring, wincing, and picked up the phone, nodding, forming two vertical lines between his eyes. "Nessa, stop worrying. But, but, but," and he slammed down the receiver, glancing at Freddy with his fingertips resting on his cheeks. "It's Nessa's fifth call today."

* * *

Karla sneered, crossing her arms. "Albert, you've drunk too many beers."

"I don't need you to tell me when I've drunk too many."

Millie patted Albert on the back. "Listen to Karla; you don't need another beer."

"Millie, please, one more."

Anger flashed on Millie's face, and her voice took on a hard edge. "Albert, no, I don't want to see your lunch on the floor."

Albert placed his elbows on the table and anchored his swaying head between his hands, forcing a smile. "Please, Millie, just one more beer."

A bitter smile crossed Freddy's lips, glaring at Hitler's picture on the front page of the newspaper. His lips parted as he checked the date: March 29. He cringed, gathering in less than sixty days Adolf Hitler had moved from chancellor to dictator of Germany.

"Someone please tell me I'm having a nightmare." Albert's head shook. Curt pulled closer to him. "We should move to France or someplace else safe to study law."

Albert flinched, gasping for air. "What! Are you crazy? And throw away the time we spent here studying law?"

Freddy's mouth opened, and he belched, releasing a whiff of sauerkraut into the air. Despair etched into his face, and he eased himself off his chair, with Hitler on his mind, and edged up to the bar and threw change before Ren. "Glass of bitters, please."

He stayed put, sipping the black liquid with a detectable licorice aroma, seeing his long-faced friends in the mirror behind Ren. Fear drank with him as he struggled to cope with denial and anger. His body shook, tormented by a mind full of mysteries, and he craved fresh air. He grabbed his coat and bag, said his farewells, and burst out the door into daylight, with chilly air fanning his face. He shivered and buttoned his coat, and with a pained expression lingering on his face, he wandered the streets till the city lights brightened, giving him a vision of where he wanted to be. Twenty minutes later he stopped, facing the convent door, and he rubbed his hands together until he got the nerve to ring the bell.

"Oh, Freddy," said Halina, opening the door and taking a step back. "What a surprise; I wasn't expecting you tonight."

Sister Rosa's voice boomed from another room. "Halina, who is it?"

"Aunt Rosa, its Freddy," sang out Halina, with excitement in her voice, beaming at Freddy.

Sister Rosa eased herself into the room, planting a smile between her chubby cheeks. "Have you eaten? There's still warm food in the kitchen."

"No thank you, sister, I'm not hungry."

Sister Rosa clasped her hands together, showing Freddy a crisp nod. "I'll leave you alone. If you change your mind, Halina can prepare you a plate."

A wide smile lit up Freddy's face. "Humph, she likes me."

Halina's eyes brightened. "Yes, she does; she knows you make me happy."

Freddy's smile wavered; he recalled the fear that had brought him to Halina's doorstep and bowed his head.

"What's wrong?"

His voice locked in his throat, and his legs weakened, and with his gut doing somersaults, he inspected Halina's blue eyes. His headshakes grew in intensity. And he shivered with unfocused eyes, unable to shake a horrible thought. *The devil has become king.*

Halina seized his hand, softening her voice, making strong eye contact with him. "What is it? You look sick."

Speechless, Freddy hung his head, fearing an apocalypse under Hitler's rule.

Halina's lips trembled, filling her eyes with tears. "You're scaring me; what is it?"

He lifted his head, cringing, unable to shake his shocking notion. "Halina, my dreams burned in the Reichstag fire. Now that Adolf Hitler's grabbed power, we're no longer living in a democracy. How can I exist in a country that abandons the rule of law? Can I live in his world? What will I do in it? I've no right to bring you into my world."

Halina straightened up, observing him. "If the man I worship wants to do something, nothing will stop him."

His tight lips danced into a smile, and he squeezed Halina's hand, taking a cleansing breath.

Halina's lips built into a smile; she said with a hint of optimism in her voice, "We'll ask God's help; he's a miracle worker."

Freddy's eyes sparkled, bringing a relaxed smile to his lips. "I'm lost without you."

Halina nudged him, uncovering her white teeth with a wide smile. "You're just finding that out?"

He grinned, enticed by her satisfied smirk. His pulse raced as he examined the smile that tugged on Halina's enticing red lips. Seduced by their grandeur and her magnificent blue eyes, he inched closer, yearning to kiss her. A tremor touched Halina's lips, and she closed her eyes. With a freaked-out heart thumping in his chest, his mouth touched her trembling lips. Warmth spread through his body, and he held her tight, feeling carefree and confident. He pulled back and gazed at her, intoxicated by her unimaginable looks. "Halina, I love you. Is it possible you might marry a poor soul with a bleak future?" asked Freddy with a childish grin. Halina held her breath, answering his question with a pink color flowing into her uplifted cheeks, shedding happy tears. The edges of his lips rose, and he inhaled a long shaky breath in a weightless state of mind. *She said yes.*

* * *

A whimsical smile reached Freddy's eyes as he concentrated on Halina walking toward Albert and Curt.

Albert commented, pressing his lips into a slight grimace. "Nero's smiling while Germany burns. It has been only a week since Rudolf and other right-wing students burned library books by authors opposed to their views. Freddy, if I ever catch you playing a fiddle, I'll break it."

"Stop! He's a right to; he's in love," said Curt, displaying a cheeky smile.

Albert's head shook, and he waved Curt away. "I am too, but you don't see me wearing a shitty grin on my face."

"Ha, that's funny," said Curt, displaying a wide grin. "I'll bet you never bought Karla flowers."

"Not funny. I'm always broke."

"Hmm, that's a surprise. With the free beers Millie and Karla give you, you could've saved money to buy Karla flowers."

Albert forced a smile, bringing attention to the gap between his front teeth. "Mind your business, shithead."

A flicker of anger haunted Curt's face.

Freddy flattened his lips, and he longed for the sound of the bell. "Will both of you relax?" Noisy enthusiasm rung out, and cheerful right-wing students herded near Rudolf, laughing and smiling. And spotting him, Krieg's mouth drew into a wicked smile. Albert's titanic legs tapped on the floor. "Look at them; they're fired up since Hitler took over the government." Albert's lips puckered, and he displayed a bear-sized fist. "This is what the Nazi shits will get if they mess with me," fumed Albert, smacking his fist into the palm of his hand.

Curt's voice tensed, and the skin around his eyes wrinkled. "A lot of good that'll do. Are you aware our numbers are shrinking?" He froze and looked the other way. "The Nazis are eradicating Communist and Jews. Who's next— Social Democrats or Catholics? If you ask me, our chances of becoming lawyers are fading fast under Hitler."

"Who asked you?" said Albert, curling his shoulders at Curt.

Lodged in between Albert and Curt, he checked the time, eager for Professor Karp to enter the room. His finger touched his parted lip; he paid attention to a suited man, whom he guessed was in his early thirties, coming through the door and walking up to the rostrum.

"Good morning. I'm professor Ludwig Sauer, I will be your new instructor. The university has dismissed most Jewish professors, along with others; Professor Karp was one of them."

Right-wing students jumped to their feet and cheered, and many of those seated gave them vile stares. Freddy's jaw dropped; he agonized over the Jewish professors. His blood boiled, and he checked Albert's and Curt's shocked faces. Breathless, with fear twisting his gut, he jumped up and rushed out the room, heading for Professor Karp's office. He arrived at his office puffing hard, finding the door locked and no name on it.

And he paced back and forth, depressed, shaking his head, agonizing over what had happened.

He rubbed his bottom lip, aware of Professor Ziegelberg's name still on his door, and tapped it three times. With a bleak expression, Professor Ziegelberg stuck his head out the door.

"Herr Bauer, it's nice to see you; please come in," Ziegelberg said, fighting to keep his voice steady.

"Herr Professor, I didn't expect to find you here."

Ziegelberg used his cane to ease himself into his chair. "Then why did you knock, Herr Bauer?"

In a quiet voice, feeling his stomach muscles contract, he said, "It surprised me to see your name on the door."

Freddy attempted a smile, noting the lines on Ziegelberg's chalky face intensifying. "I'm here because I fought in the war; if I hadn't, they'd have dismissed with the others."

A slight grimace appeared on Freddy's face. "You survived."

Ziegelberg wagged his head, speaking in a weary voice. "I'm caged in with hungry lions; my days here won't be many."

He gave his head a slow shake, examining Professor Ziegelberg.

The hapless man's nostrils widened, and he pulled on his beard. "I won't let them dishonor me."

Freddy left Professor Ziegelberg's office, catching nauseous waves in his stomach. Despair gnawed at his brain as he found his way to Professor Karp's apartment building. He lumbered up the steps, taking feeble breaths, fighting the urge to change direction. On unsteady legs, he rang the doorbell.

"Delightful afternoon, Friedrich," Nessa Karp spoke emotionlessly, with tear tracks marking her powdered face. "Stefan's expecting you. Can you find your own way? I'm not myself right now."

Upset with Nessa's condition, he found Professor Karp's doors closed and tapped on one of the glass panels.

"Who's there?"

"Professor, its Friedrich Bauer," said Freddy, swallowing the lump in his throat.

"Friedrich, come in. I was hoping to see you."

He nudged the doors open, infiltrating a space that reeked with the odor of tobacco, coughing.

"Sorry, Friedrich. I'll open the window." The pasty-faced man picked himself up and walked heavy-footed over to the window and crack it open. He sagged back into his chair, eyeing a steeple he made with his fingers, using a flat, monotone voice. "Friedrich, not the day anyone expected, was it?"

He cringed, shifting in his seat. "No, it wasn't."

"Nessa didn't take it well; she's in shock," said Professor Karp in a somber voice.

Freddy looked to the side, answering him. "I noticed."

Professor Karp's eyes welled up, and he turned his head away from Freddy. "I must give my daughters the terrible news; it won't be easy with Nessa crying alongside me."

And concluding nothing made sense in the world, Freddy shut his eyes, thinking he was being dragged through a series of surreal events.

Professor Karp's lips sprung open, but no words came out of his mouth.

Freddy sniffled, rubbing one eye. "What will you do?"

Karp's lips trembled. "Flee. What else can I do? Staying in Germany's no longer a choice for me, or any Jew. How can we trust a man who threatened us in *Mein Kampf* or speaks out in public against us?" Professor Karp's head was still with his pupils zeroing in on a ceiling crack. "Boycotts, intimidation and violence—what's next? I should leave Germany and move to New York—my sister could help us. Maybe Jerusalem. If I stay here, I'll wind up selling brushes in the streets."

Speechless, Professor Karp picked up a letter, handing it to Freddy with a shaking hand.

Freddy's eyes widened as he read over the letter. He gawked at Professor Karp, detecting fire in his belly. "Rector Rath?"

"Friedrich, they dismissed Rector Hartmann because he's not a nationalist."

Confounded, staring at nothing, he said, "Maybe I should flee too?"

"Friedrich, do you recall the biblical account of Jonah and the enormous fish?"

"Who doesn't?"

"Do you remember, after the fish swallowed Jonah, he found God, and after it discarded him, he warned the wicked people of Nineveh to repent if they wanted the city to exist in forty days?"

"Kind of."

"Well, Friedrich Bauer, Germany needs Jonah's bringing her to her senses."

Freddy gulped, assuming the worst. "I'm not Jonah."

Professor Karp leaned in, furrowing his brows. "A student said to me it's important to protect the Constitution from the tyranny of man and preserve its integrity. Do you think he was sincere?"

Freddy's cheeks burned. He forced a smile and lowered his head, softening his voice. "No, he was telling you the truth."

Professor Karp's face brightened. "I thought so."

He took up a bottle of scotch and two glasses, filling each glass until the brown liquid reached the top of his second finger. Karp handed him a scotch and made a toast. "Pray God Germany finds her way through the fog."

Freddy gagged, tasting the strange-smelling liquid with an earthy color.

"It takes time to appreciate a fine scotch," said Professor Karp.

He downed the scotch, catching a burn descending from his throat.

"Friedrich, some more?"

Freddy covered the top of his glass, looking at Karp. "No more for me."

Karp poured himself another scotch, adding one more finger to it.

Freddy licked his lips, relaxing from the sips of scotch. "I've something important to tell you—I asked a girl to marry me."

Professor Karp glowed and cheered. "We needed pleasant news. Wait till Nessa learns of your engagement. We must throw you a party. I want to meet, uh…"

"Halina Suzansky."

Professor Karp rose and walked over to the door, and opened it. "Nessa, please come here, I've wonderful news."

"Halina, what a lovely name," said Nessa, her lips smiling faintly, hearing the news. "Friedrich, is she Jewish?"

"No, Frau Karp, she's not Jewish."

Professor Karp's brows jumped, and he moved his eyes in circles. "Huh, one less embarrassing question for Nessa to bring up when she meets her."

When the phone rang, Professor Karp lost his slight grin and picked up the black receiver.

"Hello. Oh, it's you, Alfred," said the professor, cradling the phone against his ear, looking glum. "Fredrich is here, Alfred. I'll call back later. He has pleasant news; he's engaged," he said, paying attention to Herr Beiner. "I'll tell him…don't know if he knows; I'll ask him." Professor Karp rubbed his chin. "Herr Beiner sends his congratulations and asked if you set a date and wanted to know where you'll be living."

Freddy gave him an unfocused gaze. "Not before two years; we agreed to wait till I passed the state exams and can hang a sign on a door."

"Friedrich, don't underestimate the state exams, they're very difficult."

His face softened, and he gave Karp a decisive nod. "Professor, I promise not to. And will miss the times we've spent together. You've been more than a teacher to me; I'll never forget you."

Professor Karp grinned, glancing at Nessa's misting eyes. "I've always wanted a son."

* * *

"I can't do this anymore," admitted Freddy, whispering to himself, half-awake, coming to his senses. He lifted his chin, twitching his nose, catching a faint whiff of coffee, and picked himself up to head for the kitchen. He collapsed in a chair, noticing a bitter smile on his mother's face. "Freddy, you missed church again. I never know what to tell Father Graf when he asks where you are."

He pinched his forehead, unable to lay eyes on his mother. "I overslept, was up late preparing for the state exams. I must pass them."

"Halina sat by herself in church," said his mother, hardening her gaze.

He made himself smaller, closing his eyes. "I'll tell Halina why; she'll understand. Is there any coffee left?"

"I think there's a cup left in the pot," answered his mother, pouting.

And dropping the paper, his father patted his hand, grinning. "You'll pass them; I know."

His cheeks raised up, and he held his head high. "Thanks for the encouragement."

"Milk, no sugar, just the way you want it," said his mother, placing a hot cup of coffee under Freddy's nose.

Freddy glanced up, dimpling his cheeks. "Thank you, Mother," he said and sighed, noticing a slight smile.

"I asked Halina to dinner, but she said she was busy."

After a sip of coffee, he squinted at his mother. "Huh, she didn't tell me she was busy. I guess I'll find out later."

A puzzled expression emerged on his mother's face. "Oh, wonder what could it be?"

"Barbara, mind your business."

"I was curious, meant no harm."

Her face glowed as she scrutinized Freddy. "Wilhelm, I can't believe it—in two years Freddy will be a lawyer and married to a wonderful girl."

The space between his lips widened. "Mother, we haven't even set a date yet."

And shedding happy tears, she said, "But you will. Let me make you breakfast. What do you want?"

Dressed in a clean shirt, Freddy looked in the mirror, combing his hair. And he hummed a tune, advancing toward Saint Jutta's convent. He rang the convent's bell, and Sister Wanda opened the door. "Halina's helping sister superior prepare dinner for Bishop Rauch; the housekeeper's sick. She wants you to go to the rectory."

He knocked on the door, and Halina opened it, smiling, wearing a spotted apron. "You heard the cook's sick? Sister Rosa is frantic and needs my help."

"Halina, can I help?"

"Sit here; you can help by staying out of our way."

Father Graf's eyes twinkled as he wandered in, his eyes zeroing in on the Bundt cake.

Sister Rosa snarled, reminding him of a mad dog. "Father, don't you dare put your fingers on it; I won't serve the bishop a cake that looks as though mice picked at it?"

The stout man's smile faded, and he stepped back, pleading to Sister Rosa. "Please, Sister, just a pinch."

Sister Rosa's head shook. "No one takes a bite till the bishop does."

Father Graf angled his head toward Freddy. "Bishop Rauch enjoys talking with university students; why don't you and Halina join us for dinner? It would delight the bishop to talk with you."

Freddy swallowed hard, eyeing Halina. "No thank you, Father, we don't want to be a bother."

The priest gave his head a shake, stiffening his voice. "Nonsense, you're both coming for dinner and that's it. Sister superior, two more place settings please."

Freddy gave Halina a flat gaze, slumping his shoulders. "Thank you, Father."

The holy man's face brightened, picking up a bottle of red wine and two glasses. "Friedrich, follow me."

Inside his office, Father Graf uncorked the bottle and poured the wine. Deep creases formed on Father Graf's cheeks as he admired the wine. "Ah, pinot noir. It's my favorite; I hope you appreciate it."

Not understanding what to do with the wine, he mimicked the happy priest's actions.

"I see you recognize superb wine," said Father Graf, easing back in the chair.

With a fake smile, he wished for a beer instead of wine.

Freddy sniffed the wine's pleasant aroma. Father Graf's cheeks dropped, and he leaned back, sneering at him, taking a bitter tone of voice. "Halina was sitting alone in church this morning. I look forward to seeing you with Halina at Holy Communion next Sunday," said the slack-jawed priest, pulling back his shoulders, strengthening his voice.

Freddy slumped, and he pulled his knees together.

Father Graf's frown changed to a smile. "Friedrich, drink up; it's rarely we taste excellent wine."

The doorbell rang, and Father Graf rose, clapping, declaring in an excited voice, "The bishop's here."

After grace, speechless, seated alongside Halina with the impression he was being watched, Freddy reached for Halina's hand and squeezed it.

Bishop Rauch leaned forward, extending his arm. "Herr Bauer, please hand me the gravy."

And he passed it to the grinning man whose tongue popped out between his lips. "Ah, smells good; can't wait to taste it."

Freddy reached for potato dumplings, sneaking a peek at the bishop, wishing the dinner would end.

Bishop Rauch wiped his bottom lip clean with his tongue before lowering his gaze to Freddy.

"Herr Bauer, Father Graf tells me you're studying law; how interesting. What fraternity did you join?"

He squeezed Halina's hand. "Your grace, none. I wanted nothing to interfere with my studies."

Freddy held his knees together, observing Bishop Rauch's unwavering eye contact. "As a fraternity member, Herr Bauer, you could be at one of my instructive lectures. I'd be interested in what a bright law student thought of one."

With a warm smile Freddy's head rose; he said to the eminent holy man, "But I did, and found it enlightening."

Father Graf's mouth fell open, and he dropped his fork.

Bishop Rauch raised his cheeks and the corners of his lips.

Freddy stiffened, noticing the bishop's smile fade and him fixing his attention on him. "Herr Bauer, that's not enough; can't you be more specific?"

He seized Halina's hand, pondering Bishop Rauch's speech. "As I remember it, Your Excellency, you started with a joke and brought up a proverb."

Bishop Rauch formed a steeple with his fingers. "Herr Bauer, I'm concerned with the speech, not with its delivery."

Freddy's fingers tightened, and he felt a stomach flutter. "Bishop Rauch, I'm sorry, I'll get to it. You warned students of right-wing ambitions and told them to rely on their faith during anxious moments."

Bishop Rauch's mouth twitched. "Well put, Herr Bauer, precise and to the point; it's what I might expect from a law student."

"Thank you, your eminence," said Freddy, grinning as he leaned back in his seat.

Bishop Rauch's smile wavered, and his voice firmed. "Well, Herr Bauer, did you agree with me?"

He displayed a wide grin. "I did, but next time make it longer."

Bishop Rauch looked agreeable, exchanging glances with Father Graf and Sister Rosa.

Bishop Rauch cocked his head Halina's way. "Halina, why the long face?" Halina patted her lips with a napkin before speaking in a voice laced with worry. "Sorry, Bishop Rauch, I'm concerned for Freddy. When he's a lawyer; what will it be like to practice under Nazis law?"

"Freddy?"

Father Graf turned an eye on Bishop Rauch, saying, "He's addressed as Freddy informally by his family and Halina."

"Oh."

Bishop Rauch stared at Halina. "Excuse me, to return to your question, it's hard to say, Hitler just took office. Most bishops were pleased Hitler signed the concordat with the Vatican recognizing the church." The holy man pressed his teeth together, spreading his lips. "It worries me Nazis think because they signed the Reich-Vatican concordat with the Holly See, it prevents me from condemning their actions, and it disgusts me that many bishops think otherwise."

And glancing at Halina, Freddy caught the sides of her mouth dip.

Father Graf's forehead wrinkled, and he flexed his finger at the bishop. "The church comes before the Reich. I'll never keep quiet if they violate God's will."

Freddy opened and closed his mouth, and a lump formed in his throat. And he noticed a slight tingle in the stomach. "Father, is that a wise decision?"

Father Graf gave him a hard stare and crossed his arms. "I'm not afraid. God tells me what's right, not the führer."

In rare silence Freddy ate, worried the questioning might not end. He chewed fast, noticing Halina putting food in her mouth. The stillness lasted till Father Graf's smile broadened, dropping his fork on his plate, "Sister superior, now's the time to cut the Bundt cake."

* * *

"Freddy, what is this on the doorframe? It has a picture of a star and candles on it?"

"Don't know; it's on every door inside the apartment."

Halina, wide-eyed, tugged on his arm. "Didn't you ask?"

"No, I was reluctant to. I didn't want to look stupid."

"I'm nervous. You mention Professor Karp and Herr Beiner, but say nothing of their wives, except that Frau Karp has a curious mind."

"I've never met Frau Beiner, but her husband's easy to recognize; he's the man with the mustache."

Halina took on a watery gaze. "What if they're not fond of me or my Bundt cake?"

He grinned, shaking his head at her. "They'll love both," he said and pushed Professor Karp's doorbell button and backed away, hearing nearing footsteps. Nessa Karp opened the door, grinning with a twinkle in her eyes.

"Hello, Friedrich," said Nessa, gawking at Halina for seconds. "You must be Fräulein Halina Suzansky; it's so nice to meet you. I'm Professor Karp's wife; please call me Nessa." Nessa's smile widened, and she nodded at Freddy. "Friedrich, she's gorgeous."

A pink tinge bathed Halina's cheeks. "I brought you a Bundt cake."

Nessa claimed the cake and stepped back, nodding. "Oh, what a handsome couple you make. Please come inside; everyone's in the parlor eager to meet Halina."

He squeezed Halina's hand before walking into the parlor. His stomach fluttered, minding Professor Karp's and Alfred Beiner's beaming faces. Nessa lifted her head, grinning at them. "Please come with me; you must meet Frau Beiner." Nessa led them to a somber woman seated on a beet-red sofa. "Fräulein Suzansky and Herr Bauer, may I introduce my sister, Frau Mata Beiner." The somber woman rose, attempting to smile. "Herr Bauer, how nice to meet you. Albert speaks well of you. I wish you both the best; you are an appealing couple."

Halina's smile wavered, and she inspected the cheerless woman's face.

"Frau Beiner," he said, nodding with a smile, "thanks for your good wishes.

Professor Karp and Alfred Beiner headed his way with upturned faces.

His stomach twitched, and he sucked in a fast breath, waiting for the two men to arrive. "Uh, Herr Doctor Karp and Herr Beiner, I'm delighted to introduce you both to Fräulein Halina Suzansky."

As the night progressed, Halina often squeezed his hand for comfort. More than once a relaxed smile appeared on Freddy's face, relieved Halina held her own talking with the women. At one point Herr Beiner reached inside his pocket with a devilish grin and pulled out a long cigar.

Nessa flinched, raising her voice. "Please, Alfred, not in front of guests."

Alfred Beiner gave Nessa a bitter smile before placing the cigar back inside the pocket.

Professor Karp's lips spread as he eyed him. "Friedrich, don't be shy; tell us how you did on the state exams—or must I ask Fräulein Suzansky?"

Freddy gave him a satisfied grin.

Professor Karp faced Halina, rounding his eyes. "Fräulein Suzansky, how did he do on his exams?"

Halina glanced at Freddy. And she said, flashing him a smile, "few scored better."

Professor Karp raised his chin, grinning, "Excellent news. What of Albert and Curt?"

Freddy cheered, raising his voice. "They both passed."

"The superb news calls for my best scotch; gentlemen, let's retire to my study and leave the women alone to gossip." He turned toward Nessa with a smirk on his face. "That's what they do best."

Professor Karp poured three scotches and lifted his glass high. "Friedrich, here's to your engagement and hard work."

Alfred Beiner smirked. "Amen." The three glasses clinked together.

Freddy's eyes lit up in appreciation for both men.

His smile slipped, and he stared at his hands. "Rudolf von Krieg passed his exams and is a commissioned officer in the army."

Professor Karp's words weakened. "I'm confused. He passed his exams; why join the army?"

Freddy cranked up his head, exposing his neck. "His family has a history of fighting for Germany with distinction; that might be why he did it."

Professor Karp offered him a pained gaze.

Alfred Beiner downed his scotch. His eyes seemed lost. His lips puckered, bringing scores of wrinkles to them.

"Alfred, one more?" asked Professor Karp, blinking at him, lifting one cheek.

"Oh, yes please," said Alfred Beiner, woke from his trance.

Alfred Beiner guzzled his drink and went for a cigar, but changed his mind and held out his empty glass, begging for more scotch.

Professor Karp scoffed, pouring scotch into Albert Beiner's glass. "Last one for you, Alfred."

Amid the uncanny silence, his eyes shifted between the two men. A sudden flush passed over Beiner's face, and the crinkle-lipped man shook his head hard. "Stefan, it can't be. Why us? Did you see Mata's face? She hasn't smiled since it happened."

Confused, Freddy narrowed his eyes on Herr Beiner.

Professor Karp made strong eye contact with Herr Beiner, tempering his voice. "Alfred, get hold of yourself; there's no choice."

Alfred Beiner appeared haunted, and he let out a heavy sigh. "They have disbarred me, and for what, defending innocent Communists?"

"A Jew that did," grumbled Professor Karp, pulling his dark brows together, giving Alfred Beiner a brief headshake.

Freddy's tongue peaked out his lips as he evaluated Professor Karp's response.

Professor Karp grabbed two tickets from a drawer and slid them toward him. "New York—professor, are you sure?"

"Yes, Friedrich. Alfred and Mata are joining us; there's no life for us anymore in Germany."

A frown darkened Freddy's face, and he shrugged, letting Professor Karp's words sink in, darting his eyes between two somber men.

Chapter Eighteen

The Devil's in the Details

Seated in an uninhabited part of the train, Freddy watched it pull out of the station. A smile flowered on Halina's lips and her eyes shined as she twisted her gold wedding band. She nudged Freddy, drawing air between her perfect white teeth. "Imagine it—I'm married to a handsome lawyer."

With a relaxed smile, Freddy raised his chin, giving a squeeze to Halina's hand. "In two years, to become a criminal lawyer, I clerked for a judge, worked for a law firm and the government, and passed rigorous state exams. Imagine doing all that with you on my mind the entire time."

Halina blinked, bouncing her alluring red lips into a smile. "But Freddy, wasn't I worth the wait?"

"Every minute," said Freddy, with a smile dancing on his lips.

Halina's lips bounced, and she said in a soft voice, "Freddy, I love you. I'm so proud of you; you're a member of the bar and can hang out your shingle."

She pressed her hands against her cheeks with a sheen in her eyes. "Oh, Freddy, you'll look so handsome in your lawyer's robe."

With a sinking feeling in his stomach, Freddy dropped his head. "I hope I don't disappoint anyone."

Halina leaned over and kissed him. "I'm proud of you. Out of four hundred and twenty-five people taking the law exams, only one did better than you."

Shiny-eyed Freddy lifted his chin with grinning lines slashing his cheeks.

Dull-eyed, Freddy gave Halina a slight headshake, speaking in a monotone voice. "I wish Professor Karp and Albert Beiner were at the church. I miss them; someday we should visit them in America. Professor Karp and Nessa send their best wishes, and I'm glad he loves teaching at New York University." Freddy ruffled his hair with a lengthy breath and firmed his voice. "He asks of Leo Herzfeld, but I don't know any news for him. No one knows what happened to him. And if I responded, I'd worry the Gestapo could read the letter." Freddy's brows jumped, sending slight creases along his forehead. "Halina, I wish I'd seen his face when he read my placement on the law exams."

Halina pressed her hand against her chest, saying with a voice matching the smile on her face, "Freddy, it was a wonderful wedding. You were so handsome, and your mother never stopped crying. Curt's cologne was overpowering; Father Graf glanced at him, often pinching his nose. Curt was very nervous. He kept rocking, unable to get comfortable."

Freddy flashed a smile. "He wasn't nervous; he was sobering up after spending two nights getting smashed at the Slippery Pig."

"But Freddy, you were sober."

"Millie didn't care if Curt got drunk but made sure I didn't."

Halina said, giving Freddy a quick nod, "Smart woman, that Millie."

Freddy released a heavy sigh and glanced out the window. "It's unfortunate Albert and Karla were not at the wedding."

Halina's eyelids sagged, and her voice was sad. "The Nazis consider Albert a crossbreed because of his mother. He and Karla are safe in Amsterdam. Who knows, they might even get married?"

Dull-eyed, Freddy nodded. "Hope so."

Halina's eyes sparkled, and she sunk her white teeth into her bottom lip, watching Freddy pull a piece of rice from her hair. "Oh, Freddy," she said, "your mother pulled two pieces of rice from my hair; you know what that means, don't you?"

Freddy read her thoughts, and his stomach fluttered. "I do, and I want three sons."

"What if I want three girls?" teased Halina, grinning at him.

Freddy covering his ears said, "I didn't hear you; what did you say?"

Halina slapped his knee. "Ouch!"

"Halina, what's wrong?"

"Darling, my hand still hurts from sawing the log."

"But it was fun. It's our first trial after we wed; that's why we do it. It's a custom, and everyone enjoyed watching it." Freddy giggled, a whimsical look in his eyes. "Oh look, I see more rice in your hair."

Halina smiled and nudged Freddy, lifting her brows in amusement. "Freddy Bauer, I'm not falling for that."

The train braked, and Freddy smiled at the idea he'd make love to Halina that night as he gazed at her. "We'll be at the lake soon."

A teasing smile crossed Halina's face, and she gave Freddy a playful pinch on his cheek.

In hushed serenity, inching along the water's edge, wearing foolish grins, Freddy and Halina kissed.

A smile spread across Freddy's lips as he admired a golden glow that embraced the horizon. Halina looked up with love flickering in her eyes. "Oh, Freddy, isn't it breathtaking?"

"I can think of something better."

Halina blushed, touching her chin to her chest.

Freddy lifted her chin, compelled to press his lips against hers.

"Halina, I love you," professed Freddy. "I can't imagine life without you."

Halina's lips gave Freddy an inviting smile, and she closed her eyes. Freddy tasted her warm lips once more.

Weightless, with his heart beating a new rhythm, Freddy steered Halina back to the room.

Inside the room Freddy and Halina flung themselves on the bed and kissed. His heart racing, Freddy stroked her inner thigh, imagining what might happen next. Halina stopped him. Her smile faded, and she sat up, fanning her face. Freddy brushed Halina's ample blond hair over her shoulder, softening his voice. "You're nervous?"

Halina fell back, resting her head on Freddy's chest, weeping. "I don't know what to do."

Freddy's face tightened. "Uh, no one explained it to you?"

Halina whined, bouncing her chin on her chest. "No, no one ever did."

Freddy stroked her hair, desiring her the entire time, declaring in a quiet voice, "Halina, I love you. Trust me; you'll figure it out."

* * *

Halina's eyes lit up, and she unveiled a devious smile.

"Freddy, it's a surprise. Wash up, but don't you dare peek in the kitchen."

Freddy relaxed on the sofa and closed his eyes, saying *hmm* more than once, mulling over the three judges' decisions. Kissed by Halina's warm lips, Freddy welcomed her with bright blue eyes.

"Freddy, I've something important to tell you," said Halina, squeezing Freddy's hand.

"Uh, what is it? What's wrong?" asked Freddy with a low rumbling sound coming from his stomach.

"We're going to have a baby," said Halina, shedding happy tears.

"Imagine that; I will be a father," said Freddy, with his face and neck flushing color. "I can't wait to tell everyone."

The doorbell rang, and Freddy's mouth fell open; he gave the door a questioning stare. "Uh, wonder who could that be."

Halina's face lit up, and she placed her hands over her chest. "Freddy, I invited your parents for dinner to tell them."

Freddy's blue eyes brightened, and he opened the door, smiling, bouncing on his feet. "Guess what? I'm going to be a father!"

His mother flinched and grabbed his father's arm. And she ignored Freddy, edging toward Halina.

"Congratulations! I'm happy for you," she said, smiling, giving Halina a hug.

Freddy's spirits soared, and he thrust out his chest.

"We're thrilled," said Freddy's mother. "How nice, the baby arrives in summer; do you want a boy or girl?"

Freddy's fingers brushed back his hair, and he glanced at Halina. "A healthy boy, right?"

Halina's lips puckered; she shook her head. "I want a baby girl."

At dinner, a glimmer of satisfaction came to Freddy's eyes and he placed his fork on the table. "Halina, they're delicious; what are they?"

His mother tilted her head at Halina, and said, adding excitement to her voice. "Halina, I love them."

Halina's eyes twinkled. "Mother, I'm glad you enjoyed them. Poles call them *Pyzy*; my mother taught me how to make them when I was young."

Freddy wolfed down his *Pyzy*, wanting more, heaving a sigh, observing his father take the last one.

"Oh, I forgot, I've dreadful news," she said with a bleak expression bowing her head. "I just heard that Bettie Wurst died."

She gazed at Halina, brushing a tear drop from her eye. "Bettie and Fritz Wurst used to attend Saint Jutta's; her husband worked with Wilhelm until business slowed and they sacked him."

Halina glanced at her hands and closed her eyes. "I'm sorry to hear that."

Freddy said to her, "Mother, how old's Carly now?"

Halina bit her bottom lip, widening her eyes.

His mother placed her hand on top of Halina's. "Halina, Carly's Bettie's daughter. I guess she's seven by now."

Speechless, Halina squeezed his mother's hand, sighing.

A slow smile built on his mother's face as she observed Halina. "Who else knows of the baby?"

Halina lifted her head, making unwavering eye contact with his mother. "You're the first we told."

His mother's fingers touched her mouth, and she said in a curious tone, "Not even Sister Rosa?"

"No, I wrote to my parents to inform them; we'll tell Aunt Rosa and Father Graf after mass tomorrow."

Freddy rubbed his finger across his sleepy eyes, coughing and moving his eyes from side to side. "Sorry, it's been a hard day."

Halina crossed her arms, assessing Freddy, and hardened her words. "Darling, perk up; most of the time I'm asleep when you come home."

Freddy's mother touched Halina's hand, giving her head a slow shake. "Halina, he'll never change; he's committed to everything he does. It surprised me you're having a baby."

His father cast an eye on Freddy. "Halina told mother you've more clients than you can handle; that's excellent news."

"I should, the Nazis purged most Jewish lawyers and left-leaning prosecutors," said Freddy, having in mind vacant law offices once inhabited by lawyers.

His father stared at his hands, speaking in a flat voice. "Oh! I didn't know that."

Freddy swallowed hard, saying with a voice hard as steel, "Under Adolf Hitler's sense of justice, there're no winners, only losers."

Confusion toned down his father's voice. "Freddy, what does that mean?"

Freddy's lips crinkled; he sized up his father and shot fast glances at Halina and his mother. "Hitler's will replaced the rule of law. My clients lost their rights, and now their fate lies with ruthless judges appointed by the Nazis. At the moment a petty theft conviction brings you five years in a prison or concentration camp." Freddy paused, and a slight smile drifted across his lips as he had a thought. "I fight for my clients; they're fortunate I'm not one of the charlatan lawyers who only want their money."

Freddy's mother scratched her head, tensing her voice. "Freddy, five years in prison for petty theft sounds harsh."

"That makes no sense," said Halina, tilting her head at him.

Freddy breathed before saying in a deliberate voice, "It does, because judges ignore briefs and dispense justice in ten to twenty minutes to please the führer."

Freddy caught sight of uncomfortable body movements and open-mouthed gazes.

His mother leaned in lowering, her eyes, "Freddy, why don't you complain?"

Freddy's shoulders dragged lower, and he hung his head, taking a wistful tone. "Mother, I can't. In America a jury dispenses justice; here the führer's thumbs on the scale." Freddy's fingers tapped on the table, and he spoke in a monotone voice. "Germany wasn't in this state when I became a lawyer. If she had been, I would have chosen another profession."

Halina clutched Freddy's hand. "Freddy, don't give up hope."

His father made eye contact with Halina and gave her a decisive nod. "Halina, he's faced adversity before and always gets through it."

* * *

Halina's stepmother grimaced at Freddy's mother, saying to her, "Barbara, look happy it's your first grandson's baptism party."

His mother frowned at the petite woman with grayish-hair. "I'm sorry, Irena, something terrible just crossed my mind."

"Well, what is it?" asked Freddy, clasping his hands together.

His mother's lips twitched. "It's nothing; forget it."

Freddy turned an eye on his father. "Do you know what's the matter; did someone die?"

His father bowed his head. "Freddy, it's not the time to tell you, it's Wilhelm Rolf's baptism celebration."

Freddy brought a hard smile to his lips. "I'm not letting it go till someone tells us what's wrong." After a quick glance at people fussing over the baby, he pressed his lips together and glared at his mother, lifting his voice a notch. "Mother, tell me what's wrong."

His mother sat up and grimaced a little and spoke, tensing her words, "You heard Father Graf during mass; he denounced the Nazis' sterilization position again. I wish he'd do it in confidence, not in public. He makes me shake when he does it; I expected the Gestapo to burst into the church and arrest him."

Sister Rosa showed a pained expression on her face. "He's stubborn; they won't silence him."

Freddy frowned, crossing his arms, speaking with a tinge of cynicism in his voice. "He's always spoke his mind. Mother, what else?"

Her face saddened, and she pulled out a letter, passing it to Sister Rosa.

Sister Rosa's eyes skimmed the letter, and she shook her head. "The police arrested Father Vogel."

Freddy wrung his hands, auditing her expressions. "Sister, may I see it?"

Freddy's nostrils flared as he read the letter. "Irena, he's the village priest that married my parents and baptized me. The Gestapo arrested him during his sermon and dragged him out of the church."

Irena's facial muscles sagged, and she glanced at his mother before her eyes settled on Freddy. "What did the priest do?"

In a reluctant tone of voice, Freddy spoke, avoiding her gaze. "They branded him a homosexual."

Halina's muscular father arrived and placed a beer in front of Freddy, laughing. "Who died?"

"Not funny, Timo," said Irena to her tawny-faced husband, "Someone wrote Barbara the Gestapo arrested the priest back home."

"Oh, sorry to hear it. What he'd do?"

"Timo, they accused him of being homosexual," said Irena, scrunching in the chair.

Timo stared at her, protruding his circled lips, slouching his head sideways.

"Mother, it surprised me to read that Werner's in the army and Maria's home pregnant."

She gave him a watery gaze, pulling on her hair. "Yes, and Uncle Dieter hired someone to replace him. Manfred's getting old and can't work any harder."

A finger swept across Freddy's brow to the bridge of his nose as he pondered what war had done to Karl, Gunter, and uncles Heinz, Manfred, and Otto. He handed back the letter with his voice taking a hard edge. "Will the madness ever end?"

Nef Muller beamed, placing two plates on the table, and pulled back a chair for Carrie, a delightful woman with shoulder-length brown hair, who was Halina's best friend. Nef examined Freddy's down-turned mouth, raising his brows above the rims of his spectacles. "Uh, Freddy, how's the food taste?"

Freddy grinned, denting his cheeks with two dimples. "We were waiting for you and Carrie to sit before we ate."

A pink color rushed into Nef's cheeks. "Freddy, I'm honored you chose me to be Wilhelm Rolf's godfather."

Freddy locked his eyes on him, adding a hint of arrogance to his voice. "Nef, remember Wilhelm Rolf expects lots of expensive gifts from his godparents."

Carrie's eyelashes fluttered, and she faced Nef. "Herr Muller, you didn't tell me what you do."

Freddy made a funny face. "Carrie, he's a physicist; he makes up numbers to prove things that no one understands."

Fish-eyed, Carrie studied Nef. "Oh, how nice."

Timo licked his lips. "The pork tastes good; who made it?"

"You're right." Nef seconded the statement.

Sister Rosa frowned at Timo. "I did; you don't remember my cooking."

Freddy planted himself alongside Halina, beaming at the attention she showed Wilhelm Rolf.

Halina flinched, rocking the baby, "Freddy, Father Graf said the Nazis are closing the kindergarten."

Freddy displayed a pensive smile, saying, "I'm not surprised, nothing they do does. Where'd Father Graf go?"

"He's visiting a patient at the hospital; he said he'll be back."

Nodding, Freddy paid attention to Berta Koch and Millie. A relaxed smile crossed Millie's face. "I didn't know Berta worked with you when you interned."

A grin cut through Freddy's cheeks. "She did and made it easier for me working there."

Berta turned a small crack between her lips into a wide grin.

Curt smirked, gazing at Berta. "Poor woman, he must have driven you crazy."

And Carrie beamed at Halina. "Don't keep the baby to yourself; let me hold my godson."

Curt glowed, brushing back his slick black hair. "I've wonderful news—Helga agreed to marry me, and I want you to be best man."

Freddy's smile broadened. "I'm so happy for you both and honored to be your best man."

Millie eye's bulged, and her lips shaped into a sarcastic smile; she gazed at Helga. "At least one of you won't be living in sin."

Helga's face softened, and she gave Millie a genuine smile. "Millie, they love each and will get around to it."

Freddy's shoulders collapsed, and with a lump in his throat, he examined Curt. "Shall we have a beer?"

Curt pursed his lips and poured two beers. "Freddy, want to tell me what's bothering you?"

Freddy hung his head, feeling his body numb. "Friday another client received a harsh sentence from the judges. They didn't investigate to see if it justified the charges. The lead judge screamed at me when I asked for proof the man committed a crime. Curt, if this keeps up, I'll go out of my mind."

Curt drew his lips into a straight line, moving his head from side to side. "Freddy, you're being hard on yourself. They dealt us a lousy hand when the Nazis came to power." Curt curled his bottom lip, moving his head closer. "Look at me. I'll spend my life hounded by countless regulations put out by them. They visit the plant often to check the books. Business is booming, and we added a new building to meet army contracts, but our costs are rising, and we're reluctant to raise prices. We don't want to suffer the consequences of the Nazis branding us profiteers." Curt eyeballed Freddy, giving his head a soft shake. "Sorry, I imagine its worse for you."

Freddy froze, seeing Father Graf approach. "Friedrich, you look upset," said the priest, drawing his brows together.

"Upset, Father?"

The priest pulled on his collar. "I'm sorry. I should learn to mind my business."

"Father Graf, the Nazis, who else?"

"Yes, the Nazis, who else?" said Father Graf, giving everyone a decisive nod. "Friedrich, Bishop Rauch tells me he's been seeking your opinion. How nice."

A gleam came to Freddy's eyes, and a laugh broke through his lips. "He does, and if he keeps it up, I'll start charging him."

* * *

346

Freddy stepped inside Gestapo headquarters at Prinz Albrecht Strasse and made a beeline for a youthful woman at the front desk. "Heil Hitler."

"Heil Hitler."

"Excuse me. The Gestapo arrested my client, can I see him?"

Unfazed, the woman gave him a blank stare. "Who are you, and what's your client's name?"

The long-faced woman wrote the name on a pad. "Herr Bauer, please sit till I summon you."

Freddy settled in a chair, mindful a shifty-eyed priest walked in, examining the room. The spectacled priest wrung his hands, narrowing his eyes on Freddy before slipping out of sight behind a bend in the staircase.

Freddy kept his vision on the vacated space, disbelieving his eyes. *What's a priest doing here?*

"Attorney Bauer, please come back to the desk," said the cantankerous receptionist, cutting short his thought.

Freddy jumped up and stormed over to the desk and crossed his arms.

The pucker-lipped receptionist eyed Freddy, saying, "Herr Bauer; no one has time for you."

Freddy's view narrowed, and his muscles tensed. He firmed his voice. "Tell them I need a minute and am not leaving till someone speaks to me."

The receptionist sighed, pointing to a row of seats, hissing. "Sit over there, Herr Bauer."

Watching the woman squint, Freddy questioned his tenacity.

The receptionist hung up the phone, unblinking, and scribbled something. "Herr Bauer, go upstairs and see Major Amsel; here's his room number."

Freddy stood inside room number 304, glaring at a bald man wearing gold-wired glasses and gray-green uniform displaying an odd twist to his mouth. The man slipped the paper he was reading into a folder and eased it onto a messy desk. He rose, sticking out his right hand. "Heil Hitler. Major Amsel at your service."

"Heil Hitler, Major."

"Herr Bauer, please sit."

Balanced on the edge of the seat, Freddy glared at Amsel, drawing his brows together. "Major, the Gestapo arrested my client Ernst Kessler just after three judges found him innocent of extortion."

Amsel concentrated on Freddy, tightening his smile. "Huh, what do they know?"

Freddy glared at the Gestapo officer. "Can you tell me what Kessler did?"

Closed-mouthed Amsel's body stiffened. "It's Gestapo business, which makes it none of yours or the court's."

Freddy's voice faded, and he avoided eye contact. "Major, can you tell me what crime he committed?"

Amsel's teeth bit out the words. "Attorney, didn't I make you understand? It's not any of your concern."

"Please, Major Amsel, let me spend a moment with him?"

Amsel's cheeks ballooned, then a burst of air blew through his mouth.

"You can't help Kessler; he's on his way to a concentration camp. We interrogated him, and he admitted to distributing Bolshevik leaflets," said Amsel, giving Freddy an angry stare. Amsel inspected Freddy, bright eyed, crossing his arms, softening his voice. "Attorney, I'm overworked and understaffed. I might need your help."

Freddy's mouth fell open while his eyes checked the room. "Um, Major, what do you mean?"

Amsel uncrossed his arms. "Someone in your position might help me weed out dissenters."

He locked his eyes on Amsel. "You want me to spy for you?"

Amsel focused on Freddy and raised his voice. "Attorney Bauer, it's your patriotic duty to do it."

Nausea took root in Freddy's stomach. "Find someone else. I'm busy."

Amsel gave Freddy a bitter smile. "Think about it; if you change your mind, come see me."

Freddy winced, leaving Amsel's office, spotting the nervous priest scrambling at the other end of the hall until he vanished from the stairs.

* * *

Berta Koch knocked and peeked in. "Uh, Freddy, your mother's here with someone, won't say why she's here."

Freddy jerked his head back, widening his blue eyes. "Oh, it's okay to show them in, Berta."

On his feet Freddy dropped his shoulders, eyeing two listless women. "Mother, what a surprise. Take a seat."

Freddy examined a frail woman sagging into a chair for a moment and lifted his gaze toward his mother. "What can I do for you?"

"Freddy, meet Frau Klein, Herr Klein's wife."

Freddy's stomach fluttered, and he gave his mother a blank look.

"Um, Frau Klein, I'm honored to meet you," said Freddy, narrowing his eyes on the frail woman wiping her nose.

His mother pulled back her head and swallowed before uttering, "Freddy, the police arrested Herr Klein."

Freddy's mouth fell open. "What!"

Frau Klein's voice vibrated with her nerves. "Herr Bauer, it was in the afternoon; they bashed the window in, and a mob rushed into the shop and sacked it. They called us unthinkable names, and people stood outside cheering. One was a customer. What did he do to her? Oskar tried stopping them. They laughed at him and pushed him aside."

Freddy's voice weakened. "Frau Klein, nothing. He did nothing to her."

Words stuck in the terrified woman's throat, and she wiped away tears, before blowing her nose hard. "Herr Bauer, in the morning we were sweeping up broken glass when two police officers pulled up in a van and arrested Oskar."

"Frau Klein, I'm sorry you saw it. I can't imagine what went through your mind when it happened."

His mother glared at him, raising her chest with a noisy breath, saying, "Decent folk won't forget that awful day."

Freddy gulped, rehashing her words. "Nor will the criminals who did it." He scrutinized the tormented old lady's red eyes. "Frau Klein, will you be okay?"

Frau Klein's lips trembled, and she closed her eyes. "Yes, Herr Bauer. I'm living with my sister and her husband. Thank you for asking."

"Frau Klein, what will happen to the store?"

She hung her head, sobbing. "Herr Bauer, we're destitute; we can't pay the rent or our creditors, and the government's confiscating our insurance money."

His mother frowned, crossing and uncrossing her arms. "Frau Klein needs your help."

While Freddy stared at Frau Klein, he cleared his throat. "Ahem. Did you go to a Jewish lawyer?"

Frau Klein said, facing his mother, "There are few allowed to practice, and everyone is afraid of the police."

Freddy evaded the distraught woman's eyes. "Humph, Frau Klein, I'm sorry, I don't think I can help you."

His mother took a hard breath. She looked away and raised her voice, astounded. "Freddy, why can't you help Frau Klein?"

Freddy slumped in the chair, thinking over her question. He shook his head, questioning his judgment, with Major Amsel on his mind. His ribs tightened, and his head dropped; he then concluded he couldn't help the woman. Feeling his heart beat in his throat, Freddy said in a faded voice, "Frau Klein, they'd disbar me if I helped a Jew."

Shocked, Frau Klein pressed on her breastbone, sobbing. "What will happen to my Oskar?"

His mother's icy gaze made Freddy wish he were somewhere else. He ignored his headache with a downcast expression and looked away. "Mother, I'm powerless against them."

* * *

A smile creased Bishop Rauch's face, and he fingered his cross, saying in a cheerful tone of voice, "Thank you for coming, Friedrich. I knew I could count on you."

Freddy's gut quivered, and he twisted his wedding band. "Your Excellency, I'm at your service."

Bishop Rauch rubbed his chain, dropping his smile, concentrating on Freddy. "Let's walk in the garden."

Freddy stuck his hands inside his coat, skirting plants awakening from winter. Bishop Rauch stopped and wiped his nose, giving Freddy an uneasy stare. "It's safe here."

Freddy flinched, displaying a grave look on his face. "Safe?"

Bishop Rauch gave him a brief smile and inched closer, lowering his voice. "The Gestapo watches me." He squinted, constricting his lips. "There's wickedness in my ranks. Many bishops sent Hitler birthday greetings."

Freddy backed away, lowering his brows. "I saw a priest at Gestapo headquarters."

Bishop Rauch cringed, putting his hand over his heart. "Judas!"

The bishop agonized, rubbing his thumb against his cross, firming his tone. "Let me ask this, can a devout National Socialist serve God if he's consumed by hatred? Nazism is not a religion; it's a plague that's consumed Germans willing to give up freedom to follow." Bishop Rauch's voice rivaled his angry glare. "No, I won't apologize for them." The bishop's cold eyes held Freddy's attention. "It took God six days to make the world. I wonder how long it will take the sacrilegious devils to destroy it."

Bishop Rauch backed off with color ebbed into his cheeks. "Hitler's been in power six years." The holy man's eyes clouded, and he softened his tone. "I can't stand by without doing something."

Freddy's brows squished together. "What do you mean?"

The bishop opined, glaring at Freddy, "In good conscience I can't overlook state terrorism. I have a moral obligation to steer my priests and parishioners in the right direction, no matter what the cost to me. I don't fear the Nazis and won't endorse antisemitism or godless behavior; no, I won't do that."

Freddy kept his head still, shifting his eyes.

"Friedrich, we must answer to the Almighty for our sins."

Freddy paused with a slack expression on his face, saying, "It's not wise to express your opinion, openly?"

The bishop's lips trembled, and he moved closer to Freddy, hardening his words. "Friedrich, was it wise of them to feed us propaganda and impose censorship on us? Decency ended in Germany when they did."

Bishop Rauch tightened his fingers on his cross, giving Freddy a frightful stare. "I worry Berlin might suffer the same fate as Sodom or Gomorrah." The man of God swept his head back and forth hard. "Hitler cleaned up society's filth but also put us in a fresh hell."

Freddy shivered, pondering the thought.

"It might be different if my predecessors had stood up to the Nazis. Now it's too late, and I'm left holding the devil horns," said Bishop Rauch, lining his face, speaking in a tired voice.

The holy man attempted a smile, hardening his gaze. "Friedrich, why were you at Gestapo headquarters?"

"I was looking after a client there and met with Major Amsel."

"Him. Hope it went well with him."

Freddy stepped back, dropping his head. "Bishop, it didn't, not at all."

Bishop Rauch ran his hand from his forehead to the back of his neck. "Nasty man, isn't he? He's called on me often."

Freddy gulped. "He has?"

Contempt laced the Bishop's tone; he tilted his head away. "He warns me to keep my nose out-of-state affairs."

"Your eminence, be careful what you state in public. The Gestapo might arrest you for it."

The cleric frowned, uncrossing his arms. "They won't chance detaining me; they're afraid a jailed bishop will upset most Catholics. But they won't hesitate to arrest a local priest, since 1933 they have hauled many to concentration camps."

Freddy opened and closed his mouth, trying to digest the bishop's words, darkening his blue eyes.

Bishop Rauch grimaced at him, bringing his head and shoulders forward. "Herr Bauer, I carry a heavy burden."

Freddy swallowed before speaking with a touch of sympathy in his voice, "Bishop, I understand and don't envy you."

The bishop's smile raised his cheeks high. "Herr Bauer, you're an honest man. I look forward to the next time we meet."

A relaxed smile spread over Freddy's lips as he leaned toward the bishop. "Thank you, bishop."

Bishop Rauch pinched his chin and inspected him, constricting his brows. "Herr Bauer, I respect your opinions, but can I trust you?"

A casual smile crossed Freddy's lips, and he inhaled, pondering the bishop's words.

Bishop Rauch narrowed his eyes on Freddy and moved closer to him. "Who knows what lies ahead; my world grows smaller each day. I need to know I'm in the company of people I can trust. Are you one of them?"

Freddy swallowed, weighing the bishop's words. His chest tightened, and he gave the bishop a flat gaze, softening his voice. "Yes, you can always count on me."

Freddy's stomach churned, and he accepted the bishop's handshake, mirroring the holy man's smile.

Chapter Nineteen

1939: War Begins

Halina's full lips trembled, and a rose color resembling a French wine spread through her cheeks. She glanced up at him with a nervous smile, blinking fast, and covered her ears. "Will someone please turn off the radio?"

Freddy hugged her. "Sit. Your mother and father will be fine."

"Darling, why would the Polish army want to attack a German radio station?"

His stomach sunk, and he ran a hand through his hair, agonizing over Halina's words. "I don't know; it makes no sense."

Halina gave him a probing gaze. "What will happen to Poland now?"

He grew quiet, holding air in his throat, wishing it could be different.

"Are my parents in harm's way?" said Halina with a few tears escaping from one eye.

Freddy's throat constricted, and he displayed a fake smile on his mouth. "Halina, don't worry. I'm sure they'll be fine."

Willy woke crying, struggling to free himself from Freddy's mother, and his father picked up the antsy child, grinning at him. "Willy, let's go outside to play; we might see a dog."

Halina kept her eyes on the door after they left. Her voice trembled, and she rubbed her hands together. "Freddy, what if something happened to them?"

He made strong eye contact with her, saying with soft undertones in his voice, "Halina, let's pray they're okay."

Halina stood up, cradling her baby bump. "I'm with child; I should be happy, not sad."

He attempted a smile and hugged her, whispering in her ear, "They'll be okay, I'm sure we'll be together for the baby's baptism."

Halina's eyes darkened, and she reclined, displaying a nervous smile.

His throat constricted. He grew still, pursing his lips. "Can I get you a drink of water?"

She attempted a smile, but nodded instead. When the doorbell rang, her eyes shut, and she covered her mouth. Freddy opened the door, and Sister Rosa burst inside with a deep note in her voice. "England and France declared war on Germany."

Sister Rosa locked eyes on her, jutting out her bottom lip. "Oh dear, Halina, you're not looking well; take a sip of the water."

Halina's hand shook, and she spilled drops of water while lifting the glass to her lips.

Sister Rosa hesitated before giving her a warm smile. "Honey, they'll be all right."

Halina dropped her head, giving Sister Rosa a pensive smile. "Aunt Rosa, you don't know that."

Freddy's shoulders dropped as he spoke to the serene nun. "Has Father Graf heard any news of the attack on Poland?"

Sister Rosa frowned, fumbling with her black rosary beads. "Bishop Rauch told Father Graf many clerics support the war."

Upset, Freddy shivered, glaring at Sister Rosa, speechless.

The bleak nun concentrated on Halina, saying in a firm tone, "Halina, did you eat? I don't want you sick over this."

"Who can eat?" said Halina, twisting her wrist.

"Nonsense, I'll make you something," said Sister Rosa with a hint of a frown.

Freddy's parents returned with Willy asleep in his father's arms and put him to bed.

His mother nuzzled next to Halina. "We passed Klein's, the stores managed by a young couple. It was sad to see Herr Klein not standing behind the counter. The Kleins are living in Warsaw with relatives. What will happen to them now?"

Halina, could not blink, her eyes bulging; her chin and lips trembled, and she covered her face with her hands.

* * *

Halina rubbed her baby bump, observing Willy walking his toy dog. Freddy laughed and picked up Willy, whirling him in a circle.

And his father wound up Willy's toy drummer boy. *Rat-a-tat, tat, rat-a-tat, tat, tat, tat.*

The child beamed, flapping his hands, tottering to his grandfather.

Freddy's mother cheered, sticking her head out of the kitchen, "The roast's done, and I've baked cookies for Willy."

"I'm starved; when do we eat?" said his father with a goofy grin on his face.

Halina's eyes audited Freddy's face, and she seized his hand, letting out a faint breath.

His brows wrinkled, and he whispered. "Are you okay?"

She let go of his hand, darting her eyes. "No, how can I be? I don't know if Irena and my father are alive."

"Halina, don't give up hope. Bishop Rauch is making inquiries, but he must be careful—the Gestapo's watching him."

Empty-eyed, she wrung her hands. "How can I bear not knowing what happened to them?"

Freddy tightened his grip. "Listen, it will be fine."

Unable to smile, she pondered him, fumbling with a strand of her golden hair. "I pray you're right."

"Wonder what's keeping Sister Rosa?" said Freddy's mother, peeking out of the kitchen.

With a sad demeanor, Halina bowed her head and messaged her pregnant belly.

"Halina, is it the baby?" said Freddy, lifting a brow, worried.

She said, closing her eyes with a slight tremor in her voice, "No, its nerves."

Willy dropped the soldier and pulled on Halina's leg. "Mama, eat. Mama, eat."

Freddy's father's face lit up, and he said with excitement in his voice, "Barbara, the roast smells good; can we eat?"

Freddy's mother walked out, crinkling her lips. "No one eats till Sister Rosa arrives."

Halina's voice cracked as she worried over Sister Rosa. "She's never late; where could she be?"

Freddy fastened his eyes on her, wrinkling his forehead. "It's near Christmas; maybe Father Graf needed her to do something for him."

Minutes later Sister Rosa arrived, holding her head high, sniffing the air before smiling.

And smiling and nodding, Freddy's father rose. "Sister Rosa's here; now we can eat."

Freddy's mother walked from the kitchen drying a plate on her apron. "Dinner's ready," she said in a joyous voice. "Sister, you're just in time to eat."

Warmth filled her chest, and she focused on Freddy's mother. "Good. What smells so good?"

"Sister, it's a roast!" replied his father, widening his eyes, laughing.

And while Freddy's father sliced the savory meat, there were two knocks on the door.

Freddy opened it, digging his eyes into Father Graf's grave face, catching the priest drop his head. "Friedrich, Bishop Rauch thought it best I give you the news."

Freddy took a quick, shallow breath. "Please come in."

"Freddy, who's at the door?" asked Halina, shouting from the kitchen.

"It's Father Graf!"

Halina burst into the room, cheerless, glaring at Father Graf's pursed lips. The priest froze, hanging his head. She covered her mouth, falling on the sofa, crying, gluing her eyes to Father Graf. Freddy wiped his clammy hands on his pants and sat alongside her, holding her hand, drawing air, fearing the worst.

Sister Rosa led everyone out of the kitchen.

Father Graf frowned, spotting Willy. "Wilhelm, take the boy to his room."

And sitting in silence for a moment, Father Graf glanced at Sister Rosa, speaking in a monotone voice. "The SS arrested Irena and sent her to a forced labor camp near here."

Halina's mouth slackened, and she placed her hands against her breastbone. "What of my father?"

Father Graf moved his head slow sideways. "Halina, he's dead. They were hiding in a church when a Luftwaffe plane attacked it."

Her eyes filled with tears. Halina shook her head. "It's not true; you must be mistaken," she whimpered, cradling her face in her hands. "No, no, no, no, no, no—it's not true."

Father Graf tilted his head at her, swallowing before speaking. "Irena made friends with a supervisor at the camp, and he passed her message to his priest."

Tears flowed from Halina's eyes, spotting her dress.

The solemn cleric sighed. "I know its grim news, but at least Irena's alive."

Halina's voice weakened to a near whisper. "When can I see her?"

"You can't; its prohibited," lamented Father Graf. "Like an animal she's gaged behind barbed wire, with no rights."

And Sister Rosa rolled her eyes, her face reddening. "The Nazis should rot in hell."

Speechless, Freddy's mother sat in silence.

"She's an old woman," said Halina, looking in his eyes for answers.

Freddy's mouth hung open; he gathered his thoughts. "Halina, we mustn't give up hope. I'll do everything in my power to help her."

She sniffled, wiping dry one eye, saying in a brittle voice, "I-I know you will."

And catching Willy's cries, she rose, easing herself toward the bedroom.

In eerie silence Freddy caught sight of long faces looking for a solution.

* * *

Rain beat hard against the window; Major Amsel jumped up, making eye contact with Freddy, stiffening his right arm, thundering his speech. "Heil Hitler."

With a slight shiver and his chest tightening, Freddy pinned his eyes on the impassioned man's face, saying to him in an apathetic tone, "Heil Hitler."

Amsel's smile wavered, and he angled his head toward a coat rack, speaking to him in an assertive voice. "Attorney, hang up your wet coat; did you reconsider my proposal?"

"I haven't changed my mind, Major," said Freddy, catching a few twitches in his stomach.

Amsel's posture sagged, and he tensed his jaw. "Then why are you here, attorney?"

"My mother-in-law is missing."

Amsel didn't blink, rubbing his chin. "That's not my concern. Why bother me? It's a police matter."

"But it's not. She's a Pole, married to a German citizen, living in Poland at the time the army overran the country."

"She's Polish?" asked Amsel, deepening the lines on his face.

"Yes,"

"Is she a Jew?"

"No, she's not a Jew," he said, blinking hard at the Gestapo officer. "The woman's a Catholic."

With a steady head, Amsel lifted his eyes, breathing through his nose, squeezing his chin. "Where's the woman's husband?"

Freddy slumped with a pained expression on his face. "He's dead, killed in a church the Luftwaffe bombed."

Amsel held his arms to his sides, squinting at Freddy. "How do you know she survived the bombing?"

"The parish priest said they took away her in a German Army truck."

Amsel crossed his arms, sneering at Freddy. "What a pity."

Freddy's lips pursed, and he felt warmth under the collar. "Why is it a pity?"

Major Amsel's straight lips changed to a grimace as he drummed on the desk. "She survived, not her husband. Poles are inferior to Germans." Amsel gritted his teeth, leaning his head forward, flicking his hand. "Attorney Bauer, go, you've wasted enough of my time."

* * *

Willy brought a smile to Halina's face, admiring a magnificent male lion.

Freddy's father grinned, pleading to his son in an appealing voice, "I'm hungry, Freddy, let's go for beers and something to eat."

"Willy want a pretzel?" said Freddy, flashing his teeth, lifting him in the air.

Willy giggled, "Ya, Papa."

"Then it's settled," said Freddy's mother, rocking Friedrich, "we're going to the beer garden."

At the beer garden, he nodded, with laugh lines stretched from the corners of his eyes. Warmth infused his body, eyeing Halina nursing Friedrich.

"Freddy, what are you thinking?" asked Halina, blinking, smiling warmly.

"It's rarely I spend a splendid day with my family."

Two servers dropped off four large beers, sausages, potato salad, and pretzels on the table.

Handed a pretzel, Willy perked up, and his tongue attacked the salt on it.

Freddy's eyes followed the sounds of laughing children to the lake. And he gasped, surprised by the water sparkling as if filled with diamonds. "It's breathtaking, isn't it?"

"Um, what's breathtaking?" said Halina, squishing her eyebrows together.

Lines bordered his cheeks, and he said to her in a cheerful voice, "Why, the sparkling water, but it will never compete with your grandeur."

Halina's lips twitched, with a dash of pink coloring her prominent cheeks.

His expression darkened as he eyed Friedrich in his mother's arms, recalling the day at the lake he nearly lost Halina.

Halina's curious tone brought him back from that other world. "Freddy, what's on your mind?"

"Nothing, just daydreaming," he confessed, wincing.

"Does he get enough sleep? He never did at home," said his mother matter-of-factly, beholding Halina.

"Mother, he never stops working," said Halina, giving her a pained gaze.

"Freddy, make time for your family," said Freddy's father, tightening his words, raising up his shoulders. "You can't make up the time you lost with them."

Freddy uncrossed his arms, glancing at him with a nervous smile, upset with himself.

Freddy's mother fanned herself with a smile, disappearing. "Wilhelm, Gretchen sent me a letter. Mother liked her birthday present. The blouse fit her. She says Werner's fighting in France and little Dieter asks for his father often, but still no word on Father Vogel."

Freddy's throat thickened, and he noticed Halina's smile fade as he concluded the priest was spending his days in a concentration camp.

His mother clasped her hands and shut her eyes, releasing a heavy sigh, catching Freddy's face with the drift.

"Mother, what is it?" he asked firmly.

"Now that Charlotte's married, it will be difficult for Andrea and Tomas to manage the farm. Look what happened when the army tore up the fields on maneuvers. If Dieter and Manfred hadn't helped them, they couldn't have replanted the fields."

Freddy assessed his aunt and uncle's dilemma.

A tight-lipped smile appeared on his mother's face. "Gretchen wrote Dieter made more money when the Nazis first raised farm prices, but now fertilizer, machinery expenses, and taxes have eaten into his profit." And she glared at Freddy's father. "Wilhelm, how long can Tomas and Andrea hold on to the farm?"

"They could sell the farm to Uncle Dieter and work for him," interrupted Freddy, reading into things, making eye contact with his mother.

His father's brows jumped, and he turned up his mouth's edges. "Hum, that's an idea."

And gazing at Halina, with a gleam in her eyes, his mother said in a silvery voice, "When Friedrich is older, we can visit the farm; it's pleasant there."

Startled by boisterous laughter coming from nearby soldiers, Friedrich woke up crying. And Freddy shook his head, concentrating on beating drums. "Do you hear the drums?"

Wide-eyed, Halina nodded, facing the noise.

A wrinkle appeared between his father's brows. "Um, I hear men singing."

"Um, they stopped singing," said Freddy's mother, stroking her chin.

The tempo of boots in cadence, pounding the ground, grew louder.

High-spirited people left their seats, flanking marching soldiers, yelling, "Heil Hitler" with gusto.

A tight-lipped soldier stood up at a neighboring table, flaring his nostrils. The baby-faced soldier lowered his brows at Freddy and shot his right arm in the air, shouting, "Heil Hitler."

The gap in his mother's mouth grew larger, and she snatched Willy in her arms, turning away from the soldier.

Freddy sprang up, with adrenaline shooting through his system, and threw out his arm, shouting, "Heil Hitler."

The soldier turned his head toward Freddy's father with an evil eye, curling his bottom lip. His father picked himself up and rocked sideways on his feet, jutting out his jaw. "H-Heil Hitler."

The soldier puffed out his chest, displaying a wide grin, and dropped into his seat.

Perched on the edge of his seat, Freddy angled his head away from the soldier, breathless, and squeezed his eyes shut. *Germany's gone mad.*

* * *

And recognizing loud sirens, Freddy sat up, driving his eyes left-to-right fast, coming to his senses. "No! This can't be happening, I'm dreaming?"

"Is there a fire, Freddy?" asked Halina, yawning and stretching, opening her eyes.

Freddy bolted to the window, and stopped breathing, catching sight of antiaircraft shells exploding in the sky. He monitored flashes of light going off along the horizon, growing sensitive to the noise. He stepped back, trembling, taking shaky breaths. "Children, Halina, get out of bed—we're being bombed."

Halina rose, shaking, and wrapped herself in her arms. "The children!"

Willy screamed, waking Friedrich, and Halina threw on a robe and snapped up the crying baby. Freddy hugged Willy, hoping to quiet him. "Halina, hurry, we must run to the cellar."

And Freddy breathed hard, aware of the loud antiaircraft fire, facing Halina with fear twisting in his gut. "Halina, are you all right?"

Her body trembled, and she shook her head, holding Friedrich tight against her breast.

Confined in a musty space with four brick walls, a huge black boiler, cobwebs, and dust-covered overhead plumbing, claustrophobic, Freddy watched Willy fall asleep in his arms.

Loud bangs startled Willy, and he jumped, screaming, twisting his body. Willy's hysterics stopped as he heard loud knocks and turned an eye on an old man, tapping his cane on the cement floor. A smile built on Willy's lips, and he lunged forward, reaching out for the cane.

"Children love the lion's head; I don't mind if he wants to play with it," said the old man, holding the cane steady, a conspicuous letter *A* on his gold ring.

"Thank you. Are you sure you want him playing with it? He could break it."

"Yes, of course. He won't damage it; children play with it when I go to the park for fresh air," said the gray-bearded man, looking pleased. "What's the boy's name?"

"Wilhelm, but we call him Willy."

Willy's eyes sparkled as he examined the lion's head.

The old man's eyes danced; he waved his cane in Willy's face. "Little boy, do you want to play with my stick?"

Friedrich cried, stirring Halina, and she woke shivering with a face turning an ashen color. "Is it over?"

Freddy swallowed, tightening the muscles in his chest. "Halina, I don't know."

The old fellow's eyes focused on Freddy. "There's chocolate in my pocket if you need it to quiet the boy."

Freddy's eyes softened, and he felt his stress lighten up. "Thanks, only in a pinch."

And with Freddy chatting with the old man, Halina breastfed Friedrich.

The old man wiped clean his dripping nose. "Since my wife passed, I spend most of my time reading and staring out the window. I was a professor at the Ludwig Gymnasium before I retired ten years ago."

Freddy shivered, and his jaw fell as he envisioned Leo and Rudolf.

A slow smile came to the elder's lips, pinching his beard. "Sir, if you don't mind me asking, what do you do?"

Freddy's face softened, and he gave the old man a firm nod. "I don't mind. I'm a lawyer."

The professor smirked. "Ah, that makes sense, with the long hours I've noticed you keep."

A smile dug into the old man's cheeks as he said in a quiet voice, "Pardon my manners, folks, I'm Professor Edmund Ackerman, at your service."

"I'm Attorney Friedrich Bauer, I live on the second floor."

Professor Ackerman stroked his cheek, fixing his eyes on him. "Did you study law at the university?"

"I did, professor."

Professor Ackerman scrutinized the steam pipes running across the ceiling.

"Come to think of it, there were two students I taught who I'm thinking were your age who went on to university to study law," said Professor Ackerman. "The two hated each other. One was a devout Communist, the other a hardened nationalist. The nationalist possessed an angry temper and thought it might cause him trouble. But here's the irony in it—one-night walking home I caught the Communist's sister holding hands with the nationalist."

A shutter went through Freddy's body, and he glanced around the room. "Professor, you're wrong!"

"No, I'm not mistaken, I'm sure of it," said Professor Ackerman, pressing his lips together.

A slow burn materialized in Freddy's gut.

Professor Ackerman gave him a decisive nod.

"I'm sure, young man. The Communist once introduced me to his sister. She was lovely."

Freddy brought a shaky hand to his forehead. He shut his eyes, concluding what appeared to be nothing—that is, Jette on the corner outside the café gazing in Rudolf's direction—was in fact something.

His eyes opened at the sound of Halina's voice. "Freddy, you okay?"

Dull-eyed, he stared at her, feeling his insides unravel.

* * *

Freddy hung up the phone, giving Berta an incredulous stare. "Uh, that was Bishop Rauch. He wants to see me right now."

"Um, it sounds important," said Berta, stiffening in the chair.

He scratched his head. "Said it can't wait and sent a car for me."

Not long after, a white-haired, spectacled priest with a weak chin entered his office. Freddy's eyes narrowed on the man; he thought he had run into him before.

"Good afternoon, Attorney Bauer. I'm Father Franke; Bishop Rauch said you were expecting me."

"Yes, Father, I was. You look familiar; did we meet someplace else?" he said, squinting at him.

"Don't think so," said Father Franke, examining him, shaking his head.

"Father Franke, do you know why Bishop Rauch wants to see me?"

Father Franke shrugged, giving his head a slight shake. "He didn't say."

On the trip to the bishop's residence, Freddy's mind struggled to place the priest's face. Under a long shadow, Father Franke pulled the black automobile up to the residence. And he made haste, leading Freddy through a long corridor to the bishop's door, knocking twice and peaking inside. "Your Excellency, Herr Bauer is here."

A spiritless voice answered, "Father Franke, please bring him in."

And after sighing, Bishop Rauch motioned Freddy into a chair, gazing at the priest. "You can leave, Father Franke."

The holy man pressed his cross against his breast, examining Freddy, and lowered his voice. "I got word Irena Suzansky died. I left a message at the rectory for Father Graf to call me; he should be the one to tell Sister Rosa."

"Bishop, what happened to her?" asked Freddy, voicing confusion with a quivering stomach.

"The work supervisor at the camp divulged to his parish priest Irena caught pneumonia."

Freddy could not draw a breath; his eyes darkened with his words. "How can I tell Halina this? Hasn't she's suffered enough?"

Bishop Rauch winced, narrowing his eyes. "May God help you."

The phone rang, and Bishop Rauch answered it. "Let them wait. I'll see them in a few minutes."

Freddy removed his palm from his mouth, giving the holy man a vacant stare. "Forgive me. I've taken up too much of your time."

Bishop Rauch bowed his head. "Friedrich, the Gestapo are waiting outside. They arrested two priests. They caught them listening to broadcasts from London."

Freddy's muscles tensed as he pondered the gravity of the crime. "Bishop, if found guilty, they will be lucky if sent to a concentration camp."

Bishop Rauch crossed his arms with a grim expression, collapsing his head. And he walked Freddy to the door, saying in a comforting tone, "Please convey my condolences to

Frau Bauer; tell her Frau Suzansky's in my prayers. Father Franke will bring you back."

"Father Franke!" Freddy blinked, shook his head, and stepped back with flared nostrils. "No, it can't be. No."

Bishop Rauch squinted. "What is it, Friedrich?"

Freddy gave him a flat gaze, hanging his hands by his side. "Father Franke's the priest I saw at Gestapo headquarters."

Bishop Rauch lowered his brows. "Are you positive?"

"I'm convinced." Freddy's voice was firm as he eyed the holy man.

Bishop Rauch crossed his arms. "Judas Iscariot, now I know whom he's loyal to."

An unexpected knock startled Bishop Rauch, and he cut his eyes toward the door and heard Father Franke say in a pumped-up voice, "Your Excellency, Major Amsel's waiting."

Freddy's eye bulged, and he musced, "Major Amsel?"

Bishop Rauch gave him a fake smile. "Come in, Father Franke."

Bishop Rauch's eyes avoided his betrayer, and his voice strained. "Take Herr Bauer home."

Father Franke showed him out. And discovering Major Amsel seated outside the door, in plainclothes, he stopped wide-eyed, recoiling his head. He continued, hoping he wouldn't see him, and walked past him without breathing.

"Attorney Bauer, is that you?"

Discovered, Freddy cringed and swung around, rubbing his fingertips against his palms. "Is that you, Major Amsel, I didn't recognize you out of uniform?"

Amsel's brows wrinkled, and he edged toward Freddy. "Attorney Bauer, what a surprise to see you. What are you doing here?"

With a hard smile, Freddy avoided his question. "A surprise, isn't it—what a coincidence."

"Attorney Bauer, you didn't answer my question," said Amsel, tightening his eyes on him.

Freddy gave Amsel a brittle laugh. "I was visiting with Bishop Rauch."

A coy smile crept over the major's lips.

Freddy's stomach tightened, and he put on a bogus smile.

Big-eyed Amsel scrutinized him.

He swallowed hard, enduring Amsel's hard gaze.

"I'm a busy man, Major; I should head back to work."

Amsel grimaced, stiffening his body, sticking out his right arm. "Heil Hitler."

Freddy mirrored his salute and walked away, thinking the despicable man stood for everything he loathed.

Chapter Twenty

The Agony of Two Robes

Father Graf finished reading the scripture and stepped back, pinching his lips together, glaring at his flock. His lips puckered, and he shook his head at rows of empty seats before giving a line of soldiers a quick stare. Through narrowed eyes, the looming priest held back his words until a mother fled with a screaming child.

Freddy seized Halina's hand, focusing on the priest, worried he might speak his mind. The reverend's lips parted, and he took a lengthy breath, hardening his gaze over the congregation.

"A mother dared to say the state murdered her son. I asked, 'What did he do?' She replied, 'He was in an institution for twenty years. What crime could he commit?' The state told her he died of meningitis, but she told me he was fine while visiting with him just before." Father Graf placed his hand over his chest and squinted, pursing his lips. "Is it God's will that the state decides who lives or dies? I ask you, If it's not God's will, whose is it?

"Would God want a deformed person sterilized? Would he want an alcoholic sterilized? Where does it end?" The priest's head shook hard, and he cast a wicked glance over at the parishioners. "Well, if it's not God's will, then whose is it?"

And he wrinkled his thick gray brows, nodding, sounding confident. "Many priests believe the church's commitment to the Reich should eclipse its duty to God. I don't quarrel with National Socialism's right to govern its citizens, but I won't say amen to its godless measures. If you asked which came first, I'd declare with certainty that God should."

Freddy's stomach muscles tightened as he heard a whisper from someone condemning the angry priest.

Father Graf's brows furrowed, and he leaned in, letting out a heavy sigh. "Let us pray for Jews, priests, and other poor souls imprisoned in concentration camps by the government."

An angry soldier jumped up, flaring his nostrils and pulling back his lips, exposing his teeth. "I won't pray for Jews."

Father Graf ignored him, mumbling words under his breath before speaking more loudly. "Let us offer prayers for the souls of Bolsheviks, and pray they change their godless ways."

The soldier's lips curled, and he marched to the back of the church, facing the doors. And he stopped, reversing himself, pounding a foot hard, shouting with a stiff arm, "Heil Hitler."

In dead silence, Halina sniffled, lowering her voice above a whisper. "The Gestapo might be in church."

Open-mouthed, Freddy picked through the assembly, gulping a breath, fearing she might be right.

* * *

Shallowly breathing, standing on tired legs, Freddy turned the door key, shouldering the door open. Halina woke, lifting her head off the sofa, rubbing her eyes, exposing a brief smile. And she rose, gliding her head back and forth, saying in a soft tense voice, "Freddy, how…how awful. Berta told me what happened in court."

Speechless, he hung his head, staring at his hands.

"I can't imagine what went through your head when you heard the verdict." She squeezed Freddy's hand and kissed him. "Go check on your sons; I'll get dinner ready."

Despair weighed on him, and he collapsed in a chair, sniffing *at Pyzy*, with sadness clouding his facial features.

"You must be hungry; eat the *Pyzy* while their still warm," said Halina, nodding at the table.

He peered at the plate, tormenting himself over the verdict. "I'm not hungry."

She reached across the table, patting his hand. "Do you want to talk?"

His shoulders dragged lower, and his Adam's apple bounced, and his voice cracked, betraying his true feelings. "It's my fault. They will execute Henrik Traeger in the morning. How will I sleep tonight?"

Halina tilted her head sideways. "You did what you could for him."

"I'm living a bad dream. How can a postal worker with eight children living on a meager three-hundred-mark salary a month pays with his life for stealing inexpensive items out of damaged packages?"

Halina's eyes moistened, and she tightened her lips.

He winced, feeling a pain in his gut.

"The prosecutor argued Henrik Traeger's committed petty theft before. The lead judge's lips curled. It did not look good for Henrik."

"How awful."

"That's what I said after the judge read the decision. He told me to sit and be quiet. Justice doesn't exist; sentences depend on handpicked men intent on pleasing Hitler." And his lips widened; he tapped his fingers hard against the table. "Huh, not what they taught me in law school."

Halina shivered, wrapping herself in her arms.

"Halina, maybe I should've chosen another profession."

She looked up, giving him a flat gaze.

"I couldn't visit Henrik. What's going to happen to his family?"

She squeezed his hand, showing him an understanding nod.

A flush carried over his cheeks; he scrutinized her for a few moments and covered his face. "The court prosecutor reported me to the Court of Honor."

"Why!"

"I didn't salute Hitler at the beginning of a trial. He told them it was not my first time."

"That was a foolish mistake; what were you thinking?"

His eyes gleamed, welling up with tears. "I hate Hitler."

"Freddy, you don't have to approve of him, just say the words. They could disbar you. Did you consider your family?"

He lowered his head, haunted by guilt, replaying what had happened. "I'm sorry. They don't disbar first-time offenders, usually give them a slap on the hand and a scolding."

Halina's straight lips pressed into a grimace, and her tone became bitter. "That's not comforting. Don't do it again."

His head pulled back, and he crumpled in the chair, hating himself. "I promise."

"Eat your *Pyzy*; they're getting cold."

"Can't eat; go to bed," he said, fatigued, of the opinion he deserved his headache. "I need to be alone, with three fingers of Johnnie Walker."

* * *

Dressed in his black lawyer's robe, Freddy invaded Berlin District Court, hurrying for the attorneys' office and dropped in to see Archie Betz, the senior law clerk of the Bar Association. He relaxed across from the fat-cheeked man with thick silver hair. Archie folded his arms, unmasking tobacco-stained teeth, taking notice of him. "Friedrich, wish this day was over—found out Judge Danner delayed the Dell case two hours."

"Oh, is anyone here to play chess with Archie while I wait?"

Archie's expression appeared pained.

"Something wrong, Archie?"

"The Gestapo arrested Heinrich Stuckart and Bernt Rust late yesterday afternoon."

"Why, Archie, what did they do?"

Archie placed his hands against his fleshy belly, stretching his neck to glance over his shoulder, and sat up, leaning forward, crinkling his lips. "There were whispers they forged passports."

Freddy's stomach quivered; he feared the worst-case outcome for Heinrich Stuckart and Bernt Rust.

"Freddy, isn't Bernt's wife's Jewish? Is it possible they did it to help Jews escape Germany?"

"M-makes sense, Archie," said Freddy, feeling a chill, making strong eye contact with Archie.

Archie cringed, turning his head. "The Gestapo will torture them."

Freddy gave the room a quick glance. "Archie, someone here might be a spy who reported them. The Gestapo has agents everywhere."

Archie gave him a stony stare, ringing his pupils in a sea of white.

"Freddy, do you socialize with Heinrich and Bernt? Major Amsel asked, do you?"

Freddy, his hands ups, shaking his head, said, "No, I'm not."

Archie lit up a cigarette with a shaking hand.

An image of Major Amsel at Bishop Rauch's residence crossed Freddy's mind.

Freddy's voice sounded strained. "Archie, what else did Major Amsel ask you?"

Archie's mouth opened, and he glanced at the ceiling for a few seconds before dropping his head.

"Freddy, he asked me who your friends are and if I doubted your loyalty to the führer."

"And?" Freddy asked, worried.

Archie's shoulders sagged, and he scratched the back of his neck. "I spoke the truth, told him you were an excellent lawyer and well liked at the Bar."

"Archie, are you suspicious of me?"

Archie's head recoiled; his arms crossed his chest.

"Freddy, you know I'm not." He gulped, pulling back in his chair. "But Major Amsel is; be wary of him."

* * *

A shadow covered Freddy's desk, and he glanced at Berta, bobbing his head. "Huh, Berta, the newspaper says rain."

"Go home, Freddy; have dinner with your family. You're going to be thirty-two tomorrow. The Deckert case can wait."

He closed and reopened a folder labeled Ludwig Deckert, stuffed full of papers. "Maybe I shouldn't," he said, minding the folder.

She moved her head forward, pinning her eyes to him. "It can wait; go home."

And he gave Berta a hard stare as he descended into despair. "I can't; I've too much work."

Berta's serene stare turned into a disdainful glare.

Freddy's mouth fell open, and his head twitched as he heard the telephone's loud ring. And gave Berta an incredulous stare, placing the receiver against his ear. "No. Is she okay?" He listened to Halina's sobs. "When did it happen?"

Freddy listened to Halina for a longer period. "Please calm yourself. Tell Aunt Rosa; I'll call Bishop Rauch."

Freddy appeared shocked as he hung up the phone.

"Freddy, what's wrong?"

He said in a disbelieving tone, "The Gestapo arrested Father Graf."

Then he answered a call with a shaking hand. "Hello. Attorney Bauer speaking."

"Attorney Bauer, it's Father Frei, Father Franke's replacement, Bishop Rauch needs to see you. Can I come for you?"

Freddy swallowed; his blue pupils darting back and forth. "No, it's better I take a taxi."

Freddy stood, sat, and stood gazing everywhere till his eyes settled on Berta. "Uh, I won't be back. Uh, Bishop Rauch wants me."

Inside the bishop's office, the high priest backed up from the window, fixing his eyes on Freddy with a sad demeanor. He gave the holy man a fake smile, knotting his stomach.

"I warned Father Graf not to speak out against the government, but the stubborn fool argued it was God's will. The Gestapo, or one of their spies, most likely were at Sunday Mass when he railed against Hitler." Bishop Rauch wrinkled his face, pulling his brows closer, angling his eyes on him. "Were you there?"

Freddy's chin fell, bouncing on his chest. "Yes, I was."

An image of Father Graf's pained stare the day he told him he had missed mass came to mind.

Bishop Rauch's lips straightened; he gave Freddy an unwavering glance. "I'll take Father Graf's place at Sunday Mass."

Freddy grimaced with a slight nod.

Bishop Rauch sank into his chair, praying to himself, clutching his cross. And with steadfast eyes, he said, pitching his voice higher, "This time he overdid it, and I wasn't able to save him. The Gestapo gave me time with him. We prayed together, and afterward he said he'd do it again given the chance."

Dull-eyed, Freddy mused over Major Amsel, cupping his knees with his palms, scrutinizing the priest. "Who arrested Father Graf?"

Bishop Rauch's lips pulled back in disgust. "Major Amsel!"

And experiencing a slight headache, Freddy flashed him a bitter smile. "He frightens me."

The bishop's lips made an oval shape, and he cut his eyes at him, speaking in a breathy voice. "Friedrich, I might have placed you in danger."

"Bishop, I'm sure of it," he said with a slight frown. "The man's suspicious nature irritates me." And he pressed his lips into a line. "I'm not sure how to handle him."

* * *

Freddy gawked at Saint Jutta's smoldering remains, catching a whiff of drifting smoke. He faced his family, pleased they were safe. Two boys and a girl he figured to be ten years old played in the remains of a bombed apartment building unsupervised. His vision blurred, and he tightened his grip on Willy's hand whispering, "Where are their parents; it's not safe."

"It's gone; where will we go to church?" his mother said, agonizing, resting her fingers on her cheeks. "What's next, the entire city?"

Willy pulled on his coat, pointing at a massive pile of bricks and smoldering wood in front of a half-collapsed wall. "Papa, church fall down."

"I can't imagine what went through Father Graf's mind hearing the news," said Freddy's father. "Saint Jutta's was his life."

Friedrich pulled on his mother's dress. "Mama. We go home."

His father smiled, gathering Friedrich in his arms

Halina wept, inhaling a shaky breath. "Thank God Aunt Rosa wasn't inside the church."

"Are you okay?" Freddy said, tightening his grip on Willy's hand.

Halina wept. "Saint Jutta was part of our lives."

"Papa, Mama's crying," said Willy.

"Mama's sad because the church is no longer there anymore."

Freddy's facial muscles slackened, and he gave a second glance to the destroyed church and the shattered buildings nearby.

"Will they rebuild Saint Jutta's?" asked Halina, using a weary tone, her words just loud enough to be heard.

"Yes," said his mother, answering her, sniffling.

Freddy drew back, spooked by the loud sirens from a firetruck that sped along a street behind him. He riveted his eyes on a small girl helping her parents push a carriage stacked with belongings.

Halina drew Friedrich close. "Freddy, where will they go?"

"I don't know; let's hope they're blessed with family near here," he said, dejected, keeping the vagrants in sight, imagining the total city in ashes. His mind ran through different scenarios, and he winced, sensing there was no hope. "Halina, you and the boys must leave Berlin; it's no longer invincible."

Halina's lips spread, and she darted her eyes between Freddy and his parents without moving her head.

Freddy gave her a curt nod, firming his voice. "It's final; my mind's made up. You can stay at the farm where it's safe."

"Freddy, you're right," said his father, frowning, stiffening his body.

* * *

Freddy's lips parted, and he wrung his hands together as he considered Prosecutor Conrad Drexler.

His eyes closed; he gently shook his head. *No, I won't put the state's interests before Katrina Schubert. Let them condemn me for it.*

The beady-eyed prosecutor displayed a toothy grin, lifting his chin to drag his index finger across his neck. Freddy flinched, bulging his eyes and pushing out his jaw. *I hate him.*

He jumped, hearing an abrupt noise. His heart thumped as he monitored the door, waiting for the judges to arrive.

His chest tightened. *Did the judges read the psychiatrist's letter I put inside my brief?*

The veins in his neck corded as he found Major Amsel in the crowd. And he gasped, turning white. He faced Katrina, who was crumpling her slight frame in between two pouting police officers, covering her face. *God, please don't let her die.*

The judge's door opened. Bug eyed Freddy dragged his fingers down his cheeks: *God, spare Katrina's life.*

Three black-robed men paraded single file into the room, positioning themselves between Conrad Drexler and Freddy. Freddy glanced twice at the senior judge, guessing he might be younger than him. He rose, wanting to be somewhere else, preparing to give the Hitler greeting. The senior judge threw out his stiffened right arm, and in unison the judges raised their voices. "Heil Hitler."

The judges dropped into their seats and huddled together. Tight jawed, the senior judge nodded at the expressionless police officers. They lifted her up, and they brought Katrina in front of him.

Katrina's body shook. Freddy's face turned white, mindful of her dirty face and clothes.

The lead judge gave Katrina a harsh squint. "Katrina Schubert, the Public Prosecutor Conrad Drexler for the Special Court of Berlin has charged you with committing the crime of looting."

Katrina displayed a nervous smile as the officers held her up.

The judge's eyes bulged and his expression darkened as he read Conrad Drexler's complaint. "It says here you entered a burning building during an air raid and stole food. Is that right?"

Katrina twitched.

"Stop doing that; answer my question," said the head judge.

Katrina shivered. "They'd burn in the fire if I-I didn't take them."

"Ah, so you, Katrina Schubert, admit you stole food during an air raid?" said the judge, baring his teeth.

"I clean rooms; I'm a widow. My children need to eat," said Katrina with sweat breaking out on her face.

"No excuse. Katrina Schubert, the state gives you money for your children," said the judge, crossing his arms.

"It's not enough." Katrina whimpered. The judge whacked the desk, making her head shake hard.

"Katrina Schubert, you're a worthless individual; you stand before me and tell me the money the state provides is not enough," said the judge in a taunting tone as he studied Katrina.

Freddy's throat constricted, running through a thought. *What if the judges pay no attention to the psychiatrist's letter?*

And when the judges rose, Freddy tasted something awful brought up from his stomach. The senior judge, Dr. Christoff, gave Katrina an icy stare. "In the name of the German people, the Special Court of Berlin in the proceedings against Katrina Schubert charged with looting a building on the Sixteenth of December 1943, the judges have reached a decision."

Worried, unable to sit still, Freddy glanced at Katrina; he was nauseous seeing black spots.

Dr. Christoff's voice took a frightening tone. "Katrina Schubert born on the Tenth of July 1913, I sentence you to death, this day, December the Twenty-third, 1943, for looting during wartime. Katrina Schubert, you trespassed into a burning building to undertake a crime,"—he smirked at her—"and you will pay court expenses."

She whimpered, shaking her head. "It was only two cans of soup. What will happen to my girls?"

Freddy scowled at the judges, fixating on the senior judge's callous face.

"This isn't justice," he protested loud enough to make Dr. Christoff give him an angry stare.

And he bared his teeth, digging his eyes into the judge, clenching his fist. The cold-blooded man gave him a smug smile, saying, "Attorney Bauer, is there something else?"

* * *

Berta wandered into Freddy's office with a deadpan expression.

"What's wrong?"

"Katrina Schubert's brother's here to see you."

Freddy winced. "Berta, please show him."

Katrina's brother cowered in a seat, bringing a shaking hand to his forehead.

"I'm sorry for your loss. I did everything I could for Katrina, Herr."

"H-Herr Ingman, Tasman Ingman, H-Herr Bauer. I believe you. Katrina said you were a good man."

"Herr Ingman, how can I be of help?" asked Freddy, softening his voice with an ache in his throat.

With gleaming eyes, Herr Ingman handed Freddy a paper. "Herr Bauer, I make little money and care for a wife and three children, along with Katrina's girls. I don't know what to do. I can't pay it."

Freddy eyed the seven hundred and fifty mark sum at the bottom of the itemized bill from the Reich Office of Prosecutions. His eyes jumped back and forth from the first and fourth lines. *What—a three hundred and five mark death sentence fee and a hundred and fifty more to execute her?*

The tip of his tongue protruded, and he concentrated on the grimacing man. "Herr Ingman."

Tasman Ingman raised his head, staring at him, holding his hands together in front of his crotch. "Yes, Attorney Bauer."

"If you let me, I'll pay the bill."

Tasman Ingman gasped and covered his mouth with shaking hands.

* * *

Freddy wiped moisture off the outside window and looked inside, beaming at cheerful people gathered around the Christmas tree. His smile broadened as he noted his sons playing with toys he had brought from Berlin. And he caught a whiff of Halina's sweet-scented perfume, feeling lightness in his limbs. His lips spread more, mindful of her face, which caught light from the fireplace. Its rhythm intoxicated him. His heart beat faster. "Halina, I love you."

He moved closer and kissed the lips he had missed and desired while living alone in Berlin.

His eyes welled up. "I missed the taste of your lips."

She gave him a silly grin.

"Merry Christmas," he said, pulling a box from inside a pocket.

Her jaw dropped, and her eyes sparkled; she placed her hand over her heart.

"Halina, open it."

Her fingers fumbled with the ribbon while she opened the gift. Her voice choked with tears. "Oh, Freddy, it's gorgeous; it matches the butterfly clip in my hair," she said, shedding tears.

Freddy put the necklace around her neck, noting the dance of light on it from the fireplace's flames.

"It's a marvelous gift," said Halina before giving him a warm kiss.

His heart raced, and he admired her stunning face.

She said, bringing a slow smile to her lips, nodding, "Freddy, I love you."

Friedrich tapped on the window, laughing, bouncing from foot to foot.

Freddy stuck his thumbs in his ears, wiggling his fingers, making a funny face at Friedrich; he noticed Grandma Petra and Aunt Andrea approved.

"Halina, it's getting colder; do you want to warm up inside by the fire?"

Halina shed a happy tear and placed her head against his chest. "No, it's our only chance to be alone." And she sniffled, hugging him. "I couldn't bear losing you. I cry each time I hear they bombed Berlin and pray every night the war ends."

A slight chill dashed through Freddy's body. "Don't worry, I'm safe underground."

A nagging thought held his attention.

"Freddy, why so quiet; is there something wrong?"

His chest grew heavy, and he lowered his shoulders.

"I know that look," said Halina, stepping back, twisting a strand of her lengthy hair. "There's something bothering you."

He hung his head, on the verge of tears.

"Freddy, you're worrying me; say something."

"I want to give up practicing law," said Freddy, facing away.

She sighed. "Freddy, I don't understand; how could you do that?"

He pictured the horror on Katrina Schubert's face dragged from court.

He was nearly crying; his voice cracked, and he said to her, "I stayed in bed the day they executed Katrina."

"But Freddy, it wasn't your fault; you did everything possible for her.

"But it was useless," he protested, wearing an intense expression. "The judges showed her no mercy." And he shuddered, mumbling his words. "Heartless sentences are the norm."

"The man I married isn't a quitter," she said, removing her face from the fireplace light, crossing and uncrossing her arms and bowing her head.

His throat thickened; he was fraught with self-loathing. "Forgive me. I'm still the man you married."

A smile bloomed on Halina's lips. "I never doubted you."

And when he heard drumming on the window, he faced Willy and Friedrich, glowing from ear to ear, with tears shining his eyes. "Halina, looks like we're wanted," he said, savoring the moment in his mind.

Chapter Twenty-One

First Half 1943

A wintry wind brushed Freddy's face as he watched Father Frei stop the bishop's black automobile in front of him at Gestapo headquarters at Number 8 Prinz Albrecht Strasse. Seated in the back, Bishop Rauch lowered the window with a dark expression on his face.

"Friedrich, please come inside with me."

In pensive thought, the bishop thumbed a piece of paper. Freddy pressed his lips together, waiting out his silence.

The bishop audited him. "I just received terrible news."

Freddy's voice dropped to a murmur. "I'm sorry—only thing we get these days."

The grave expression on the bishop's face mutated into a forced smile. "The note in my hand says Nazis are deporting Jews to Treblinka."

"Um, Treblinka?" said Freddy, wrinkling his forehead, studying the bishop's bleak face.

The bishop leaned back, raising his lifeless eyes, saying something undetectable.

Freddy's eyelids drooped, with a flush coming to his cheeks. "Your eminence, did I say something wrong?"

Bishop Rauch's face saddened; he stared at the note in his hand. "Jewish Poles are being gassed and cremated at a concentration camp near Warsaw."

The bishop's words circled in his brain trying to make sense out of them. "No, that's not true; it's impossible!"

Bishop Rauch said in a soft voice, "I pray for them."

Freddy's body froze. He gave the bishop a sideways glance, feeling disbelief.

"Friedrich, are you okay?"

He shook his head. "We're powerless against them, aren't we?"

A bit of optimism wormed its way into the bishop's voice. "Yes, we're at their mercy, but it doesn't mean we give up fighting them."

Freddy gave him a dim smile, exhaling, deciphering his thoughts. "Why should Amsel want to see both of us?"

Bishop Rauch responded, "Friedrich, it can't be positive."

Seated within reach of Bishop Rauch in Major Amsel's office, he gathered a long breath to calm his nerves. On the other side of the desk, Major Amsel's body stiffened, and with an icy glare, his eyes darted back and forth between Bishop Rauch and Freddy. Amsel unmasked a fake smile.

"Bishop Rauch, we've transported Sister Rosa to Dachau for condemning the führer in public. A saleswoman called for the police when she criticized the führer to her. We picked up Sister Rosa and brought her here for questioning." Major Amsel's nostrils flared. "She admitted telling a woman the führer ruined Germany," said Major Amsel before slamming his hand against the desk, bunching skin around his eyes. "Attorney, you can't help her."

Freddy glared, refusing to break eye contact with him. "Was Sister Rosa questioned or tortured?"

Amsel crossed his arms in front of his chest. "Attorney, watch what you say to me—you might be sorry."

Freddy gave Amsel an incredulous stare and leaned back, tightening his fists. He wondered what he'd tell Halina.

"Major, can I see Sister Suzansky?" asked Bishop Rauch, drawing his brows together.

Amsel faced him. "I'll consider it."

Bishop Rauch frowned, clutching his cross. "Major, is there something else?"

Amsel examined a stack of folders, drawing his lips into a straight line.

"There is, bishop," he said, morphing his lips into a fake smile that baffled Freddy.

Amsel's eyes probed Bishop Rauch for a moment, then he looked toward Freddy.

"Attorney, several things disturb me," said Amsel, squinting at Freddy.

Freddy's jaw dropped, and he felt a burst of heat move through his body. "Uh, I don't understand."

Amsel opened a folder and ran his eyes over the first page, stabbing the middle of a page with his index finger. "Ah, Ernst Kessler—why don't we start there?"

Freddy rubbed his sweaty palms against his legs, realizing hard thuds in his chest. "Why him? The judges acquitted Ernst Kessler."

Amsel frowned. "A confessed Bolshevik whom you defended."

A thought stuck in his mind. *What if Amsel discovers I helped Alfred Beiner defend Communists?*

Amsel examined Freddy, saying with a curious tone, "Is there something wrong, Attorney Bauer?"

He concentrated on Amsel's folder. His elbows pushed against his sides, and he heard his stomach growl. "Is that file on me?"

The man twisted his lips into a wry smile. "The entire file."

Freddy's dry tongue sanded the roof of his mouth.

"It can't be," Bishop Rauch said, narrowing his eyes. "Herr Bauer's a lawyer; he upholds the law."

Major Amsel glanced over at another page.

Amsel's voice took on a dangerous tone. "Ah, says here Prosecutor Conrad Drexler turned you in for not saluting the führer."

"My fault. I apologized to the Honor Court, and they censured me for it; you're barking up the wrong tree."

"Huh, barking up the wrong tree? Attorney, what does that mean?"

"Sorry, it's an American expression meaning you're looking for answers in the wrong place."

Amsel glared at Freddy, taking short, noisy breaths. "Am I now? You grew up in America, doesn't that raise doubts?"

Freddy could not wrap his mind around Amsel's thought.

"And then there's Father Graf," said Amsel, disgusted. "A traitor who vilified the führer and often prayed for the Jews." Amsel clenched his fists. "Or Sister Rosa, who served him."

Amsel gave Bishop Rauch a hostile stare; his face whitened.

"Bishop, the state hasn't overlooked the fact that you place God's law above the state in your sermons. Pity you don't live in a cell next to Father Graf."

Bishop Rauch jerked his head back. "Major, you're losing the war. If you arrest a bishop, people will be angry. Do you think that's a wise decision?"

A tremor touched Amsel's lips. He shot a hard smile at Freddy. "Attorney, you and your wife's close relationship to the clerics and Sister Rosa brings you under suspicion."

"It shouldn't. Sister Rosa's my wife's aunt, and Father Graf's our parish priest; he introduced us to Bishop Rauch," said Freddy. "It adds up to coincidences, not crimes."

"Is your association with Jews a coincidence too?" inquired Amsel with a hint of mockery.

Freddy gave Amsel a bitter stare. "Uh, what Jews?"

Amsel studied him. "Rector Rath says you were a disciple of Professor Stefan Karp."

"Was that a crime?" fumed Freddy, raising his voice. "He was a wise man who mentored and inspired me; I considered him a friend."

"And he's a Jew," said the Major, pulling back his lips.

Freddy bit his lip, worrying Rector Rath might have mentioned Rudolf von Krieg's name to Major Amsel.

"Were Heinrich Stuckart and Bernt Rust close friends?" Amsel's voice matched the bitterness of his gaze.

Freddy turned white. "Were?"

"They forged passports for Jews."

"I played chess with Heinrich Stuckart, waiting in the attorney's office for trials to begin, nothing more. I'm sure Archie Betz confirmed it when you questioned him, am I right?"

"Major, all you have is a bunch of coincidences that amount to nothing. Where's your evidence I committed a crime?" Freddy said.

Contempt crept into Bishop Rauch's voice. "Major, is Attorney Bauer's inquisition over? I thought you brought us here to tell us you arrested Sister Rosa. Can we go now?"

Amsel glared at Bishop Rauch and steered his head to the door, pointing at it. "You can leave."

Freddy followed behind Bishop Rauch, and as he heard a loud noise behind him, he envisioned Amsel whacking his desk.

* * *

Freddy stirred, wakened by loud air raid sirens. He fixated on the office door, sensing danger.

He snatched his coat and hat and dashed into the biting night air, glimpsing at beaming lights crisscrossing in the darkness. And he strung along with a family, heading toward a bunker. Inside Freddy leaned on the concrete, checking his surroundings. He eyed a nervous man and woman with two adolescent girls seated in front of them.

A flush appeared on his cheeks. "We'll be safe underground," he said, reassuring the youthful couple with a nod.

The man attempted to smile.

Freddy cowered while loud explosions shook the ground beneath him. The woman and children screamed. One girl covered her ears, and the other clenched her father's arms. Freddy cringed, knowing he had made the right decision about sending Halina and the boys away.

A bomb exploded overhead, shaking the ground, causing bits of concrete to fall. Dust lingered. And people let out ear-piercing shrieks. Another bomb followed, knocking out the lights. In compete darkness, people screamed and called out God's name. A man without vocal skills sang out, playing his accordion soothing nerves.

Hours later, the overhead lights flickered. Freddy scratched his head, reckoning the loud sirens signaled an end to the air raid. He dusted himself off and caught sight of dazed and shocked faces on the family in front of him. Freddy closed his eyes; and a slow smile crossed his lips. *It ended; and I won't have to listen to the irritating accordion player's voice.*

The youthful man shuddered, clutching his daughter tight.

Freddy checked the time. "Hold on; it should be over. I figure they need to fly home before sunup."

A smile slowly appeared on the youthful man's mouth. "Think so. Hope you're right."

Freddy yawned, rubbing the whiskers on his chin.

Exhausted, he vacated the bunker, picking up the booming noise a firetruck made, which was pulling up to the flaming remains where a building once stood. The air reeked with the stench from the burning fires, and he and pinched his nose.

On the walk back, Freddy froze, noticing fire in his apartment's direction. "Oh God, no, it can't be," he said, gasping.

He arrived at the apartment short-winded, mindful of loud sirens, and slapped his hands over his ears, probing the flames. "It's gone."

With a fluttering stomach he stared at two firefighters pouring water on flames that moved at the whim of the wind. Freddy pressed his fist against his trembling mouth, shutting his eyes, repeating a thought over and over in his brain. *What if I hadn't sent them away?*

Freddy stayed put till the last drop of water came out of the hose. His legs wobbled, and he edged himself toward piles of charred bricks and wood where three buildings once stood. He shed a tear, convinced part of his life had died in the building. *Maybe a photo survived.*

Firefighters approached with a body on a stretcher. His skin tingled, and he removed his hat and ran his fingers through his hair.

"Do you know who it is?" Freddy asked a blackened firefighter.

"He shouldn't be hard to name. He wore a gold ring with the letter A on it."

Freddy covered his mouth and backed away. "No, it can't be him."

* * *

Berta frowned, handing Freddy a cup of coffee. "It's your fourth cup."

"I can handle it."

Berta's eyes teared. "Freddy, I'm glad there's a place you can sleep," she said, letting out a huge breath. "I made room for a cousin and her daughter. A bomb hit their apartment."

Freddy clasped his hands together, considering her words, whispering to himself, "No home in Berlin is safe from bombing anymore."

Berta's nose scrunched. "What's that odor?"

"Last night's dinner scraps; I slept here last night."

Berta sat, scratching her temple. "Why are you sleeping in the office?"

"Is there any scotch left?" he said, staring down at the coffee with a pained expression.

"Uh oh, when you want scotch, it tells me something's wrong," said Berta, scrutinizing him. "What is it?"

Expressionless, with a glimmer in his eyes, he lowered his head. "Berta, can you get the scotch?"

Berta frowned, placing the quarter-full bottle in front in front of him. "Freddy, what's wrong? You're scaring me."

Freddy handed her a letter.

And after reading it, she slumped, wearing a somber expression. "What, you're ordered to report for duty? Aren't you too old; don't they want boys?"

Freddy looked away. "I guess not if you're losing a war."

"Huh, you slept here because you didn't want to tell your parents. Does Halina know?"

"No, only my mother, Archie, and you."

"Your mother?"

"I called home this morning."

"It's not right," Berta said.

A loud phone ring startled Freddy. "Attorney Bauer speaking; how may I help you?" He paused. "Good afternoon, Bishop Rauch."

The receiver shook against Freddy's ear. By the time he hung up, he was crying.

"Why didn't you tell him?" asked Berta, weeping.

"It's Father Graf; he's dead," said Freddy.

"Oh no!" said Berta, drawing her head back.

His heart drummed hard inside his chest, and his chin was trembling. He drew in a lengthy breath, releasing it slowly. "Berta, Archie Betz found a job for you at the bar."

Berta's brows jumped up and her fingers touched her parted lips while tears ran over her cheeks.

Freddy smiled. "Berta, it's been more than a month since Easter; won't Halina and the boys be excited when I turn up?" Freddy's smile wavered. "We can have a picnic and pick flowers before I report for duty."

Berta let out a heavy sigh, concentrating on Freddy. "Promise me you'll take care of yourself?"

Freddy examined Berta, remembering how she changed through the years. "We've been together for a while, haven't we?"

"Yes."

He studied the scotch, shifting in his chair. "Pour us scotches?"

"No thanks. Never liked the stuff."

"Try some, you develop a taste for it."

"I'll pass."

Freddy opened the scotch and poured himself a glass two fingers high.

"Berta, do you think Major Amsel is behind the letter?"

"Would that surprise you?"

Freddy sipped the scotch with a shaky hand.

Chapter Twenty-Two

September 1943-October 1944: The Eastern Front

F ired up, the black beast's powerful steam engine thundered, puffing smoke, hauling greenish gray uniformed troops with its motoring wheels, making loud click-clacks, speeding under splendid moonlight. Later it confronted a driving rain, making it hard to see out the windows, and the train reduced speed till it ended. Freddy's head ached, and he frowned. He held his breath, fixating on the question, reckoning the answer might come soon. He pressed his lips together and furrowed his brows. *Can I kill a man?*

He gathered, checking the time, he traveled over four hours without filling his belly.

"Hey, big-shot lawyer, are we in Russia yet?" said Casanova, a chain-smoker whose face resembled a pig and who kept a picture of a nude woman inside his helmet.

"I'd guess we arrived in Russia an hour ago. The words on signs along the tracks are different."

A backpack fell off the overhead rack, bouncing off Casanova's leg. A red tinge crossed a young soldier's cheeks as he picked up the bag and shoved it back on the rack.

"Next time it happens, I'll give you a kick in the ass, momma's boy," fumed Casanova, giving a youthful teenager with hair the color of hay an angry look.

Finn's mouth twisted as he measured Casanova. "Leave the kid alone."

Casanova was speechless; his face whitened, and he turned his head. Freddy figured he wanted no part of the huge muscled man with cropped hair who worked in a slaughterhouse. And he winced, reminded Casanova never let Jorg forget he cried for his mother his first night at bootcamp. He sighed, promising himself to look after the boy soldier.

Surprised by loud explosions, he flinched, hyperventilating. His pulse raced hearing the brakes screech, stopping the train hard.

Sergeant Weber, a tall, handsome young soldier with copper-colored hair, no older than thirty, jumped up. "Sit tight, I'll see what happened."

Outside the window, Sergeant Weber approached an officer and saluted him. Freddy's stomach hardened and his fists clenched as he watched the men's lips move without hearing their words. The officer shook his head and pointed his revolver up the tracks.

The sergeant yawned inside the car, inspecting everyone, owl-eyed. "Fall in outside, right away. Partisans blew up the tracks just ahead. We've got a long march ahead of us."

And he puffed clouds in the frigid air, gathering together with his comrades.

"Fall out!" shouted Sergeant Weber.

Freddy lined up, shaking, needing to relieve his bladder. He pissed in a muddy puddle, haunted again by the nagging question. *Can I kill?*

Jorg stepped back and said, buttoning his pants, "I'm hungry; when do we get something to eat?"

Minutes later, the Luger-waving officer came back in sight. "Soldiers, fall in. Sergeant Weber will march you to the next station. Watch out for partisans. They just blew up the tracks ahead of you."

Freddy marched in puddles, splashing mud on his polished black boots. He hiked parallel to railroad tracks, constricting his fingers on his rifle, passing a crater with pieces of metal tracks and wood covering the ground near it.

"Be careful," screamed Sergeant Weber, "partisans might still be in the area."

Shallowly breathing, Freddy formed an affection for his rifle's trigger. The crunching noise from stepping on leaves or twigs spooked him. A short walk up the road, flashes of light emerged from the woods and cracking noises whizzed past him. Freddy dropped, tasting a mouthful of dirt, spitting it out with saliva, bargaining with God. *Let me live. I've led a righteous life; my family needs me.*

Freddy fired at specks of light, losing track of time. The flashes and bangs from the trees ceased, but German soldiers kept firing at blackened spaces.

Sergeant Web screamed, blinking hard, "Go after them; bring back prisoners if you can."

Freddy rose, his lips trembling, and he headed for trees with Jorg, Casanova, and Finn running near him. A bullet whistled past his ear. Freddy hid behind a tree, and gave Jorg a second look, gratified he hadn't snapped. "Jorg, let's go."

His heart pounded as he edged forward. And he turned, motioning Jorg toward him, noticing that Casanova and Finn were with him. He edged forward with the others near him. Just over a ridge, bullets whistled past him, inches from his head. He dropped, hypervigilant, his gut twisted, panting. He eased his head above the ridgeline, viewing clouds of smoke in front of trees.

Breathless, he aimed his rifle and squeezed the trigger, firing off a shot. The others fired, too.

"*Sdacha! Sdacha!*" Freddy shook his head, assessing the words, gulping for air, stroking the trigger. He took a quick, shallow breath and crawled over to Finn, unable to blink.

"Um, Freddy, did you hear that? What does it mean?"

"I don't know."

Freddy peeked above the ridgeline, spotting a partisan coming out from behind a tree with raised hands, and rose, aiming his rifle.

Freddy picked up a girl's frantic voice. "*Sdacha!, Sdacha!*"

Two more resistance fighters showed themselves, dropping their rifles.

"*Sdacha! Sdacha!*" shrieked the two men, raising their hands high in the air. Freddy nodded to himself, reckoning he knew what the words meant.

"They surrendered," sputtered Casanova, rising with his rifle directed at one of them. "Sergeant Weber will be proud of us."

Freddy, doing a double take, muttered, "Why, they're Jorg's age."

Speechless, Jorg swallowed.

The youthful girl clawed at her cheeks and fell crying. The boys sobbed; one wet himself.

"Let's get back; this place gives me the creeps," sputtered Finn, puffing clouds in the air.

And returning, Casanova stuck his rifle nuzzle in the girl's back and pushed the wailing girl toward Sergeant Weber. "Sergeant, look what we have?"

The sergeant's head recoiled as he glared at the prisoners. "What! They're kids."

A line of trucks pulled up, full of soldiers. Nerves stirred in his stomach, noticing a frowning SS captain exit a truck and come his way. He froze, stiffening his muscles, eyeing Sergeant Weber saluting the captain.

"What happened, sergeant?"

And digging his eyes into the officer, Sergeant Weber stood at attention. And he said, in a loud voice that held a tremor, "Sir, partisans ambushed us, killed two soldiers, and we took three prisoners."

"Sergeant, did you interrogate them?"

"No, sir," yelled Sergeant Weber, monitoring the captain's eyes.

"Why not, sergeant?"

"Sir, these four men just captured the prisoners," said the sergeant, pivoting his head in Freddy's direction.

The captain's voice took on a light tone, making eye contact with Freddy and the others. "Good job, soldiers. Sergeant Weber, write them up for their bravery."

"Yes, sir, right away!"

Jorg made eye contact with the captain, lifting his chin. "Sir, we followed Private Bauer; he deserves the credit."

"Sergeant Weber, write that down," said the officer, slanting his head at the men. "Which one of you is Private Bauer?"

Tight-lipped, Freddy stepped forward, standing at attention.

A smile built on the captain's lips. "Good job, private."

The officer's smile dropped and a corded vein protruded from his neck as he glanced at the prisoners. He advanced toward the captives. He planted his feet wide apart and compressed his lips, eyeing each boy.

"Where are you from? Do you understand me?"

The boys wailed, raising their trembling hands, palms in the air, shaking their heads hard. He pivoted toward the girl, yelling the same question. She clutched her chest, gasping for air.

"*Ya ne ponimayu*," shrieked the girl.

The officer drew air between his teeth and pulled out his revolver, shooting the girl in the head with a hostile expression on his face. The boys hollered horrific, blood-curdling cries until the officer shot them.

Freddy's mouth sprung open; he wanted to scream. *God, why me? I don't deserve this.*

Jorg's mouth flew open, and he heaved vomit on himself, leaving a funky smell in the air.

"Pity they don't speak German," snorted the officer, looming over the bodies, holstering his revolver.

At noontime Freddy arrived hungry in a large camp struck by a hard rain, cursing himself for not putting a snack in his backpack. An MP checked Freddy's papers and ordered him to stand outside in the rain with the others until a truck came by for him. Tired and nauseous, Freddy sped over bumpy roads, cringing whenever his mind pictured what had happened to the partisans. At camp, he polished off a can of meat and sipped a harsh cup of hot coffee, with warmth spreading through his body.

* * *

Freddy carried his eyes over rows of barbed wire and hidden minefields, assessing endless green hills, figuring no one at home had heard of the Kuban Peninsula. He sighed, envisioning Halina and his sons. His stomach tightened, and his back brushed against the wall before he dropped to the ground. He stared up at the blue sky. *"God, why me?"* A smile reached his lips as he envisioned Halina and the boys, and he drew their pictures from his top pocket. His eyes twinkled; he fumbled through each one with shaky fingers.

A cheery-young Romanian soldier intruded on his space, waving a baby's picture in his face. Freddy smiled, eyeing the picture with laugh lines at the corners of his eyes, and handed his pictures to the man. The Romanian kept his smile, glancing at the pictures. When he finished, he gave them back and held out his hand, speaking Romanian, *"Numele meu este Cristian."*

In broken German, his comrade spoke. "He said his name is Christian."

Freddy's lips bounced, and a weak smile crossed his lips. "Friedrich."

The brown-eyed Romanian handed back the pictures and saluted him with a broad smile before crawling to his waiting comrades.

Dull-eyed, pursing his lips, Freddy let out a lengthy breath, worrying over his family. His eyes flickered shut, and he imagined the trench walls were closing in on him.

A voice whispered in his ear. "Are you nervous? If you say no, I won't believe you."

Freddy grimaced, opening his eyes.

"I was too, my first time," said a willowy soldier with a dimple fitted in the middle of his chin, lounging alongside Freddy with a cup of coffee.

"How did you get through it?"

The soldier's smile wavered. "It's difficult coping with fear and anxiety. If you accept it, it might increase your chances of surviving the war."

Freddy's head hurt, and he envisioned a vise closing around it. He looked at the soldier. "I-I killed no one."

Freddy observed six men falling inside the trench, speaking foreign words. And his lips pressed into a slight grimace, eyeballing the strangers, aware three were without rifles. "Who are they?"

"Hiwis, Russian POWs who want to fight with us rather than go back to their comrades."

Surprise crept into Freddy's voice. "What, Russian POWs? Suppose they run away?"

"Don't think so; Russians torture traitors before they hang them. You'll find them and Romanians everywhere on the front. We need them; we don't get enough replacements from home to cover our losses."

"Losses?"

"The Seventeenth Army has high casualties."

"A-are they dependable?" he said, pulling his head back slowly with a vacant stare.

The soldier gazed up a second and dropped his eyes on Freddy. "The Russians are better fighters. After the defeat in Stalingrad, they mixed in the Romanians with us. An officer complained they weren't any good by themselves."

"Some Russians don't have rifles?"

"They can find parts for their rifles. They'll take rifles from dead soldiers."

The soldier lifted his chin. "I'm Lance Corporal Albrecht, from Ulm. Call me Dolf. What's your name, private?"

"Friedrich Bauer, but call me Freddy. I'm from Berlin."

Jorg grinned, hunkering beside Casanova, returning from relieving himself.

Casanova sniffed the air and pulled back from Jorg. "Kid, you stink."

A rush of pink crossed Jorg's cheeks as he sniffed under his arms. "Sorry."

Casanova pursed his lips. "Jorg, shit smells better than you do; when's the last time you washed?"

Jorg's eyes teared, and he angled away from him.

Casanova shook his head and lit a cigarette.

Dolf shot a grin at Jorg, holding out a cup of coffee. "My name's Dolf. Here, take it."

"Thanks, Dolf, I'm Jorg."

A smile danced on Freddy's lips as he glanced at the kind man.

Jorg smiled at him and took a sip. "Dolf, h-h-how long have you been a soldier?"

"Since early forty-one."

Jorg planted his eyes on Dolf. "Wow! Did you kill lots of Russians?"

Dolf said nothing.

Jorg frowned, thinking Dolf had ignored him.

"Kid, why do you think we're called the Seventeenth Army?" said Jacob, a recent acquaintance who was listening to the conversation. "It's because that's how many of us will stand when the fucking war ends."

Jorg's eyebrows jumped up, and he swallowed hard.

Dolf snarled, hardening his tone. "Jacob, you're scaring him. He's a kid. Do you want him to run away?"

"He'd better not," said Jacob. "If he tries it, I'll shoot him in the back."

The whites of Jorg's eyes surrounded his pupils, appearing haunted.

Freddy spoke in a soft tone, patting Jorg on the back. "Listen up, I'll get you through the war."

"And who will get you through it?" said Casanova, snorting.

"Be on guard; scouts reported Ivan's stirring. Pass it on," said Sergeant Weber.

Rows of steel helmets bobbed along the trench, passing on Sergeant Weber's words. Dolf jumped up and peeked outside. He picked up a rock and tossed it at something. "Wake up, assholes. Reds are on the move."

Freddy stood up and looked outside at men in a machine gun nest waving their fists at Dolf.

He picked up rifle fire, and taking rasping breaths, observed swarms of advancing Russians screaming words he didn't understand, which terrified him. Dazed, he made a grunting sound, holding a shaky finger against the trigger. Bullets whizzed over him, and he kissed the trench wall, crying. He inched his eyes over the wall, breathing hard, catching rifle bursts. He aimed and fired a shot. The man he targeted dropped to his knees in pain before collapsing on the ground. Freddy pulled back the bolt, and a spent shell jumped out the rifle's chamber, and he shoved it forward, firing a bullet at another charging Russian, witnessing his fall. He fired three more times, believing he shot two more Russians. Pale with fright, with beads of sweat on his lips and his stomach churning, Freddy dropped his head. *Yes, I can kill.*

Bullets kicked up dirt near him, clearing Freddy's mind. He crouched and reloaded, finding Jorg on the floor, shaking, holding his helmet. Anger and nerves shook his voice. "Jorg, stand up; get ahold of yourself."

Jorg stayed put, with tears running off his cheeks. "No, I won't."

"Get up, Jorg," screamed Freddy, hyperventilating.

Jorg stayed in place. Freddy leaned over and slapped Jorg's face, handing him his rifle.

Freddy hollered, blinking hard. "Jorg, if you don't put on your helmet and start firing, an officer will shoot you."

"No! I can't."

He yanked Jorg to his feet. Glassy-eyed, with a deadpan expression, Jorg fired his rifle helter-skelter. Freddy smacked Jorg's helmet, thinking of the consequences if the boy didn't aim his rifle.

Freddy shot a Red in the head who kneeled, firing a shot at him that missed.

He gasped, seeing Jorg aiming and firing his gun at targets.

Countless Russian soldiers appeared over a hill, firing their guns. Their loud screams made his knees shake. With an eye narrowed on the gunsight, he fired at a few easy marks, watching them fall. And with bulging eyes, he witnessed rows of Russian infantry fall ripped apart from the buzz saw sound of machine gun blasts. He looked at dead and wounded Russians piled on the battlefield. More Russians charged; many died. Freddy questioned the sanity of their officers.

Three Russian armored vehicles blasted their cannons, approaching the minefield. Freddy flinched, catching loud bursts from German artillery. His eyes bulged as he beheld shells zeroing in on the tanks, striking them, making them belch black smoke. One's turret flew in the air, becoming a ball of fire. Two soldiers jumped from a burning tank on fire, running in circles, trying to extinguish the flames with their hands. A German machine gun nest found them, ending their suffering. He froze, breathing gunpowder smoke and inky clouds released from burning tanks, coughing tainted air. Freddy noticed two Russians taking cover behind dead soldiers. He blinked hard, trembling, picking up loud screams from Reds who had made it through a break in the barbed wire unscathed. He cried, pulling the trigger with a shaking finger. A Russian with a tommy gun fired, hitting Cristian and two more Romanians before Dolf blew out his brains. Rifle fire and stick grenades halted the Russian advance. One angry Russian cursed at Freddy, firing a shot that deflected off his helmet. Breathless, reaching out from the trench, he seized him by his ankles, yanking him inside the trench. He gasped hard, twisting on solid earth with the Russian warrior. His pupils enlarged as he wrestled on top of the screaming man, pulling out his knife. His nostrils flared, and he grunted loudly, muscling the knife between the soldier's ribs and twisting it, bloodying his hands, hearing him moan, "Ugh!"

When it ended, after looking at the dead Russian's face, he laid eyes on his bloodied hands and started shaking,

"Freddy, superb job; you'll live to see another day," Dolf said with a smile, nodding, after the fighting finished.

One of the Hiwis raised his eyebrows, finding something as he picked through the dead Russian's pockets before tossing him over the wall, and crawled away with the soldier's submachine gun.

Freddy reexamined his blood-stained hands, unable to blink. *Did he have a wife and children?*

* * *

Freddy made a face, scratching at mites who had found a home under his belt. "Who knows the date?"

With a gleam in his eye, Finn said, "It's Friday, August Thirteenth, and after four brawls with Ivan, I'm still breathing."

Freddy stared at nothing, haunted by terrible memories, and clamped his eyes shut. *Countless men died here, many cried out in pain, many from my bullets.* And said in a stupor talking to himself, "Sergeant Weber took a bullet and lived; hard-luck Jacob took one in the head and left his brains where he stood."

"Ivan's budging. Keep your eyes in front of you if you want to live," yelled out Sergeant Weber with a blood-stained bandage wrapped around a slight head wound.

Freddy's head recoiled, and he squeezed his eyes shut, catching heartbeats. "Dolf, can we keep them back? We've lost many men."

Dolf took on a concerned look. "Afraid not."

Freddy looked up. *The Russians lose more men than we do, but still keep coming at us.*

Dolf's straight lips changed into a bitter smile.

Freddy dove to the floor, hearing a Russian shell zooming above him. The foul taste of stomach bile reached his throat, and he rolled his fingers into fists, revisited by his constant companion—fear. Images of Halina and the children tore through his mind. He heard a booming voice near him.

"We're moving out; pass the word on," screamed Sergeant Weber.

* * *

Packed into a boat by midafternoon, Freddy released a pent-up breath, catching sight of Crimea.

"Glad we're getting out of Kuban," crowed Casanova, putting a cigarette in his mouth and running his eyes over the Kuban shoreline.

Finn snorted, fixing his eyes on Casanova. "I'm sure you are. All you could do is gaze at Trudy's picture."

Jorg smiled, baring his gums. "That's funny!"

Casanova said, shaking his fist in Jorg's face, "Shut up, Jorg, or I'll—"

"Or you'll do what?" said Freddy to Casanova. "Leave Jorg alone."

"Is it ours?" Finn stroked his chin, watching a plane pivot over open water.

Freddy froze. "It's not ours."

Confined within four metal walls, seeing a Russian Sturmovik drop from the sky and head for him. Hearing men's screams, Freddy expected to die.

Boom, boom, boom, boom fired a German flak gun at the diving Sturmovik. *Boom, boom, boom.* Another gun let loose a barrage of shells at it. Freddy's muscles slackened as he zeroed in on a flaming ball of fire splashing into the water.

* * *

Flames frolicked from a crackling fire, and a bottle of vodka made the rounds. Drunk Finn rose, rocking, swallowing vodka before falling on his ass, giggling. "Merry Christmas, everyone."

Casanova wet his lips, glancing inside his helmet. "Merry Christmas, Trudy; I love you."

On all fours, Finn crawled to him. "Can I see Trudy?"

"No, she's for my eyes only."

"She…she must be a pig if she's your girlfriend," sputtered Finn, relaxing.

Casanova mumbled something under his breath, rubbing the back of his neck.

Dolf snorted and puffed on his cigar. Jorg drank his vodka and grabbed the cigar out of Dolf's hand and took a drag from it. Moments later, Jorg turned pale and chucked up what had found a temporary home in his stomach. Dolf caught Freddy gawking at him and dropped his head.

Freddy's eyes twinkled as he stared into the darkness. *I wish I could tell Halina and the children I love them.*

"Freddy, do you want more vodka?" asked Dolf, high cheeked.

His eyes stinging with tears, with a hollow feeling in his chest, Freddy sighed. "No thanks, Dolf. I'm heading inside, to write my wife a letter."

He pulled up a chair and lit a candle inside four walls covered with a tarp.

Dear Halina,

I'm delighted we will have another child—maybe a girl this time? It's Christmas, I miss you and the boys more than ever. I hope everyone at home is well. Glad to hear Werner's alive. He's retreating east, and I'm heading the other way. Maybe we'll touch backs at the end of the war. I'm fine. Don't worry about me. The weather outside feels comparable to Berlin at this time of year.

Freddy snapped his eyes shut, rehashing words he overheard from an officer. "They'll attack when the weather warms and the clouds lift." He ran his hands through his hair and breathed hard, deciding not to tell Halina the truth.

I've not seen combat, and Sergeant Weber told me he thought we might be home next Christmas. Did you and the children enjoy Christmas? My parents are fine, but I'm sure you know this. They won't leave Berlin. I hope they change their mind. Mother writes the bombings are getting worse, but Father feels safe in shelters. A second, minute, or hour doesn't pass that I didn't wish I held you in my arms and tasted your warm lips.
Your loving husband,
Freddy

* * *

"How lucky can you be? We're in the front," said Casanova, pulling back in disgust, scrutinizing trenches behind him. "Reminds me of what I read in *All Quiet on the Western Front*. Hope I remember where the mines are if I retreat?"

"Huh, the perv can read." said Finn, glancing at his watch.

"Today's April Seventh," said Jorg, beaming. "It's my birthday; I was born in Twenty-Eight."

"Shit, you're only sixteen?" said Casanova, glancing at the others.

A lump formed in Freddy's throat, and he tucked in his upper lip. Dolf shut his eyes, generating a quick headshake.

Finn sipped coffee and spit it out. *Ptui, ptui, ptui.* "Soapy water tastes better than this."

Freddy caught sight of banana-shaped objects crossing the sky. "Um, hope the planes are Messerschmitt's."

Dolf brushed against Freddy. "Let me see."

"Dolf, are they ours?"

"Don't know."

Freddy grimaced as he spotted three Russian fighters turning toward them. His nostrils flung open and his voice cracked. "Drop, three Sturmoviks." He dove headfirst inside the trench, hearing loud engines and blasts from their cannons. And he faced the sky, taking rasping breaths, picking up a howling engine, and caught a red star on the wing of a Sturmovik shooting past him. He jumped up, gulping for air, feeling claustrophobic, and peeked outside the trench, seeing two Sturmoviks rockets destroys an artillery position.

At twilight, pestered by a mosquito, he eyed the nuisance and slapped it before it could settle on his arm. Dull-eyed, he took a shallow breath, picturing Halina tucking in the boys under their sheets. He spent a restless night haggling with God, offering the deity promises if he survived the war.

At 0800 hours it rained artillery shells. Freddy's eyes bulged, and he kissed the ground under him. His body trembled, and he cried, terrified by noise from screaming rockets, whistling mortar shells, loud explosions and swarms of buzzing Sturmoviks. The earth shook underneath Freddy, and dirt and rocks showered him. Jorg cried and shook his head hard. Dolf squeezed his shoulder. Big-eyed, with ashen white faces, Casanova and Finn looked like ghosts.

At 1030 hours Russian artillery scattered smoke bombs ahead of him. White surrounded Freddy's blue pupils, and he was breathless as he listened to the gunfire. Adrenaline rushed through his veins, and bile burned his throat. He rose, cycling his bolt action rifle quickly, firing at invisible soldiers, masked behind smoke. He caught a few emerging through the smoke. *Bang, bang, bang, bang, bang.* Three soldiers dropped. Freddy reloaded and shot two more.

Jorg breathed hard, firing his rifle at screaming soldiers coming out of the smoke curtain.

Rockets screamed overhead, and the earth under his feet shook. He saw in the distance a flamethrower shoot fire at a German machine gun nest. He aimed and fired his rifle at whatever moved in front of him. His eyes welled up, and he cried when German artillery found a few advancing Russian tanks.

"We're outnumbered; we should run," screamed Casanova, gasping for a breath, shifting his head sideways.

"If you do, I'll shoot you. They ordered us to hold our ground," shouted Dolf, releasing a hard breath, pulling back his head in disgust.

"Freddy, duck," screamed Jorg, killing a Russian before the Russian could shoot Freddy.

A Red fired inside the trench, killing a Romanian. Dolf wrestled a Red to the floor, and Casanova shot him in the back.

Freddy grabbed a Red's rifle before he could pull the trigger and yanked him inside the trench, shoving a knife hard into his gut, the knife slipping off bone.

Freddy jumped up, bug-eyed, firing at approaching Russians, hyperventilating, sensitive to noise from gunfire and explosions.

Russian tanks held up in the minefield, with a few losing their turrets—easy marks for fixed gun artillery shells.

A German officer raised up, pointing his revolver at destroyed buildings. "Pull back, to Armyansk."

Freddy stared at Dolf, open-mouthed, becoming disoriented.

"Fall back," said Dolf as he fled.

Freddy cried, hearing arriving artillery shells. And he hit the ground, tasting dirt in his mouth. After it ended he rose, making a face, spitting, nauseated from the funky odors, and ran toward Armyansk. His eyes stung, and his nose tingled as he sprinted past bloodied decaying soldiers' and horses' bodies. He passed blown-up trucks and artillery pieces, catching whiffs of burning rubber. And he fell behind a wall in Armyansk, weeping, spooked by bullets whizzing overhead. His face turned pallid, and he assumed the worst as he heard bullets whack the wall. Terrified by the sound of tanks, he winced, detecting a bang and whooshing sound and men's screams. He trembled, peeking through a crack, discovering a Russian flamethrower torching soldiers hunkered in a ditch.

"Baa," said Finn; he fell over without his helmet, missing a part of his head.

Jorg fired quickly, his face white from fear. "Bastards."

Nerves shook Dolf's voice. "We can't hold out here."

Russian infantry broke through the right flank. Freddy yanked a stick grenade from under his ammo belt and flung it and grabbed another. Dolf shot two men, and Casanova threw a stick grenade at a group of excited Russians, tossing them in the air.

"Fall back," screamed Dolf, backing away, firing at advancing Reds.

A half-mile walk past the minefield, short-winded, fingering a stick grenade behind what remained of a collapsed wall, he hunkered close to Dolf, Jorg, and Casanova. And he shut his eyes, shaking, reckoning he might die soon.

At sunup Freddy woke, rubbing gunk from his sleepy eyes. And his head recoiled. "No." He heard bullets overhead, and a noisy tank engine. Casanova, sat up, opening his eyes wide, breathing hard. He peeked above the wall and dropped, flashing brown stained teeth, firming his voice. "We'll die if stay here; I'm leaving."

"Wait for Sergeant Weber's orders," said Dolf, placing his hand on Casanova's arm.

Casanova pushed his hand away, giving him an icy stare. "My mind's made up; I'm going. See you in hell."

Casanova shook his head. "Last chance, suckers," he said, leaving. Sergeant Weber rose from behind a wall and fired two shots into Casanova's back, and he fell dead.

A short time later, Dolf peeked out and dropped, scraping the wall with his back. "Ivan's moving up the road."

"Pull back," screamed Sergeant Weber, pointing to ruins on a hill.

"We'll get shot if we do," said Freddy, shaking, seeing black spots.

Dolf sniffed through his slender nostrils. "Freddy, you and Jorg run for it; I'll cover you."

Freddy's chest tightened and his stomach knotted as he darted his eyes between Jorg and Dolf.

"Go, before it's too late," screamed Dolf, rising and releasing shots.

Freddy dove to the ground, hearing incoming artillery shells hit and shake the ground. He jumped up, crying, choking on fumes, and blinked, paying attention to smoking vehicles, fixating on torn bodies. He looked up to the heavens whispering, "Please Lord, let me live another day." And he ran off with Dolf and Jorg, concentrating on the loud noises from exploding artillery shells behind him.

"Ha, it's April Tenth," said Dolf, staring at a rose-colored sunrise. "We made it through another day."

Freddy grinned, flashing his white teeth on a muddied face. "Dolf, I hope I hear those words tomorrow." As he laid eyes on retreating horse drawn artillery and open trucks filled with exhausted and wounded soldiers, his chest caved in, and he felt numb.

* * *

"It's May, and its warm; it's going to be a splendid day," said Freddy cheerily, catching sunlight through cracks in the ceiling.

There was a light note in Dolf's voice. "Good, let's go for a swim. Oops, sorry, I forgot we're in Sevastopol and Russian snipers made going to the beach their hobby."

Freddy grinned and shook his head at him. He realized he might be one of the lucky ones who survived if the navy rescued him.

"Chocolate, canned meat, and wine—there's more left. They opened the officer's storehouse because they didn't want to leave the food for the Reds. I grabbed as much as I could carry," said Jorg, ducking inside with his pockets and arms full of food. "When we're done eating, I should go back for more."

Jorg yanked the chocolate out of Dolf's hand. "The chocolate's mine."

Loud explosions flanked Freddy. Stunned, he hit the floor, noticing machine gun bursts getting louder. His body shook, and his breathing sped up as he concentrated on the buzzing noises overhead. Frozen to the floor, he smelled rancid smoke infiltrating the nooks and crannies of the walls. He gagged, inhaling munitions smoke, reckoning he'd die if he didn't flee. Once it ended, a smile spread on his lips and he nudged Dolf's arm, with tears building behind his eyelids.

Afterwards, offering a bemused smile, Dolf opened red wine and wolfed down half the bottle. "It's excellent wine. Want a swallow?" said Dolf, waving it in front of his face.

Jorg spit chocolate. "Let me take a drink."

Dolf handed Jorg the bottle and reached for a can of meat.

Jorg drank some wine and belched.

Freddy gave Jorg an incredulous stare, frowning. "Jorg, give me the bottle."

Freddy wiped chocolate off the bottle's mouth and finished the wine.

Moments later, Dolf yawned and nodded off to sleep.

Mellowed from the wine, Jorg tumbled beside Freddy.

He blinked hard, dipping his chin. "Freddy, can I ask you something? You're the only one I could ask that won't laugh at me."

Freddy scrunched his eyes together, keeping his voice low. "Jorg, I give you my word. What's so important?"

Jorg gave Freddy a slow smile.

"Um, what do you do when you're alone with a woman?" asked Jorg, edging closer.

Freddy's eyes brightened at the words; he imagined holding Halina in his arms.

"Jorg, it's an indescribable feeling when your bodies touch; you'll know it if you find the right woman."

"What I'd miss, Freddy?" said Dolf, yawning and squinting. Speechless, Jorg cringed, reddening his ears.

"Ivan's been quiet; you hadn't slept long."

* * *

A week later, fired upon, Freddy raced on bomb-cratered streets in Sevastopol, moving closer to the Black Sea.

Sergeant Weber's voice strengthened, offering hope. "There're ships waiting to carry you to Romania." He wiped off a drop of blood that fell from a minor arm wound. "Keep going; it's not far."

Freddy, nosedived into a ditch detecting the whistling sound of an incoming shell. A loud boom shook the soil, burying him under dirt. Airless, in eerie blackness, he thought he was going to die. He choked on a mouthful of dirt, unable to budge, weighed down by the heavy earth. Hands brushed dirt off his face, and he opened his eyes, coughing, tasting dry earth.

Dolf lifted Freddy's head, gazing into his eyes. "Are you okay?"

Freddy built saliva in his mouth, dislodging grit with his tongue, and spit. On his feet, he dusted himself off and rinsed out the rest with water from his canteen, collecting his thoughts. "Dolf, where's Jorg?"

"Freddy, J-Jorg's dead. Stay put; you don't want to see Jorg," replied Dolf, bowing his head, eyeing the remnants of a wall and a pile of debris.

Freddy winced and fell to his knees, unable to focus on any of the thoughts racing through his brain. A lump formed in his throat. He shook his head, and he rose breathless, taking small steps. An uncontrollable shudder hit him as he viewed Jorg's mangled body, and he fell to his knees, tasting something brought up from his stomach. "Dolf, he's not whole." He looked hard at the heavens, angry with God. "Why him?"

Loud explosions came closer, along with rifle shots.

"Freddy, we should leave Jorg. Someone will bury him. We'll die if we stay here," said Dolf, pulling on Freddy's shoulder.

"I won't leave him."

"Freddy, there's nothing we can do for Jorg; maybe medics will find him."

"You go. I'll bury him by myself," said Freddy, dismissing the blasts, taking noisy breaths.

"I won't leave you, but let's hurry."

Freddy muscled a makeshift cross in the ground at the head of Jorg's grave. And Dolf hung Jorg's dog tags and helmet on it. Both men bowed their heads, with Freddy saying a quick prayer. With gunfire approaching, passed by retreating infantry, they grabbed their rifles and glanced at each other before facing the sea and running for it.

"Freddy, there's the ocean, boats are evacuating troops."

Freddy's smile wavered, with what happened to Jorg stuck in his mind.

Dolf's cheeks dimpled. "Freddy, you'll see your wife and boys."

Kaboom!

* * *

Inside a darkened tent, in pain, Freddy passed in and out of consciousness. Dolf's crisp voice breached his thoughts. "Freddy, stay alive; there's a wife and children at home waiting for you."

Soaked in blood, with his vision blurring, he screamed, noticing a masked man with a knife standing over him. He blinked hard, observing Dolf with a blood-stained bandage wrapped around his head, holding a lantern.

Freddy's eyelids drooped; he heard the masked man tell Dolf, "Soldier, good job; he'd be dead if you hadn't stopped the bleeding. We've used up our morphine; he'll be in pain, give him some of this brandy."

Freddy gritted his teeth, feeling a stinging pain in his side. "God help me!"

Dolf's loud voice rung in Freddy's ears. "Hold on, Freddy, the doctor's fixing you."

Light-headed, he shrieked and blacked out. He woke up bawling, aware something was digging into his leg. A chill ran through his body hearing the rasping noise a saw made and a man scream in pain. Unable to close his eyes, he stared at nothing, tortured by scraping sounds. Freddy released a strangled cry. "Don't cut my bones."

"Nurse, get rid of the leg," said a high-pitched voice.

"We're finished with him; he's in God's hands." said a doctor, attending to the other man.

Dolf yelled, "Freddy, don't give up. Think of your family."

Touched by something on his chest, he closed his eyes, drifting off into unconsciousness.

Hours later, dressed in fresh bandages, he woke, catching the odor of something antiseptic in the air.

"Where am I?" asked Freddy, grimacing from soreness in his wound, discovering his legs moved.

"On a destroyer heading across the Black Sea for the Romanian port of Constanta."

"Where's Dolf?"

"Who's Dolf?"

"He's my friend; he was with me when the doctor operated on me."

"Soldier, if he's lucky, he's somewhere on the boat."

Freddy squinted at him with a mind growing numb from jumbled thoughts.

* * *

Having finished putting down the baby, Halina faced him. Her cream-colored silk nightie clung tight to her body, and she edged closer with sensuous charm, drawing attention to her delightful curves and the pleasant smell of her perfume. Her lips parted, and her breaths quickened; she removed her laced gown, exposing a magnificent body. She examined Freddy, running her fingers through her lengthy blond hair, bouncing her breasts, breathing. And she released a long sigh, dropping under the covers, placing her soft quivering lips against his mouth. "Freddy, I need you; make love to me."

Freddy shivered, sliding on top of her warm body. On the verge of tears, perspiring, he fell off her, locking his eyes on a crack in the ceiling. Haunted by glimpses of death, the walls of the shadowy room closed in on him, and he closed his eyes, grimacing. Halina placed her head on his chest, rubbing the insides of his leg. His eyes froze, with images of death speeding through his brain. He bit against his bottom lip, reliving Jorg's last moments in the Crimea. He wept, recalling a joyful moment with the boy soldier. His stomach churned, reliving driving his knife into the Russian's gut, picturing the dead man's eyes. The muscle in his wounded leg tensed as he envisioned his bloody hands after killing the soldier. *Why won't the nightmares go away?*

"Freddy, what's wrong?"

Speechless, Freddy touched his hurt leg, shifting his eyes across the ceiling.

Halina stroked his inner thigh with her soft fingertips. "Freddy, make love to me."

Freddy's chest thumped and his cheeks burned with the urge to flee. Tears bolted from his eyes. *She doesn't know what I did; I'm a terrible man.*

Halina kissed Freddy with her soft lips. "Talk to me. Don't you want me anymore?"

"Halina, I'll never stop wanting you. I'm not myself. I need time to sort out my problems."

Halina's fingers found Freddy's wound and caressed it. "Does it hurt?"

Freddy's eyes welled up as he fought the demons in his head. "I wish it were worse and kept me from going back."

Halina, pursing her lips, turned on her back. "Why did you lie to me?"

Freddy's stomach tightened. "I didn't want to worry you; you were pregnant."

"Freddy, please tell me what happened?" Halina wept.

Freddy's voice cracked. "I can't. I did horrible things I can't forget. There are nights I can't sleep, preyed upon by voices of dying men." With clammy skin, he seized the sheets, tightening his fingers, sensing the mattress pulling him in it. His dark eyes moistened, and he winced, picturing what had happened to Jorg with a thought tormenting his soul. *Dolf, he's not whole.* Freddy's voice weakened with his nerves. "Halina, I wish I were dead."

"Freddy, stop blaming yourself; it's not your fault. God knows they did not give you a choice."

Freddy's lips shook, and he burst into tears, sweating, gasping for air.

Halina squeezed Freddy's hand. "Freddy, it'll be all right. Pray to God; he works miracles."

"It won't stop me from returning to the front," said Freddy, in a frail voice. "Maybe a bullet will end my misery."

"Freddy, never speak those words to me. I-I couldn't live without you; what will happen to the children?"

Freddy closed his eyes, hating himself. "Halina, I'm sorry. Forgive me?"

Halina's breathing quieted. "Freddy, why don't we run to a place where it's safe?"

A lump formed in Freddy's throat, and a sharp pain shot across his chest. "We can't do that. If we're caught, they'll shoot me, and you and the children might wind up in a concentration camp."

Halina's lips shook, and she wiped her eye, softening her voice. "Freddy, I'm scared you might not come back."

Halina's words tormented him, and unable to draw a breath, he figured the odds of returning were poor.

Halina wiped her nose. "Freddy, I love you."

The baby's coos interrupted his focus. Halina brought him his daughter. A sob caught in his throat as he admired her. "I love you, little Alise." His face flushed red. "Halina, I'll never get back the lost time with you and the children. It's laughable, isn't it, the entire time fighting for a cause I detest?" Freddy held back tears. "Alise is a pleasant name for a girl."

Her eyes gleamed. "It was my mother's name."

Freddy felt overwhelmed, his vision blurry. And his hands shook, putting his daughter in Halina's arms.

Chapter Twenty-Three

November 1, 1944-February 25, 1945: Cloak-and-Dagger

Dear Halina,

This is my last letter to you from Poland. Tomorrow I leave for a training base, in Grafenwöhr, Germany, with a head full of unanswered questions. I'm being sent there as an English interpreter.

I'm glad the boys are getting along and Alise is crawling. Thank you for the sweater, I needed it. I shared the chocolates and cookies with friends. I hope the war ends soon and agree with Uncles Dieter and Tomas if the Russians approach Bautzen, head for Dresden. Americans would treat you better than the Russians.

When I have answers to my questions, I'll write. I promise I will come home. I love you, give kisses and hugs to the children for me. Your loving husband,
Freddy

Freddy stood to attention, firming his voice. "Heil Hitler."

The SS officer inspected Freddy, returning a half-hearted salute.

"Sit, private. I'm Captain Wolter, here to test your English," barked the bald officer, removing his glasses.

Captain Wolter listened to Freddy speak the English sentences he gave him. Speechless, the SS officer kept nodding.

"Excellent. You carry no accent; where did you learn to speak English that well?"

Freddy gave him a hard gaze, fast-blinking at him. "Sir, in America."

The officer stared at him and shrugged, flattening his voice. "Here, soldier, you need to sign this pledge."

With his heart hammering inside his chest, he read over the pledge.

"I-I will face a firing squad if I divulge the mission to anyone?"

The officer snorted out loud, folding his arms across his chest. "Sign it!"

"Yes, sir," said Freddy.

"One more thing, soldier," said the officer, "you're forbidden to write letters."

Freddy fast blinked. "Yes, sir."

The officer's body stiffened, and he said in a firm voice, "Good. See Major Rudolf von Krieg."

Freddy exhaled a loud breath, followed by a low moan. "Major Rudolf von Krieg?"

The officer sneered at Freddy, tapping his fingers on his hand. "Yes, Major Rudolf von Krieg."

* * *

Freddy stuck out his right hand, clicking his heels hard, feeling his heart flutter, bolstering his voice. "Heil, Hitler."

Major Krieg rose and returned the salute, doing a double take at Freddy's Iron Cross. "Let me see your paybook."

Freddy's skin flushed as he handed Major Krieg the book. Krieg yanked the book out of his hand, jutting out his chin.

"Hmm, never expected to see that; you're written up for bravery capturing partisans. Um, by yourself?"

"No, sir, I led three men."

"Didn't think so," said Krieg tauntingly, easing himself back in his chair. A sly smile appeared on Major Krieg's mouth. "It surprised me seeing your name—thought you might flee to Switzerland."

Freddy's stomach tightened.

"What happened to your Jew friends?" said Krieg, poking his tongue into his cheek.

"Jew friends, sir?"

"I'm no fool," said Krieg, fixating on Freddy. "Answer the question."

"Sir, yes, sir. Don't know what happened to Leo Herzfeld. P-Professor Karp's living in New York," said Freddy, giving the bully a fevered stare.

"Do you correspond with him?" asked Major Krieg, frowning at him.

"No, sir, I don't."

Major Krieg glanced down his nose, twisting his lips with scorn. Freddy swallowed, guessing he didn't believe him.

His chin quivered as he recalled Professor Ackerman's words in the cellar. And with the words haunting him, he glared at Krieg, watching him look over his paybook. His body grew heavy, and a lump formed in his throat as he agonized over the Jette and Krieg connection.

Major Krieg sighed, shaking his head. "Where's Paul Bunyan?"

"Sir, do you mean Albert Haas?"

"No, don't answer; I'm sure it'll be a lie," said Krieg, breaking a pencil in two and throwing it at him, hitting his chest.

The major snarled, glancing over at a paper with a bold swastika at its top. "You're English is splendid. Where you're going, you'll need it. Your name was on a list of English-speaking soldiers. You're perfect for the operation."

He could not breathe, and charged-up, anxious thoughts raced through his brain. A lance corporal emerged, clicking his heels.

"Lance Corporal Schlegel, show Private Bauer to his barracks."

Major Krieg gave Freddy a hard stare before handing him back his paybook.

* * *

Sergeant Dirk, a squinty-eyed man with a wolfish face, strained his voice. "Fall out."

Freddy dropped his backpack, gasping for air, guessing he had outlived the others by at least five years. "I bet we hiked ten miles."

"Feels like a hundred," said Sparky, a lean, long-legged man, huffing and puffing.

Wolfgang, a dimpled-chinned soldier, placed his hands on his knees. "It's the middle of November, and we do nothing but drill and practice English. I'm sorry I signed up for this."

"Stop bitching; you make me sick," heaved Sparky. "Did you think it would be easy?"

Eck, a solid soldier, unmasked a wide smile. "I hope we see action soon."

Freddy frowned, catching a smile building on Sparky's face.

"Hmm, Friedrich, you and Wolfgang were the only ground pounders that volunteered who spoke decent English."

Freddy stared at Sparky. "I didn't volunteer."

"I'm here to fight, not waste time improving my English," protested Eck.

Wolfgang made a wry face. "Hey, anchor head, you heard Captain Wolter—except for Friedrich, we need to work on our accents."

Eck shook his head. "It's always Friedrich; if he's not the best English speaker, he's the best in close combat training or hooking up explosives,"

Sparky spat and snorted. "Hope Friedrich is with me when we go to war."

Wolfgang made a *hmm* noise in his throat. "Think the rumor's true, we're heading for Paris to capture Eisenhower?"

"Makes sense to me. That explains the tanks, trucks and guns and why we need to speak good English," replied Sparky with a hard nod.

"An American firing squad will shoot us if we're discovered wearing one of their uniforms," warned Freddy, a chill racing through his body.

"We were told it's a dangerous mission," said Wolfgang, concentrating on Freddy.

Freddy's gut twisted; he reckoned his odds of returning home in one piece had plunged.

"Fall in for target practice," screamed Sergeant Bier. "Hope your aim's better than you drill."

Freddy marched to the rifle range, dry-mouthed, picking up the sound of his heartbeat in his ear.

"Listen up, shitheads, in my hands is an American M-1 Garand rifle. It's semiautomatic, not bolt action. Learn how to use it; your life might depend on it," said Sergeant Popp, spreading his legs and knitting his brows.

Freddy's throat constricted as he marveled at the rifle.

Without warning, Sergeant Popp tossed the rifle to Freddy. "Catch, soldier." Freddy caught the rifle with a warm smile. "Excellent, soldier, it's good to see you're alert."

Freddy handed Sergeant Popp the rifle, conscious of its lightweight.

"Catch, soldier," said Popp, grinning, throwing the rifle to Eck, who dropped it. Eck's face blushed, and he picked up the rifle and presented it to the sergeant.

Sergeant Popp frowned and yanked the gun from Eck.

"What's your name, soldier?"

Eck stiffened, firming his words. "Seaman First Class Eck Alt."

The sergeant gave him a dirty look. "Uh, Eck, never heard the name."

"Sergeant, Eck's short for Eckernförde, where I'm from," shrieked Eck, tight-shouldered.

Sergeant Popp lowered the rifle's muzzle.

"To be specific, the M-1's light. It's automatic, gets eight shots off with the pull of a trigger."

Eck's face reddened, and he glared at Freddy, talking to himself.

Freddy's mouth fell open and his gut fluttered, spotting Major Krieg grinning behind Eck.

* * *

Freddy departed Grafenwöhr crammed inside one of an endless row of railroad boxcars. Unable to blink, looking haunted, he tilted his head. "Wolfgang, do you think it's true we're going after Eisenhower?"

Wolfgang's lips puckered, and he gave his noggin an unhurried shake. "Uh, not sure, heard yesterday we could head for Dunkirk or Lorient."

Freddy's jaw dropped.

Eck's eyes glowed; he stared at nothing. And Sparky seemed content, uncrossing his arms. Freddy closed his eyes, questioning the sanity of the hardened men.

"Sparky, why did you sign up for this?" asked Freddy.

Sparky widened his eyes, pinching his chin. "I was a sailor on the Prinz Eugen when it rammed the Leipzig in heavy fog on October Fifteenth. I volunteered at Gotenhafen, deciding it was better choice than getting killed on a docked ship fixing its wires."

"That's funny!" said Freddy with a laugh.

"What's so funny?" Sparky frowned.

"Just figured out why you're nicknamed Sparky."

Sparky checked out Eck and moved closer to Freddy, softening his voice. "Eck was a submariner. He loaded torpedoes and manned the gun when it surfaced. Poor fellow lost his family in 1943 when the RAF bombed Hamburg."

A pained look crossed Freddy's face as he glanced at Eck.

Eck blinked and snapped out of wherever his mind had gone.

"What'd you say, Wolfgang? Dunkirk or Lorient?" said Eck. "Doesn't matter which one as long as I can fight."

"Be careful what you wish for; you might not come back," replied Wolfgang, flashing him a brief smile with arrogance brightening his eyes.

Inside the darkened boxcar, Freddy agonized over different outcomes, concluding each one could be terrible.

Major Krieg stood up. "Men, give me your full attention."

Freddy narrowed his eyes on Krieg, squeezing his stomach muscles, picking up short, dull sounds from the steam engine.

A relaxed smile appeared on Major Krieg's face as he gazed over the men, and he picked up his voice to compensate for the trains noise. "Listen up, men, we're headed for the Ardennes Forest. We will assemble there for a special mission ordered by the führer. Our assignment is to seize enemy bridges and disrupt their communications before the crucial assault begins."

Freddy bared his teeth, believing his fate rested in Major Krieg's hands.

* * *

Unhurried by the wind, gray clouds floated in the sky. Soon light faded from above the forest's snowy canopy, hushing nature's voices. Freddy made peace with God, filling his eyes with tears, sensitive to the noises surrounding him.

Sparky patted his leg with a weak smile, pulling out cigarettes from his pocket. "Want a smoke?"

Freddy felt the excess saliva making his tongue sticky. "No, you know I don't smoke."

"Thought you needed one now," said Sparky with a hint of a frown.

Freddy's upper teeth dented his bottom lip; he felt nauseous, focusing on a bothersome thought. *It's nine days till Christmas.*

Sparky exhaled a long puff of smoke through his nose. "Friedrich, anyone waiting for you back home?"

"A wife, two sons, and a baby girl," replied Freddy, with moist eyes, his voice cracking. His shoulders slumped as he assessed his fate. *How can I survive dressed in an American uniform behind enemy lines?*

He fumbled with the cyanide capsule in his pocket.

Sparky raised his head, building a meager smile. "What's with you and Major Krieg?"

Freddy eyeballed him with an in an intense gaze, consumed with anger and indignation for Major Krieg. "What do you mean?"

"I see pain and anger in your face when you observe him," replied Sparky, turning his head.

"We were in the same law school," said Freddy, giving Sparky a nervous smile. "I never got along with the arrogant bastard."

"You're a lawyer? Why are you here?" asked Sparky, grabbing his arm, frowning.

He let out a heavy sigh, glaring at him. "Major von Krieg."

"But, why'd he want you on his commando team?" said Sparky, shaking his head.

Horror bulged Freddy's eyes as he pondered the illogicality of the situation.

Engines roared, filling the air with thick smoke. Lights turned on, beautifying snow crystals on the white-covered ground. Wishing time would stop, Freddy ran his eyes over chalky white armored vehicles, assault guns and infantryman minding an 88 mm gun hooked up onto the back of a truck.

Sparky nudged his shoulder. "Grab your rifle, and wake Eck."

Freddy heaved himself in an American jeep, gazing through the window with a facial tic, his back facing Eck and Sparky, serenaded by a symphony of loud engine noises.

"Hurry, major, I'm ready," said Eck, bouncing in his seat, growing a slight smile.

Major Krieg approached with a map and took his last puff from a cigarette.

"Don't disappoint me, Private Bauer," said Major Krieg, curling up behind the wheel, switching on the ignition.

Freddy's fingers clenched into fists, blinking hard.

Major Krieg grew still, making strong eye contact. "No fuckups."

Later, Krieg pulled up behind dense trees and checked the time. "It's five minutes before the artillery barrage starts."

Loud booms preceded explosions of light dancing across the horizon, tormenting Freddy's brain till they ended.

"We're behind enemy lines; get rid of your jackets," said Mayor Krieg, eyeing everyone.

Eck jumped off, collecting the German jackets, burying them under leaves, kicking snow over them.

Krieg checked his map and sped up the jeep. A half hour later, he pulled into a heavily wooded area. Loud explosions kept Freddy awake. At midnight two American tanks led scores of soldiers over a dirt road. Early morning Krieg pulled out field glasses and checked out the road. "It looks safe, but stay alert."

He steered the jeep onto a muddy road and picked up speed till he reached a sign pointing to Mont Rigi.

Major Krieg glanced up after reading his map. "Private Bauer, point the sign the other way."

An hour later Krieg came to a stop, looking over his map before he radioed his position.

"Put the minefield sign there." Krieg lashed out, glaring at Eck and Sparky. "We're behind schedule."

Late afternoon Major Krieg left deep tracks, hurrying on a muddy road flanked by snow-covered woods, directing his sight toward MPs at a crossroad.

"Don't say a word," warned Krieg, driving toward the MPs. "I'll handle them."

Freddy caught Eck placing his finger on the trigger, pressing his lips together.

"Where you headed, major?" inquired the sergeant, squinting at Freddy, Eck, and Sparky.

"Where going to Verviers, sergeant; are the roads safe to travel?"

"Sir, can I look at your papers?" After perusing the papers, he eyeballed Freddy first, then Eck and Sparky. "Huh, I don't catch many officers traveling with three soldiers."

Krieg handed over his papers and tightened his grip on the steering wheel.

"Sir, wait here while I call command," said the sergeant. "Last I heard Germans were at the Baugnez crossroads."

Freddy's eyes bulged as he watched the sergeant give the papers to an officer. A pain shot through his chest when the officer faced the jeep, displaying what seemed a fake smile.

Krieg faced him, cold-eyed, sweeping his head back-and-forth. He floored the pedal, forcing Freddy's head back. Freddy heard bullets whiz past his head. Krieg bounced the jeep off the road and headed for a shadowy woodland. Krieg lurched to a stop at a point bordering trees. Freddy's heart pounded in his chest, and he jumped off the jeep, holding his M-1 in a shaky hand. His head jarred, and he saw Eck's blood-soaked face.

"I'm hit," cried Sparky, holding a bloody hand over his stomach wound.

He cringed, noticing Sparky struggling to breathe. "Sparky, think you can walk?"

Sparky winced in pain.

Major Krieg assessed Sparky, rocking with a faraway look. His eyes broadened, and he withdrew his Colt 45, firing two shots in Sparky's chest. Freddy gasped hearing Sparky emit odd noises.

"We couldn't take him with us."

Freddy's eyes darkened, and he recognized the hard thumps in his chest.

Boom, boom, boom. Freddy ducked, widening his eyes, searching for the source of the shots.

Bullets pinged against the jeep, with one whizzing past his ear. Freddy and Krieg glanced at each other and ran away inside the woods, slipping on snow-covered leaves before finding a stream and following it, mindful that the light from the gray sky was dimming. Short winded, he moved forward, wheezing, cutting his eyes toward every sound, often catching a foul taste in his mouth.

"We can't stop." Krieg motioned Freddy ahead with his revolver. "We can't stop,"

Freddy followed him along the water's brim, many times losing footing on wet stones. At the sight of flashlights, Krieg and Freddy nosedived into a ditch, hugging the ground till the danger passed.

Krieg's voice softened after he swallowed water from his canteen. "We must keep moving; it's not safe staying long in one place."

Freddy gargled water and spit out the rancid substance, glaring at Krieg, wary of woodland noises.

Major Krieg ate a Hershey bar, taken from captured Red Cross packages, measuring Freddy with crazed eyes.

Freddy fell back on his elbows, unlocking his ankles, avoiding eye contact with Krieg. "Huh, the mission failed; all we did was change road signs."

"Shut up, or I'll shoot you," fumed Krieg, aiming his Colt 45 at Freddy.

"You won't, because the noise might bring American soldiers. What will you tell them wearing one of their uniforms?"

Krieg's eyebrows dropped, and he made grating noises through his nose. "Shut up!" he screamed, waving the gun at Freddy.

"Your wars ending; they will write its history in blood and tears, caused by hate and evil," taunted Freddy, feeling his body numb, squinting from the force of his grin, boring his eyes into Krieg.

Krieg whacked the side of Freddy's head with the revolver, drawing blood. Freddy rubbed the wound, inspecting blood on his fingers. And he gave him an intense, fevered stare with his fingers forming claws.

"That's treason. You're a coward," said Krieg in a rage. "I'll make sure you face a firing squad when we return."

"That won't happen; there's a better chance the Americans will shoot us first," said Freddy, holding his palm against his wound, noting heartbeats in his throat.

The veins in Krieg's neck throbbed, and his face reddened.

"After the war, what will become of Germany?" said Freddy, glaring at him. "How many will have died?"

Mayor Krieg pressed the gun against Freddy's forehead, pulling the corner of his lip up and back. "I was right— you're a coward."

Freddy drew air between his teeth and lunged at Krieg, wrestling him to the ground, fighting for the revolver. The gun fired, and a bullet brushed Freddy's head, stunning him. Krieg freed himself and rose, aiming the gun at Freddy with loud snorts intensifying. "That was stupid."

Freddy respired hard, with fear burning in his gut. "Go ahead—it's what you wanted."

"My father cursed at me and forbade me to see Jette when he found out she was a Jew. I loved her." Krieg said, sneering, followed by a laugh. "I ran into Jette at the train station; we walked outside. She told me she was in love with you. I pictured her with you. It drove me mad. I pushed her into an alley and strangled her. After it I smiled, imagining your face when you found out she was dead."

"You're crazy," he screamed at Krieg, flushing red. "I'll kill you."

Krieg's grin widened to a squint. "Did you forget? I'm holding a gun."

With pain building in his chest, Freddy embraced the worst-case scenario, surrounding his pupils in white. And he lunged for the revolver, wrestling Krieg to the ground. Krieg lost control of the gun when Freddy rolled on top of him. *Thump, thump, thump.* Freddy's heart pounded, and he whacked Krieg's mouth, wanting to kill him. He hit him again and again. Krieg's eyes bulged as he tried to twist himself free. His fingers curved around Krieg's neck, with his thumbs stiffening, pushing harder. He bared his teeth, breathing loud and hard, constricting his fingers. Krieg gagged, trying to pry his hands free. He squeezed harder, catching the ashen faced man's breaths diminish and his strength weaken till he stopped fighting. And for moments he nodded his head, with his face flushing with pleasure, recognizing his heartbeat.

In complete darkness, frightened by noises, he shivered from the chill in the air. He followed a bubbling stream in darkness until it funneled into a wider channel. His breaths shook as he moved along the water's edge, and he fell, winded, for a drink of water and a bite from a chocolate bar. His insides twisted at the unexpected racket from machine gun fire, explosions, and whining plane engines. After taking a few quick gulps of air, he dragged his feet forward, directed by the racket. At the edge of the forest, taking rasping breaths he discovered a burning truck, with infantry sprinting past the flames and burning bodies. His throat constricted, and he stepped backward, then crumbled to the ground, leaning on a tree.

"They won't believe me if I tell the truth," he whimpered to himself, catching a flush of heat in his face. "If I don't lie, they'll shoot me."

Freddy rose, with a sinking feeling in his stomach, and peeked at German tanks and soldiers moving over a snow-covered field. His heartbeat sped up, and he dragged his dry tongue over his mouth, visualizing Halina with the children. He wheezed, widening his eyes, slanting his brows up, and exposed himself, saying, lifting his hands high above his head, "Don't shoot me, I'm a German soldier."

* * *

Dear Halina,
I'm back fighting in Poland with the Seventeenth Army, glad my tour in Grafenwöhr has ended. Dolf's alive. I should have expected it. He knows how to look after himself. I'm lucky he's a friend and feel safe when he's with me. You and the children never leave my thoughts. Holidays are cruel without you. Tears came to my eyes, looking at the pictures you sent me.
I love you and miss your warm lips.
Your loving husband,
Freddy

Sergeant Weber kept his tone soft, passing alongside soldiers hunkered on snowy ground. "We move out at four thirty."

Dolf's lips creased as he edged closer to Freddy, quieting his voice. "Freddy, March is two weeks away. I thought I'd be in hell before I saw it."

Freddy gazed at Dolf, rubbing his nose. "We made it this far; let's hope our luck continues."

The expression on Dolf's face darkened. "Freddy, Hitler won't quit till he kills everyone."

Words stuck in his mouth, and he eyeballed Dolf, unable to blink, envisioning Krieg dying.

"Is something wrong? You're white as a ghost."

Freddy's mouth fell open; he focused on Halina as he tightened his grip on the rifle.

Sergeant Weber relaxed alongside Dolf, offering him his chewed cigar. Dolf smiled and puffed on it twice before giving it back. "British and American planes bombed Dresden for three days. The lieutenant was told two hundred thousand people died there."

Freddy grabbed the sides of his head. "No, No, he's wrong." Dolf's hands snatched his shoulders and shook them. "Freddy, what is it?"

A pain swept through Freddy's chest. "I told my family to head for Dresden if the Russians approached."

Dolf's said in a consoling voice, "Maybe they weren't in Dresden."

Freddy swallowed and drifted his head back. "What if they were there?" said Freddy. "They're my world. What would I do without them?"

Sergeant Weber's face lost its color, and he smashed his cigar in the snow. Freddy hung his pounding head, letting tears cloud his vision.

* * *

"I heard Lieutenant Glas has lost his nerve since his return from the hospital," pointed out Dolf, nodding. "Joppe caught him crying when we attacked the Poles near Gorlitz."

The lines between Freddy's brows lengthened. "I don't care."

Dolf leaned forward, grinning at Freddy, "It's the first of May; the war can't last much longer. You might head home sooner than you think."

Freddy was expressionless.

Lieutenant Glas raised his voice to near a shout. "Move out."

Freddy gnawed on his cheek, checking the time. He rose, trembling, gripping his rifle hard. Freddy hiked a brief time and left the road, following a tank heading for an open field, talking to himself. "Stay calm; you can get through this."

Flares lit on both sides of a German tank, sending Freddy to the ground, dizzy, seeing spots. A bomb exploded overhead, showering metal fragments. He saw some hit the ground near him and heard them strike the tank, making clinking sounds.

Dolf cried out through clenched teeth, "Shit, I twisted my ankle."

Eyes wide, frightened, blinking hard, Lieutenant Glas jumped up and fell dead, shredded by metal missiles from another exploding overhead bomb. A soldier screamed in pain, hit by the falling metal. The ones missed by them left their guns unnerved, running away. Freddy watched the tank leave, carrying the wounded man by itself.

"Dolf, can you walk?" asked Freddy, spotting blood on Dolf's chin. "You're bleeding."

Dolf wiped his chin with his coat sleeve. "It's just a scrape; how lucky can you get?" Dolf placed his hand on Freddy's shoulder. "Leave me, you've a family to consider, you might get killed if you stay with me."

"I won't leave you. I'll take my chances," protested Freddy, picking up more explosions.

"No, think of your family," said Dolf, his eyelids sagging.

Fear dried Freddy's throat when the shelling stopped. "Dolf, stay put; I'll get branches to make you crutches."

Dolf's face brightened, and he lurched forward, gripping tight tree limbs Freddy made into crutches. After a half day's slow walk, Freddy and Dolf stopped, spotting thousands of German prisoners afoot on the autobahn. Freddy's cheeks dimpled as he patted Dolf on his back. "I think the war's over for us."

Chapter Twenty-Four

Godforsaken Places

Freddy scooped the last bit of shit-soaked mud out of a hole brought by an afternoon shower. The pungent odor in the muck conjured up memories of manure in his grandfather's barn. A late sun materialized, hardening the space Freddy called home. He crawled into it with a bellyache, shielding his vision from the intense sun. Dizzy, taking shallow gasps, he imagined being home with Halina and the children.

"Freddy, can you make it to the river? Martin's puking—the idiot mixed grass and weeds in his soup."

"Will he get through it?" asked Freddy, dropping his eyebrows.

"How should I know? I'm no doctor, but I heard fifty men died yesterday."

"Who told you that?"

"Hans. They forced him to load bodies in a wheelbarrow and shovel lye on them before putting them in bags."

Freddy's slow headshake quickened, and he exhaled, replaying Dolf's words.

"Dolf, who's taking Martin's place?" asked Freddy, attempting to wet his dry lips with his tongue.

"Sepp said he could do it."

Freddy's jaw dropped as he realized piss hitting the ground behind him. He sat up, grimacing, feeling his skin tighten. His empty belly growled. He belted his wrist with his thumb and index finger sighing at the space between them. *Shit, I'm wasting away each day.*

Loud voices raced past him, and he peeked out of his pit in the earth, minding tattered POWs who formed a circle, laughing loudly at something. Freddy edged between two chuckling men, watching two detainees battle for cigarette butts tossed over the barbed wire by grinning sentries. Freddy's head jerked back, and he cringed, tensing his body at the sound of a few unexpected rifle shots. His lips twisted into a grimace, and he backtracked, forgetting to take a breath of air, spotting a still prisoner on the other side of the spiky wire puddling blood. A voice in the crowd spoke in a weary tone. "If he had a drink of water, he would not have ran for the river." Freddy gathered with other captives along the pointy fence, observing two guards throw the man's corpse in a green bag and lug it to a tent near the front gate. A man with a deadpan expression shook his head at Freddy. "We're caged animals. Alby went mad from thirst and hunger."

Freddy noticed two prisoners wrestling for an apple thrown into the camp by a guard.

Late that night Freddy inched below barbed wire, beneath a starlit inky black sky, spooked by noises made by nocturnal animals. He inched ahead, weary, hounded by rapid heartbeats. He spotted Sepp heading back with a sack full of food. And he crawled forward, happening upon shiny boots. His body shivered; he reckoned he could get shot. His upward look ended at a young guard's face. The boyish man stepped aside. "*Snell, snell.*"

Freddy pivoted on his back, hushing his tone of voice. "Soldier, I speak excellent English."

The young guard took a quick breath, eyeing Freddy. "Hurry, if I'm caught letting you pass, I'll be in trouble. If I see you, I'll toss you an apple. There's food for you in camp, but they won't let us give it to you. General Eisenhower gave orders not to treat prisoners as POWs; they do not allow the Red Cross inside the camp."

Freddy made a face, marking the ground with his fingertips. "Why? The war's ended."

"One officer said it nauseated him inspecting a concentration camp."

"Soldier, it sickened me when I heard what they were doing."

Freddy's face softened as he examined the youthful soldier. "I grew up in Detroit. Where did you learn to speak German?"

"From my grandparents and in high school."

"What's your name, soldier?"

"Corporal Harold Smith, from Wisconsin."

Freddy spoke in an amused voice. "Ah, your mother's family's German; if we meet again, call me Friedrich."

A smile lit up Corporal Smith's face, and he nodded his head.

Freddy frowned, puzzling over a thought. "Corporal Smith, sometimes I wake hearing rifle shots at daybreak."

The boyish serviceman sneered, keeping his rifle nozzle facing the ground. "They shoot SS soldiers if they find them. You better not be in the SS; they'll know if you're one of them."

Freddy's throat constricted, and he gave Corporal Smith a glassy stare, feeling his stomach rumble.

The young soldier said with a touch of concern in his tone, "Tell whoever is giving you food to be careful; they're stepping up river patrols."

Freddy turned on his belly, crawling for the Rhine, spooked by animal noises.

He reached the wide river, beaming at a woman rowing a boat from behind bushes. "Here's bread; eat it quick."

Freddy wolfed the bread fast, eyeing the fair woman, and held out his hand, hiccupping. "Give me water?"

She smiled, handing him a jug. "Hurry drink it. I can't stay much longer. If I'm discovered, they'll put me in jail."

"Then why do you risk it?"

"Because you need my help. I was twenty when my husband died at Stalingrad two years ago. If I can lessen the pain for one less woman, I'll smile."

"I'm sorry. You're a brave woman for doing this."

She smiled, removing her headscarf and soaking it in water.

"Here, wash. You stink. It's dreadful what they're doing to you; the war's ended."

A relaxed smile crossed his mouth as he took the wet scarf from her.

She watched Freddy clean himself, fluttering her eyelashes. She smiled a little, with her words taking on an amorous tone. "You're very handsome; I can hide you in my cellar."

Freddy's smile dropped; he could read her thoughts. "Men at camp need the food."

Her voice took a wistful tone, saying, "Come back, I'll wait for you."

Freddy gave her a pensive smile, answering her, "I can't. I'm married. My name's Friedrich Bauer, b-a-u-e-r, from Berlin. Can you find out if someone is looking for me?"

Her head dropped, and she said in a quiet and tense voice, "Berlin's in ruins. Many soldiers and civilians died there when the Russians seized the city."

Freddy's jaw unfastened and slumped, and he moved his head slowly back and forth, picturing his parents.

The woman inspected the shoreline. "Hurry, I must leave."

"Be careful, a guard warned me more soldiers will watch the river." He grimaced, turning his head to the side. His voice cracked. "Please help me. I have three children. Don't forget my name—it's Friedrich Bauer, b-a-u-e-r."

He breathed hard, shoving carrots and white asparagus under his shirt and in his pants and forced rolls in his pockets.

Freddy kept low and moved slowly, hindered by the food he carried on him, heading for the barbed wire, hoping to find Corporal Smith waiting there for him. When he reached it, the guard smiled and held it up high enough for him to wiggle under it. "Thank you, Corporal Smith. It was a pleasure meeting you; I'll remember your kindness."

The soldier's eyes twinkled, and he whispered. "Gute Nacht, mein Freund."

* * *

Awakened under a warm blue sky, Freddy's tongue peeked out his parched lips. His stomach somersaulted, and his insides blew out, his mouth covering him in puke. With a bitter taste in his mouth, he ran his tongue over his dry lips, spitting out chunks of vomit. And he wiped clean his lips with his sleeve and rubbed puke off the shirt in the dirt, leaving it to dry under the sun. Dolf wheezed, inspecting Freddy wide-eyed. "The slop smelled awful."

"I can't recall the last time I ate actual food," said Freddy, weak, straining to get out the words.

He felt a flutter in his stomach, picking up heavy footsteps. "Corporal Friedrich Bauer!"

He pulled his chest against his knees, hearing his name repeated. He dug his eyes into two soldiers walking with rifles close by. "I'm Friedrich Bauer and can speak English."

One guard made an awful face, sniffing the foul air. "You stink. Head for the gate; Captain Goldstein wants you."

Freddy rose on unsteady legs. He struggled for air, clutching his stomach. He dragged himself forward, touched on and off by a rifle's nozzle, heading to a green tent. "Move faster; you're too slow."

Freddy tripped over his feet, hurrying. The guards yanked him up and dragged him the rest of the way. He slumped with his fingers trembling; he looked at a red-faced officer, noticing Corporal Smith grimacing and cowering alongside his superior. The officer grunted, sticking a picture of piled bodies before him. Freddy's tongue pushed out of his mouth, and he turned his head, tasting a bit of something his stomach heaved and swallowed it.

"Don't you dare look away," the captain screamed, pounding the desk. One MP seized Freddy's head, directing it toward the photo.

"Corporal Smith, tell the prisoner my grandmother died in one of his concentration camps," he screamed, spraying spit on Freddy.

Freddy's lips trembled. "Not my concentration camp. I speak English."

The officer's face muscles slackened as he eyed Freddy.

"Corporal, give me the folder." The captain yanked it from Corporal Smith's hands. With a down-turned mouth, he leaned back, darkening his eyes. "Corporal Friedrich Bauer, if that's your rank, are you a member of the SS?"

Freddy let out a quick gasp, and his eyes bulged, connecting his brows with a crease.

Freddy's eyes raked his face with a spike of adrenaline speeding through his veins. "No, I was a foot soldier in the Seventeenth Army and fought on the Eastern Front; read my paybook."

"Ah, the fucking German paybook. I'll get to it shortly. But first tell me where you learned to speak English?"

"I-I lived in Detroit till I was fifteen," he said, swaying in place.

"Corporal Bauer, were you stationed at Grafenwöhr?" said Captain Goldstein, giving Freddy a pained stare.

Freddy closed his lids, rubbing his tongue inside a dry cheek, tasting bitterness. "I told you—I was a corporal in the Seventeenth German Army."

A vein twitched in Captain Goldstein's neck. "What was your occupation?"

"I-I practiced law in Berlin until conscripted."

A fake smile came to Captain Goldstein's face, and he picked up Freddy's paybook, eyeing him and the picture in the book twice. "So a thirty-five-year-old corporal in the German Army who is a lawyer expects me to think he's not suspicious? Admit it, you're in the SS and put your picture in a dead soldier's paybook to hide your actual identity. You might as well confess; there's more evidence against you."

Freddy's eyes darted from one green tent wall to the other, sensing his body warm. Terrified, he stared at Captain Goldstein. "That's my paybook. What evidence?"

Captain Goldstein leaned in. "Your name appeared on an SS document captured at Grafenwöhr. Corporal, I bet you're surprised we possess it."

He gulped for air, picturing himself facing a firing squad at daybreak. "M-my name? I don't understand."

"Neither do I," said the officer. "Parts of the document were missing, but your name was on it; that implicates you."

"Fr-Friedrich Bauer is not an uncommon name."

He squinted at Freddy, pinching his lips. "Were you a member of the Nazi Party?"

Freddy closed his eyes, shaking his head.

"Say it, yes or no!"

"No, I'm not!"

The captain threw his hat to the ground, tempering his words. "I don't believe a word you said; sergeant, take him away."

Handcuffed to a tree, he sat alongside another man under a scorching sun.

The other prisoner's voice hardened. "I'm proud I served in the SS."

"Keep quiet, you idiot," Freddy said, shouting, curling his fingers.

Corporal Smith kicked his foot, sneering at him. "Were you an SS officer?"

"No, I'm not, believe me," whimpered Freddy, taking rasping breaths.

"Captain Goldstein's convinced you're an SS officer; they might shoot you in the morning."

Freddy's brows shot up. "Corporal, come close; I must tell you something."

The boy soldier's mouth slackened as he listened to Freddy's words. Once he finished, Corporal Smith hurried away.

* * *

Freddy woke at dawn, picking up footsteps in the dirt. He felt thuds on his chest and cried in agony. "No, not me. I'm innocent, an honorable man."

His hand cuffs removed, Freddy struggled to his feet on shaky legs, hyperventilating alongside the other prisoner. The quiet MP pulled Freddy's hands behind his back, reattaching the handcuffs around his wrists. Carried away, on a bumpy road, inside a truck full of soldiers glaring at him and the SS man, an uncontrollable shudder swept through his body. He departed the truck and guards led him to a post. Once his handcuffs were off, a soldier secured his ankles to the post. Spots danced in his eyes; his prayers sped up. A gasping man blindfolded him. In darkness Freddy sniveled, aiming his eyes to the heavens. "God forgive my sins." His body quivered, and he wept, picking up noise from marching footsteps. He heard voices after a momentary hush.

A voice shook with fury. "Sergeant, stop, release him."

Clumsy fingers removed Freddy's blindfold. He blinked from the light and focused on Corporal Smith's face. The junior soldier grinned at Freddy. "Bishop Rauch is alive and insisted you'd kill yourself before joining the SS."

As they headed back to camp, gunshots rung in Freddy's ears, and he covered his face. "No!"

Corporal Smith squeezed his arm, mumbling in his ear, "God's on your side."

Half-smiling, weeks after Freddy faced a firing squad, Corporal Smith edged over to the fence and turned his back on Freddy, strengthening his voice. "Friedrich, you should know French soldiers will come for you in a few days; the French government requisitioned POWs."

* * *

Freddy fixated on truckloads of curious armed French troops pulling through the gate. "No, Corporal Smith was right."

"Shut up, let me sleep," said Dolf, pushing dirt at his feet.

"Dolf, French troops are here to take us away."

Dolf rubbed an eye and sat up, grimacing at the sight. "Uh, why?"

At the roaring command of a French officer, the soldiers hurried off the trucks, forming two straight lines. An American officer drove through the gate slowly, with Corporal Smith seated on a jeep's hood beside a loudspeaker. It stopped, and the boy soldier spoke German. "Move inside the soldiers lines."

Fear crossed Freddy's face, and he concentrated on dazed and confused men in tattered clothes, many standing on wobbly legs, assembling between two lines of French soldiers. The soldiers ignored those too weak or sick to crawl from the holes they called home.

And swallowing a soggy mush for breakfast, he picked up Corporal Smith's loud voice again. "Obey the soldiers. They're here to take you to a French POW camp. You've nothing to fear."

With a terrible accent, a loud-speaking French officer moved up the line yelling in German, "Prisoners, stand and march in line with the soldiers."

Pushed along by rifle butts and angry words, Freddy lumbered on a dirt road, stopping for a weak prisoner who had fallen unconscious. And observing two guards drag the man into a ditch, he winced in pain when they murdered him with their rifle butts. Seated alongside Dolf in a cramped railroad car heading for France, he agonized over the other prisoners who had died during the march, hearing their cries; he burst into tears.

* * *

"Dolf, open your eyes," Freddy said. "We need to eat before moving out."

Dolf's eyebrows rocketed up, and he rolled over, holding his stomach. "Freddy, look, my ribs are showing."

Freddy's brows knitted, and he measured his wrists. "Shit."

Freddy and Dolf inched ahead until they reached a POW ladling out a boiling watery brown soup from a filthy pot. Freddy's gut tightened, and he let out a brief gasp.

"Please fill the cup to the top," said a trembling prisoner standing ahead of Freddy. A French guard overheard. He spoke loud French words and threw the man's cup to the ground and punched his face. Freddy wheezed and moved forward with slow steps. He bowed his head, feeling his cup warm, and returned to the ditch, followed by Dolf. The soup cooled, and Freddy finished the repulsive brown liquid in six swallows. A short time later, the front gate siren screamed, constricting Freddy's throat. "Dolf, how many will die today?"

"Freddy, concentrate on what you're doing; don't let the guards rush you in the minefield," advised Dolf in a pained voice, blinking quickly. "Poor Christian, he was only sixteen; he should be in school, not picking fields for mines."

Freddy bounced inside a truck, heading for a place he visited every single day. He pinched his lips together, noticing a yellowish ribbon across the horizon, recalling his piss once resembled the color. Sleepy Dolf's head bobbed even with his slumped shoulders. Freddy shut his eyes. *Another day in hell.*

"*Snell, snell,*" screamed the French sentry, bastardizing the only German word in his vocabulary. Freddy jumped off the truck, following weary captives up to a soldier handing out digging utensils. Lined up with prisoners in an open field, Freddy heard the two words that haunted him: "*Snell, snell.*" He fell to his knees, flanking Dolf, heaving with sobs, easing the tool into the ground with a trembling hand, searching for mines. The line advanced, orchestrated by the two words. "*Snell, snell.*" His pulse raced as he inched ahead, mindful a mistake might end his life.

* * *

Freddy clung to Ernst, burying his face in his smelly back, desperate for warmth amid the icy darkness. Dolf released his grip around him. "Freddy, time to change places." Freddy moved to the outside, numb and freezing, sniffing pungent odors.

He stirred, shivering at the sunrise, opening his eyes to a pee-colored horizon. Dolf yawned, releasing a funky breath. He pulled himself away, wrapping himself in his arms from the bitter chill. His body shook. *I'm no longer afraid of dying. What will happen to my family? Will they remember me?* His empty stomach bubbled and let out gas.

Dolf gave him a hopeless gaze, emitting a weak sigh.

"Dolf, eat," he said, with a tingle in his limbs from fatigue.

"Leave me alone: I'm too tired to eat."

"Dolf, eat," said Freddy, bringing a shaky hand to his forehead, inspecting his friend with half-opened eyes.

"I can't, go away."

Freddy detected sets of noisy footsteps. Shadowed by a heavy-breathing man with a weak chin, he frowned, unable to grasp the soldier's words. The sentry snarled and kicked his leg hard. Both men yanked him to his feet. One of them smacked his face hard, smiling. Weak-kneed, he wobbled, tasting blood. The guards grabbed under his arms, shouting harsh-sounding French words.

"He did nothing wrong," shrieked Dolf. "Leave him alone."

The weak-chinned guard whacked Dolf in the head.

And the two guards dragged him through the barbed wire gate into a wood building.

Inside, the soldiers walked him to a fat-cheeked man pecking on a typewriter. He warmed, concentrating on the dreadful typist. The soldier sneered at him and continued typing. A silent civilian with glossy crow-black hair parked alongside the typist inspected him; Freddy reckoned he might be his age. The typist handed the civilian what he had produced. Tight-lipped, knitting his black brows, the stranger signed the paper and glanced at Freddy, smiling. Freddy's heart beat faster, believing his existence neared its end. Unable to blink, and with his shoulders arched, he held in a lungful of air. The four walls were closing in on him, and Fat Cheek's stare lacked warmth. *Why did the stranger keep smiling?* He grew dizzy, and his legs started trembling. And he inhaled a nervous breath, gazing into the stranger's eyes. The stranger spoke French.

Freddy shook his head.

The man flashed his teeth. "Do you speak English?"

"I d-did nothing wrong," he said in English, with his entire body quivering.

"I'm sure you didn't," said the Frenchman in a gentle voice.

Fat Cheeks gave the Frenchman a revolver, shifting his pupils to Freddy.

The guards pushed Freddy out the door, shoving him in the front seat of a gray van. The black-haired Frenchman dropped behind the wheel and started the vehicle. Once the van passed through a checkpoint, it picked up speed. Freddy rubbed his fingernails against his sweaty palms. "Where are you taking me?"

"To Lyon."

"Are you going to kill me?"

The Frenchman shook his head, keeping his eyes on the road. "No, you're safe. My name's Charles Bouchard; you'll work in my bakery. Inside my pocket is a paper issued from the government giving me custody of you for two years. Don't run away. If you're not killed, they'll send you back to the camp. I don't think you want that." Charles Bouchard slowed to make a sharp turn. "Prisoner, do what you're told, and we'll have no problems."

Freddy displayed a fake smile, weighing the danger. "Why choose me?"

"Friedrich, a guard said you were a pious man and an excellent worker."

Freddy eased a breath, staring through the front window, believing his life changed.

"Where did you live in Germany?"

"Berlin," he replied, looking straight ahead.

"Oh, not much left of it now. Do you have any family there?"

"My parents do. I sent my wife and children to a safe place when the English bombed the city."

"What did you do?"

"I was a lawyer," he said.

Charles Bouchard slammed his foot on the brakes, stopping the van. "Were you a Nazi?"

"No, I'm not a Nazi," he said. "I despise them and everything they stand for. I defended hopeless people they prosecuted."

Charles Bouchard grinned, pushing his foot on the gas pedal. And gave Freddy a quick glance before speaking his mind. "A friend told me and my parish priest that guards mistreated prisoners. It upset us and went to see the authorities. Because I'm considered a hero in France for fighting in the resistance, the government grants me favors, and you're one of them. But I might change my mind if you don't get cleaned and wear clean clothes."

The Frenchman wiped the smirk off his face, shooting a glance at him. "I killed Germans; did you kill Frenchman?"

"None," said Freddy, on the verge of tears, noticing a stomach ache. "Many Russians and a German."

"German?"

"He was going to kill me."

Charles gasped, widening his eyes, giving a quick glance. And moments later he handed him bread from a basket. A smile blossomed on Freddy's lips, and spilling tears, he bit off a chunk and chewed it, feeling his body lighten.

"Charles, I know another good man."

* * *

Two years later spring flowers bloomed, filling the air with sweet-scented fragrances. Two men left a gray Citroen van parked in front of the Lyon train station. Teary-eyed, the driver extended his right hand to the other man. He let out a heavy sigh and shook it, sobbing. "Charles, you saved my life; I'll never forget you."

"Stop, you'll make me cry. It's been two wonderful years. I believe God put you in my hands for a reason. Freddy, I'll miss you." Woeful sadness placed lines on Charles Bouchard's face. "I pray your family lived through the war."

Freddy's fixated on Charles Bouchard's words. "Charles, I don't know where I should look."

* * *

A long black locomotive reached a West German train station on a quiet Sunday morning. Few passengers departed the train. A blue-eyed stranger with uncombed, sandy blond hair stepped off the train and glanced sideways. He placed a finger over his lip, lifting his brows. And his fingers combed his hair before smoothing wrinkles on his coat. He met a man on the corner and handed him a paper with something written on it. The man shook his head and gave it back. He wandered the sleepy town until he found a place to eat. Three other people handed back the paper, shaking their heads. Outside, a fourth man's face lit up, pointing over to a road.

The man walked for hours before reaching a small village. He met an old woman sweeping her steps and asked a question. Her broom pointed to a dirt road. His cheeks rose, and his body tingled. He hurried up the road, mumbling words, serenaded by birds and nature's intoxicating scents. On restless legs, he stopped, admiring a farmhouse fenced in by green trees. With eyes welling, he continued. Within range of children's voices, he stopped crying. He watched a small blond-haired girl giggling on a swing, being shoved by a young boy. An older boy with curly light-colored hair spotted him and stopped dribbling a soccer ball. He stepped closer, measuring the stranger with unwavering blue eyes. The boy gave a slight headshake to the stranger. "Papa?" His eyes sparkled, and he sprung toward the door. "Mama, Papa's home!"

The door opened, and a wide-eyed blond woman with long, wavy hair burst out onto the porch. And seeing the man, she covered her mouth, spilling tears.

The man's heart raced, and he fell to his knees, crying, "Halina, I'm home."

Epilogue

F riedrich Bauer learned the Nazis conscripted his father in Berlin in the last days of the war, where he died defending a cause he detested. The heartbroken man never learned what happened to his mother. And he spent sleepless nights hoping she didn't suffer at the hands of crazed Russian soldiers.

No one ever heard what happened to Berta Koch. Grandma Petra, Uncle Tomas and his family, Bishop Rausch, Professor Stefan Karp, and Albert Beiner, lived long lives. Heinz, Manfred, and Werner Hoffman didn't. Werner rests in a cemetery in France among countless rows of crosses. Father Vogel never left the concentration camp, but Sister Rosa did, devoting the last fifteen years of her life to orphaned children. A day never passed when Friedrich Bauer didn't thank his uncles for camping outside Dresden on those terrible nights planes bombed the city, setting it up in flames, causing an unfathomable number of deaths. Friedrich Bauer never discussed the war with his children, but there were nights his wife understood his pain when she woke to find him weeping.

In 1949 a man visited him whom he long believed had perished in a concentration camp. The rabbi, who lived in London, brought his wife, Sara. He never learned he had killed the wrong man.

A committee of renowned judges selected Judge Bauer to the highest court, the Federal Court of Justice, and he wore the dark red robe with pride and distinction till his death.

In his last days, many close friends stood beside Judge Bauer's bed. Nef Muller's widow, Carrie, the godmother of his children, comforted his wife.

The rabbi and his wife wept at his bedside. Both kissed him. Judge Bauer's cheeks dimpled.

A tall man with red eyes and a conspicuous space between his front teeth cried, squeezing Judge Bauer's hand. His wife bowed her head, sniveling, and wiped her nose. Judge Bauer's eyes brightened.

Two men from Lyon, France, arrived; one spoke German, the other did not. Judge Bauer smiled at them with glassy eyes, reminded both had saved his life. The German's lips trembled, and he grinned at Judge Bauer, saluting him, holding back tears. The Frenchman held Judge Bauer's hand but couldn't hold back his tears. Judge Bauer smiled at them and let out a weak breath.

Curt Krause's widow wept and stroked Judge Bauer's cheek and kissed his forehead. And tears rolled out of her eyes. Judge Bauer struggled to stay awake.

In his last moments, Judge Bauer's family gathered near his bedside. His sons, Wilhelm and Friedrich, along with his daughters Alise and Barbara, and his loving wife, tried to smile. Judge Bauer's breathing became labored. His wife, Halina, leaned over him, dripping tears on his cheeks, and wiped them dry before gazing into his blue eyes and kissing him. Judge Bauer smiled at her, releasing pent-up tears. "Halina, I love you." Those were the last words ever spoken by Judge Bauer.

From the time a midwife of great standing brought Friedrich Wilhelm Bauer into the world on a frigid February night in an old farmhouse eighty-one years before, he lived a remarkable life. He endured the throes of rebellion and war and lived long enough to realize a persistent dream, a reunited Germany. The night he died, the priest at the village wrote in his diary: "The wind howled, shutters rattled, and doors blew open." Almost the exact same words Father Vogel jotted down in his journal the day Friedrich Wilhelm Bauer was born.

CPSIA information can be obtained
at www.ICGtesting.com
Printed in the USA
BVHW071116250423
663000BV00012B/875

9 781638 372929